# WAYFARER

Join the discussion: #Wayfarer

# WAYFARER

## K.M. WEILAND

*To Timothy,*
*who will always be*
*my favorite brother-in-law.*

*(Romans 2:11)*

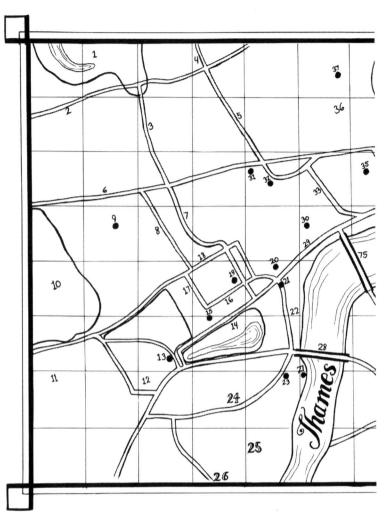

| | | |
|---|---|---|
| **1. Regent's Park** | 15. *St. James Palace* | **29. The Strand** |
| 2. *Marylebone Road* | 16. *Pall Mall* | **30. Covent Garden** |
| 3. *Portland Place* | 17. *St. James* | **31. Soho Square** |
| 4. *Hampstead Road* | 18. *Piccadilly* | **32. Seven Dials** |
| 5. *Tottenham Court Road* | 19. *St. James Square* | **33. Drury Lane** |
| **6. Oxford Street** | 20. *Trafalgar Square* | **34. Temple Bar** |
| 7. *Regent Street* | **21. Charing Cross** | **35. Lincolns Inn Fields** |
| 8. *Bond Street* | 22. *Whitehall* | 36. *Bloomsbury* |
| **9. Grosvenor Square** | 23. *Westminster Abbey* | **37. Foundling Hospital** |
| **10. Hyde Park** | 24. *Westminster* | 38. *Clerkenwell* |
| 11. *Kensington* | 25. *Millbank* | 39. *& 40. Holborn* |
| 12. *Green Park* | 26. *Chelsea* | **41. Chancery** |
| 13. *Buckingham Palace* | 27. *Houses of Parliament* | **42. Fleet Prison** |
| 14. *St. James Park* | 28. *Westminster Bridge* | **43. Fleet Street** |
| | | **44. The Temple** |

# CHAPTER 1

I N THE HAMLET of Affery, folk cherished the plague. Will Hardy was not one of those folk. In all truth, he held no belief whatever in a plague he'd never had sight of in all his life.

That was why he ran, head up, arms pumping, directly towards the source of it.

After last month's barley harvest, the fields lay in barren contentment, even with his feet flinging soil clods. The sun burnt through the crisp autumn breeze and heated his face. He was belated, and considering what awaited him, that was far worse than any fabled plague.

He reached the stile in the midst of the tumbled stone wall. In one stride, he leapt the three steps. The second stride would have been no difficulty—save for the singularly lovely face that distracted him from the corner of his eye. He caught his toe on the bottom step, and from there it was top over tail into the road.

In a flurry of green skirts, the girl scarcely halted before tripping over him. "Oh!"

The thought of her falling atop him had him flushing—and then flushing the harder because he was flushing.

A golden goddess, she was—clean and sparkling in a wide-brimmed straw bonnet tied off under the slightest of dimples. She could not be more than eighteen—no more than a year younger than he.

A small oaken chest thumped into the dust at her feet, and she hastened to right it. Still bent, she looked up from beneath her hat brim. Dark lashes highlighted wide, slightly almond eyes. And weren't they the smokiest of blues?

He reclaimed his feet. "All well, my lady?"

A spot of red burnt each of her cheeks. "A lady? Pray, do not be ridiculous." She fiddled with the box's lock.

True enough, she didn't dress as a lady. She wore a plain frock—fustian of the low-waisted style he'd seen on his own mother. Even truer, her brown coat was patched at the elbow. But the material hardly looked threadbare, and the patch was raised, as if placed atop cloth, instead of a raveling hole.

He had seen her about, but always in the fields, never the village. In point of fact, she seemed always to be near to the barn where the furtive Dr. Silas did whatever work he so closely guarded. 'Twas where Will was bound at this very moment.

He raised an eyebrow, somewhere between challenging and teasing. "Had I known you weren't a lady, *miss*, I wouldn't have done you the honor of throwing myself at your feet, would I?"

She frowned, perhaps deciding if she would put him in his place as any lady certainly would. "Well. You have done no harm, so we shall say farewell, shall we?" The twitch of her mouth seemed amused, whether at him or her failed ruse. "May I suggest the next time you believe you have encountered a lady, you throw yourself with less enthusiasm?"

He risked a grin. "Don't you suppose a lady might be worth a bruise or two?"

Her eyes widened—scandalized, of course. But make no mistake, the smile twitched her mouth again.

He glanced across the road.

A two-room cottage sat within a cleft in the up-and-down swell of the countryside. Heather and gorse overgrew every corner of the garden, save for the muddy path betwixt the front door and the barn. The barn was stone, sunk halfway into the hillside.

To judge from the sun overhead, the day had long passed the mid-hour. If Will were to reach Dr. Silas before his opportunity were lost, he must put wings to his feet.

But then, one hardly left goddesses to manage baggage.

He reached for the chest's leathern handle. "Shall I help you, my—miss?"

She jerked the chest away. "Oh—no!" Then she half-smiled, embarrassed. "Thank you, but I am equal to it. I am traveling no great distance. And you seem in haste. You are going far?"

He grinned. "Aren't I, though? To London." He touched his forehead and ducked in the tiniest of bows. No sense paying even goddesses too much obeisance. "Perhaps we'll meet there, my miss."

In the distance behind her, a closed carriage rumbled into view. Lord Carstone probably.

His stomach twisted, as always when aught of Lord Carstone's crossed his path. *why? QU.*

The girl flinched a look over her shoulder at the carriage. "I think I will. . . cut short across the field." She spoke quickly and hefted her trunk in both hands.

Perhaps she was a lady's maid, taking to her heels after stealing Lord Carstone's silver.

Well.

Sweeping the trunk from her, he climbed the stile and set it on the other side. He hopped over to assist her, hand at her elbow patch.

He grinned. "Enjoy the shortcut, my miss."

Then he darted across the road, grasped the top of the opposite stile, and swung over the stone wall. He landed at the other side, already running. Positively no tripping this time. Her ladyship could think on that, if she wished to think on aught that had passed between them.

He crossed the muddy barnyard.

Folks hereabouts swore their legendary plague—which had struck the village forcefully in decades past—came from this farmstead.

Will knew that to be the devil's own lie. Because hadn't he been born on this farmstead?

From within the barn, a cow bellowed.

Trust Dr. Silas—who was down from London and strange as a moonlit night—to be too heedless a farmer to let the livestock out to graze.

*That* was the sort of tenant Cyrus Barbary, the Right Honorable Earl of Carstone, preferred to Will's father.

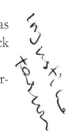

From inside, the cow called again. A chicken chittered. Something man-sized rattled about.

Will knocked. "Sir? 'Tis Will Hardy. I've come about the assistance you requested."

Even the cow quieted. Then: more banging. Something crashed and broke.

Footsteps approached. There issued forth a considerable scrabbling of iron, as if the doors had been locked and locked again.

"Sir?"

The door cracked, and the fruity stench of decay wafted out. Will stepped back. But he refused to hold his breath. There was *no* plague here. Never had been in all his life.

Dr. Silas poked out his head and squinted. "Oh. *You're* Will Hardy then."

Will was no hulking lad, but this Dr. Silas undercut even him by at least a hand's span.

The doctor scowled over the half-lenses nestled into his stiff nose. "Not a bit plague-touched, are you?"

"There is no plague." Will knuckled his forehead. "Begging your pardon."

"Mmm." The doctor sauntered out. He wore the graying wig and green velveteen breeches of fifty years past. "Your tongue's out-swollen your brains, I see." He seemed a bird sizing up a worm—and disdaining it for not being fat enough.

Might be Will wasn't the tallest or the broadest. But he'd swung a hammer in Tom's forge since first he could lift one. Might be that was about *all* he knew how to do. But the world was still young. And he was the man to meet a proper chance halfway.

He raised his chin. "My apologies—sir. That there's no plague has merely been my impression, having lived here as a boy."

The doctor's eyes lit up. He grinned, revealing a full yellowed set of teeth. "Now we come to it. Do you know why I asked you here?"

"Your note suggested you'd pay the fare for a likely lad to transport something of value to London."

"Anyone could do that for me. All that's special about you

is that here"—he pointed down to the mud—"you were bred, here you were born, and here you have lived your life."

"Only the first eight years, sir."

"Ah, yes." Dr. Silas shut the barn door and walked a circle about Will. "I know the sad story of the parents, two sisters, and one small brother evicted. For debts, yes? Then dying of the plague." He was almost leering. "And yet, here *you* stand, alive and well. Immune, perhaps?"

Will gritted his teeth. "They succumbed to gaol fever, sir, not any plague. I'm here merely because I was spared the workhouse and its agues." A familiar weight settled in his belly. It was all so long ago. Eleven years now.

Dr. Silas waved dismissively. "Had they no odd symptoms before they left?"

Will shifted. "No."

"And you? No oddities in all these years?"

"There is no plague. Never as long as I've lived. Never as long as my parents lived. They died of the fever, but that had naught to do with this place." He swallowed. "I'm a good worker. Anyone hereabouts will tell you. Ask my master at the forge, Tom Colville."

Dr. Silas scowled. "You're no good for going to London if you're bound to a master blacksmith. The magistrate would not appreciate my colluding with runaway apprentices."

"My term's almost finished. Tom granted I could go." It wasn't what Tom *wanted* to grant, but he had to finally accept that Will had no wish to be a blacksmith.

"Well." Dr. Silas sniffed. "You're no good to me in any event."

"What?"

"I'm only interested in those with the plague."

"What's that to do with transporting goods? I'm strong enough to see to nearly anything, and I'll take my oath I'm trustworthy." He'd fight to his last fingernail to gain London. The world started there, and the world was the very place he needed to see. "I've waited all my life for this opportunity." *And I need it. Tom needs it.* But he swallowed those words. There'd be no begging, no matter the stakes. "I . . . know this farm. I could tell you things about it." He strove to think of something worth the telling.

Dr. Silas raised an eyebrow. "Things such as how crops never grew well here—*save* adjacent to this barn? Things about how the animals were always sickly?"

"But not with the plague," Will said, in spite of himself.

"Hmp. 'Where plants perish and animals are absent, there thou should not live. The place is unhealthy.' Know who said that? Nostradamus said that. Know who Nostradamus is, boy? Of course, you don't."

"I know him. I've had my learning." The name was familiar at all events. Doubtless, Tom had made Will read something about him. "What of the stone behind the barn? Do you know of that? How water seeps direct from the rock? Tastes better than any county well."

"Pish posh. You're not here to educate me, boy. You're here to show me proofs."

"Well—they say folks around here used to fall down ill, their livestock along with them."

"Why do you think I'm here? I know all about that."

"But 'tisn't the interesting part, is it? The interesting part is the ones who survived were supposed to have found old ailments made well." He tried to remember. "Umm . . . things like blindness, swollen joints, even one old farmwife who couldn't have children."

"Hah!" Dr. Silas laughed in his face. "Maybe it's *you* who doesn't know. There were others affected. They were not merely cured. They were *changed*: two-headed calves, dogs that could smell meat cooking at the far side of the village, men too tall, men too short, women too strong. That's what I want to know about. Tell me about that, why don't you?"

"Those are mere fables."

"The plague, boy! Never been a natural discovery like it." Dr. Silas snapped his fingers. "Or is it the fairies a-dancing? I heard that too. But did I credit it? No."

"The rector says 'twas the devil's work."

"He's wrong. They're all wrong. But you—you're a wonderful disappointment. I was counting on you, and here you are, with no symptoms a'tall. You're certain your family hadn't aught strange about them? Extra digits on their hands?"

Will jutted his chin. "Sir. I have no more to say about my family—or the godforsaken plague."

Dr. Silas's bristled cheeks turned red. "You want to rattle the world? That's well, my boy. So do I—and by heaven and earth, I'll *do* it. You don't believe in the plague? You don't believe in miracles either, I'll venture? Well, you're going to see miracles, boy. And you're going to see them happening right here, because right here you shall be—and ne'er in London. I, for one, haven't a use for lads who think they're princes and forget they're the charity wards of poor common debtors such as Tom Colville."

"This isn't to do with Tom Colville." Will clenched his fists. "Tom Colville's the only reason I'm not dead in the ground with my parents."

"Tom Colville's one more reason you're still in Affery and not on your way to London." Dr. Silas tossed his head, nearly dislodging his wig. He stomped to the barn door and pulled it open, then looked back. "But do tell me if you remember any symptoms." Then he disappeared inside and slammed the door.

The stink of decay—along with a strange sharpish smell— wafted once more to Will. The chains scrabbled against the door, the locks snapping back into place.

Was it ended then? As swiftly as that? Will trembled.

Dr. Silas was madder even than the rumors said. From the rank smell of it, whatever he did in there *was* the devil's work. He was as likely as not to bring the plague—the real one, the Black Death one. Then he could study it all he wanted, whilst hoping and praying for his miracles.

But what did the madness of Dr. Silas's pursuits signify? A madman could have given Will what he wanted as easily as a sane one.

A ride on the mail coach up to London—a letter of introduction to a shipping agent or one of those folks who were always discovering gold in Abyssinia or wherever—those were not opportunities coming to Affery boys every day.

And there Will was, opening his mouth and letting out his temper. He couldn't have pulled his forelock and shuffled his feet and said, "My humble honor, sir. Anything you say, wise sir"? *No.* He had to spit it back into the duffer's face.

He made his feet move. He turned from the barn.

Then he halted.

The closed carriage he'd seen before now sat parked in the road.

Lord Carstone witnessing his shame? His heart stopped.

But the matched pair of blacks weren't ones he had seen before—and working at the forge as he did, he knew all the horses in the parish.

Seemed it wasn't Lord Carstone the young lady had feared encountering after all.

The door opened. A man leant out. Doubtless, he'd heard every word of Will's degradation.

Heat spread up Will's neck.

The man studied him, eyes an intense blue beneath a tall beaver hat. His face was boyish, but he must be as old as two score years. Honey-colored hair curled at his neck, stylishly short. He wore a dark blue coat, buttoned twice above fawn breeches. The reflection of the roadside rowan trees gleamed in the toes of his two-toned top boots.

With his ebony cane, he gestured Will nearer.

Will hesitated, then altered his steps.

"Your pardon." The man's London accent was authoritative but not uncivil. He nodded to the barn. "The loud gentleman—was that not Dr. Theobald Silas?"

So he *had* heard.

Well, then.

Will wasn't ashamed of *what* he'd said, only that he'd been daft enough to give it voice.

"Yes, sir."

"He is investigating Affery's infamous plague, yes?"

"So he says, sir."

"And he is experimenting upon animals, is he?"

"That I couldn't say, sir. Perhaps."

"I could not help overhearing. As I said, the gentleman was loud. I believe he mentioned you once lived here?"

Why was that of such interest all of a sudden? He shrugged.

"Well." The man smiled, small at first, then all the way to the

crinkled corners of his eyes. "No doubt you've heard that regard is something you must earn." He unbuttoned his coat and
withdrew a silver shilling from his waistcoat. "This is *what* you
earn." He filliped the coin into the air.

Will caught it.

The man withdrew into the carriage and closed the door. He
looked at Will through the window. "I am the Honorable Mr.
James Fitzroy. I will be staying at the Pirrup Inn. Should you
desire a chance to begin earning what needs to be earned, you
may visit me this afternoon. Good day." He rapped his cane
against the ceiling.

As the carriage rolled away, Will stared in wonder at the shilling in his palm.

# Chapter 2

WHAT WAS A lad to do when a stranger handed him a shilling?

Will crossed the field, back to the forge. A shilling wasn't fare to London. But shillings added up. Where there was one already, another might follow. That all depended on what Mr. Fitzroy thought Will could do. Already, Mr. Fitzroy had given him more than Dr. Silas had offered. Tossing the coin, he caught it, then tucked it in his trousers.

Near the forge, the breeze carried the sound of hammering. Of late, they hadn't been hearing that nearly enough.

He rounded the cottage.

Its single story was split down its midst with a wall separating home from forge. The forge was at the far side, double doors open to the distant village. Judging by the two chimneys puffing away, tea must be on the hearth in the house and the coals must be hot for work in the forge.

As he reached the forge doors, the blind bulldog Tip growled. Will scratched the dog's hard wrinkled head, then entered.

Without slowing his hammer, Tom glanced up. "Ah, just the time. I half thought you'd be atop the mail coach. You can give the fire a pump." He nodded back to the great bellows.

Will tied on his leathern apron. "That doctor's off his head. He'd no notion of hiring a lad a'tall. All he could go on about was the plague." He reached for the bellows handle. "He thought that's how my ma and pa died. Hasn't an ounce of respect in his whole mouth."

Tom stopped hammering. "And *your* mouth is so properly full of it? When a man sets up your bristles, it don't mean you have to set up his right back. Care too much for the praise of a man, and I can give you my oath you'll be disappointed every time."

Will grasped the bellows with both hands and pumped mightily. As a boy, he'd had to stretch to reach and then dangle off the handle to pull it down.

"You wait. If I earn my fortune, it will all be different."

"Can't buy a man's regard, lad."

Will touched the shilling in his trousers. "Never seen the rich man who wasn't saluted by every cottager he passed."

"And I've seen plenty of men who didn't *need* to be saluted at every turn."

"All I want's a civil tongue from every man, same as I give them. Why is that too much to ask?"

"The Lord's no respecter of persons, and He gets by on that principle handsome enough."

"Well, you can't deny the practicality of it. A little bit of fortune around here'd go a long way to paying the debt."

"We'll pay it off. You want to talk about fortune, this order here's a fortunate one. Whilst you were out, Squire Grainger stopped in, wanting new gates, as big as those at Lord Carstone's Lightwood estate. Finish on time and we'll be fine as an Easter morn. And then there's this." He drew a sooty paper from under his apron bib.

Will took it with his free hand.

The note was from Lord Carstone himself, granting Tom an extension on the debt, "in light of your known good Character and past Dependability in all matters as an Honorable freeholder in the village of Affery, and your Admirable record in service of His Majesty during the conflict on the Peninsula."

Tom looked Will in the eye, serious despite half a smile. "That kind of regard, even in the face of a debt, that's worth more to me than money in the hand."

Will shook his head. "From Lord Carstone—"

"From any man."

Tom went back to hammering, the muscle expanding beneath his rolled sleeve. Around town, the general opinion of the womenfolk was that Tom Colville was handsome enough—

the unkempt dark hair, the quick-fire smile that sometimes belied the equally quick-fire temper. But he'd never married. There'd been a girl long before Will could remember, but she'd turned jilt and Tom had lost patience with the whole idea.

Tom lost patience with many things, but never those he truly believed in. Those he kept hammering away at, same as he hammered the iron—skillfully, resolutely, and, eventually, triumphantly.

That was the unsettling thing about disagreeing with him.

"Maybe that's true." Again, Will fingered the shilling. "But it's still money keeps a man from debtor's prison, and I'm going to help you get it."

"You are helping. Keep pumping."

"Out at the farm . . . I met a gentleman. He's staying at the Pirrup in the village. Might have a position for me."

Tom cast him a long look, mouth firm, then landed another blow on the iron rod. "I say you're your own man, Will Hardy. Have been since you were eight years old." He raised the rod in the tongs and examined the flattened end. Satisfied, he plunged it into the leathern water bucket. "But I'd have a care before doing business with a man about whom you know naught."

From outside the forge's open doors, a golden voice piped in: "But do you not find that is, on occasion, the most interesting sort of man?"

Tip loosed a belated bark.

Heat flooded Will's face, almost before he could turn.

Still hoisting her little trunk, his wayward goddess stood in the doorway, backed by the afternoon sunlight.

She turned her smile away from Tom to acknowledge Will's presence for the first time. Her recognition was immediate, and she proceeded to make everything slightly better by coloring to the tip of her nose.

A grin started at the corner of Tom's mouth. "Well, now." He touched his forehead. "My la—"

"Miss," Will interjected. He released the bellows and approached her. "If you crossed the field to come *here*, you were a long time coming."

"Yes, rather." Her blush was already fading, but her smile

remained fixed. "I walked to the village, only to be directed back here."

"Carrying that load all the way?"

"Well, take it from her," Tom said.

Will managed not to flush even more. He raised both eyebrows, asking permission.

She laughed nervously and finally held it out. "Yes, thank you. It requires a slight repair."

"And then where might it be off to?"

She tossed her head. "Back to its owner, of course. Then to London."

"London?" Realization struck him. "This belongs to Dr. Silas?"

Her smile faded. She twitched her gaze sideways. "Who?"

It was as obvious she knew Dr. Silas as was obvious she didn't live in the hamlet.

"And he's a great oaf to have you carry this about the county for him."

She raised her chin. "*Farm girls*, I think you will find, are quite up to carrying things all about."

This time, he dared a full grin. "Oh, right you are, my miss."

Her chin rose even higher. "The clasp must be in its best condition for the journey." She nodded to the dangling brass at the box's front.

With what he hoped was a courtly bow, he took the trunk. His fingers couldn't help brushing hers just a bit. He carried the trunk to the brick counter beside the deep well of the hearth. Its weight was not great, but its contents rolled about, shifting the center of balance from side to side. The clasp was a simple slotted tongue fitted over an eyelet. The tongue was nearly rusted through at the top.

"I've precisely the thing for you." He rummaged the cobwebs in the shelf above the counter until he found the ornate steel clasp he'd made last winter. Locks and such minute metalwork were his specialty. Tom hadn't the patience with the fine, small work, so he gave most of it over to Will's nimble fingers.

This one was decorated with the four-pointed North Star.

"It is lovely," she said. "Like the compass on a map."

"Aye, 'twas the idea. A compass'll take you anywhere. We'll

hope it will take your box to London." He used a chisel to pry away the broken clasp.

She leapt forward, reaching with both hands. "But you must not open it!"

What did she have in there? Not the Carstone jewels if she was working with Dr. Silas. But then who knew why that old buffle-head would have a young lady carting trunks all over the county for him.

Will glanced at Tom.

His master kept hammering, but slower now, with steady little taps. His gaze scarcely left Will and the lady, and a tiny grin scarcely left his mouth.

Will scowled. "This won't take but a minute to repair, but you know I'll have to open it to secure the new clasp?"

Her eyes implored. "Must you?"

"I do if you want your lock affixed all the way to London."

"You must not look inside. Promise me?"

He hesitated. But what choice had he?

"Anything for a lady."

She *must* be a lady. Even genteel maids couldn't be this barmy. No wonder she kept company with Dr. Silas. Probably, they were both escaped from Bedlam.

With two raps of hammer and chisel, he knocked off the old clasp. The brass clanged against the cabinet, but there was another sound too: a skittering—like Tip's claws against the floor.

He frowned.

From the corner of his vision, he could see the smoky blue of her eyes watching him shamelessly.

*That* didn't seem quite the thing for a highborn lady to be doing. Not that he'd know. He'd only observed from afar on the rare occasion when one passed through the village. Most spent their time staring demurely at their own folded hands or simpering behind lace fans.

This one seemed different. And wasn't she lovely though? Fair took his breath standing next to her. Brazen eyes or not, she was a girl any gentleman'd be proud to bear on his arm.

As for Will, *he* was the sort of lad who'd probably offend her if he so much as offered.

She cleared her throat. "Your business across the field was successful?" A dimple appeared in one cheek. "No more tripping, I trust?"

"You'll be relieved to hear there were no more young ladies at whose feet I could throw myself."

"You . . . made no mention of me? Not to . . . the man in the carriage, or anyone?"

This time he looked her full in the face. "You're not in difficulty, are you?"

"Oh, no, not at all. Nothing like that. I merely—" She glanced at Tom, then back. "I would appreciate your forbearance in mentioning my being here. I would count it a great favor." She gave a little smile and nod, trying to make it all sound innocent.

"Of course, miss," Tom said. "We've no reason to raise the subject."

The smile she gave him was genuine. Then she turned to Will, brows raised.

"Of course," he said. But the mystery of it all would remain with him longer than even her lovely face.

With four taps of his hammer, he fixed the new clasp onto the box.

More skittering emerged from inside.

The girl laughed, too hastily. "It is such a beautiful day, is it not?" She spoke too loudly. "I love these genial September days in the country."

As compared to September days in the *city*? A farm girl would be knowing all about that contrast, wouldn't she?

Will struck the second nail once again, enough to knock the box back a full inch on the counter.

More scrabbling.

The girl turned to Tom, voice still raised. "Do you not find Surrey the most congenial place in the world?"

Will lifted the lid, only an inch, because he'd promised not to look, and felt through the crack for the raw ends of the nails. Pain pierced first his forefinger and then his middle finger—but not from the edge of the box where the nail tips were placed. These stabbed his hand from *inside* the box lid.

He yanked away, unintentionally flinging open the lid. "Ow!"

With a screech, the girl darted to his side.

In the box, a white ferret stared up, thin lips drawn. One needle-sharp tooth offered a drop of blood.

Why in the name of sanity would Dr. Silas have this girl toting a common ferret bound for London?

Will blinked—and the ferret was gone. Not *gone* as in jumped from the box and scurried from the forge. Simply *gone*.

"What . . . ?"

The girl slammed the lid. "You promised you would not look!"

"I . . . didn't." He held his bitten hand. "I didn't. But it bit me."

Her glare was more reproachful—and panicked—than angry. "You saw." She flicked his new clasp closed and clamped the padlock over it, locking it with a silver key. Then she lifted the box in both hands. She turned back to him and huffed a resolute breath. "*What* did you see?"

Perhaps better put—what *hadn't* he seen? "A . . . white ferret."

"That was all?"

He opened his mouth to tell her that *absolutely* wasn't all. But what was the point? She'd deny him an explanation and stomp off, believing he'd looked on purpose.

"That was all. But you might have warned me before I stuck my hand in there!"

Her features softened. "Are you injured greatly?"

"No." He wiped the blood on his trousers. "No, I'm fine."

"Well, I am glad of that." The dimple flashed briefly. "What is just recompense for wounds whilst working?"

He managed a tight smile. "Consider it a gift to a farm girl."

Her straightforward gaze bore into him once more. Finally, she nodded. "Thank you. I mean that. You are very good." She smiled at Tom. "Both of you."

Tom inclined his head. "At your service, miss."

She turned and left.

This time, Will gave no offer to take the trunk.

He looked at his hand. Two tiny punctures, beaded with blood, marked his fingers. Disappearing ferret, indeed.

"Well." Tom spun his hammer. His eyes sparkled. "Had I

known making a fortune was as simple as giving away hard-wrought iron work, I'd have been rich long since."

Will scowled. "What has she to do with Dr. Silas? And why send a ferret to London?"

"If 'twas your business, you can be sure she'd have told you."

Down the path, her green homespun swished through the dust.

Mr. Fitzroy said Dr. Silas was experimenting on animals. Cows, for a certainty. But ferrets too, apparently. Such a girl shouldn't be involved with something dangerous enough to kill animals.

She wanted no one telling about her? That was fine. But if Mr. Fitzroy could give Will an opportunity to raise himself up in the world *and* solve the puzzle of Dr. Silas's doings, that was too good a chance to pass by.

He turned to the hearth and stirred the fading coals with a poker. "Let's finish up. I've decided I'd like to hear whatever it is this Mr. Fitzroy has to say."

# CHAPTER 3

WILL STOOD OUTSIDE the Pirrup Inn's oaken door and took a deep breath.

It wasn't someplace he'd ever had much cause to visit. It hosted the well-to-do tradesmen, such few as were in Affery. Farmers and laborers were more welcome in the Hammer and Tongs at the other end of the village.

But surely he'd as much right to step inside as any.

He kept his floppy woolen cap on his head until he crossed the threshold into the warm dustiness and its smell of ale.

Tables lined the wall, flanked by high-backed settles such as a man might use before the hearth to contain the heat. Here, the chairs provided privacy for quality guests.

The innkeeper, Mr. Bayham Pirrup, set a tankard upon the front table. "Master Hardy. What can I do for you?"

Will stood straight, cap in hand. "I've come to see the Honorable Mr. James Fitzroy."

The man who had just been served looked out around the edge of his settle. He angled an elbow to block Will's path, whilst leaning the other elbow against the table.

"Gentleman, is it?" Young Richard Grainger looked Will over, from hat-mussed hair to Sunday boots. His eyes sparkled in his lean face. "Did the *gentleman* know for whom he was asking?"

It *would* have to be Grainger, today of all days.

Will faced him. "That isn't for you or me to say, is it?"

Two years older than Will, Grainger was the squire's son. The old man was a good sort, for a toff. But his son had made it his business to incessantly flash his position in Will's face.

There had been one particular incident—which Will did not recall with much pride—when Grainger pushed his cheek too far and cracked Will in the face with his riding whip. Will had pulled him from his horse before the entire village. Had it not been for Tom's grip on his arm, he would have thrashed the fellow with his own whip.

You could bet a ha'penny Grainger had forgot that day no more than Will had. The slight scar on Will's cheekbone quivered.

Grainger gestured elaborately for him to continue down the row of tables. "By all means, let us see what the gentleman says."

Will walked through.

As Will passed, Grainger shifted and leant into his path, jostling his own arm. Ale sloshed over the tankard's brim and splatted onto his glistening Hessian boots.

"You sorry oaf!" His tone was stony. "You have no business in here in any event." He snatched Mr. Pirrup's rag from his apron band. "Wipe it up like a good lad and we will say no more."

Will stiffened. Heat crawled up his neck. "A man should clean up after his own carelessness."

Grainger further extended the rag. "You have a considerable opinion of yourself, Master Hardy."

Will clenched his teeth. "I'm not the only one."

The laughter left Grainger's eyes. He stood. "There will come a day when you will learn your place in this world. God made the order of men. There is no shifting that." He waggled the rag. "It might even be blasphemy." He jutted his chin, as if desiring Will to strike him. Then he could call in the magistrate and get Will set up in the stocks.

Will swallowed. "God made you, and God made me. And I've it on good authority, He's no respecter of persons."

"And neither are you?"

"I respect them that respect me."

Grainger's cheek twitched. He threw down the rag. "You insolent cub. You refuse to learn? Perhaps whipping is still what you need." He reached to the table for his riding crop and snapped it in Will's face.

Reflex saved Will. He caught Grainger's wrist and held it—squeezing the wrist bones together.

Grainger's eyes bugged. "You—"

*That* would teach Richard Grainger about blacksmith apprentices.

Behind Will, a chair creaked; a boot clomped the floorboards. Grainger's eyes widened further. "Mr. Fitzroy."

So Mr. Fitzroy had been there all along—overhearing yet another conversation in which Will hadn't bitten his tongue hard enough.

Will released Grainger's arm and turned to face the gentleman. "Sir."

Mr. Fitzroy's boyish face was stern now, the lines around the frank blue eyes as hard as any king's.

What did he see?

It was a fair question. Sometimes even Will wasn't sure what he saw of himself in his own millpond reflection. But a lad had to start someplace, and here in Pirrup's Inn, with a fool and a fop such as Grainger, seemed the place he must start.

Why should he apologize for that to any man?

He squared his chin.

In Mr. Fitzroy's eyes, something flickered. "Well, then." He looked to Grainger. "You will excuse us."

Grainger stepped back towards the door. "Yes, sir. Your pardon." He left.

Mr. Fitzroy beckoned Will. "Now then."

With a last glance at Grainger, Will came forward to stand beside Mr. Fitzroy's table.

"Please, sit."

Will slid into the high-backed seat across from Fitzroy. He clenched his hat. This time, so help him, he'd keep his mouth shut until spoken to.

Mr. Fitzroy watched him, strangely. Then he smiled. "Forgive me. You remind me a bit of myself at your age."

No reprimand? No reminder to heed his betters?

"Oh." Will released his cap. "Thank you, sir. But I'm certain you were never a blacksmith's apprentice."

"I was *not*." The words were decided, almost aggrieved. "But we are hardly here to discuss such, are we?" He leant back. "Did I hear Master Grainger name you Master William Hardy?"

"Yes, sir."

"Am I wrong in thinking you have never heard of me?"

"No, sir."

"If you moved in any circle of import in the City, you would answer differently."

Mr. Fitzroy wasn't nobility, or the arms on his coach would have said so. But neither did he seem a wealthy tradesman. He didn't quite seem like any sort of gentleman Will had ever seen. This was a man who looked Will straight in the eye as if he were an equal—someone to be weighed and measured, counted worthy or found wanting on the basis of himself, not the money in his pocket or the handsome words in his mouth.

"What is it you'd like me to do for you, sir?"

"You mean, what is it I can do for *you*?"

"I daresay I mean something whereabouts the two meet."

Mr. Fitzroy's laugh lit up his face. He leant forward and lowered his voice. "Well, then, Will Hardy, what I need from you is a service."

"Having to do with Dr. Silas?"

"Dr. Silas indeed. He is a puzzling fellow. I am interested in his activities—in part, because I have no trust he will take proper responsibility for the care of them—and in another part, because I believe they have the potential to do considerable good in this world."

"Just what is he doing, sir?"

"Magic, I rather think." Mr. Fitzroy watched him. "Or so your locals might call it."

Will kept his face straight. "You mean the plague."

"The plague is the result, not the cause. Do you know what a trackway is?"

Will shook his head.

"It is a path upon the earth's surface—a perfectly straight path no one can see but some say they can *feel*. Some say it is the highway of the spirits."

"Sir," Will spoke carefully.

"You may not know that in our recent Peninsular War, it became a superstition amongst campaigners to sleep only where first a cow had lain—because cattle sensed the healthiest of these lines. Lying there would prevent the rheumatics, or so they said."

Will's face must have shown his incredulity.

Mr. Fitzroy smiled. "I do not believe in spirits, magic, or, in this instance, plagues."

"Neither do I, sir." Nor in invisible paths you could *feel.*

"I believe in logical inquiry. I also believe that although our Dr. Silas may be irresponsible, he is not necessarily incorrect."

Will frowned. Surely such a man as Mr. Fitzroy could not be considering Dr. Silas's rubbish?

He shook his head. However mad Dr. Silas might be, Mr. Fitzroy certainly was not. After all, what did Will truly understand of Dr. Silas's work? Whatever it was—if indeed it was anything a'tall—it must, of course, possess a sounder explanation than what Dr. Silas himself offered.

"You think his experiments have to do with this . . . trackway?" he ventured.

"I do."

"But he experiments upon animals."

"And perhaps more."

The golden girl. She'd known what Dr. Silas was about. But certainly the old man wouldn't conduct any of his barmy trials on her.

Will straightened. "Why entrust me with this secret, sir?"

"It *is* a secret. But it is also nothing other than a well-constructed hypothesis. What I desire is to transform the secret into fact. Unfortunately, Dr. Silas would not take kindly were I to invite myself for tea."

"He'll take no kindlier to my arrival."

"The idea is for him to have no knowledge of it."

"You want me to spy?"

"Yes."

"I'm no sneak-about, sir."

"There is more to this than idle curiosity." Mr. Fitzroy drank off the last of his Madeira and thumbed a drop from the corner of his mouth. "The rest is delicate. The granddaughter of a great friend of mine appears to be . . . *too* acquainted with Dr.

Silas. I do not say the man would harm her." He rubbed his forehead. "But I cannot say he would not either."

Will's heart turned over. "She's in danger?"

Mr. Fitzroy's penetrating gaze seemed to see straight through him. "Perhaps, perhaps not. At all events, I am not only investigating this fascinating secret, I am also inquiring discreetly before she should be damaged—in any number of ways."

If the goddess knew Mr. Fitzroy, she *must* be a lady after all.

An unexpected wave of disappointment ran through Will. He looked down at his hands and fiddled with his cap. It was already sure enough a girl such as her would never look at him—not whilst he was little better than a plow-boy. But if she was a fine lady, then that seemed too firm an answer for him to even bother raising the question.

He looked up. "It's true I'd want no harm to come to a girl. But why not recruit someone who knows already what's happening? If there's rumors about, someone must know."

"I want the truth from the source." Mr. Fitzroy straightened the high fold of his stiff cravat and took up his hat. "Information can be a difficult thing to come by for a man in my position. Either people are inclined to hide the truth, or they lie."

"But not to a man in my position, is that it?"

Mr. Fitzroy flashed that smile again. "Perhaps that may not always be so in your case." He slid from the chair.

Will scrambled to his feet. "I haven't said whether I'd do it or not, sir."

"And you needn't." Mr. Fitzroy reached into his waistcoat pocket. This time, he came out with a golden sovereign. "This is not a contract between us. This is an opportunity. If you decide to take the opportunity and *if* you find aught worth the telling, use this sovereign to come to me in London, Number 12, Soho Square. I will be returning there tomorrow morning."

Will tried not to gape. That sov would pay his way to London *inside* the mail coach, instead of on top.

"If you do," Mr. Fitzroy said, "I can promise there will be more opportunities." He set the sovereign on the table. "But make no mistake, if you bring me something, it must be solid." With a last smile, he started for the door.

Will looked up from the sov. "You failed to say, sir: why are you trusting me with this?"

Mr. Fitzroy turned. Shadows from the windows behind him played across his face. "Because if someone had given me this chance at your age, I would have done what I think you will do." He touched his cane to his hat brim. "If I am as correct about that as I believe I am about Dr. Silas, I shall see you in London within the sennight."

# CHAPTER 4

THAT EVENING, SQUIRE Grainger canceled his order for the gates. *moves plot along treader ou* The September twilight had fallen in layers—first ever so slightly green like the fading leaves, then golden like the sun, and finally rosy like the edge of the sky. Shadows always grew inside the forge faster than they did without, so Will had learned to do a deal of work by the light of the hearth coals.

Alone at the anvil, he had spent forty minutes hammering another piece for the iron gate frames. The end glowed orange. He steadied it with the tongs and raised the sledge one considerable swing at a time. He hadn't Tom's height for the extra leverage, but he could hammer out a rod quite as swiftly.

Tonight, all the old restless energies, stored up ever since his parents left him with Tom, ran amok.

It had seemed clear this morning that Dr. Silas was a mad old buffle-head, best left alone. But if even the likes of the Honorable Mr. James Fitzroy thought he wasn't so insane with his talk of plagues and miracles—then what if there *were* something to be discovered? Not the long-dead plague and not that superstitious nonsense about invisible trackways, of course. But something.

He smashed the hammer into the molten end of the rod.

And what of the girl? No proper lady would be without a chaperone. Did that mean Dr. Silas had seduced her? She was in love with him? Ridiculous. At all events, what did love have to do with secret ferrets that disappeared before your eyes? He gave the rod another great crump.

One thing was true enough: Dr. Silas was not a man Will would have wanted in the company of his sisters, had they lived. How much less a girl such as that—with no chaperone, no protection, maybe even run away from her family? That was the most certain kind of destruction for a lady, even if no actual harm came to her.

Of course, Mr. Fitzroy held his own secrets in this matter. But if he'd said Will reminded him of himself, then it wasn't a stretch to say James Fitzroy was the sort of man Will wished to be in another score of years.

Still, playing the spy on Dr. Silas—even if he were living in Will's old home—didn't sit easily.

Tom walked through the doorway and halted, blocking the remaining light. Outside, the squire's carriage rumbled away.

Will looked up. "What did he want?"

"What he doesn't want anymore are the gates."

Will forbore hammering. "What?"

Tom crossed to the brick cabinet beside the hearth, leant both hands against it, and hung his head. "No explanation, simply—no gates. 'Tis a bad twist, Will lad, I can't lie."

Will's heart began pounding. "This is his son's doing." He stabbed the rod into the water bucket. The hiss of steam sounded apiece with the blood rushing in his ears. "And my doing."

Tom looked over his shoulder. The coals lit his face. "What's this?"

"Richard Grainger and I . . . had words this afternoon."

Tom groaned. "Not seriously, Will? That popinjay breathes naught but trouble—and he isn't worth the fight."

"I didn't start it, I promise you."

"But you couldn't let it go?"

"No. I couldn't." Will clunked the sledge atop the anvil. "What is it you want me to do? Knuckle and scrape to these arrogant fancy men every time they snap their fingers? I don't see you doing that!"

Tom pushed up from the cabinet. "I don't *have* to. I live my life and work my trade, so I can wake every morning and be at peace with myself. There isn't any other man on this earth whose approval I need. An honest man will have it in him to respect another honest man, whatever his station. And any man who isn't so honest isn't a man whose soft words I need in my ears."

"And that will save you from debtors' prison, will it?" Will yanked his apron over his head and threw it onto the flat top of the bellows. "All this respect you don't need from *honest* men such as Squire Grainger won't keep you from dying of gaol fever, as my family did after *honest* Lord Carstone ripped our land and our work from us."

"Lord Carstone had a right to do what he did, and you know it. 'Twas your father and his great dreams that wouldn't pay the rent for that miserable place."

They'd argued this before. Fairness, always fairness with Tom. Always trying to see both sides.

Will's breath came in hot draughts. "My father and his great dreams would have paid his debts ten times over if given the chance."

Sympathy—and exasperation—flickered in Tom's eyes. "But they didn't."

He was right enough, and Will knew it. But only because his father had been too much a dreamer and not a doer. Just as Tom was too much the doer and not the dreamer.

Will stalked to the door.

"Where are you going?"

"To see if *my* great dreams can't save *your* skin."

"Meaning what?"

He slammed the forge door.

Still breathing hard, he ducked around to the house to gain a coat against the chill of the autumn darkness. Then he crossed the plank bridge over the millpond stream. Once in the field separating Tom's forge from the old Hardy barn, he ran.  ˗

Even in the half-dark, he could run this field without fear of falling. He'd run it time and again, whene'er he was in a fume or frustrated or sad. Back and forth betwixt the home Tom Colville had given him and the home that remained a fierce reminder of where he'd come from and where, so help him God, he was going.

He reached the stile over which he'd tripped earlier, jumped without faltering, and crossed to the opposite stile. There, he slowed and climbed the steps, up and down, in silence.

The cottage stood within an encirclement of crumbling stone markers. Those stones had been erected by the druids themselves, so insisted Will's father. The cottage glowed faintly. Will knew the look of a hearth fire in the windows; he'd seen it many a night when helping his father tend livestock.

He swallowed. He was *not* his father, too full of dreams to save his family. But neither was he Tom, too stubborn to save himself.

So here he was—spying on Dr. Silas after all. Tom wouldn't approve. But better Tom in disapproval than Tom in prison. And if Dr. Silas was up to tricks with the girl, that was worth a bit of spying too.

In his trouser pockets, he found Mr. Fitzroy's shilling alongside the golden sovereign. He rubbed them together—for luck.

Something gleamed in the grass, and he halted to gather a handful of sluggish glowworms. They always seemed to glow brightest here around the old farm. He pocketed them and crossed the garden, straight to the one small window in the near side of the barn.

It was boarded over. Not surprising, given the number of locks on the doors.

But he hadn't spent his boyhood here to no purpose. Grasping the deep ledge above the windowsill, he hoisted himself high enough to get a foot on the lower sill. From there, he found the overhanging eaves and gained the roof. At the far end, the same old plank was still loose. He pushed it aside.

A stench floated against his face, and he gagged before peering deeper.

The waxing moon cast silver and shadows throughout the barn. This side of the building was an open corridor; the far side, built into the hillside, was divided into stalls.

Something shuffled. A cow lowed weakly.

Beneath, a ten-foot trestle table held the clutter of physician's implements, along with inky papers and all sizes of boxes, jars, and satchels.

He shot one more look at the dull glimmer of the house,

then lowered himself through the hole to crouch on the table. Careful to disturb nothing, he fished the glowworms from his coat pocket. By their light, the papers strewn over the table were covered in a wild scrawl, indecipherable despite his schooling. He pushed aside one paper and found another bearing a different hand—delicate, with deep scrolling loops. The girl's perhaps? But the letters she wrote formed no recognizable words:

*"Sic detectus est completum. Quod quidem verum est, et mundus commutatur."*

The glowworms climbed onto the back of his hand, and he scraped them into his palm. One dropped onto a trunk about the same size as the girl's. Locked, of course.

He rattled it.

Inside, something scrabbled.

The moonlight showed six more trunks lined up on the table.

He hopped to the ground and walked down the line, shaking each trunk. All but two offered scrabbling from within. More ferrets bound for London?

His heel bumped something, and the stench swirled worse than ever. He turned.

The stiff carcass of a cow, huge and bloated, filled the corner.

He scrambled back, tripped over a low spot in the dirt, and flailed. His hand knocked a trunk to the floor, and he landed on his backside beside it.

The trunk's hinges cracked completely off—as rusty as the clasp on the girl's box. Amidst the fallen glowworms crawling about the crack, a pair of small black eyes glinted. A furred head emerged.

This time, it was an otter.

It saw Will, hissed—and fled.

It moved faster than any living otter had a right to. In a streak of darkness, it crossed the floor and disappeared into the far stall.

Heart thundering, he scrambled back, crab-like, on hands and feet.

He was seeing things. Old village folks said that was part of the plague. But disappearing ferrets and storm-fast otters—it was all impossibilities and madness!

Mr. Fitzroy said this wasn't the stuff of magic and fairy-folk. But it certainly seemed little enough like natural science. He shoved to his feet. Perhaps the rector was correct after all: perhaps it was the devil's workshop. He stepped back. Surely this'd be enough to interest Mr. Fitzroy—and maybe bring the magistrate down on Dr. Silas for . . . something.

But first he needed proof.

From behind him, light gushed over the corner of the table, revealing half a dozen amber bottles stoppered with cork and wax. Before he could turn, something hammered into his shoulders, grazing the base of his skull.

He slammed into the table. The amber bottles scattered and fell.

From behind, Dr. Silas shrieked. He hit Will again, across the lower back.

Again, Will smashed against the table. His right hand shattered a bottle. Pains stabbed his palm. Warm, thick liquid seeped over him, either the contents of the jar or his own blood. Likely both.

He shoved up from the table and faced the light, hands before him. "Stop!"

Dr. Silas had a spade cocked over one shoulder and a lantern hooked over an elbow. The gray wig sat askew on his head. His eyes glinted in the gyrating light.

"You . . . ! You mongrel! You cur! How dare you? This is my property! You're trespassing! You're spying! You'll go to Newgate for this!"

Cold sweat sprang up at Will's hairline. Lads such as he could be deported, or even executed, on little more than a gentleman's condemnation. His hands shook. The pains in his head, back, and hand all congealed in his stomach.

"I've as much right here as you," he gasped out. "Tom Colville owns half this barn."

The farm belonged to Lord Carstone, but at least half the barnyard edged onto Tom's land. Tom had never minded, of course. The barn caused him no difficulties, and he wasn't the sort to inconvenience a neighbor.

"What is happening here?" Will said. "How are you doing these things to these animals?"

Dr. Silas scoffed. "*You* could have no understanding of the glories I have wrought here. You who grew up on this place—atop the most powerful reservoir of earthly energy I have ever encountered—and still ignorant as a chimney sweep!"

Will's head spun. "What are you talking about? The plague?"

"And you were so certain there was no plague! It *has* been a plague to some, make no doubt. But it is no illness to be given from one man to another. It is a change deep in your bones, as unpredictable as aught I have ever seen." The twist of the doctor's lip straightened. His eyes shone. "Some bodies do wonderful things with it. Some don't." The twist returned; his eyes refocused. "*Most* don't."

And those that didn't died as the cow had?

A dark thought seized Will. "What have you done with the lady?"

Dr. Silas leant back. "What lady?" He blinked. "Don't be daft. It's not ready to be tested on a man yet, much less a lady! Not yet."

The pain in Will's stomach crawled to his heart. "You filthy old man. A girl such as her? A *lady*? In this place?" His breath came hard. "You're the one who'll rot in Newgate!"

The mania in Dr. Silas's eyes faded, distilling into simple rage. "You had your chance to do me service. Now it's the squire I'll be visiting!"

"Not until you've told me what's happened to the girl!"

"Oh, the knight gallant? Well, you needn't have a care for my lady. She's a soul all alight, even if I'm the only one who knows it! She's a scientific mind in a weak vessel, a visionary in angel's form! She understands more than you will in a lifetime."

The pain in the back of Will's head pounded up into his temples. "The squire will be hearing about her—what's happened to her, what you've done with her. He'll be interested in what you've done in this barn!"

"I'll fire it, I'll blow it up with gunpowder." Dr. Silas snapped his fingers. "'Tis prepared already. I go to London to complete my trials, and no one will use this place whilst I'm gone. And *no one*"—he leant forward—"will credit the likes of you, the trespasser and the spy, the troublemaker and the rebel."

That was likely true, especially after his altercation with young Grainger at the Pirrup. The squire wouldn't cast a kind eye upon Will's sneaking into another man's locked barn. A rivulet of shame ran through him. Tom had been correct about that: a dishonest act was hardly grounds for an honest man's regard.

But Dr. Silas was no sane country surgeon, calmly advancing natural science. He was dangerous.

"Wait—" Beneath Will, the world spun. He caught himself against the table. The fallen amber bottles rolled about, rattling one against another. One toppled off the edge and splintered against the floor.

Dr. Silas squeaked. Then his gaze darted from Will's face to the bottles to Will's bleeding hand. "*You . . .*"

Nausea washed through Will's innards. He tried to straighten his knees, but the barn tilted crazily, like a ship at sea. The once-cold sweat upon his brow now burnt like coals. His vision darkened down to pricks of light, then swirled madly back to full view.

He panted. "What's . . . happening to me?"

Dr. Silas dropped the shovel and rushed to him. "You fool, you fool, what have you done?" For the first time, he sounded a concerned doctor. "'Tisn't ready for man! I told you that." He knelt and seized Will's chin.

Will dragged at the heavy, stinking air. It refused to enter his lungs. "What . . . is it? What was in . . . there?"

Dr. Silas pried open his eyelids and raised the lantern, peering deep into his eyes.

The light pierced to the back of Will's head in a blast of agony. He cried out and pulled back. "What is it? Tell me what it is."

Dr. Silas grasped his throbbing hand. "My discovery, boy, my discovery. Your magic rock and its spontaneous water? The minerals from the ground beneath your feet? You had no idea the treasures you were scorning. But *I* have transformed them. I have transformed every animal who drank from them!"

Animals such as the ferret and the otter? Or animals such as the cow?

At last he gained a breath. The carcass's bloated stench filled his body. His stomach bucked, and bile swarmed his throat. He freed his hand and grasped the table.

With every particle of his strength, he hauled himself up. "What's happening to me?"

"The battle of life, boy! Death or transformation!"

Then the plague had been *real* all along? How many times had he been exposed before? He'd always survived it—until today, when he'd returned for no good reason.

He staggered. "I have to go, I have to go."

Dr. Silas clenched his shoulders. "No, my boy, no. What happens could change the world, do you understand? Never mind the trespassing. I'll not tell the squire or the earl. You're part of this now! If you live—if you are transformed—you will share my glory!"

The room went dark save for a pinpoint of light swirling 'round and 'round.

Will forced one foot forward. "Transformation?" His voice echoed, at a distance. "What do you mean? What does that mean?"

"We never know. It depends on the body, it depends on *you*." Dr. Silas pressed harder against Will's shoulders. "You *must* stay. You're not fit to travel anywhere. I must observe you. It is for natural science, boy. You have sown your fields, through no choice of mine. Now we both must reap the harvest, whatever it may be!"

"No." He must leave, must go home, find Tom, tell him he'd been correct, tell him he was sorry. Find a real doctor, someone who could help. He had to breathe, find some air he could breathe. BreatheBreatheBreathe. That was the only thing left to matter.

He tried to push Dr. Silas away. "Le'go."

Dr. Silas dug into Will's coat lapels. "You must remain!"

His lungs burnt. He scrabbled at Dr. Silas's fingers, couldn't loose them. He started forward.

Dr. Silas clung to his coat. "Stay, you blighted fool!"

Will moved. He had to get away, had to run. And suddenly he *was* running. His feet moved, much faster than he expected them to. He tore free.

Dr. Silas yelped.

Will slammed into the half-open door before he could stop himself, before he could even see it. It swung open under the force of his contact, and he sprawled in the mud outside.

"Wait! You're seriously ill, boy! Don't you understand?"

That was the one thing Will *did* understand. He gained his feet. And then he *ran*—faster than ever he'd run in his life.

Maybe even as fast as the otter.

# CHAPTER 5

THROUGH THE WEED-eaten garden, Will ran. Up and over first one stile, across the road, then the other stile. The night air cut through the sweat on his face. Even as he ran, his teeth rattled cruelly.

For the first time since he was a lad running this field at night, he caught his toe and fell on his face. Before he hit the soft soil, his stomach erupted. He vomited, and then he vomited again. The stars in the sky spun and spun, in every direction, up and down, in front and behind.

On hands and knees, he dragged himself forward, barely gaining his feet.

This time, there was no running; indeed, he could scarcely walk. He splashed into the knee-high stream before its gentle splashing even registered in his ears. He crossed without looking for the bridge. He would have been unable to see it in any case.

He staggered up to the house. His vision had gone completely dark, so maybe there was no light in the window.

"Tom . . ." he croaked.

He reached for the latch, but his hand overshot it. He tried again. Same result. None of his limbs functioned properly. With every movement, they darted all about, his reflexes overreacting violently.

He lurched from the house and supported himself, both hands on the wall, around the corner to the forge. He pushed past the door and stumbled through the darkness until he crashed into the hearth where Tom had banked the coals. Fever roared through him, and new sweat scalded his skin. He fell to his knees, vomited again, then rolled over—and passed into blackness.

———————

Light stabbed Will's eyelids. He shivered awake enough to hear the twittering of nuthatches outside. With a start, he opened his eyes and jerked up. Light flayed his eyeballs and gouged his skull—whether from Dr. Silas's clout upon his head or from the plague.

The plague. Dear God.

He dragged his shaking hands before his face and squinched his eyes open again. The left hand had swelled twice over. His skin was purple, nails brown. Gritty black blood covered his palm and down his wrist. He flexed his fingers open, and new blood oozed from the red graves in which the amber shards were buried.

He was surely going to die. If Dr. Silas's plague failed to kill him, then the rot of his hand—already impossibly decayed—would be his end. He was going to die a disgraced pauper, same as his father. And Tom was going to prison.

Dr. Silas had said he would die . . . or be transformed. But transformed into what? There was no transformation here. Merely corruption and filth and stench. Same as the cow carcass. He squeezed his eyes shut.

Nothing for it now. He must tell Tom, must make some sort of effort to survive. With his good hand, he gripped the hearth and gained his feet. The world swirled him into dizziness once again, but maybe not as badly as last night.

In the doorway, he dared a searing squint outside. The light was faint and gold: the morning was early. With any amount of fortune, perhaps Tom would have overslept the day.

He tottered to the stream and submerged his hand in the nauseous cold. Panting so hard he almost wasn't breathing, he prized out the biggest of the glass pieces with a knife he'd brought from the forge. Blood ran betwixt his fingers, warm and sticky.

He could keep his eyes open for only seconds at a time before the dizziness swirled him back into sickness. The blood on his hand smeared all across his vision, until he could hardly pinpoint the glass shards. Once again, his uninjured hand refused to cooperate. It darted about with more quickness than his brain asked of it. He stabbed the center of his palm and clamped his eyes shut.

Hand in the stream, he leant forward, head almost touching the ground. "What is happening to me?"

He must tell Tom. He must warn him about the plague. If Will were about to die—and surely he was—then he must first tell Tom.

Somehow, he managed to regain his feet and start back to the house.

By the time he reached the garden, voices filtered out to him.

"—apprentice, Master Will Hardy?"

Dr. Silas.

Will halted around the corner from the door. He leant against the wall, eyes closed.

Tom grunted. "Will said you hadn't use for him yesterday." He sounded muffled through the wall, not so loud as Dr. Silas, standing outside.

"Oh, yes, that. We had a misunderstanding. But everything is different now."

"How so?" Tom thumped nearer. "You've seen Will? He failed to come home, as I know of."

"Did he? Well." The doctor sounded uncertain. "Did he . . . tell you of my work?"

"Nothing worth the memory." Tom's voice deepened, still civil, but also demanding. "You know where he is?"

"Ah, no. No, I am afraid I do not, Mr. Colville." Will could almost see the manic quiver of the doctor's eyes as he calculated how to find his new experiment whilst keeping all on the hush.

Will shivered.

"I'm just leaving." Dr. Silas crunched through the grass. "Apologies for disturbing your morning rituals. But you will dispatch the lad my way, yes? It develops I have a better opportunity for him than we were able to agree upon yesterday."

"I'll tell him." Tom sounded as if he'd swallowed a green persimmon. "But that choice is his."

Assuming Will *had* any choices.

"Quite right, quite right," Dr. Silas said. "Good day to you." He retreated.

Will straightened from the wall and held steady. He must get away from here. There had to be a cure somewhere. There had to be *someone* other than Dr. Silas who could tell him what was happening.

Someone such as . . . Mr. Fitzroy.

Of course. Mr. Fitzroy wasn't leaving until this morning. Perhaps Will might yet catch him. He'd found proof enough of Dr. Silas's strange doings, that was certain.

He tugged his coat cuff over his bloody, swollen hand and forced his eyes open. One step at a time, he reached the door.

It was open. Thank God. Who knew if his flighty hands could even manage the latch?

Tom knelt before the hearth, boiling coffee and frying the last of the eggs they'd got in payment for Mrs. Summerson's ladle.

He glanced back. "Will, lad." He rose. "You've had me anxious half off my head! That Dr. Silas of yours was hither. What's happening? Where is it you've been?" He drew back. "What ails you?"

"Tom—I'm leaving." He managed to sound only faintly winded.

"What?"

"Yes. I've an . . . opportunity. With Mr. Fitzroy. He leaves this morning. No knowing when we'll return."

Tom drew his brows. "You didn't mention it last night."

"No. It's of a sudden." Will released the door frame and stepped back. "I must go now. He's leaving straightaway."

"You have no things." Tom frowned. "You won't eat a last meal here?"

Will shook his head. Even that rocked the earth beneath him.

"What's afoot here, Will?" Tom's voice deepened. "Is it drink? This gentleman of yours had you crooking an elbow all night?"

"Tell you all about it when I return." God willing. "Goodbye, Tom."

"Wait—"

If he waited, he'd collapse.

He ran.

"Will!"

But Tom wouldn't follow. He wasn't the sort to force his bidding on another. He'd let Will make his choices, whether he agreed or not.

Pain coursed through Will. He gritted his teeth and kept running, faster and faster. The world blurred. The wind dashed tears from his eyes and snapped his clothing. He kept upright, one stride after another, and by some miracle, he did not fall.

He gained the principle road from Affery where it passed the gates to Lightwood—Lord Carstone's grand estate. Half a mile down the road, a four-horser journeyed north.

He put on an extra burst of speed and reached the carriage door. "Mr. Fitzroy—sir—"

Through the window, Mr. Fitzroy's expression was first startled, then piqued, then shocked. "What—?"

The latch turned in Will's hand, and the door opened. He tripped and fell into the hard road. The team shied.

"Stay the horses!" Mr. Fitzroy demanded.

The carriage halted, dust clouding.

Mr. Fitzroy descended, hatless, and half-ran back to Will. "What is this?"

Will fought for breath. "Dr. Silas—you were correct—the plague—"

Mr. Fitzroy waved off his driver and the other servant who had been riding atop the carriage. "Come." He helped Will to the shade of a roadside tree.

Will devoted himself to keeping his heart from beating out of his chest. "I don't know what it is or how it can be. But you were correct. You were correct. He's doing things there. 'Tis impossible, but he's doing them."

"Slow yourself." Mr. Fitzroy gripped Will's shoulders and peered into his face. "Tell me what has occurred."

Will jerked back. "I've the plague." Again, sickness crept from his stomach's pit. Darkness closed in. If he couldn't get a proper breath, he'd faint.

Mr. Fitzroy stared. "There *is* no plague. I told you that." He looked at Will's swollen hand. "The doctor inflicted this on you?"

"Yes. No. I cut it. His bottles broke. His . . . concoction. He *has* been experimenting on animals. He's doing things to them." His thoughts ran faster than words. "I saw one *disappear*. I saw one move faster than aught could ever move."

"Calm your mind. Speak slowly." Again, Mr. Fitzroy reached for his shoulder.

Will shot up his hand. He pushed Mr. Fitzroy away. The reflex was so sharp, so fast, he nearly spun Mr. Fitzroy around.

The gentleman's mouth came open.

Striking a man such as Mr. Fitzroy? He *must* be losing his senses.

"I apologize, sir, I apologize."

A new light entered Mr. Fitzroy's eyes. He closed his mouth firmly, as if Will had never touched him.

This time he gripped Will's forearm. "Be calm. You have done very well indeed. You will come to London with me today. The best surgeons in all the world will examine you. You will be made well. I promise you. And then you will be given a chance—a *real* chance to do something with your life. Perhaps something none of us has ever done before." He leant back. "But first you must do one last thing for me."

He turned Will about and pointed to the gates of Lightwood, barred as they were to the common world of Affery. "Run to the gates. Run as quickly as you can."

"Run?" He'd already run all the way from the forge. The very air burnt his lungs.

Mr. Fitzroy smiled, encouragingly. "Run."

And so Will ran.

He pounded his feet into the road, every step faster than the last. He reached the gates in seconds and found he could not check himself. He smashed into the iron bars and fell back.

What little air remained in his chest exploded from his mouth. Darkness clamped his skull. He dropped his head to the ground, and the nothingness of a swoon claimed him.

# CHAPTER 6

WHEN WILL OPENED his eyes, nothing made sense. He floated on a cushion of air, surrounded by yellow as if in a field of cowslips. He was warm as steam pudding, and not a thing hurt.

Voices murmured, but not Tom's.

Raising his head required more effort than it should have, but when he did, he found himself in the handsomest room he'd ever seen. His heart skipped, and in response his left hand jabbed pain. The hand lay beside him atop a silken counterpane. It was bandaged.

*The plague!* He'd been polluted with the accursed plague, and then . . . Mr. Fitzroy . . .

He looked about.

In the doorway, Mr. Fitzroy was speaking with a small white-haired man.

"Ah, the patient awakes." The stranger approached and clamped a hand to Will's forehead. "Quite as I said. Heart and lungs sounded quite normal." He smiled, red cheeks puffing. "Your hand improves steadily, my boy. But you had a ticklish few days of it."

"Days?"

Behind him lay a black cloud of sweat and dreams. Prior to that—Tom's concerned face.

He sat—faster than he intended. "I've been here for days?" His head swam, but not as before.

Mr. Fitzroy remained in the doorway. "Dr. Hawkins, you are satisfied?"

"Very. Interesting constitution you have, young man." Dr. Hawkins's eyes twinkled. "Some porridge and a spot of wine would be the thing, I believe. You will be your old self in no time."

Mr. Fitzroy looked Will over, carefully. He offered the corner of a smile. "Perhaps. Perhaps not." He ushered the doctor out. "I will see you in a moment, Will."

Will sat up carefully.

The bed was curtained in bright yellow. To his left, a hearth of ivory and green marble dominated the wall. Before him, two tall windows flanked a mahogany writing table.

If this was how Grainger and Lord Carstone lived, then little wonder they never saw him as aught but a common lad.

He flexed his bandaged hand, carefully, lest his body run away with him as it had seemed so wont to do in his fragmented memories. His palm throbbed dully, but his fingertips were a healthy pink. Whatever he'd been infected with seemed not to have got the better of him.

And yet, within him, a strange energy hummed, a sense of urgency marrowing his very bones. His limbs seemed under control now, but there was *something* different.

Gritting his teeth, he eased from bed, found himself in naught but a nightshirt, and shrugged into the red silk banyan coat waiting for him on the chair.

Across the room, the windows revealed a street lined with mews houses that reached upwards of four stories—not counting their half-submerged ground floors.

He unlatched the window. Into the room crashed the clatter of traffic and, from afar, multitudinous voices. The smell was thick and faintly putrid: horse and smoke and a vague scent of waste. Even the fanciest of men hadn't money enough to escape that.

He found himself grinning, in spite of everything.

London. He was *in* London.

He leaned his head out and looked up and down.

Mr. Fitzroy's house was a buttery yellow, like the bed curtains. Black iron balconies adorned every opening on the first floor and again around the downward stairs to the servants' entrance.

Behind him, the door opened, and Mr. Fitzroy entered, followed by a gentleman in a white wig and knee-high stockings. The be-wigged fellow carried a tray with Will's porridge and wine.

Will faced them.

"How do you find yourself?" Mr. Fitzroy asked.

"Well, sir."

"That *is* a pleasant change." He gestured to the servant. "This is the butler, Tite. He will aid you during your stay."

Tite was a sharp-faced sort of perhaps thirty and five years. He offered the slightest bow possible. "Your servant, sir."

"Thank you." With any luck, that sounded as if it were the exact tone Will *always* used in such cases.

Tite left, closing the door noiselessly.

"How do you find your head?" Mr. Fitzroy asked.

"Clear. In fact"—he thought about it—"I've never felt better." He raised his bandaged hand, still carefully. "Save for this, and even that feels much restored."

Arms behind his back, Mr. Fitzroy circled Will. He looked as if he were doing hard sums—wondering, studying, calculating. His face was slightly flushed, eyes bright.

Then, as ever, his sudden smile transformed his face. He clapped Will's shoulder. "Eat. Then find me in my study. We have much to discuss."

---

The study was even finer than the bedchamber. Paneled in mahogany, it featured an eight-foot painting of a woman with intense eyes and, at her knee, a bored-looking boy. The desk was a massive slab—mahogany again, with gold reliefs. It was framed by chairs upholstered in brilliant blue.

"Well," said Mr. Fitzroy. "You look the part."

A valet had bedecked Will in fine clothes. He'd even trimmed Will's hair and given him a silver watch.

"Thank you, sir. I wasn't at all sure."

Mr. Fitzroy laughed. "My boy, it is easier than breathing to make something appear what it is not. You are an excellent example."

A spot of heat touched his neck. He'd seen himself in the

mirror: he looked a fop. Tom would surely have guffawed, even though they couldn't have paid for this rig with a year's wages.

Mr. Fitzroy approached. "What I mean is you look a normal young man. But you are not, are you?"

"Sir?"

"You have stepped beyond the ordinary, Will. You are something extraordinary now."

His heart started pounding. "I . . . don't believe I know what you mean, sir."

"Shall I tell you what I witnessed?"

Will nodded.

"But perhaps I shall not." Mr. Fitzroy smiled. "Perhaps I shall allow you to demonstrate." He raised a gold pocket watch. "Take it."

Will reached out.

In a twinkling, Mr. Fitzroy spun the watch away, flicking it finger to finger like a gaming man with a coin. The watch disappeared around the back of his hand, and he tugged each empty sleeve in turn. "You must be quicker." He reached behind his back and returned with the watch, which he again tucked into his waistcoat's fob pocket. "Take it without my knowing. Deftness is key."

"You mean . . . pick your pocket, sir?"

"Like this." Again, Mr. Fitzroy raised his hand. From the crook of his thumb dangled the silver watch given to Will by the valet.

Will had felt not even a whisper in his waistcoat.

The man was a magician!

Mr. Fitzroy laughed. "Swift mind and swift hands never serve a gentleman amiss. Now"—he faced the window—"take mine."

Will wet his lips, not quite certain what he hoped would happen. A lifetime of hammering at the forge wasn't the sort of work to sustain a man's quickness. And if the plague had altered him in any way, then it should only have further dulled his reflexes.

Hesitantly, he reached with his unbandaged right hand.

Mr. Fitzroy dodged without looking. "Faster."

Faster indeed. Will darted out his hand.

Quicker than a blink—quicker almost than his eyes could un-derstand—his fingers closed upon the watch chain and jerked it free.

Saints in their heavens.

He dropped the watch as if it were a hot coal.

Half a second more and it would fall to the rug, crack its case at the seams, and scatter delicate machinery all over the floor.

Even faster than before, he grasped at the watch. He caught it midair before it fell more than a foot.

Mr. Fitzroy turned back, brow raised. "Interesting, yes?" He reached out and returned the watch to his pocket.

This time Will needed no prompting. Almost before Mr. Fitzroy averted his eyes, Will snatched the watch.

Mr. Fitzroy must have felt something, because he started to turn back.

Quite as fast, Will restored the watch.

Mr. Fitzroy looked down to find the watch still nestled in its pocket. He seemed unsurprised. "Well, well. You have never possessed such reflexes, have you?"

Will's blood pounded in his ears, strangely. "I . . . couldn't say, sir."

"Then I *shall* tell you what I saw you do back at the Affery road. I asked you to run to the Lightwood gates, you recall? Well, you did. Even giddy and feverish, you ran as I have never seen man run."

That bit was all a-fog. But he *did* remember running through the field from Dr. Silas's to the forge—and from the forge to find Mr. Fitzroy. The world had blurred around him.

He shook his head. "How could that be—even with the plague?"

"We must investigate further, of course, to understand the extent of what has happened to you. But believe me when I tell you I have been watching you these past days and studying this matter, and I have no doubt whatsoever." Mr. Fitzroy's nostrils flared. He looked like a general about to rally a charge. "There *has* been a transformation here."

Will straightened. "That's what Dr. Silas said. That I would die or be transformed." His mouth was ash dry. "What does this mean?"

"We must discover that together, you and I." Mr. Fitzroy looked at him steadily. He held himself as calmly as ever, but the energy humming within him seemed palpable. His own movements were also somewhat quickened, as if he wanted to explode with the excitement of it, but held himself in, as was only proper. "I *believe* it means you are singular, young Will. I believe you possess the ability to move more quickly than almost any other man on this earth."

That was impossible. Plague or no plague. Remarkable reflexes or no remarkable reflexes. Will shook his head. And yet...

He looked down at his hand.

"This is significant in ways far beyond your own life, Will. This discovery is incredible. The possibilities for revolutionizing our world—natural science, war, politics, even social injustice—are fascinatingly endless. I have spent your convalescence contemplating them incessantly."

Will couldn't stop shaking his head. Difficult enough to consider such an idea at large. But this wasn't something occurring in the distance. This had occurred to *him*.

"I can hardly credit what you say, sir. All these changes you believe will happen. How can this . . ." He raised his hand. His fingers were shaking. "I've little interest in war. Social injustices, perhaps."

"A worthy cause." Mr. Fitzroy's excitement stilled and drew in on itself, curling into focused determination. "That is only the beginning, I promise you."

"Sir?"

His eyes grew intent. "It is my wish that history remember me as someone who bettered mankind. That is why I first stood for Parliament. It is why I sought out Dr. Silas. Now, I look at you, and I see a man—young and in need of guidance—but one who also wishes to be remembered well. Am I wrong?"

No, he wasn't so wrong. But he wasn't quite correct either. So much had changed of a sudden. More than Will could yet hold in his brain.

"Sooner or later," Mr. Fitzroy said, "there *must* be a social revolution in this country. Would it not be remarkable were you and I to have some say in shaping it?"

"Social revolution." That rather smacked of Frenchmen running amok with cleavers. "What is it you wish to reform, sir? You wish to lessen the burden of poverty?" That much he could embrace.

"Not at all." Mr. Fitzroy looked at Will levelly. A tiny spark lit his eyes. "My desire is to wipe it out."

Will blinked. "That sounds fine, sir, and I *would* like to have a part in it. But all I can do is pick your pocket and maybe run faster than most. How am I to aid you in this?"

"You are to stop here at Fitzroy House, as my guest. I told you I have use for intelligent, ambitious lads. That holds true now more than ever. Something I may not have mentioned is a good chance of the Prime Ministry coming my way before long."

That should have shocked Will. He was standing in the study of the next *Prime Minister* of the entire country? But somehow, on this day of impossibilities, it seemed a matter of course.

Mr. Fitzroy moved to the desk and lifted a handful of papers. "I must first gain Dr. Silas's loyalty. During your recovery, I arranged to secure the land upon which the trackway rests."

He wasted no time, that was certain.

Will eyed him. "Lord Carstone would sell to you?"

"I have been a valuable friend to him for many years."

"Not all the land belongs to Lord Carstone. Tom owns the edge where the barn is built."

"Does he?" Mr. Fitzroy pursed his lips. "Then this might put him in the way of some profit."

"Tom wouldn't sell merely for the idea of gain." However much he could use the money. "The land's always been in his family."

"Indeed." Mr. Fitzroy looked to the window. He looked for so long Will almost began to think he had forgot him.

Then he spoke, his voice a murmur. "Never have I been able to fathom men who are averse to bettering themselves. There exist two ways to move in this world: up or down. One cannot remain still. A man who refuses to climb is a man with no self-regard whatsoever." He looked back. "You do not speak of your master as being such a man."

"Not a'tall, sir. Tom just has no care what people think." Will bit his lip. "But . . . he has a burdensome debt."

"Ah. Well, that does influence a man. I shall look into it for him."

Will licked his lip. "You care so much about those beneath you, sir? Why?"

Nothing in Mr. Fitzroy's posture changed: head still bent to his papers, one hand raising a corner of the topmost leaf. It was the room itself that stilled around him.

He looked up. His eyes met Will's, and it were as if a shutter closed behind them. All the light left them, all the expression—except for a tiny flicker of deepest pain.

Then, quite as quickly, a smile ghosted his mouth. "Yes. Why indeed? Let there be clarity between you and I." He faced him. "Will, I am a . . . relentless man, let us say, and I do not deny it. I believe in what I believe in, and I offer no apology for it."

"Nor should any man, sir."

"I believe a great enemy undermines our society. But that enemy is not poverty." Mr. Fitzroy's hands seemed almost to tremble against his papers. He lowered them to his side. He continued, expression calm. "But poverty is its mask. There are many poor who have no choice." He inclined his head towards Will. "But there are as many who remain poor and trap others in poverty with them, because they have not the self-regard or strength of character to raise themselves."

He lifted his chin, eyes deep with purpose. "Let us create a clean slate, where men cannot fool themselves into believing their lifestyles are an excuse for allowing themselves to be held back."

Why had Tom never been like this? The thought swirled up from Will's depths. He attempted to quash it, but it popped back up.

He swallowed. "I believe in these things you're saying, sir—I do. But what is it to do with me?"

"What has happened to you is the key to a larger door, which may unlock many possibilities. The secrets of all the world could open to us. Surely, we are not the only ones to discover these things."

That caught Will off guard. "You mean others have had this happen?"

"Indeed. Perhaps Dr. Silas has found a hint as to how our ancestors built the great monuments—Stonehenge, Avebury. Some believe these places lie upon the trackways, you know. What else did our predecessors know that we have yet to remember? Could they fly?" He tapped his temple. "Was the capacity of their brains augmented? What else can this strange magic accomplish?"

What *else*? Will glanced down at his hand, still trembling slightly. This wasn't enough then? What else *could* there be? A feeling welled within him, between panic and excitement.

Mr. Fitzroy came back around the corner of the desk. "For now, such future possibilities are neither here nor there. I ask *you* now because, thanks to your encounter with Dr. Silas, you have become one of the most remarkable people I will ever meet." He extended his hand, almost one gentleman to another. "You are a prodigy, Will Hardy, and the world will fall at your feet. Give me your aid, and I shall give you mine."

It all seemed too grand.

But what kind of daftness was that? His life had changed overnight—like a wish from a fairy—and he was cut up because he'd got *more* than he requested?

Or perhaps it was the manner in which he'd left Affery?

He hesitated, then took Mr. Fitzroy's offered hand. "I should ask Tom. I'm not sure what I left him thinking. And . . . I owe him that."

Mr. Fitzroy nodded. "Write him. If all goes well, we shall return to Affery within a day or two, to close the land sales and speak with Dr. Silas."

From behind Will, a diffident knock sounded.

The door opened to reveal an artfully tousled head, belonging to a man of perhaps five and twenty. He saw Will and widened his eyes. "Our mysterious convalescent! Quite the rotter, sir. Lying abed, not even deigning to satisfy irresistible curiosity in return for our hospitality."

Golden hair a shade darker than Fitzroy's and sky-blue eyes a shade lighter framed a sharp-featured, rather flushed face. He wore a high-collared scarlet coat over a cream waistcoat embroidered with a dizzying vine pattern. Instead of boots, he displayed high silk stockings and buckled shoes.

"But," said the newcomer, "the gods of fortune smile upon you. You're on your feet in time for the grand ball—if you are equal to cutting a figure."

Mr. Fitzroy frowned. "This is Mr. William Hardy from Surrey. Will, my son Henry." He tapped his papers together against the desk, then started for the door. He glanced at Will as he passed. "This ball is a private gathering, so it is a simple thing to secure you an invitation. But only if you feel yourself restored." He raised an eyebrow, as if he expected Will *to* be restored, even after his days in bed.

Strangely, Will found he *was*. Energy surged through his blood, feeling as if it would explode out of him. Whether it was the plague or merely the revelations of the hour, what he needed was to go outside and *run*—to discover what he was actually capable of. Dancing, however, would suffice in the pinch. He was hardly likely to know the steps. But to attend a London ball, just as if he were quality like all the other guests?

"Yes, of course, sir. I'd like nothing better."

"Good lad." Mr. Fitzroy continued to the door. "See to him, Henry. He brought no luggage, so you will ensure he has everything he needs, hmm?" He left.

Henry looked Will over, from head to toe. "Dashed if I can understand the governor on this one. Not exactly from London, are you?"

Will stiffened, but Henry's expression wasn't mockery: more lazy curiosity.

"No, not London. Affery."

"Ah-ha, I know the little place. My adorable betrothed hails from there—or she is *nearly* my betrothed. Lord Carstone's granddaughter, you know?"

Small wonder then that Mr. Fitzroy was Lord Carstone's "valuable friend."

Will strained for something suitable to say. "I've heard she's lovely." He'd seen her, from afar, riding through the village in an open carriage once or twice.

Henry shrugged. "Would have been jollier to have a say in the matter, what? But when the governor makes up his mind, the governor makes up his mind." He yawned against the back of his hand. "Appears he has made up his mind about you, at any odds. Pleasant for him to have a chap such as you as an associate, I daresay."

"I . . ."

Henry lowered his voice. "I never had a head for all that *associating*. The governor forgot he was supposed to explain it to me one of these days."

"What kind of business is he in? Other than Parliament."

"Why none a'tall. No respectable gentleman does business." Henry tapped his nose. "We're in Polite Society. How we got there is a proper mystery. But where there is money enough, questions disappear. Confidentially, it's all a matter of well-placed shipping ventures."

Will eyed him. "Rather a valuable secret to share with a stranger."

"Why not?" Henry turned to the door. "The pater is all about trust and loyalty." His tone flattened. "But a street bears traffic both east and west." Hand at the latch, he looked back. "A spot of advice. Things are not always as they seem with my father. People believe what he wants them to believe." He flashed a grin. "Occasionally, it is even true."

# CHAPTER 7

THE GOLDEN GODDESS was at the ball. What's more, Will had been introduced to her.

Henry did the honors. The lady curtsied diffidently, glancing past Will without recognizing him. The sound of her name was obliterated by the din of two hundred guests and the clash of the orchestra behind ornamental shrubbery at the top of the room. Judging by her blank smile, she missed his name as well.

Then the whole party—Mr. and Mrs. Fitzroy, Henry, and Will—moved on, propelled into the swirling throng. But the introduction *had* happened, that was the essential thing. Will might speak to her now, perhaps even ask her to dance.

His heart hammered with dangerous speed, surely faster than ever before. That was one not-so-prime aspect of this new life of his.

At least he was remembering to breathe as he stood across the room and watched her flirting her fan at several young men. A plump woman with yellow curls at either temple looked on from a seat behind her young charge.

Between Will and the goddess, couples lined the room, swaying through patterns far more elaborate than aught he had danced at the harvest celebrations.

Henry snatched another sherry off a passing servant's tray. His cheeks were already rosy. "Have no anxiety, my buck." He slapped Will's shoulder. "They are certain to play you a familiar air before long. Then you may ask one of our angels for the pleasure." His gaze wandered to the side of the room, where a dozen young men gathered. "Or perhaps you would rather join my tribe for a chance with the dice."

If Will went with Henry, he might lose sight of his still-nameless lady. But if he stayed, he would lose his guide to this dazzlingly foreign world. His heart raced even faster.

Who would have guessed this should be so strange? Little wonder the nobs were uptight. All these clothes for a start. He shifted within the rich weight of his white waistcoat and black coat. He'd exchanged this morning's boots for stockings and buckled shoes—polished until he could see his chin in them.

As he and the Fitzroys had disembarked from the carriage, Henry had leant over to him. "Say as little as possible, keep your back straight, and bow to everyone. That would get even the King of Circassia through the night unremarked."

Throughout the journey, Mr. Fitzroy had seemed distracted. But he spared Will a nod. "As my guest, no one will look down upon any peccadilloes."

Almost as soon as they entered the grand house, Mr. Fitzroy had patted Will's shoulder and departed into a smoky side room. Will had spied Lord Carstone's patrician head looming at the far end above the crowd of men.

Will kept trying to put his gloved hands in his pockets, only to be brought up short by the fact he *had* no pockets. Mimicking those around him wasn't so difficult, but the powers of observation could carry a hamlet boy only so far.

Back at Fitzroy House, when he and Henry had descended the staircase, he had heard Mrs. Fitzroy ask her husband, "Are you certain of this, James? Who is this boy? What can he accomplish but making a fool of you at table?"

Mr. Fitzroy grunted.

"James." She lowered her voice, entreating. "Have you thought on my request? A tour of the Continent—together?"

Will had stepped into view to find a petite woman with a pile of black curls. She wore a gown of orange and gold, a mass of jewels about her neck. Whatever beauty she had possessed was careworn now, like a gilt frame wanting new leaf.

She flinched towards Will, guiltily. Something heated lurked in her face.

Her silence brought Mr. Fitzroy's head up from his papers, even as a liveried footman helped him into his topcoat. "What was that, Esther my dear?" He glanced at Will, smiled approval, then returned to his wife. "Oh, the tour. I am sorry. It must be postponed again. Something important has arisen." He inclined his head to Will. "Has it not, Mr. Hardy?"

Even Mrs. Fitzroy's jewels seemed to diminish. "Something important." When she looked again at Will, her expression was of a combatant sizing up an opponent.

She said nothing more until they reached the mansion where the private ball was to be held. Even then, she only breathed in her husband's direction, "This is so very foolish, James."

Will had clenched his jaw and marched on behind Henry. Still, he couldn't disagree.

He needed to return home and tell Tom what had happened. Tom would make sense of all these impossibilities.

But first he needed to get through this night without making an utter fool of himself. The easiest way to do so was to observe Henry's counsel: speak to no one.

That advice, however, had been given before *she* appeared.

Again, Henry clapped his shoulder. "See you in a bit, yes?" He headed for his gaming chums.

Will started after him, then stopped. He needn't be nursed as an infant in napkins. He could care for himself. He'd spoken to her before. Why not again?

Across the room, she stood out as would Minerva herself, in a high-waisted white dress embroidered with gold across the short sleeves and bodice, and overlaid in the skirt like a toga. She spoke to a young man, the swish of her fan petulant.

Will approached, dipping his head to anyone he passed. The first few times, even that movement made his body try to dart away with him. He nearly tripped over a dowager's train.

He planted each foot deliberately, and it became easier to anticipate his body's reactions.

The need to move burnt within him. He needed to get outside, run, jump, sweat, until his body and his lungs were afire, until his heart was too done up to beat so.

But first came his lady. The real question was what to say to her?

*Good evening, we've met before, remember?*

Or, *I say, how's your invisible ferret?*

Or, *Might you be interested in a small experiment your friend Dr. Silas accidentally enacted upon me?*

What *did* a gentleman say to a lady at a ball? Perhaps this was too forward, even though they'd been introduced. Perhaps she wouldn't look at him.

But she did.

She looked straight at him, over her partner's shoulder, and she broke out in a shining smile.

She recognized him? He nearly tripped again. But surely if she *had* recognized him, pleasure wouldn't be her first reaction.

"There you are." She extended her hand, gloved to the elbow. "I was telling Mr. Lammle you had bespoken this dance." Her fan tickled her nose. "I feared you forgot me."

So that was it. She didn't remember him—she only needed rescuing.

Her young man—handsome enough, though with a thin hairline and a sour mouth—surveyed Will. "Your pardon, sir." He drew out the words, then looked back at the lady. "You will introduce us?"

Her fan froze. "Ah."

Time for extraordinary bravery.

"The lady and I were introduced earlier," Will said. "But in all honesty, I do not believe she was able to hear my name over the clamor." He bowed again. "I am . . . the Duke of . . . Veneering."

Seize it. *Was* there even a Duke of Veneering? Why not tell her "plain Mr. William Hardy"? Surely, there were scads of "Misters" here.

Her smile scarcely faltered. "Of course. That is precisely what I thought was said, Your Grace."

He held out a hand, and, for a wonder, it did not shake.

The gentleman scowled and moved in front of him.

Almost without thought, Will sidestepped and took the lady's hand. His motions were swift, although mercifully not so swift as to knock anyone over. He gave another scant bow to the gentleman and led his prize to the floor.

She gently slipped her hand from his and instead placed it

on his forearm. Slyly, she glanced at him. "I am aware of your secret."

His heart sped up. "You are?"

"You are *not* the Duke of Veneering."

He stopped.

Her laughing eyes still held no recognition.

How could she *not* recognize him? They'd met twice, exchanging more than a few words at both occasions. Of course the light was different now. Despite the extraordinary chandeliers, the result was a dark flicker compared to daylight.

Or was it that a common village lad hadn't merited looking at closely—much less remembering?

No odds now. He would be that lad no longer.

He grinned. "I'm not the Duke." He leant in. "I'm his son. But I thought it might sound better in helping you complete your ruse." He strove for the stiff accent the Fitzroys used. "Is it always your practice to tell untruths?"

"Oh, blatantly." She laughed. "If I refuse a partner, I must, of course, sit out the rest of the evening. Ruins a good ball."

They had almost reached the dancers—which would be his unmasking as a country clod who had never once waltzed in his life.

Then the set ended, and the orchestra smiled upon him by striking up a country dance. No doubt, they danced it more strictly here, but at least he knew the steps.

He moved away from her to arm's length and extended his hand. "Shall we?"

They wove through the pattern. For the first few minutes, he devoted himself to watching his too-nimble feet, her own small feet, and the feet of the gentlemen before him. With fifty couples filling the floor, the dance offered many moments of stillness whilst waiting for the others to complete their parts.

Finally, he looked up at her.

She studied him curiously, as if trying to fit the missing puzzle piece. When their eyes met, she smiled—genuinely.

Now, they were supposed to converse. He cleared his throat. "You are recently returned to town?"

"For the Little Season—until the fox hunt begins in November. But how did you know I was away?"

Ah, yes. No one here was likely to know about her dabblings with Dr. Silas. Nor would she desire them to.

"Word is you are interested in . . . things."

The pattern reached them, and she wove past and around him, twirling at the arm of the adjacent gentleman, then gliding back into place.

"Well, yes," she said. "I find most people are interested in *things.*"

"I mean things such as . . . natural science."

She laughed. "A lady should hardly admit to that."

"Why not?"

"Most partners would be disgusted by the indelicacy."

"Not I."

The teasing left her eyes. She seemed surprised. She *almost* seemed impressed. "Well, more specifically then, I fear my grandpapa does not appreciate the glories of the topic."

"But *you* find it glorious?"

"Oh, yes." The sheen of practiced hauteur faded. "There are things possible in this world—things you cannot imagine. So much we do not understand, and yet so much we are at the brink of discovering."

He took her hand and stepped to meet her in the middle, then back again. "What sort of discoveries?"

A dimple appeared in the corner of her mouth. "Superior men, perhaps? I suspect they may exist already, in all corners of the world, if only our eyes might be opened to them."

"And what traits might these superior men of yours possess?" He retained a serious tone. "Considerable intellect? Supernatural ability? Physical enhancement?"

She raised perfect eyebrows. "I see you spoke truly. You are not disgusted."

"Not at all." He met her in the middle once more, halting very near this time, their joined hands raised above their heads. "I would be most interested in meeting some of these gentlemen. Is that so singular?"

"Not exactly. I should think *I* were the singular one."

"Because you'd rather tell untruths and dance with me than curry favor with that other chap, who no doubt wants to marry you?" He blurted the words before he'd time to properly think them.

Her eyebrows rose even higher. *"Really."*

"I apologize. I . . . thought it was the occupation of young ladies to find husbands."

As they stepped back, she gestured dismissively. "That will all be arranged for me. I make better use of my time pursuing my interests whilst I may."

Most girls, even poor ones, cared heartily enough whom they married. At the least, any girl peculiar enough to run about the country risking her reputation in pursuit of natural science, of all things, would surely resent any marriage that might curtail her diversions.

"You're the strangest girl I ever clapped eyes on."

She reared back. But the dimple seemed in danger of resurfacing.

She uttered a small, rather well-practiced laugh. "Indeed, sir. Well, I am certain *you* are nothing like any duke with whom I have ever had the pleasure of partnering." She performed a devastatingly slow blink. "And I have danced with most of them."

He grinned. "Any of them superior men?"

"I can hardly say otherwise, since I must marry one of them."

No wonder she'd not looked twice at Will Hardy, blacksmith's apprentice.

"Don't you bother a'tall about the person you will marry?" he asked.

"Why should I? The decision is hardly mine. We all marry whom we marry, and we make the best of it."

This time, when the dance allowed him to take her hand, he gripped it longer than he was supposed to. "Are you so cynical about everything?"

She looked up, surprised. "Not cynical. Factual."

"Maybe you should look *beyond* your superior men."

She laughed. "Do not be absurd. I could never marry a working man. That would be approximate . . ." She shrugged. "To returning the gold to the ore."

He halted half a step before the dance ended, leaving himself sticking out from the line of gentleman dancers. "You mean that?"

"Of course." The dimple resurfaced completely. "The best sort of people always rise to the top." She glanced about the glittering room, then back at him. "*We* are here, are we not?"

She *would* judge a man by his rank, same as every other member of the fancy! The heat of indignation burbled in his throat. She would spurn Will Hardy at the back of her heel, but not the Duke of Veneering's son? The heat balled in his windpipe.

And yet, she was correct: he *was* here. He *was* dancing with her. For today—and maybe for every day for the rest of forever—he would walk in the society of such a lady as this. He was one of her superior men and she didn't even know it yet. Someday she *would*. If ever he walked down the street with a goddess such as this at his arm, the likes of Richard Grainger would never dare jostle him again.

"I believe the dance has ended." She pointed to where the woman with the yellow curls used a lace pocket-handkerchief to fan herself. "My aunt sits there."

Which meant he now must return her whence she came. He offered his right arm. Alongside the other couples, they promenaded the edge of the room.

With the exertion of the dance behind him and the most beautiful woman in the room at his side, his heart began beating away again. The glimmer of the hundred candles in the hanging chandeliers sparkled everywhere: on the ladies' jewels, the gold needlework on his partner's gown, the crystal goblets lofted on silver trays. It was fair blinding.

Of course, the chandeliers dripped wax here and there, and the headdress feathers drooped in the heat, and more than a few gentleman—Henry among them—wobbled from drink.

He glanced at his partner. Even she—passing strange as she was—casually bore the scars of her upbringing.

Strange that Mr. Fitzroy should be so different.

She looked up at him, coyly at first, no doubt aware of his admiration. But then she must have recognized the rest—that he wasn't thinking merely of her beauty. Her smooth brow knit, and her expression deepened. For the first time, she *almost* seemed to recognize him.

She slowed. Perhaps—just perhaps—she was as loath to reach her aunt as he.

She gestured to a tall window. "The streets are beautiful at night, are they not?"

"Indeed."

At either side of the cobbled street below, gas lamps cast both light and shadow in a quivering cotillion across the pavements. Even now, lines of closed carriages rattled past, depositing late-arriving guests at other bright mansions.

A sudden wash of dizziness spun through his head. His knees turned to air and nearly dropped from under him.

"Sir!" She caught at his arm. "Are you unwell?"

Darkness edged his vision, and he staggered back. Blinking hard, he whirled from the window. His vision cleared only in time to dodge the footman carrying a tray of champagne.

The man's shoes skidded against the waxed floor. He lurched backwards, then forwards—and loosed his tray directly at the lady's head.

Will moved, and the world stopped moving around him. Time slowed. Before she could raise her gloved arm in defense, he stepped betwixt her and the tray.

Time resumed.

The tray and its goblets collided with his chest. Glass shattered; a shard nicked his chin. Everything, including the footman, clattered to the floor.

People turned, belatedly.

His blood thundered in his ears.

The lady stared at him. "How . . . precipitant of you." She reached towards his chin. "Oh, you are injured!"

His brain had yet to quite catch him up. He stepped away from her and dabbed the blood with his white glove.

Henry wandered over and shook a finger at the footman. "Clumsy, clumsy." He hauled the red-faced servant to his feet and directed him to wipe Will's sopping suit. "See the man put to rights, yes?" He glanced at the lady. "All dry, Isabella?"

She waved off his impertinent use of her first name as she might wave off a fly. She stared at Will, not with solicitude only, but with deep attentiveness. "Are you well?"

"Quite." But his heart beat again with that same need—to run, run, *run*. A wisp of black dizziness still floated in his head.

He backed up. "Allow me to attend to myself."

"But of course."

He took another step back, remembered barely in time to bow, then hastened to the door.

# CHAPTER 8

OF ALL THE hob-brained things to have done. Will had no idea the proper etiquette for escaping a ball. But escape he must—at least for a few minutes. In his champagne-soaked coat and neckcloth, he waved off the footmen and managed to pass through the massive front doors onto the cobblestones.

A few coachmen glanced at him, perhaps expecting their masters.

He kept each step careful and precise until he could halt in the lane of shadow betwixt the grand house's wrought iron fence and the gaslights bordering the street. With both hands, he gripped the railing. He lowered his head and breathed in the smoky night.

Good heavens. Had he made it through a fancy ball, even an entire dance with the finest lady in the house, only to tangle feet with a servant and end drenched in champagne and broken glass?

He closed his eyes against the remains of dizziness and drew deep, calming breaths. His heart slowed.

Perhaps he *hadn't* embarrassed himself quite so much. After all, he had saved her. Better he drenched than she. And she had been much struck by his actions. Not every man could have done what he had.

He opened his eyes. This thing that had happened to him—*was* happening to him—perhaps it was the great opportunity Mr. Fitzroy suggested. Straightening, he found a grin on his face. Had the plague been capable of this all along?

He could now run very quickly across roads and fields. He could pick pockets and catch falling objects. He could save damsels from drenching. What more?

From within the shadows next to the house, a darker spot moved. Oval eyes glinted. A ragged, woebegone cat opened its mouth and hissed.

On impulse, he leant over the fence and grasped at it.

Almost faster than comprehension, his hand closed in the matted black ruff. He snatched the cat off the ground, over the fence, and—foolishly—against his chest. It happened with such speed that, for a full heartbeat, even the cat lay in his arms, silent and shocked.

Will stared at it.

It stared back, half-moon eyes grown appallingly full. With one breath it spat, and with the next it screeched. It swiped at Will's already bleeding chin, then dug all eighteen claws into his chest and leapt away.

Once more, Will reached out—and once more, he caught the animal in mid-air.

The cat froze again, but only for a second.

Before its claws could find his hand, Will released it.

The cat landed on all fours, shot him a murderous yellow glare, then fled.

He'd caught it? Who would have thought? He looked at his palms. They held steady now, nary a tremble. He darted one hand out and then back, then both hands. They responded with what certainly seemed impressive speed.

Again, the need pounded in him: run, run, *run*.

Perhaps he might dash to the corner. If he remained in the shadows behind the gaslights, who was to see?

Busy with conversation and snuff, not a single coachman looked his way.

Well, then.

He launched off his back foot, and he ran. The shiny buckled shoes clapped the pavements. At first, it felt no different from running across the field from Tom's forge.

And then, of a sudden, it felt very different.

The bright mansions with their Palladian columns blurred

past. The still night became a gale, snapping his clothes, ripping tears from his eyes.

God help him, but he was fast! Faster than any man, surely. Faster than a galloping horse!

That thought nearly toppled his balance. One of those daft shoes went flying. He staggered, flailed, regained his stride.

His stocking foot met the pavement and pushed off, sure and strong. The night air roared power through his lungs.

This was magic. This was grandeur beyond any glittery ball-room. He threw back his head and laughed.

He pumped his arms, and his shoulders strained against the confines of his new coat. Scarcely slowing, he stripped the coat from his arms and let it fall. He would retrieve it later.

He turned down another road.

Judging by the slackening number of bright lights, perhaps these houses were not so fine as those behind in Grosvenor Square.

He flew past a man and woman disembarking their coach. The lady squealed.

But not to worry. She wouldn't be able to bespeak *what* she saw, much less whom. He laughed again, then let the noise explode from his chest in a whoop. Let Tom see him now! Tom would gape in wonderment—and then what a belly laugh there would be.

The ground surged beneath his feet. He must have covered miles already.

The street narrowed. No iron fences surrounded these houses.

From the shadows, a carriage bore down at him. Or rather, *he* bore down at it.

The coachman shouted. The horses threw up their heads, shying.

Heart in his throat, Will dodged to the side of the street. His speed was too great to allow him to slow for the wall of the house. Instinctively, he put out his foot to catch himself against the bricks. His legs kept running. He did *not* smash into the wall. Indeed, he did not halt a'tall. His momentum carried him, running *on* the wall, for all of five strides.

The carriage thundered past, and he stumbled back to the flat road. He pumped his arms harder. Again, he tilted to his right and stepped onto the wall. Again, he managed it: merely a short arc, but he ran *on the wall*.

"Huzzah!" he shouted.

Ahead, the overhang of a single-story roof jutted into the darkening street. If he could walk on walls, why not roofs?

In four strides, he reached the building and jumped.

He landed, not hanging by his fingertips, but on his feet.

For a tremendously long second, he teetered and thrashed, heels suspended over the eaves. Then he leant forward enough to right his center.

Behind him, the street loomed fifteen feet below.

"Saints and martyrs."

He took off again, across the rooftop. He leapt the gap to the next roof, up to a second story—and on and on.

At last, he halted.

Before him stretched an ocean of black, speckled with as many lights as the midnight stars back home. All these foothills and mountains of rooftops, undulating with the black smoke from thousands of chimneys—now *there* was an adventure! *There* was an uncharted land made for only him to discover. All his dreams were to be had out there.

He looked back.

What lay behind appeared no different from what lay ahead.

In fact . . . he hadn't the slightest notion where he might be. He hadn't run merely to the corner and back. He had run for miles—in a strange city, where he knew naught but one man.

A chill cooled his sweat.

He walked to the eaves and swung down to the street.

No cobblestones here, and no streetlights. No lights a'tall, save an occasional rushlight glimmering behind a dirty pane. Not a soul was in sight, although the clamor of traffic and nocturnal voices buzzed louder here than in Grosvenor Square.

His breath failed to come as easily as before. His lungs burnt, and his calf and shoulder muscles felt as if they might fall off his bones. He leant against a house, wheezing.

Swift, yes. Invincible? No.

What did all this mean to his body? As yet, his heart and

lungs seemed pleased to sustain his speed. But had the plague enhanced them as well, or were they struggling to keep pace with his feet?

Uncertainty wriggled through him. He knew absolutely naught about what was happening to him. He might yet die from the plague for all he knew. Only Dr. Silas knew.

From behind, a great clattering of hooves and wheels thundered down at him.

He dodged aside, and a closed coach careened past.

Two lanterns beside the driver's seat showed a team of horses snorting wraiths of steam. They were headed in the general direction of Grosvenor Square, which meant he could steal a ride at least part of the way home.

He leapt. Weary muscles propelled him high enough to grasp the luggage rack 'round the carriage's roof. He kicked off the footman's step and hoisted himself to the top.

The driver seemed oblivious. He slashed at the horses with his whip. He, too, seemed eager to leave these environs.

Ahead, a flickering streetlight broke the darkness. In the center of the street, within the dim circle of light, lay a dark heap.

A girl child.

She lay facing up, palms flat against the street, legs straight.

The driver leant back at his reins. "God save us!"

The horses skidded on their haunches. They would never be able to halt in time.

One more surge of energy burnt through Will. He launched himself over the driver—almost over the team. He caught a step against the near horse's shoulder, just enough to propel him past.

The horses staggered, now scrambling as much sideways away from him as anything. Their change in direction might be enough to keep them from the child.

His feet hit the ground, and he stumbled to catch up with his own momentum. He reached the girl and grasped her arm.

Wide-open pale blue eyes stared from a filthy face. Her mouth went round. "Cor! Where'd you come from?"

He half-dragged, half-flung her sideways, away from the horses. He slid back on his tailbone, the girl on his lap.

Now fully within the circle of light, the horses slammed against each other, tripping over their traces, grunting volubly. The carriage listed onto two wheels. Abandoning his whip, the driver leapt free, only to crack his head against the ground. The coach toppled to its side, hauling the horses along with it. The axle fractured, and the team staggered free.

The girl spun up into a crouch, gaping at the wreck of the carriage. Then she turned her stare on him. "What was that?" Her voice was piping.

"That's what I should like to know!" he rasped. All his new-found energy drained from him. He fought the need to collapse flat on his back.

She eyed him, from his sweat- and champagne-soaked waist-coat and shirtsleeves down to the raveled silk stocking on his shoeless foot. "Warm cove for these parts, ain't you?" She leant in. "What're you grabbing me for?"

"What were *you* doing in the street? You could hear the coach a mile distant!"

She snorted. "'Course." Turning her head half away, she observed him through one eye. Even within the filth of her face, 'twas a keen little eye. "Well." As suddenly as that, a smile lit the corners of her mouth. "I ain't never seen the like, eh?" She touched both thumbs to her chest. "And I've seen every bit there is to be seen. Jumping off a runnin' coach, bouncing off the horseflesh. You're the lucky one not to be trampled to specks."

Dirty wisp that she was, she couldn't be more than nine years of age. Long moon-pale hair framed a scarred forehead, a pert nose, and a sharp chin. Knobbed elbows and knees protruded at angles from beneath the faded frock. A woman's blue shawl was knotted over her stomach.

She pushed against her knees to gain her feet and shuffled over in huge boots. She grasped his arm and leant back to haul him to his feet. She smelt of wet straw and the leavings of rats.

He allowed himself to be hauled. What *was* this creature? Her words and those eyes could have belonged to a person at the end of her life rather than the beginning.

"Haven't you parents?"

She shrugged. "You're a performing tumbler, are you?"

He waved that off. "Did I save your life?"

She looked him over admiringly. "Didn't you just?"

"Then best you tell me what demon possessed you to lie in the middle of the street in the middle of the night with a mail coach coming!"

Her face closed up. "Ah, well . . . that I couldn't be saying." She glanced at the upended coach.

Will had all but forgot the poor driver. The man must be tended, if he weren't already killed.

Indeed, he lay prone in the street.

The coach, however, offered more than enough activity to compensate for any lack on the driver's part.

Two men had flung open the coach door, so it was now erect in the air. They lugged out mail sacks and, with a muted shout, a small strongbox.

"Hie!" Will cried.

The girl snatched his wrist. "Now, don't be rowing." She glanced almost frantically down a side alley behind the lamppost. "If there's trouble now, Mr. Monarch'll plant you in some dark pit."

Within the alley's shadows, a rotund figure in a tall hat slunk back into the obscurity of the night.

Will's heart started up again. He looked at the girl. "They made you lie in the street in hopes of overturning the coach?"

Her shrug came a second too late to be convincing. "It always stops."

Amongst what sort of men had he found himself? Gentleman highwaymen were rogues of one turn, but to capsize a coach in a narrow street with no concern for the driver or, had there been any, the passengers?

His throat burnt, and he freed his hand from the waif's clinging fingers.

The two men at the coach door watched him as they worked. The taller—a hulking man with a protruding jaw—glowered. The shorter grinned provokingly.

Will could run away, of course. Even done up, he could outrun these wretches. But that wasn't what Tom would do. Tom would dive in, fists swinging, and likely lay both men at his feet. Will stepped up.

The girl hauled at his sleeve. "Already been a hero once, ain't you? That's enough to level the ledger."

"Will they punish you for what I do?"

She pursed her lips. "Nah, I did my job aright."

"Well, then." He shook free and stalked to the carriage.

From the far side, the big man growled.

"Ah, stow that, Bull," said the shorter. His unshaven face was round as a cheese wheel. He wore a patched waistcoat beneath a long brown coat and a battered shovel hat with a gleaming square buckle.

Still hauling out bags and handing them over to his imposing partner, he grinned, displaying two toothless black holes to the sides. "The bloody clunch, aren't you, mate? *Quite* the bloody clunch, I'll give you that. Ain't never seen the like. But what you need to risk your crag for, eh? Little Rose, she's always prime." He raised his voice. "Ain'tcha, my chit?"

Rose offered a deep snort. "Hah. Ain't I? You're a blinker, Lifty! That'n would've had me, and you know it!"

Will advanced. "She's a child!"

"Ah, now. Don't give her no slight." The round-faced Lifty laughed. "She's bang-up." He looked at the other man. "Ain't she, Bull?"

"Shut your chops." Bull caught the last mail bag in his thick arms, dug his fingers into the canvas, and ripped its seams. Letters scattered. "Do the job like Mr. Monarch says."

Will stepped forward.

"Don't," Rose whispered.

"Cease what you're about. Or I'll call the . . . authorities."

Lifty pawed through an open bag atop the coach. "What— the Bow Street Runners?" He snorted. "You're a lovely chaw-bacon, ain't you? Just going to holler out and hope those Robin Redbreasts scuttle to your beck, eh? Like as not, they'll take *you* under the king's warrant."

"They'd have no just cause."

"Reckon they don't need one. If they can find a way to gain a reward, what more do you think they need against folks such as us?"

Will straightened. "I am not such as you."

Lifty looked Will over. "If that rig's supposed to tell folks you're the stuff a gentleman's made from, you'll have to give me pardon for not quite believing it."

"He's a gen'leman, true enough," Rose said. "You ever seen the flash cove what jumps before a mail coach to save me?" She crossed her arms and raised her chin. "At all events, he smells of champagne."

Lifty sobered. "Does he now?"

Bull threw down his mail bag and glared at Rose. "Cork-brained mort. You do the job true and there ain't no complications, is there?" He reached across the broken axle to seize her arm. "You think Mr. Monarch'll be glad for this?"

She squealed. "Le'go!" She slapped at his hand and, when he hauled her off her feet, started kicking.

Will acted immediately—because speed was truly the only factor in his favor.

He burst forward, slamming his open arm around Rose's waist and snatching her from Bull's grip. He dropped her in the street, then whirled back. Lowering his shoulder, he ran straight into Bull's abdomen. The force of his speed alone slapped them both to the ground.

Rolling away, Will sprang to his feet even before he could finish registering the pain in his shoulder. He gritted his teeth. Lucky not to have disconnected the joint.

With a deep moan, Bull raised himself to his elbows. He blinked and shook his head, then slowly swiveled his glare towards Will.

Will rushed him again and landed a kick with the heel of his remaining shoe. It smashed into the man's heavy jaw and catapulted him all the way over onto his stomach. It didn't, however, render him unconscious—which it should have.

Will turned to Lifty. "Give me the strongbox."

Lifty looked from Bull groaning on the ground, then to Rose lying open-mouthed at a distance, then to Will standing before him. "Blimey."

"And *that* will be just enough!" a nasal voice bellowed through the street.

Rose screeched. "Horneys!"

Almost as quickly as Will might have done it, Lifty shoved the box into Will's arms. He spun about, hauled Bull up, and together they fled into the shadows.

Will turned to find Rose vanished as well.

From across the street, half a dozen men in red waistcoats clomped into the light. One knelt to check the unconscious driver. Two raced around the carriage in pursuit of the thieves.

The other three closed on Will.

Their apparent leader was a scarecrow of a man in perfectly squared clothing: black broadcloth coat, red broadcloth waistcoat, white linen shirt, black broadcloth trousers, white leathern gaiters. In the dim light, his hair was also very black and very square, just as his face was equally very white and very square.

Will swallowed. "Are you the Runners?"

The scarecrow squinted down his nose. "*Principle officers*. If the quarry were the intelligent sort, he'd know better than to insult us."

The strongbox in Will's hands grew heavier. "Quarry?"

Another of the Runners tucked a gilt-topped baton under his elbow and produced a set of manacles. "We are officers on His Majesty's warrant—and you, sir, are under arrest for thieving from the Royal Mail." He clapped on the manacles, then wrested away the box.

Oh, stupid. Will reeled. This couldn't have worked out better for those three reprobates if they had planned it.

"I'm no thief. The coach was about to crush a young girl. I pulled her to safety, then I forced the thieves to give over at least these valuables. I was about to come in search of you."

The leader sniffed. "Yes, I saw."

Had he also seen Will's inhuman speed? "You . . . did?"

Was that a good thing or an evil thing? Mr. Fitzroy had warned him to veil his new abilities. Certainly allowing this policeman or magistrate or whatever he was to glimpse them was an egregious lapse of that.

The leader cocked his head. "Interesting fish, aren't you, my lad? I can see why flash coves might like your sort at their elbow." He scanned Will's disheveled length and raised heavy black eyebrows. "Constable Henderson Pish, of the Bow Street office. And you?"

Will clamped his mouth. But why not say? He *was* innocent. "Mr. William Hardy."

Pish pursed his lips.

"I'm a guest of the Honorable Mr. James Fitzroy."

"Ah. The Tories' man, is it? Ambitious, charming, a little furtive perhaps. Eye on the Prime Ministry."

"You know him then?"

"Many know of him. More to the point, *anyone* might name him. And even *more* to the point, knowing a wealthy and respectable man is no vouchsafe for respectability in one's self."

Pish removed his black hat and withdrew from its depths a quire of paper and a graphite stub. "Now." He replaced the hat, licked his finger several times, and applied it to the papers until he found the desired page. "Tell us what has occurred here."

"I *told* you."

"Yes, yes. Girl in the street, saved the girl, overcame *two* flash coves." Without raising his chin from his writing, he cast Will a questing glance. "Saved the valuables." He finished with a flourish of the pencil. "Now perhaps you can tell us how a gentleman from Soho Square comes to be off Charing Cross Road in the middle of the night—and without half his togs."

Will opened his mouth, then closed it. The truth would never do. "It's all rather . . . foggy."

Pish grunted. "Well, 'tis London, isn't it?"

The other officer rattled Will's elbow. "Reeks of spirits, this one."

Pish leant in for a sniff. His stare started out intimidating, then remained to grow downright thoughtful.

Will's stomach cinched into a tight ball. "If I were to tell you the facts, sir, you wouldn't believe me."

"Hmm." Pish leant back. "Were you to spend any time a'tall in my company, Master Hardy, you would learn the only thing in which I am *able* to believe is a fact."

"The facts might not be as believable as you're accustomed to think them."

"Give them a try, why not?"

Out of nowhere, the yellow-haired waif appeared at Will's side and sank her teeth into the hand of the officer holding Will.

"Try *that*, cully."

# CHAPTER 9

PERHAPS IT WOULD have been wiser for Will to remain and demonstrate his innocence by pointing at this girl as one of the true robbers. But for all Constable Pish's devotion to facts, the look in his eye said what he was *truly* inclined to believe was a thief in his hand. No doubt he would like two thieves—and two rewards—even better.

At all events, Will's first reflex regarding anyone who manacled his wrists was to flee—and his reflexes were rather good these days.

The moment Rose bit the officer's hand, Will had leapt back, snatching the key from the man.

Howling, the officer grasped futilely, first at Will, then at Rose.

Will unlocked one wrist, freeing his arms enough to catch Rose by the waist.

It all happened in a blink. Pish and the other Runners could take but a single step.

Will lifted Rose's whisper-thin frame and sprinted away. He looked back just once as he left the circle of lamplight.

This time, Pish's lips weren't pursed in disbelief: they were wide open in shock.

Well, the man had just witnessed a *fact*, and true to his word, he appeared to believe it.

Of course, the other fact Pish had witnessed was Mr. William Hardy running off with one of the thieves.

He ran until his lungs burned, which after his evening of exertion, required hardly five minutes.

Under his arm, the girl wriggled. "Stop! You've passed up Lifty!"

Will staggered to a halt and set her down. Black encircled his vision, and fire engulfed his throat. He sagged, hands at his knees.

Oh, seize it. How daft was he? If he'd been half as smart as he sometimes liked to think himself, he would have left her to her fate.

Still leaning upon his knees, he looked at her in the light of a lantern from the nearby eaves.

She cocked her head. "And now I've saved your skin."

"Is that what you've done?" he said dryly.

If he hadn't reacted to her interference, perhaps she would have escaped on her own. Perhaps the magistrate would have chosen mercy. Perhaps the Runners weren't so mercenary as Lifty suggested.

And perhaps the moon was made of gold sovereigns.

She giggled, and then she laughed. "I don't believe I've a word to call you by."

"You'd plenty of words before."

"Aw, most of my words are for things that ain't so agreeable. But you . . ." Her eyes positively sparkled. "There should be a prodigious word for the likes of you. You saved my life—which, believe me, nobody's ever done before. You thrashed Bull—which nobody's ever done neither. And you picked the key from the hand of a Bow Street boy and ran like a madman, clean away."

Her smile faded. She chewed her lip. No doubt, she was searching for the same question every person for the rest of his life would want to ask: *How?*

Unfortunately, he hadn't yet any way to explain it.

Straightening, he unlocked the other cuff.

From behind, footsteps trotted down the road.

He whirled.

The short man in the shovel hat—Lifty—stared at him. "Thought I'd never catch you up. You're a swifty devil, ain't that the truth?"

Will clenched the manacles. They were his only weapon. "Where's your friend?"

"Pointed hisself home. Wasn't too keen on saving the likes of you, believe it or not." Lifty circled Will.

Rose followed in his wake.

Might it be she had pulled him from the fire to the furnace? In Affery, passing London coachmen told stories of children hired to lure unsuspecting men into the darkness. "Moon-cursers" they were called.

Will swiveled to track them. "But *you're* keen to save me?"

Lifty shrugged. "I'm not the sort to hold a hard feeling. Besides you raise a mite of curiosity."

A tiny pressure delved into Will's waistcoat. It felt suspiciously akin to when Mr. Fitzroy had picked his pocket. He looked down in time to see his silver watch disappear into Lifty's voluminous coat.

But then, quite as quickly, Rose's hand followed the watch into Lifty's pocket and nipped it back into Will's waistcoat.

Too surprised to catch Lifty's hand, Will managed to snatch Rose's instead. "What are you doing?"

It was a ludicrous thing to say. They were criminals, weren't they?

Lifty laughed and slapped Will's shoulder. "What am I doing? Seeing if you're awake with your eyes open." Even as he spoke, the pressure tickled Will's pocket once more. Silver flashed between them and vanished into Lifty's pocket.

This time, Will shot out his hand so quickly he closed his fingers 'round the watch and dragged it back out even before Lifty's hand left his pocket.

Lifty's eyes popped. "Ain't you full to your brim with the king's own surprises?"

Rose stared up at Will, her own empty hand suspended betwixt Will's pocket and Lifty's. "How do you do that? 'Tis like . . . magic."

Will pocketed the watch and shrugged out from under Lifty's friendly grip. "Maybe 'tis."

Lifty clapped his hands—clad in fingerless mittens—and laughed. "Ain't that marvelous? And country lad that you are too!" He leant in again. "You are, ain't you? 'Cause blow me down if you'd know your way *to* Seven Dials, much less *around* it. And yet here you are picking pockets with the fingers of the fairy folk."

Hand still on his watch in its pocket, Will turned to go.

"Now that you're on the bolt and all," Lifty said, "I don't suppose you'd be wanting a proper job? Mr. Monarch'd be happy of a hand like yours. Reckon he ain't seen the like since the days of his prized Blue-Eyed Jem—and that was years before me."

Will shook his head. "If I asked you to point me towards Grosvenor Square, I don't suppose you would?"

Rose crossed her arms. "You don't know about Blue-Eyed Jem, do you?"

Lifty blew a vulgar noise. "Jem's gone and long gone. Legend says he filched enough to sail away and become a sheik in Araby or such like." He tapped his nose. "Around here, when folks have that said of them, it don't mean something quite so cushy."

Will began walking.

Rose skipped to match his pace. "Jem couldn't have been no older'n me when he flitted." She whistled through her teeth, then glanced at him nonchalantly. "Think of that."

Lifty moved in on Will's other side. "Greatest geezer Mr. Monarch ever trained, eh? Mr. Monarch probably made the whole bloody thing up, I say. But he'd be happy to have a truth like you replace his dusty old legend. I could fix you right up. Get you in his trust, swift as that. How say you?"

"No."

Lifty stopped walking and let Will pass him by. "Your mistake, matey. Because there'll be trouble waiting if you're going back Grosvenor way."

That was true enough. Like a daft fool, Will had given the constable his name *and* Mr. Fitzroy's name.

Mr. Fitzroy would help him. He would. He wasn't like the rest of his class.

But he wouldn't be pleased.

As far as Will knew, he'd been traveling east when he left the ball. If he kept in a westward direction, perhaps he'd find a kinder neighborhood where he might ask directions. As soon as he was free of these two, he could jump to a rooftop where he could travel out of the way of criminals.

Rose still trotted at his side.

"And where are you going?" Lifty called.

"Thought I'd go along and see this Grosvenor Square."

"Ah, you've seen it and you know you have. Mr. Monarch'll want the likes of you back safe and snug."

Will looked at her. How soon before they had her lying down before mail coaches again?

This was her home. He could hardly take her away. As it was, he might have difficulties enough regaining entrance to Mr. Fitzroy's house.

"I'm sorry," he said, "you can't come with me."

They reached the crossroads.

Without protest, she halted and once more clamped thin arms over her chest.

He turned left and walked five steps.

"If you're going to Grosvenor," she said, "you might like to know you'll never get there going that way."

Ah, yes. West. He was supposed to be traveling west.

He halted and turned slowly. As he walked back past her, he touched his forehead in a small salute. She didn't deserve to be left with this lot. But what was he to do?

She lifted one pale eyebrow. Something in the shadows of her eyes seemed reproachful.

Oh, fie. He turned back.

Doubtless, this was all a stratagem. Lifty and his Mr. Monarch trained her to look doleful, then put her at the corner with a bandage over one eye to beg pence.

Still, he pulled out Fitzroy's shilling. 'Twas a pittance, and 'twas pitiful. But at least it was something.

"Here."

Halfway down the street, Lifty blew through his lips again. "And how'd I miss that?"

She took it in her cupped palms and crooked a smile—both gratified and in some measure amused. Then she shook her head. "Keep it. Somebody'd only be pinching it from me."

"Hey now." Lifty clomped down the street. "That'd buy a short gin, it would."

She upturned the coin into Will's hand. Her smile grew to full bloom, and she looked him in the eye, as if he'd suddenly met her standards.

Lifty came up behind Will. "If she's too daft to have it, you can be sure it won't go to waste with me."

Will pocketed the coin, still looking at Rose. "Is there some way I can help you?"

"Nah." Her smile faded only slightly. "But might be ol' Pish'll send you my way and I'll see you again."

"Hey, now," Lifty said pleadingly. His hand came down on Will's shoulder.

Will managed a small nod for Rose. Then he turned in the direction she'd indicated. With one deep breath, he took to his heels, pulling out from under Lifty's hand so quickly he left the man staggering.

---

By the time Will found his way back to Fitzroy House, the night had sunk into that deep darkness just before sunrise. The scullery maid—awake to light the morning fires—allowed him into the basement kitchen. The cavernous room was empty save for her, another sleepy-eyed maid, and the butler looming in the doorway.

Tite looked Will over. "You seem rather diminished by your night out . . . sir."

Will kept his chin up. "I fear I became lost."

Tite sniffed. "Among other things. Sir." Probably, he smelled the champagne on Will's shirt.

After finally wending his way back to Grosvenor Square, Will had been unable to identify which of the great houses hosted the ball. It hardly mattered, since all the mansions had been reduced to no more than the occasional flicker of a bedtime candle. He managed to extract directions back to Soho Square from a disreputable-looking street wanderer.

Now he stood to be judged by the butler.

His stomach growled.

The maids giggled.

He squared his shoulders. "If you'd show me to my room, I would appreciate it." His stomach growled again. "And I'd have a morsel to eat if it isn't inconvenient."

One of the maids—Kitty—moved to slice bread.

Tite turned sideways in the door and gestured Will to precede him. "If there is any inconvenience to be borne, I assure you it is borne by Mr. Fitzroy. He waits in his study."

Oh, seize it.

Upstairs at the study door, Tite knocked and turned the latch. "Master Hardy has returned, sir."

Will marched forth.

The gray light of approaching dawn silhouetted Mr. Fitzroy against the windows. He stood at the end of the desk, leaning upon it with both hands, shirtsleeves rolled to his elbows.

Tite shut the door.

Silence clogged the room, broken only by the rumble of early handcarts in the street.

Darkness obscured Mr. Fitzroy's face.

Will tried to stand tall. "I'm sorry to keep you from bed, sir. I hope I have not caused anxiety. I got turned about in the streets."

"You are apologizing?"

"Yes, sir." He sounded every bit as abject as he felt. It was not a pleasant feeling, although Tom would say 'twas good for one's innards.

Still, Mr. Fitzroy did not move. "A man apologizes for one of two reasons. Either he wishes to forestall wrath even though he does not, in the particulars, believe himself in the wrong. Or else he speaks in sincerity because he has truly done something regrettable. Which is it, young Will?"

"Sir, I found myself in a strange situation and could see no proper way out of it. But I hope with all my heart to have caused you no more than an inconvenience."

Mr. Fitzroy laughed, short and dry. "Sadly, a futile hope." His voice deepened. "I have enjoyed a call from Constable Pish of the notorious Bow Street Runners."

Seize Pish. He wasted no time, did he? Doubtless, he had cast Will's involvement in the worst light possible.

Will rubbed his palms against his breeches. "I left the ball to stretch my legs."

"Indeed."

Best to tell the whole truth. He had been foolish. Lying now would be more foolish still. "I lost my head, I admit, and I'm uncertain how far I ran. But I happened upon a crime—a mail coach robbery. The constables misunderstood. They took me for a thief. I gave them my name, and your name, sir. Then I . . . ran." His breath came choppily. Had he ruined everything already? "I believe I did the right thing, sir."

Mr. Fitzroy pushed up from the desk and walked to the window, his posture rigid. "You *ran*." He touched the side of his fist to the window, gently. "When I specifically asked for secrecy?"

Will managed to shake his head. "I did not realize the secret was of such great importance."

Mr. Fitzroy barked a laugh. "Indeed. Our secrets are power. Power is respect. Stupidity is nothing. It is worse than poverty. It is worse than obscurity, it is worse than ignominy."

*Our secrets.* Was that what Will had exchanged in accepting Mr. Fitzroy's opportunity? The right to his own secrets?

"Believe me, sir, I endangered nothing tonight—save perhaps your trust, which I would sincerely regret."

"Look at me." Mr. Fitzroy pointed at himself. "What you see, what you see of any man, is not truth. Reality is nothing, irrelevant, useless. Perception is everything. What is important is what you convince others to believe they see."

Mr. Fitzroy curled his pointing finger into a fist and held that fist at his side, very still. "The truth of your actions tonight matters not, Will. What matters is what people will think is true. And what they will think is not that my inexplicable new protégé has done a great deed in fleeing the ignominious Runners. All they will see are the shadows—the questions with no answers. What were you doing there? Why were you caught? How did you escape? And why would such as you be involved with such as I?"

Will stared. "You're a great man, sir. Greater than this Pish. Surely, you can make him see the truth if anyone can."

"Mr. Pish's questions have no good answers—truthful or not. You tell me you believe you did the right thing. I say to you it does not matter. What you *did* was perhaps irrevocably endanger any useful partnership between our two selves."

Will's head spun.

Mr. Fitzroy straightened. "Why would you do that at this great juncture in your life? Why would you do that to me after the succor I have offered?"

It was the fairest question of the night. Will tried to find a fair answer. "There was a child—a girl. The thieves were using her to stop the mail coach, they were endangering her, and the Runners would have taken her. It was not her fault, sir, I believe that. I could not leave her."

Mr. Fitzroy looked away, shook his head. "That sort—they are worth no good man's time."

"But did you not say you wished to raise them?"

Mr. Fitzroy turned back. The whites of his eyes glared. "To teach them self-respect, to teach them what it means to be human. *Not* to reward them for their infamy, their sloth, and their greed!"

The intensity of the words struck Will like the slap of a glove.

He resisted stepping back. "Yes, sir. I see that, sir." He wet his lips, trying to regain balance. Where was he to stand in the midst of so confused an issue? "I know some of their names, sir. I could perhaps inform the Runners, help them find the culprits. There was a Lifty, and one named Bull. And they spoke of a Mr. Monarch."

Mr. Fitzroy didn't move—indeed his body remained entirely still. But he *tightened*. Every muscle grew stiff.

It was as if a thunderclap had erupted in the ceiling. The air smelt all but singed. Will's very hair stood at end.

"No." Mr. Fitzroy breathed deeply. "You are never to speak to Mr. Pish ever again. The matter will be forgot. I will see to that. I will bury it."

He unrolled his sleeves and buttoned first one cuff, then the other. That done, he returned to the desk where his coat lay across the chair.

Released from the man's ferocious gaze, Will found his breath juddering. "Thank you, sir. And I am very sorry, sir. I lost my head. I should never have been there. I should have waited for you before testing my speed, just as you wished." He swallowed.

"I will wait until whenever you think proper to show you what I've discovered I can do." Even now, the memory rushed upon him and stirred his blood. "It was . . . unbelievable. I can almost outpace a horse. I can run on walls, even jump high enough to gain rooftops."

Mr. Fitzroy smoothed his coat lapels and reached inside the sleeves to tug his cuffs. "I believe our tests are at an end. I am very sorry to say I will be sending you home today."

"What?"

"I regret it. I had greater hopes even than you, I believe." He rang a bell on the desktop. "But the events of this night have proven us incompatible in every way."

The first rays of sunrise cut through the gloom. They crossed Mr. Fitzroy's face to illuminate its angles—now gone impossibly hard. His eyes were dark, impenetrable. He looked at Will as if he saw *everything*, but would allow nothing of himself to be seen in return.

"You," he said, "disappoint me."

Will's body forgot how to function. His blood forbore pumping. His lungs forbore expanding. Even his eyes refused to hold steady. The room swirled.

"Sir, I don't . . . I don't understand. I am sorry for any mistaken actions on my part. But—" His brain raced ahead of his words. *But you gave me no guidance, you gave me no instruction—save follow me and do not question.*

He raised his chin. "I do not understand you."

But he shouldn't have been caught so far off guard. Henry had warned him how little he actually knew of this man.

"I apologize." Mr. Fitzroy strode to the door. "I raised hopes within you I will not be able to fulfill." He extended his arm, bidding Will follow. "I will return you to Affery today. I have questions for Dr. Silas, so I must journey there myself."

What could Mr. Fitzroy say to Dr. Silas without Will? Will was the one who should be examined. *Will* was the one with questions.

His words refused to form themselves into either requests or demands. He followed Mr. Fitzroy to the door, his feet moving almost of their own accord.

For the first time, Mr. Fitzroy's expression eased, as if he again saw Will as a person—a boy he related to—rather than a problem to be eliminated.

He opened the door. "I promise you this: I will ask Dr. Silas if your condition puts you at any risk and if he advises precautions."

Will halted in the open doorway.

Tite was advancing up the corridor. Probably he felt the eviction of rabble too important to be entrusted to a footman.

"Sir." Will steadied his voice. "If I have acted unwisely, I apologize. And . . . I ask you to reconsider." It was as close to begging as he had ever come.

Mr. Fitzroy shook his head. "In my world, one chance is all a man is ever likely to receive. In your world, there are no chances. Already, you have got more than ever the world owed you."

# CHAPTER 10

RE NOON THE next day, the forge rolled into view. The day was gray, the leftover summer green of the hills already fading to brown at the edges. When change came, it most assuredly came in the blink of an eye.

Betwixt the stiles separating the Hardy barn on one side from the field and the forge on the other, Mr. Fitzroy bade the carriage halt.

Will had no baggage. He'd taken nothing with him, save the clothes on his back, and he brought nothing home.

He looked at Mr. Fitzroy on the facing seat. "Sir," he managed. Then he opened the door and stepped to his home ground.

Anger and confusion swirled.

Anger with himself for being so ignorant and daft.

And anger with Mr. Fitzroy for opening the golden door far enough to fill his heart with hope—and then shutting it in his face.

Resisting the urge to slam the carriage door, Will latched it firmly, then turned towards the forge. He *did* still have his self-regard, whatever Mr. Fitzroy might say.

"Will."

He looked back.

Mr. Fitzroy leant one elbow out the window. His brows were drawn, his mouth sober. "If I am disappointed in you, then perhaps you are also disappointed in me. I desire you to know one thing, and that is this: I am truly unhappy events have turned so. I possessed considerable hopes for you and for my ability to aid you."

Will's throat closed.

"I understand if it cannot be so, but I hope you will not blame me." Mr. Fitzroy's blue eyes were intent. "I always know when something will work and when it will not. I hope you will appreciate my making a move now, in swiftness, which would have become inevitable in time."

It suddenly struck Will that Mr. Fitzroy had got everything he wanted: proof beyond imagination of Dr. Silas's advances with the plague. He had no need of Will now.

He swallowed. "If I blame you for aught, it's for not seeing it sooner."

Mr. Fitzroy inclined his head.

"Now," Will said, "if you'll grant me leave, I don't believe we've more to say to one another."

"I hold you and your abilities in the highest regard." Mr. Fitzroy extended his hand through the window. "I wish us to part friends."

Had they ever been friends? Had they truly?

Mr. Fitzroy watched him, waiting. "We may find ourselves incompatible at this moment, Will. But I tell you: better a powerful friend you do not like than a powerful enemy whom you do."

Will blinked.

Certainly, there could be no threat in those words.

Was it Mr. Fitzroy who didn't wish *Will* for an enemy? Because Will could now run as fast as a horse? He snorted to himself. Or because they shared the knowledge of Dr. Silas's secret?

It mattered not.

Mr. Fitzroy had nothing to fear from Will. He *had* shown Will the world of dreams. That was worth something.

Will offered a nod. 'Twas all he could manage right now.

He turned back to the stile. Once at the other side, he stepped down into the field and looked over his shoulder.

Mr. Fitzroy's carriage drove on into Dr. Silas's garden.

Sighing, Will turned and trudged across the field, hands in his very nearly empty pockets. He bowed his head. He was supposed to have returned with enough gold to fulfill the debt, save the forge, and repay Tom ten times over. Instead, he returned with naught but the ability to run like a gust.

He kicked a clod open.

There was nothing he could do with such powers hereabouts, that was certain. He'd have to return to London. He still had the sovereign. It wasn't enough to pay the debt, but it *would* buy him fare.

This time, he'd find his own opportunities. But doing what? All he'd learned how to do thus far was to shatter champagne goblets and outrun robbers.

That last wasn't nothing. He'd already thrashed that big thief Bull. Perhaps he could hire out to those who feared such chaps. Mightn't there be interest—and money—in that? Even Tom might approve.

And by heavens, this time he'd do it without a patron.

At the end of the field, voices clamored from the forge.

He looked up from his trudging, but could see nothing past the millstream willows.

Men shouted—angrily.

Breaking into a run, he dodged through the trees, nearly colliding with several, and had momentum enough to clear the stream without requiring the footbridge. Then he checked himself and jogged around the corner of the house to the forge.

Half the village had gathered.

He stopped.

Tom stood in the forge doorway, arms crossed. His hair stood at end as if he had scrubbed his hands through it. He glared, all but snorting steam.

Before him two strangers waved pamphlets.

The foremost was a lanky man with sharp eyes and a sharper nose. "Think you're above this? You run up a debt, you pay that debt. You fail to pay with gold in the palm, then you got to pay in other ways."

Tom jutted his jaw. "That debt is not come due yet! I've assurances from Lord Carstone."

The other stranger—shorter than his partner with round brown eyes and lengthy sideburns—shook his head. "What Mr. Clem here says's true. 'Tisn't assurances that matter. Only warrants."

Lord Carstone had dispatched warrant officers? Will's whole body burnt hot. The other night at the great ball, Will had seen the earl drinking wine and laughing with his fellows, flush with more money than he'd ever need. Had he, even at that moment, been readying an arrest warrant for Tom's measly debt? The debt he'd *promised* Tom the full time to pay?

A great shudder seized Will.

He shoved through the crowd, past Mr. Pirrup the innkeeper. "What's happening?"

Tom looked up. "Will, lad—"

The sharp-nosed officer—Mr. Clem—whirled about. "You—" He pointed the warrants at Will. "You live here?" He looked at his partner. "Be quick about it, Hale. We got something on him too?"

"Will has no debt against him!" Tom said.

Clem looked narrowly at Will. "Ever stand surety for this reprobate?"

"He's my apprentice!" Tom roared. "Why would anyone ask him to stand surety?"

Hale ruffled the papers. "No, no, nothing, I'm afraid." He nodded briskly at Tom. "Only you, sir. Now if you'll be so good, we'll accompany you to the great Marshalsea Prison."

"*Prison?*" Will stared first at Hale, then at Clem. "He's supposed to be taken to a sponging house first! To get his affairs in order. What gives you authority to take him straight to prison? This whole thing's a farce!" He looked at Tom. "Why is this happening?"

Tom shook his head, mouth tight.

Under the Law of Arrest, any man could issue a warrant for the price of a mere shilling, even if the person to be arrested owed nothing. The warrant alone was enough to get you arrested until you could prove your innocence.

Will trembled. If he had a cleaver to hand, he'd join the French in their insanity. This feeling in his heart, *this* was what Mr. Fitzroy meant when he spoke of social revolution.

Clem pointed at Will. "You stand down, kinchin. Interfering with the due process of a due law isn't going to get you anywhere but into a due prison along with your friend here." He reached for Tom's arm and nodded for Hale to take the other. "Come on then. I got more warrants to serve, see if I don't. Wasting time here ain't keeping *me* farther from the Marshalsea myself."

A breath whistled through Tom's teeth. He flexed his arms.

He'd fight this. Surely, he'd fight this. He could lay these rotters flat to the ground in two blows. Then they'd run. They'd go to London. Tom would lie low whilst Will hired out as protection against thieves. Will could earn enough to pay the debt, and then Tom would be free.

But Tom didn't fight.

He released the breath. His chest deflated.

The officers gripped his arms.

"No!" Will gathered himself. He could run at them both and knock them aside before they even realized he'd moved.

His neighbors, however, reached out and stopped him.

"Don't do nothing rash, lad." Lines furrowed Mr. Pirrup's mouth, inside his beard. "Causing more difficulties won't help him. Can't you see even he knows that? You stay here, and you stay calm. If you get into trouble too, who's left to pay him out?"

Will could scarcely hear over the whump of his heart.

Tom was going to prison. Will had feared it long enough, yes, but he'd never believed it. It had always been a possibility—like dying young—but not a probability.

He yanked free of Mr. Pirrup's arm and backed away, shaking his head.

The tendons in Tom's neck were taut to bursting. He looked like, if he so much as opened his mouth, he'd explode and throw off these two popinjay officers with their shilling-apiece warrants.

He didn't. He bowed his head.

But things were different now, weren't they? After everything that had occurred, there *must* be a solution.

For one thing, Mr. Fitzroy was here.

Will caught his breath.

Mr. Fitzroy could aid them if he wanted to. Wasn't he Lord Carstone's "valuable" friend? Wasn't he interested in buying Tom's property?

Will took one step and stopped. He'd sworn never again to prostrate himself to the likes of Mr. Fitzroy.

Officers Clem and Hale prodded Tom along the path. In the road, two carts waited. A third officer sat at the reins of the one, already pointed towards London.

Will *would* grovel to Mr. Fitzroy. He would do it for Tom Colville.

Turning his back to the forge, he ran as fast as he could.

# CHAPTER 11

WILL FLED ACROSS the empty field.

Behind him, the gathered villagers gasped at his speed. Vaguely, he sensed at least some of them following, far behind.

He reached the field's end and leapt the stile. The road forced him to slow so that he needed two strides—one off the middle stile step—to get him across the second stone wall.

Then he checked himself altogether. His breaths ripped through his chest in great burning swathes.

Before him, Mr. Fitzroy's carriage sat at the cottage door. The matched pair of blacks craned their necks at Will, white-eyed. At their bridles, the footman gaped.

The barn was silent, the door slightly ajar.

So Mr. Fitzroy had secured his interview with Dr. Silas after all. Amazing how much courtesy a handsome carriage and expensive clothes gained a man.

Will swallowed the bitterness. None of it mattered now.

Odds were Mr. Fitzroy would not see fit to help him. But the man *had* asked for Will's friendship. Friendship went not one, but two ways—even when between MP and blacksmith's apprentice.

That was the truth. Please God it might also be how Mr. Fitzroy decided to *perceive* it.

Will made it only halfway across the yard.

The entire barn exploded in flame.

Heat engulfed him, and he stumbled back.

Flames leapt from the barn doors, from the small rearward

window, from the hole in the roof where Will had loosened the plank.

Behind him, the horses clattered, and the footman shouted. Farther back, the villagers yelped, still only halfway across the field.

That mad old duffer! Will rushed forward. Dr. Silas had told Will he planned to destroy the barn before departing—but Will hadn't imagined he meant it.

Perhaps a handsome carriage and clothes meant not so much to Dr. Silas after all.

The unlocked door burst open. More smoke bellowed forth, and Mr. Fitzroy staggered out.

The back of his coat smoked like the very devil. Hatless, his yellow hair glinted in the flames. He looked up, blue eyes flashing bizarrely in his sooty face.

Will reached him, caught his arm, and hauled him twenty feet back from the barn. "Sir, are you injured?"

Mr. Fitzroy stared as if he could neither hear nor see. In the corner of one eye, a red teardrop welled. It swelled larger and larger, to the size of a small pea. Then it broke and tumbled in a thick stream of blood.

"Sir! You're unwell. Can you hear me?"

Mr. Fitzroy twitched towards him, as if only now comprehending his presence. The movement freed new lines of blood from both nostrils—and then his ears.

He looked about, blearily. "I—"

"Sir, can you see? Have you been burnt?"

Aside from a few smoking holes in coat and breeches, Mr. Fitzroy showed no damage—only this ghastly bleeding, which made no sense a'tall. Unless . . .

"Sir—" Will clenched Mr. Fitzroy's arm. "Is it the plague?"

This bleeding was nothing like Will's symptoms. But the bleariness, the inability to see or hear or focus—that much suited.

To blazes with Dr. Silas!

He peered into Mr. Fitzroy's face, trying to get the man to look at him. "Did Dr. Silas do this to you? Please tell me what's happened!"

"Dr. Silas." Mr. Fitzroy dragged his gaze to the burning barn. "He is . . . there."

"In the barn?"

Flames licked through the rearward window and about the eaves. If Dr. Silas remained inside, he must either be intent on losing his life—or too insensible to save it.

Will turned to the field, where the villagers were running towards the road. The warrant officer Mr. Clem ran with them.

"Hie!" Will shouted. "There are injuries!" He took Mr. Fitzroy by the shoulders and forced him to the ground. "Sit, sir."

Then, he raced for the barn and dove into the heat.

The flames clung mostly to the rafters, since the walls were stone. But they chewed hungrily through the wooden stalls and the trestle tables. Smoke engulfed him.

He pulled his shirt over his nose. "Dr. Silas!"

Two steps in, he caught his toe and tripped face first. Only his newfound reflexes brought his hands before him to save his head from the ground.

Behind him, a body sprawled upon its back. Or, rather, it must have been a body, once. Now, it was only a blackened husk, the face and shirtfront flaking.

And this was Dr. Silas? Surely not. He could not have burnt beyond all recognition so swiftly. And yet . . . here he lay.

Will's throat closed, choking, and he gritted his teeth.

Dr. Silas hardly deserved this, even by his own hand.

Will gripped the corpse's armpits. Slippery ash slimed his palms and his hands slid. He tried again, digging with his fingernails, even as bile rose in his throat.

Movement flickered.

He looked up, eyes stinging. Through the roaring glare, the barn's rear door banged in the breeze. In the rearmost stall, a rafter collapsed. Smoke swirled and whisked away the last answers to the questions Will had not even yet been able to completely form.

With all his strength, he dragged Dr. Silas from the barn. He retreated far beyond the garden, then tripped over his own heels and fell back.

He left the body where it lay. No need to close its eyes: it had none.

Raw energy hummed through him. He turned back to Mr. Fitzroy.

The hummock was now empty.

Will pivoted.

The crowd from the village, led by Mr. Pirrup, was crossing the road. Near the cottage, the footman still struggled with the horses.

In the edge of his vision, the bluest bird he had ever seen—too large to be a bluebird—flashed. He turned to look, but there was nothing. The bird must have flown.

He turned all the way around. No Mr. Fitzroy.

Something moved again, this time in the opposite corner of his vision.

He jerked about.

There, at his elbow, stood the shorter of the two warrant officers. His round blue eyes were dazed. Hale, his name was.

"What are you doing?" Will asked.

Hale raised both hands, now empty of the warrants. He scrubbed his cheeks, frantically. Then he stared at his hands. His breath came so rapidly he seemed likely to tumble in a swoon.

Will shook his arm. "What's wrong with you?" He pointed to the charred corpse. "A man lies dead there! Mr. James Fitzroy, from London, is hereabouts. He's injured. We must find him."

Hale frowned. His sideburns rippled. "I do not understand you—"

"Help me locate Mr. Fitzroy!"

Still, Hale did not move. He looked down to his feet and flinched his arms from his body. "What is this—" Then he puffed out a breath that was almost a laugh. "Indeed, indeed!"

Was he drunk?

Will leant away. "What ails you?"

Hale's cheeks grew pink. He grabbed for Will's arm, nearly tripping. "You know me, yes?"

Will tried to free his arm. "No, I don't know you—and I've no care to."

The villagers clambered over the stone wall. Behind them, the cart driven by the third warrant officer clattered past. Another man sat with him. In back, Tom stretched to see.

Will looked about wildly. He could hardly go after Tom with the barn ablaze, Dr. Silas dead beyond recognition, and Mr. Fitzroy in a faint somewhere—especially when Mr. Fitzroy was the man he needed.

"Release me," he demanded of Hale. "We must find Mr. Fitzroy before he harms himself."

Hale let go of Will's sleeve long enough to gain a handful of Will's arm. "Murderer!" he shrieked.

"*What?*"

Hale whirled to the approaching crowd. "This boy is a murderer!" He pointed to Dr. Silas's corpse. "He has slain this man! He must be apprehended!"

Will tried to strip Hale's hand aside. "You're mad, you are!"

The man clung with more strength than his slight body evidenced.

"I had naught to do with this!" Will said. "You crossed the field behind me! You must have seen me the entire time!" His heart raced. "Why would I kill him?"

The blue of Hale's eyes glittered, feverishly. "This is the murderer!" he shouted. "I witnessed it!"

The accusation was ridiculous—farcical. But the shock nearly knocked Will off his feet. Never had anyone said such a thing about him, such a blatant falsehood, and for no reason a'tall.

Afar off down the road, the cart—and Tom in it—disappeared around the bend.

The villagers reached them, surrounded them. Mr. Pirrup and the others stared askance.

Hale's sharp-faced partner Mr. Clem pushed through their ranks and clamped a hand at Will's other arm. He peered at Hale. "Thought I told you to go with Colville, didn't I? What is it you think you're doing here?"

"I witnessed it," Hale said. "I swear it. He must be confined."

Shillings glittered in Clem's eyes. "Well, then you're under arrest, my boy."

Blood thundered in Will's ears. "For what? Just because a man's dead doesn't mean he was murdered." He looked to his neighbors. "And because I pull him from the flames doesn't mean I'm the one who did it!"

They shifted, apprehensively. These London chaps had already put the Affery folk on their heels. They were confused, heads leaned back, eyes wary.

Only Mr. Pirrup stepped forward, hesitantly. "There's no proof."

"There is my word." Hale panted. "I will swear out the warrant right here and now."

"But it's monstrous!" Mr. Pirrup said. "Why would you do that to the lad? He's no danger to you or any other." And yet even he looked at Will with some uncertainty.

Perhaps running off at inhuman speeds hadn't helped matters.

"There's no justice in this." Will tried to force confidence into his voice, but it rose at the end.

"The charges are blatantly untrue," Mr. Pirrup insisted.

The flush had faded from Hale's cheeks. His face seemed almost swollen. "I apprehended him. I apprehended him in the act. See to it he is properly confined. For . . . safety's sake." Then he released Will's arm and staggered into the crowd.

Will tried to pull free of Clem's grasp. "He didn't even arrive until after I recovered the body!"

Clem redoubled his hold and looked to the villagers. "Hie there, lend a hand! You know your duty to the Crown when you see it, don't you?"

Mr. Pirrup's round face was uncertain, his brow lined. But still, he jutted his jaw. "Is this English law?"

Clem gnawed his lip. He glanced after his partner. Then he shook his head, firmly. "Hale ain't the one to lie. By the book, he is." He looked Will straight in the eye. "And if he's telling true, then there's something in this for old Clem, you can be sure of that."

Will's heart sank.

From the far side of the crowd, a man shouted. "And here's a gentleman fainted clean away!"

The villagers parted to reveal Mr. Fitzroy, crumpled on the ground, not far from the hummock where Will had left him.

Had he been there all along? He lay utterly still, save for the rise and fall of rasping breaths. He might yet wake in time to speak a true word for Will. But not in time for Tom. Not today.

Will stared down the road where Tom had disappeared. If Will could escape Clem, he might be able to catch the cart and its running pony.

Clem jostled him. "Come on, blighter. We'll need a magistrate to sort this, just you wait. You won't get off so easy as your master. Might be your master had a hand in it too. Old Clem'll sniff it out, see if he don't!"

Mr. Pirrup caught Will's eye and lowered his voice. "This is a farce, my boy. Any one of us here can see that. These men are a common lot. They've no power to do this to you, no power a'tall. You go after your master, that's where you're needed. I will see to this here—for Tom Colville's sake as much as yours. 'Twill all be cleared up."

Will stared at him. Mr. Pirrup was a decent sort, always had been. But . . . if Will ran, would it compound the matter, as it had with Pish? Fear rattled through him. Or was this his only chance to avoid falling into the power of corrupt men? He could not depend upon the truth to see him clear, that was plain. And he could never hire a solicitor.

Tom might have told him to stay, to trust righteousness to win out. Will might even have believed that, a week past. But standing on this side of all that had occurred, he could not *know* that such was true. Staying now would be as much of a gamble as running, perhaps more. And if he were arrested, then there would be no one to aid Tom.

He met Mr. Pirrup's anxious eyes and nodded his thanks.

Then, with the strength of a blacksmith's arm and the speed of the devil, he yanked free. He darted through the crowd, past the flailing hands of his surprised neighbors.

He paused for only a half second to glance at Mr. Fitzroy's prone body on the grass and at the blood smeared all about his face. If Mr. Fitzroy would help him at all, it would not be today.

He leapt the stone wall, caught his balance in the center of the road, and turned his face towards London.

"Don't be daft!" Clem shouted. "You flee, and you'll be found, mark me! You run, and you'll never leave off running!"

Will took in one great breath and leant into the wind.

# CHAPTER 12

THE SHINING LONDON that had welcomed Will's dreams a sennight ago was not the London that met him on his return. In the street outside Fitzroy House, he stood and he shivered in his sweat-damp clothes.

Only an hour past, dawn had warmed the sky to rose-flecked gray. After the stumbling blackness of night, even that faint light illuminating the city had felt a tiny spot of hope. But then black smoke began trickling from one chimney, then another, then a thousand. Dawn blinked, turned coward, and retreated entire.

Now, brown fog drifted past the grand terraced houses. Silent as a watchful ghost, it surrounded Will so he could scarcely see across the street.

He approached Fitzroy House's railed entrance. Perhaps the railing was to protect fog-bound passers-by from tumbling into the servants' sunken entrance. Overhead in the windows, balls of light blurred, necessary even in daytime thanks to this brown blight.

He shouldn't be here. But it was the only address he knew. Indeed, the Fitzroys were the only people he knew.

At any odds, he owed the family news of Mr. Fitzroy's injury.

For the moment, however, he sagged against the railing, weary muscles melting.

All through yesterday and yesternight, he had traveled. He ran until his vision shrank to pinpricks of scarlet, but he never did catch Tom's cart. He'd got within a scant quarter of a mile when his legs—and his lungs—and his heart—decided they could run no more. He tumbled head over heels and lay, unable to twitch anything more than his raw throat, sucking in one great burning draught of air after another.

Finally, the clatter of an oncoming carriage had prodded his consciousness. He got up, and again he ran until he could not run. He collapsed, then ran again.

After crossing the river, he limped the whole way here to Soho Square, wandering about, asking directions where he might. The Marshalsea Prison, he'd discovered, was back across the river in Southwark. Still, his feet had led him hither, because once he reached the Marshalsea, there would be nothing left but to face Tom.

His innards cramped. He should have been at the forge when the warrant officers had come. Instead, he had left Tom behind whilst he sought fortune and adventure—only to return empty-handed just in time to watch Tom carted away.

Dear God in heaven, what was the purpose in any of this? Why give him this thing—this gift or curse or whatever it was—and then give him no way to use it to help anyone?

Who was to say if the plague were even finished with him? Perhaps he would yet find himself dying of it. And now there was no one whose help he could seek, no one who knew any-thing a'tall of what had happened to him. He blinked away the image of Dr. Silas's charred corpse.

Of course, there was yet the golden goddess—Isabella. His heart managed a relieved leap. He was not utterly alone in this new world then. But where was he to find her? And would she deign to see a poor disgraced boy as anything more than one of Dr. Silas's animals?

He looked up.

Through the drifting fog, the yellow façade of Mr. Fitzroy's house shone intermittently.

Only a few short days ago, Will had been bundled from this house. Pride said he should walk straight past.

Except pride would never get Tom out of prison. He gritted his teeth.

God help him.

He marched to the front door and knocked.

Before he could even slap the dust from his clothes, the oaken door pulled inward.

Mr. Tite surveyed him. "And *you* are?"

"You know who I am. I've news of your master. Is Mrs. Fitzroy at home?"

"I doubt it with sincerity." Tite offered a smile of decided *in*sincerity. "If you came to tell us of the master's indisposition, then you need not have exerted yourself." He withdrew.

Mr. Fitzroy was already home? No one would have risked moving him while unconscious, so he must have awoken. And they must not have spared the horses.

Will darted his hand to the door. "Wait."

Beneath his powdered wig, Tite drew his black brows rather confusedly at the speed of Will's movement.

Will leant toward him. His weary brain offered no immediate words.

Tite's frown deepened. He drew back.

Likely, Will appeared a wild highwayman. His eyes felt bloodshot, and no doubt his hair was streaked white with dried sweat and dust.

He coughed to clear his throat. "If Mr. Fitzroy is indisposed, I must instead see Mrs. Fitzroy or Mr. Henry Fitzroy. It is urgent."

Tite shifted his mouth.

Will clenched his teeth—and then he clenched his fist.

Tite flinched a glance between the two, then straightened. A smile pinched his cheeks once more. "Come through."

Will tromped upstairs to the drawing room, where a small fire shriveled within the hearth, scarcely enough to light the fog-shadowed windows.

"For the sake of the maids," Tite said, "I will beg you not to sit." He left, stiffly.

Will halted before the fire. The warmth—meager as it was—softened his bones. Never mind sitting, he might liquefy right here upon the hearthstone. The heat soothed the shivers, leaving an all-suffusing ache.

Was the pain from running through the chill night? Or was it because of the plague?

These were two more questions Dr. Silas would never answer. Another shiver racked his bones.

Had the doctor fired the barn on purpose? He surely couldn't have wished to harm himself. He might have been cut up about Mr. Fitzroy's intention to purchase the trackway. But killing himself?

Again, Will saw the blood dripping from Mr. Fitzroy's eyes, nose, and ears.

The fire couldn't have caused *that*. Had Dr. Silas attacked Mr. Fitzroy—perhaps crashing one of his amber jars over Mr. Fitzroy's head in defense of his property? Even that failed to explain how Dr. Silas had ended a burnt crust on the barn floor.

Behind Will, a gown swished.

He turned

In the doorway, Mrs. Fitzroy clasped her ringed hands loosely. He pulled his forelock. "Ma'am."

She surveyed him, head tilted.

Her eyes were dark and bird-like, opaque. The plumpness of her faded cheeks and the dimples at her mouth presented a soft femininity at disorienting odds with the rigidity of her movements and the staring coldness of those eyes.

"Well." She spoke with a mocking edge. "I hardly expected you, Master Hardy. Certainly not within days of my husband's returning you to your place." She smiled, falsely. "Indeed, you must have run the entire way." She wore a high-waisted gown of dark green over a loose-sleeved white chemise. "I wonder if you realize this is an inconvenient time." She crossed the room and faced him from the other side of the hearth. "My husband returned from your venture quite ill."

"Yes, ma'am. I was there when it happened."

"And what happened—exactly?"

"He did not tell you?"

"He has been feverish and racked with headaches. I believe there was a fire?"

Will took a breath. "What do the physicians say?"

For the first time, her mask cracked. She moistened her lips. "They are . . . undecided."

He hesitated. Mr. Fitzroy enjoyed his secrets. If he did not wish his wife to know what had truly happened to him, Will dared not interfere. Yet, of all people, he might be of some aid in this.

"May I ask—are his movements altered?"

"What do you mean?"

"Do his reflexes seem heightened?"

"No. Only the headaches, and—he keeps moving things about the room when no one is with him. He is confused by the fever perhaps." She flashed another empty smile.

If Mr. Fitzroy had contracted the plague, then he and Will were now the only two of their kind—so far as Will knew. *If* Mr. Fitzroy survived—and *if*, of course, Will continued to survive—they must now teach themselves about this thing that had happened to them.

That might again give them common ground.

Even if it didn't, Will could hardly walk away from the man. Mr. Fitzroy had not walked away from him during his own feverish recovery.

"Perhaps I could be of help. I've questions I would like to ask your husband. I believe he might wish the same of me."

She drew erect. "Do not presume you are in any way equal to my husband."

It always came down to that, didn't it?

"No, ma'am. I don't presume. I'm only offering."

Her eyes snapped darker than ever—as dark as the swirling fog outside. "I cannot understand why he should pull you from the gutter."

He looked away. "I never was in the gutter, ma'am. I was a blacksmith's apprentice in Affery."

"The *gutter*." She clenched both hands, her rings dazzling. "This secret knowledge you think you share with my husband, it is naught, you hear me? It gives you no hold over him."

She advanced, earrings trembling. "He has done nothing but rise and rise again, all his life. No one will ever drag him down, not now, not ever. Not you, not I." Her cheeks flamed. "He will be Prime Minister. He will rule England. And *I* will stand at his side." Finally, she looked away. "I have always stood at his side."

Hers was a sacrifice Mr. Fitzroy seemed to remark but little, if his distraction at the night of the ball had been any indication.

"I care not about any of that," Will said. For the moment, it was true enough. "A friend of mine—my master—is in straits."

She snorted softly, making it sound both haughty and genteel. "And you believe if you lend a supporting shoulder during my husband's convalescence, he will forgive whatever made him throw you off? You believe he will give you what *you* want?"

"It's not quite so bald as that, ma'am."

"Is it not?" She swished her skirt and advanced again, near enough she had to tilt her head to look him in the face. "Let me speak to you with all frankness. Believe me when I tell you it is the greatest favor I can grant."

Her bright, dark eyes became infinitely old. "My husband is unlikely to ever again be a friend to you. He is a man who is pleased only by purpose. If something—or someone—holds no use for him, then . . ." She raised a shoulder. "If you are right in what you say—that what has happened to him also happened to you—then he will not see you as commiserative. He will see you as competition."

"Competition for what?" Will could be a threat to Mr. Fitzroy in nothing.

"I know not what bond you share. But I do know the wisest thing you can do is to expect nothing more from him." She cocked an eyebrow. "Not only would you be disappointed, but you might lament the day." She stepped away and raised her chin, all stiff hauteur once again. "Stay clear, Master Hardy. My husband is a storm. If you give him the chance, he will engulf you."

The weariness in Will's bones pierced his heart. "I understand you, ma'am. But if Mr. Fitzroy will not aid me, then there is no one else."

She crossed to the door and held it open. "Then I fear there is no one."

———

The Marshalsea turned out to be not so impressive after all.

Aside from its great surrounding wall—and the iron spikes at its top—it looked hardly anything like a prison. The whole atmosphere seemed more a downtrodden boarding house. Beyond the grated door, the "collegians," as they called themselves, milled about the narrow paved yard in various conditions of dress, attitude, and conviviality.

As it developed, any man could enter. Will, however, got no farther than the turnkey, who presided over the lobby that buffered the street entry from the actual prison.

After admitting Will to this anteroom, which he called the Lodge, the turnkey returned to his wooden stool and resumed twirling a considerable key ring around one finger. He alternated his gaze between watching the revolutions of the single key and eying Will's uncertainty.

"I'd be Harry Postelwaite, in the Marshal's service. First-timer, are you?"

In his fourth decade, he was tall and lean, arms and legs both a mite too long. His face was long and lean as well, with wide, alert eyes and a narrow mouth that couldn't decide if it preferred to be amused or confused. He wore a large, flat-brimmed cap atop a bristle of black hair.

"Is there any way to see a prisoner?" Will asked. "I mean, I believe he's a prisoner."

"Of a certainty." Postelwaite moved to open the prison door, with its iron-grated window. "What'd he be in for? Debt? Smuggling?"

"Debt."

"And we've plenty of those. But if I was you, I'd watch myself. Seen a goodly number of friends sucked in hither right along. Pay your own debts, I say, and don't be pulling down your friends, if they truly be your friends."

"How else are prisoners to gain freedom?"

"Oh, there's ways and means. They might run themselves a little industry from right inside. Your friend wouldn't be a barber, would he? We could use one just now." He pushed his cap forward and scratched the back of his head. "Or could be he decides to sell his land—if he owns any. Creditors can't touch land. Only your money, your portable goods, and your person, don't you know?"

Will digested that. "No, I didn't."

At the threshold, Will halted and looked up at Postelwaite. "Could you tell me how I'd find him? His name's Tom Colville."

"Arrived this minute, he did." Postelwaite sighed. "Not so out of the ordinary, him. Every now and again, we get a baronet or such, but even they're not so peculiar, not to an old hand the likes of me. One day, we're going to get ourselves a real fine specimen as'll make the other prisons that envious."

Beyond the door, men, women, and children wandered the yard. Most thronged the shadow of the principle barracks, even though shade was almost nonexistent in the approaching noontide. A bench, a pump, even a skittle-ground at the far end filled the prospect.

But no Tom.

"Where would they have taken him?"

"Probably finding a bed for the duration."

"And where will that be?"

"Wherever he can afford."

Will couldn't stop his mouth falling open. "A prisoner must pay for his bed?"

Postelwaite grinned. "This ain't the Foundling Hospital." He hooked the key ring over his thumb and counted off on long fingers. "For commitment, there's the fee of thirteen shillings, four pence. Then there's one and one that goes to the turnkey—being meself, in this case. Bed in a single room—three shillings a week." He inclined his head towards Will, as if imparting particular information. "Only one and three if the man cares to share, and only one alone if you deign to make a bed in the common room—though it'll be another shilling yet if you can't find your own bedding."

Will gaped. "If a man can't pay to keep himself from this place, how is he to pay to keep himself in it?"

"Paying creditors is one thing. Paying to keep body and soul together, that's a second thing, I find."

Will's empty stomach rolled. Well, Tom *would* have money enough to keep together in here. And Lord Carstone would see his loan repaid. Every wretched farthing of it. Will would earn it squarely from the pockets of the city's rich, and he'd put it as squarely in Lord Carstone's hands. God willing, his strange powers would sustain him that long at least.

"Shall we to it?" Postelwaite asked. "New inductees are always in want of a spot of cheering."

Will started forward. Then he halted.

Two men emerged from the near end of the back-to-back buildings. The warrant officers, Mr. Clem and Mr. Hale.

Will jerked back, too fast.

Postelwaite raised his eyebrows. "Thought you wished to see your friend?"

He backed up again. "I think, after all, I'll visit him later, after he's settled."

Postelwaite shrugged. "However you want it, that's how 'tis here in the Marshalsea. Unless you're in the lock, eh?" He elbowed Will as he turned to lead him back to the outer door.

Will's reflexes kept wanting to nip away with him—urging him fast and far from this place and these men. He held himself in, forcing his feet to walk with slow deliberation.

Behind him, Clem's voice neared. ". . . rum business, this. Whole thing's blighted strange—especially with you going bird-witted on me in that confounded village."

"You're still on about that?" Hale said, sourly. "I told you how it was."

"What you told me and what I seen is two different things. But never mind it. The runaway apprentice is what's interesting now." Clem snorted snuff from his palm. "There'll be more'n a shilling on *him*, you can be sure. Murder always inspires prodigious sums, eh?"

Will's thoughts spun into stillness. They were proceeding with the charges. Cold clenched his innards. Would the lie of a stranger be enough to hang a man? This whole thing was madness. Why would Hale accuse him of something so far beyond the pale?

Postelwaite unlocked and opened the outer door for Will. "Sure about your friend, then? I told you a familiar face goes down well on the first day."

Will strove to keep his composure. He should never have come here. He had thought no one would recognize him, no one would be able to accuse him of aught, not here, so far from

Hale's theatrics. But if this charge could follow him here, where could it *not* follow?

Postelwaite grinned. "Not that a friendly face don't go down on the second—or hundredth—day too."

"I'm sure." Will avoided his eye. He didn't need the man thinking him any stranger than he already had cause too. Will *would* return to see Tom. There must be a way. He looked over his shoulder.

Visible in the far door's window, Clem and Hale waited until another of the turnkeys might arrive to let them out.

"Never mind about the boy," Hale was grumbling. "We won't see a sniff of any reward. If the lad was fool enough to come up here, he's the Runners' prey now."

"Hoities that they are too," Clem said. "But the beak'll still call you as witness."

Hale scowled. "Can't be a witness unless you *witnessed* something. I told you that."

Clem snorted—whether in irritation or because of his recent bout with the snuff. "Should have had that thought two days ago."

Will's heart pounded. Might Hale have already admitted to the lie? And yet Will was *still* to be hunted like a dog by the Bow Street Runners. It made no sense a'tall.

Hale shifted. Through the window, his eyes met Will's. His mouth fell open. "Hie! That's him!"

Postelwaite looked back at Hale. He frowned, then turned, slowly, to Will. He scanned him up and down as if considering Will's candidacy for that unique specimen he was awaiting. "What's this then? You're a *murderer*?"

Will's heart beat 'til he could scarcely breathe. The air in the Lodge turned to sludge in his lungs. He had to fight to make his body move a'tall. He turned away and stepped down into the street.

"Hey!" Postelwaite said.

Will paused long enough to look back. "I murdered no one."

Then he started running.

# CHAPTER 13

WILL DIDN'T RUN far. As soon as the crowds swallowed him, he slowed and attempted to regulate his gasping. He made it almost back to the Iron Bridge before the jostling changed from general crowding to a sensation that was becoming all too familiar: a hand stealing into his coat pocket.

His own hand darted to his side faster than thought. He clenched the strange hand in his pocket, and he bore down hard, grinding wrist bones together.

From behind, someone squawked in pain.

"Pick my pocket, will you?" But before Will could face the thief, the crowd leant in upon him, and he was thrust off the principle road into a narrow alley.

More hands grasped him.

"Hold up now," a man rasped. "Why you hurting our little matey here?"

Howling, the lad freed his hand from Will's pocket and grasped his wrist.

The thief had friends. Fine, then. *More* noses to break. Will seized the hand upon his shoulder and whirled.

The man hadn't time enough to blink: no doubt he was accustomed to victims with reflexes slower than his own. He was a filthy blighter, dark streaks under his eyes and a raveled scarf under his unshaven chin.

Behind him loomed two more rogues, both bigger than Will.

Will grabbed the leader's arm and spun under it, dragging it around until the joint popped.

The man wailed.

With a snarl, one of his friends charged.

Releasing the first man's arm, Will pivoted on the ball of one foot and smashed his fist into the second's jaw. Immediately, pain flared through his knuckles straight up to his elbow.

Seize it. He knew better than to hit a man square in the jaw. How many times had Tom told him? *Hit a man where it will hurt him worse'n it will you.*

He spun around to face the third and final man, who was reversing up the alley with all speed.

Good for him. He was the only one with any brains a'tall—including Will.

Gritting his teeth, Will gathered himself. For a prolonged moment, all his impossible energy sat deep in his stomach, buzzing, waiting to be released.

So he released it.

He exploded towards the third thief, running deeper into the alley.

The man ran, stumbling, gaping back over his shoulder.

At the last moment, Will planted a foot on the crumbling brick wall and launched into a leap. The alley was narrow enough for him to land his other foot higher up on the opposite wall, then bounce back. He snagged the blighter's shirt collar and used every bit of momentum to haul the man up. Someone's wash line stretched conveniently before him and he suspended the man over it, twelve feet above ground.

He continued for one bounce more to the opposite side of the alley, where a windowsill offered purchase. Crouching with a foot on the ledge, he crammed his shoulder up into the corner and grasped the overhead sill.

Below, the man flopped off the line and fell flat on his back. He lay there, choking for air and staring up at Will.

Down the alley, the others were still picking themselves from the mud.

Near the street, the lad cupped his good hand to his mouth and screeched, "Beware, hawks! It's the Runners!"

That snapped the others from their haze. They stumbled up the alley, casting fearful glances at Will as they passed beneath him.

At the alley's other end, three men in red waistcoats rounded the corner from the street. Their leader carried the same gilt-topped cane as had the honorable Henderson Pish.

Now, this *was* a predicament. If Will dropped from the sky to escape, they'd see him without doubt. And outrunning them would be no certainty in these congested streets.

He looked across the alley.

Ten feet above his head, a rickety bridge hung between the buildings. At its far end, a girl sat dangling her feet over the edge. She held an apple before her face, mouth frozen mid-bite.

It was the yellow-haired street waif he'd pulled from under the mail coach the other night.

She looked down at the Runners.

"He came this way?" one was asking.

"That's what they said at the Marshalsea," another replied.

Will's throbbing hand cramped from clutching the window-sill. His fingers slipped. Instinctively, he thrust his other hand out to the far side of the sill and caught the shutter hinge. It all sounded like a great clatter.

Rose promptly tossed her apple at the Runners' feet.

In unison, they all looked up—but at her, not at Will.

"'Ey," she said, "That's me bleedin' apple."

The lead Runner stooped to fetch it. "Then you should keep a grip on it, shouldn't you?"

She held out both hands. "Toss it here, eh?"

"Anyone pass through? A lad of ten and nine perhaps—running like the devil's at his heels?"

Will's foot slipped another half-inch. He gritted his teeth and wedged himself more firmly within the sill.

Rose shrugged. "Mob of scurvy buzzers come through. I reckon they was movin' fast enough."

The third Runner slapped his leader's shoulder. "Reward to be had there!"

"Well, and it's true enough we're getting nowhere with this." He tossed Rose her apple. "Bad neighborhood to be dropping things, love."

"Isn't it just?"

Will held his breath as the Runners exited the far end of the alley.

Rose took a huge bite from her apple and scrambled to her feet. The bridge swayed beneath her. Chewing, she jerked her head in invitation.

Carefully, he pried his shoulder from the corner. He hadn't momentum enough to jump straight up to the bridge from here, so he dropped back to the ground and performed the zig-zag leap, from one building to the other, to gain the bridge.

She waited at the far end, both hands holding the apple to her dirty face. This time around, she looked not so much shocked as impressed, in a calculating sort of way.

He resisted the urge to grasp the rope handrails. "Thank—"

"Mind that gap."

A hole, two planks wide, gaped before him. Below, the earth swirled.

He swallowed and took one long stride over. Miracle of miracles, the planks held all the way to her end.

"Thank you," he said. "I would have been in some distress had they located me."

"Went and killed somebody since last I saw you?"

He glared. "*No.* Someone is lying about me. I've yet to discover why."

"Strangers attract strangeness, if'n you know what I mean." The corner of a grin caught her mouth. "But didn't I tell you I'd see you again? Just didn't reckon on it being so soon—and all the way over here at South'ark side. You do like to go running away from your fancy friends, don't you now?"

He exhaled. "There are no fancy friends. They've cast me out."

"Shouldn't have gone mingling with the likes of us, should've you now?" She was entirely in her element, unfazed by the height, the rickety bridge, her filthy rags, or the mud-spattered apple. She cocked her head as she chewed, studying him.

She couldn't be more than nine years old, a mere child. City experience or no city experience, he was the adult here. He was the man. And that expression of hers—casually superior, a bit proprietary, and entirely amused—was more than slightly irritating.

"Well," he said, "'Twas kind of you to aid me."

She shrugged. "Owed you a good turn, didn't I?"

"If you'll excuse me, I must find lodgings."

She nibbled her apple down to its brown core. "Cheap, eh? A nethersken maybe?"

He felt his pockets. He didn't know what a nethersken was, but he still had the gold sovereign. Surely, that would stretch until he could earn wages. "Yes."

"Look here." She paused to examine the core, then pocketed it within her voluminous shawl. "I can tell you where *not* to stay. But first I want to know about them Runners. Don't much like this notion of you being wanted for murder."

"I didn't do it."

Her gaze flickered, as if she were seeing *beyond* him, into the inside of him.

Who knew what was on the inside of him? Nothing too grand. Nothing worth regarding—not yet. He shifted.

She nodded. "You're innocent."

He scowled. "And how is it you think you know that?"

"I just know."

"Who are you?" he asked.

She thrust out a hand. "Rose Gray. And you'd be William Hardy. I heard you sayin' so to them horneys the other night."

He shook the hand—sticky with apple and heavens knew what else. "About a place to stay—"

"Want my advice? Don't be taking lodgings here. Post yourself straight from London. This ain't no place for the innocent, if you know what I mean—especially when the innocent happens to have Runners barking after his tail, you see?" She performed a slow blink that almost seemed an attempt at feminine artifice. "Ain't no place for me either, would you say?"

He shook his head. "I can't leave." And he certainly couldn't have her along. "I've a friend in the Marshalsea. I can't leave him there."

"Well." She blew through her lips. "At least your sentiment's strong."

Beyond the alley, a cart clattered and a man shouted.

She dropped to her knees and squirmed through a tear in the netting that formed the bridge's sides. "It don't pay to stay in one place too long hereabouts." She reached for a narrow ladder that had been hammered flat into the wall of the building.

He stood above her as she climbed down. "Where do *you* stay?"

"Oh, Seven Dials."

"Where's that?"

"St. Giles way. Across the river, don't you know? Only five little hops from where we met t'other night."

"But that's the high end of town, isn't it?"

She beamed up a grin. "'Fraid it ain't so flash as that. And if you want one more piece of advice, it'd be that Seven Dials ain't no place for you—"

Footsteps sounded in the alley.

They both froze.

A man in a patched brown coat and a shovel hat rounded the corner. From his waistcoat, he withdrew a wad of bank notes and started thumbing through them.

Beneath Will, the ground swirled—as it had when he'd looked out the window at the ball. He groped for the rope handrail and shut his eyes. What was wrong with him?

Still clinging to the ladder, Rose whooshed out a breath. "Cobbler's awls, Lifty! You about scared me off 'n my balance!"

Will opened his eyes.

Below, Lifty's eyebrows popped. "I'll be blowed—that ain't our nimble hero?"

"The same." Rose climbed down to the last rung, three feet above ground, and jumped. "Got a mate in the Marshalsea and Runners on his trail."

"And here I'd supposed you for a toff."

Will hesitated. "Not quite."

The ground still wobbled. The sooner his feet were upon it, the better. He ducked through the hole in the bridge's net, stepped onto the ladder, then jumped the rest of the way. A thin layer of mud cushioned the landing.

He straightened and dusted off.

Lifty's eyes were wide and eager.

Eager for what? Another spectacle such as Will had been fool enough to give him the other night?

"Want a job?" Lifty asked.

Rose grabbed his coat. "*No.*"

Will shook his head. "Not picking pockets, I don't."

Lifty glanced at the notes in his hand. As if realizing they were within Will's reach, he suddenly tucked them in his collar. "Pity. You've the touch."

Will straightened, self-consciously. "I'm to *stop* pickpockets."

Lifty grinned. "That so?"

"Thieves at all events. I'm to offer protection from thieves."

"And then what? Hope the fancy will hand you a reward?" Lifty waved off the idea. "No toff *volunteers* a reward."

Rose frowned. "And why not? They pay Runners to guard theater doors, don't they?"

"That's different. Runners belong to the beak."

"Will don't belong to nobody no more. Not even that cully Fitzroy, eh?"

Lifty inspected Will. "What's this?"

Will scowled. "Never mind. I never have and never will belong to any man. Mr. Fitzroy and I were . . . friends."

"Fitzroy, is it?" Lifty fingered his chin, mouth pursed. "Heard that name, seems like." He glanced at Rose.

She shrugged.

"Yes." Lifty turned back. "Uppity toff, ain't he? House of Commons, or some like?"

Will managed a stiff nod.

"Well then, I like a man with connections."

"I wouldn't exactly call him a connection." Will tried to wrest back control of the conversation. "But I daresay I can make my own way now."

"Oh aye, and how're you going to find these robberies for doin' your good deeds? Think you're going to run onto an up-turned mail coach every night?"

"I've been here a sennight, and already I've run upon your mail coach, had my pocket picked, and found you flush with some deviltry or another." In a flash, he snatched Lifty's wad of notes from inside his shirt collar.

Lifty grabbed at him, too slow by far.

Will backed out of reach. He wouldn't keep the notes—he'd

no idea to whom to return them. But why not provide a reminder that he could beat Lifty at his own game?

He held the notes out of reach a moment longer, then
handed them over. "Perhaps *you* could aid me."

Lifty eyed Will, his expression once again somewhere between distrust and interest. "Me?"

"You're a criminal."

"No need for names. It's a professional geezer, I am." He
paused in counting his notes and saluted against his hat brim.
"Lifty Lefty, in me professional circuits."

Rose rolled her eyes.

Will ignored her. "Mightn't you two know where robberies
are likely to occur? I could . . . give you a percentage of the
rewards."

Rose's eyes lit up. "Like bleedin' Robin Hood!"

"I dunno." Lifty chewed his lip. "Ain't exactly my line. Noth-
in' hefty I can do outside of Mr. Monarch's endorsement."

"Who's Mr. Monarch?" That was the same fellow they'd
mentioned the other night. Will looked at Rose. "Your father?"

"Nah." She scowled and clutched her shawl tighter. "Mr.
Monarch ain't no kin. He's the putter-up. You know, a kids-
man."

"He runs a flash house in Seven Dials. *The* flash house," Lifty
said. "Brought us up from kinchins. He'd know about any sizable robbery. But whenever you work his territory, you have to
give him a cut."

"Why not work beyond his territory then?"

Lifty shrugged. "If it ain't him takin' a cut, 'tis another."

Will considered. "How much of a cut?"

"Might be he'd grant such as you a special deal."

Will needed earnings, that much he did know. And he needed
a place to stay. If he kept his head down amongst Rose and
Lifty's sort, perhaps the Runners would be less likely to notice
him.

But. His stomach rolled over. These people were the worst
of the worst. They'd proven that countless times just in the
short while of his acquaintance.

Of course, insofar as the law was concerned, he *was* one of
these people.

A shiver coasted his arms.

Mr. Fitzroy said this transformation was a gift. Perhaps he was correct, perhaps not. Of a certainty, it *was* a tool. If Will was to save Tom—and maybe himself—he was going to have to use it however he may.

He looked at Lifty. "Take me to your Mr. Monarch."

# CHAPTER 14

LIFTY AND ROSE guided Will back across the river, roundabout the City, past the Strand, and through the flower market at Covent Garden. This Seven Dials of theirs was only a cat's whisker from the grand environs to the east. But Rose was correct: the neighborhood was not so flash.

The place covered at least six acres. According to Rose, it was named after seven little streets intersecting at an impressive Doric pillar topped with a seven-faced sundial.

Will tromped behind Lifty, who scooted in and out of corners and alleys, navigating the twisting streets as if they didn't all look exactly the same.

In truth, they weren't the same. Around every turn, there was something new. The houses were packed together, back to back, until it was a wonder there were any alleys a'tall. Here was a building of three stories, here a shack with a single floor, here one loomed with its fourth story stretching into crumbling shingles and exposed rafters.

Chimneys puffed black soot everywhere. The muck in the streets grew deeper and fouler step by step. Men, women, and children—all reeking of gin—sprawled in doorways. Others huddled over open braziers that blazed away even at midday.

There was as much bustle of industry as in any street with legitimate businesses. Children played at the doorsteps, screaming and laughing by turns. Women shook laundry from the windows, spattering gray droplets. Men strode up and down, smoking, conferring, jingling, and eyeing one another with a sentiment somewhere between camaraderie and common wariness.

Will was dirty enough not to attract more than a second glance. Still, his palms sweated. He tucked his chin and watched sidelong. If he'd thought Southwark a foreign land, this place was beyond anything he had imagined: that people should live in this filth—that they should be jovial amidst it—that they should lead lives of crime and consider it a good day's labor.

How far he had fallen since his grand debut in Grosvenor Square.

Rose patted his back. "You don't bite them, they won't bite you. Not today anyhow."

Lifty halted before a tall, gray-brick building and opened the door upon a large room. It was surprisingly bright, thanks to a large shattered window with its shutters flung open to the side alley. At the room's far end, a ragged curtain concealed another wide doorway.

Within the first room, the only dweller was a middle-aged woman sprawled in a chair near the door.

Lifty kicked the chair leg as he passed. "Peggy, what you up for?"

She squinted and raised an unsteady hand to clear dark, straggling hair from her face. She looked at Will, without comprehension.

She was not as old as he'd first thought. Perhaps, she might even be as young as himself. Huge violet eyes stared from a pinched face. Her cheeks were flushed, almost feverish.

Her gaze traveled over to Rose. She caught the girl in her arm, half falling from her seat. "Aw, darling Rose, darling Rose." The words slurred and phlegm rattled her throat.

Rose squirmed. "Leave off!"

Peggy planted a kiss on her cheek.

Lifty hauled Rose away. "Ah, let be, Peg. You know she don't like your rubbish." He looked at Will. "C'mon then, Mr. Monarch's through here."

The rip in Peggy's skirt revealed the length of her leg, covered past the knee in a red stocking with no fewer than three holes.

Heat rose at the back of Will's neck, and he turned after Lifty. Peggy drifted her hand out to brush Will's. Her skin burned.

"Oy . . ." Her eyes had cleared. "What are you, then?"

He colored up furiously. For the love of the saints, what had *he* to be ashamed of?

Rose ran back and grasped his other hand. "Told you to leave off, Peggy. Go back to sleep, why don't you?"

Peggy grunted and slumped against the wall.

Will let Rose march him across the room. "Who's she?"

Rose faced forward, mouth grim. "That's Peggy. She's got the wastin' sickness, and she's a bleedin' poppy-eater. When you're a boy around here and you don't get out, you end up like Lifty." She snorted, only a little disdainful. "When you're a girl—well."

Ahead, Lifty swept aside the faded curtain and revealed another room, almost as large and bright as the first. It was papered in a faded shell design with diamond-patterned parquetry covering the remains of the floor. Once, this must have been a fine house.

In front of the vast hearth, a weathered plank table was covered in wooden bowls, a hacked-up loaf of bread, and baskets of mending that shone like silk.

An extraordinary collection of valuables was scattered all about: silver plate stacked in the corners, mirrors and paintings leaning against the walls, snuff boxes of varying sheen upon the mantel.

All this was contrasted with the chipped pottery beneath the table, the worn pewter spoons and rusted knives, and the stink of dust and old spirits.

A short, stout man stood upon a table bench, thrusting a fire iron into the low rafters.

He wore a burgundy velvet smoking jacket, rubbed to dullness at the elbows and across his shoulders. Pale curls straggled about his collar. His legs—judging by the perfect white silk stockings—seemed, by their owner at least, to be considered rather shapely. Or perhaps 'twas mere vanity, since the calves looked to be padded to achieve the ideal appearance. Will had heard of rich young cubs doing such.

The man looked over his shoulder with a quick, piercing gaze that took in Lifty and Rose and landed upon Will. He had a plump face of perhaps two score and ten years, his eyes a soft, clear blue, vivid even across the room. Rather alarmingly, his eyebrows slanted up, away from his eyes.

He smiled. "Well, and who might this be?" His gentle voice was smoothed by an exotic accent that Will could only guess was French. He continued to prod the poker into the ceiled shadows.

Lifty held his hat before his chest. "This'd be Will Hardy, Mr. Monarch. He's the chap what planted a facer on Bull."

As if *that* revelation were the best way to introduce the plan. Will shifted.

Mr. Monarch pursed his lips. "Yes, and now? Do you come to make to me an apology?"

Will cleared his throat. "Perhaps they've . . . told you what I can do?"

"I have heard, yes." He didn't sound much impressed—or convinced.

"I've a plan to gain rewards from those who can pay by *stopping* robberies from happening. But only if I've a source who can discover the robberies aforetimes."

The idea sounded far more ridiculous now than when he'd explained it to Lifty. Why should Mr. Monarch aid him? Robberies—and worse—were doubtless his sustenance. Likely, he would order Will murdered merely for suggesting such an idea.

Will's mouth dried out.

Mr. Monarch studied the rafters. "This is—an *intéressant* plan." He thrust out the poker in a quick stabbing motion.

Overhead, something squealed.

He dragged the poker across the beam, back towards his other upraised hand. "But why come to me? Where is there to be benefit for me?"

Lifty leant forward. "He's promising you a cut, of course. And as his partner, I'd be giving you your accustomized cut there too."

That was a new development.

Lifty glanced sideways at Will and offered a shrug.

"Well, it is *intéressant*," Mr. Monarch said. "And—original, we shall say? But also to me it seems very . . . uncertain." From between the rafter and the end of his poker, he retrieved a black furry lump, half again as large as his hand.

He stepped down from the bench, holding a battered but still chittering rat.

Rose started.

Tranquilly, he laid the poker on the table. He sat on the bench, crossed his admirable stockings, and reached for a thin, gleaming knife.

He looked Will over, leisurely. "Hmm. My *député* Bull, he is not someone to be defeated easily. You must provide to me a demonstration of your skills, yes?"

Will could only nod.

Mr. Monarch turned the rat belly up and inserted the knife into the fat bulge of fur. Blood and innards gushed. The rat shrieked, naked feet scrabbling. Mr. Monarch twirled the knife around to cut off the left front paw.

Rose lunged. "You bloody devil!"

"'Tis but a rat, my child. It can have no place in this world."

Her voice turned shrill. "'Tis Pip!" She seized his arm.

Without changing expression, he boxed her ear, the flick of his wrist elegant.

She sprawled on her knees. Her cheek was red, but she didn't touch it. Her nostrils flared to white, and she scorched him with a murderous glare.

He lowered the knife and touched its point to her nose. "Peace, my child."

In one quick motion, Will yanked her back and thrust her half behind him, heedless of her choked yelp.

Mr. Monarch's crooked eyebrows rose. "A most *curieuse* sort after all." Efficiently, he snipped off another of the rat's paws between the blade and his thumb, as if paring the stem of a flower.

The rat scarcely tremored.

The flesh on Will's arms crinkled all the way up and down. Amongst what sort of men had he found himself? Mr. Monarch would not have applied the knife to Rose. Surely, it was but a threat.

Mr. Monarch raised the rat nearer his face, observed it, then held it away from himself.

He looked again at Will. "Even still, this plan has not excitement for me. I like to have in my hands *monnaie* that is certain. To undermine my own ventures, would that not be unwise?"

At this moment, Will had no particular excitement himself. If the man disliked the plan, then he could yet leave.

Lifty elbowed him. "Tell him how it is you're good friends with Mr. Fitzroy."

Mr. Monarch looked up, sharply. "What is this name you speak?"

Will shook his head. "Lifty misunderstands. I don't know him." He'd made that mistake once before, with Pish. Never again.

"Mr. James Fitzroy." Mr. Monarch rolled the name over his tongue. "He who would be Prime Minister."

Lifty nodded. "Thought that might interest you. Soon as I hears the name on this chap's lips—and remembering he was staying in the gentleman's very house—I knew that'd be honey on your bread."

Will gritted his teeth.

"Fitzroy. *Fils du roi.*" Mr. Monarch tasted the syllables, decadently. "Well, and *he* interests me. I watch him, yes?"

"Why?"

"Because I have wisdom and I have patience, and I can see from far, far off, this is the sort of man who can be very useful to such as me." He smiled. "If only I wait." He uncrossed his stockings and rose gracefully. He extended the oozing rat towards Lifty, as if bestowing a gift.

Releasing his hat with one hand, Lifty gingerly took the rat.

Mr. Monarch approached Will, bloody hand held away from his body, palm up. His gaze paused on the grip Will still maintained upon Rose's elbow. Then he looked into Will's eyes.

Will held steady. This man was but a soft little fop. Thanks to Will's speed and surprise and his not inconsiderable forgehewn strength, he had already managed the formidable Bull. He could manage Mr. Monarch too.

But Mr. Monarch flashed his blade at neither Will nor Rose. "I think, yes, perhaps after all, you have potentialities to offer, young Mr. Will. So let us say—we will *try* your plan."

Will leant back. "Why should you?"

"I like what is singular. I like what is unexpected. It is making life *intéressant*, yes? It is how we do not allow others to perceive what we will do on every day of our lives. Do you gamble, young Mr. Will?"

"No."

"Which is most wise. But sometimes one must gamble to gain. I gamble on you now." With his clean hand, he retrieved a huge silken pocket-handkerchief from his waistcoat and smoothed the gore from his other hand. He raised both eyebrows. "So we shall talk. You will pay me . . . forty-five *pour cent*, I think."

"Forty-five? I can't afford that."

"Of course you can, because without paying, you are not earning. As I say, we try it, yes? If you don't like it, if I don't like it, then we try no more." He smiled, baring a crooked eyetooth. "It is a good deal, and I give it to you because I have admiration for what I see."

Footsteps clattered through the room behind, and the curtain was jerked farther aside. A dark-haired, hawk-faced lad of perhaps three and ten ripped off his squashed beaver-nap hat. He glanced from Lifty and the rat to Will and Rose, halting briefly at the hold they had on each other.

Mr. Monarch faced him. "Yes, my young Arthur?"

"It's Tug and his bloody pack of waterpads! They're poaching on us."

"Ah, yes, and where's this?"

"Out to the East India Docks. There's that merchantman you've been waiting for just in, and they're wangling aboard as tidewaiters whilst she's unloading." He kept twitching rearward, as if the need for haste pressed upon him. "Bleedin' thieves!"

Mr. Monarch pressed his finger to his lips. "Thieves, thieves." He looked to Will. "You would halt thieves, yes? They thieve from this merchantman. They thieve from me. You protect us both, I think."

Protecting such as Mr. Monarch had no place in this plan. Will shook his head.

But what then? If he refused, he not only lost his chance

here, but the merchantman would yet be robbed. And at this point, Mr. Monarch might well exact his own reprisal for any refusal.

Heaven help him if the entire situation hadn't wrenched from his control.

Mr. Monarch merely smiled.

Will's partnership with this criminal would advance the man, true enough. But it could help others too, far beyond Tom alone. That couldn't be counted for naught in the overall balance.

He straightened.

This was not the deal he *would* have made—shaking hands with this foul Seven Dialer. There was no black and white to it a'tall. But the world had become such a muddle. Was there any black and white to *anything*?

Perhaps back in Affery.

He swallowed and managed a nod.

Mr. Monarch bared his crooked eyetooth once again. "We will see how this partnership can work. Arthur, my hat. Rose, my shawl. Lifty, give word to Bull to care for my girls whilst I am out."

With a growl, Rose thrust Will's wrist from her. She stomped across the room to where a clothesline stretched between the corner of the hearth and the wall. She returned with a patched green silk shawl.

As she passed Will, she shook her head. "Went and sold yourself to the shop, didn't you, cully?"

# CHAPTER 15

THE WEIGHT OF a pistol hung heavy in Will's hand. He looked down at it. "I'm not going to shoot anyone." Rose crossed her arms. "Rather they shoot you then?" They stood at the northwest corner of the East India Docks. The bustling rectangular import dock hosted scads of ships, a quarter of which were currently queued for unloading. At the center, resting ships were ranged in formations of between six and twelve, their masts and spars naked.

The setting sun had at last burnt through the fog. Round and red, it bounced its light off the yellow water, pierced his vision, and set fire to the back of his brain. The brackish tidal water, smelling of dying fish, aided nothing.

His limbs quivered with weariness. The thought of a straw tick beckoned. Even a blanket in a corner would be bliss.

He closed his eyes against the infernal blare of the sun. When he opened them, black spots danced a quadrille. And yet even now, that same frantic energy pumped through him. His senses were alight, his muscles tight, ready to run and run and run. Was it possible this new instinct would run him to death?

Rose jumped up and pointed. "There's Lifty!"

Through the crowd, Lifty's shovel hat appeared, then his face. His eyes were bright—alive with the chase. But the lines around them were tight.

"Well?" Will asked.

"It's the *Willing Mind* you're wanting, three ships down. Tug's got the crew believing his lads are customs officials, and they're unpacking and filching right along. Think of the biggest, ugliest whapper ever you saw, then imagine him a little bigger and uglier. That's Tug."

Will adjusted the high collar of the black greatcoat provided by Mr. Monarch. The long skirt swung past his knees, and the double cape hung heavy about his shoulders. He had buttoned it all the way to his throat, then turned up the stiff collar to hide his face from the cheekbones down.

He stowed the pistol within the coat. "Well, then."

Lifty stopped him with a hand against his chest. "Wait. You didn't think that was *all*, now did you?"

Will glared. "*What* then?"

"The captain's having a dinner party—a welcome home no doubt. They're all at table in his quarters—his wife, ship's master, the whole lot." Lifty tweaked Will's collar. "Want my opinion, you'll leave this lark."

"This was your plan!"

Rose scowled. "If he leaves this now, Tug'll be off with Mr. Monarch's swag. How's that to get squared?"

Lifty shrugged. "Only stating facts, me."

Rose pushed Will's hip with both hands. "Go. Just remember these nasties is not your chaps back home, eh?" She nodded to the row of tall buildings along the inland side of the dock. "Mr. Monarch'll be watching."

And that was intended to make him feel the better?

He stepped tentatively into the crowd.

Lifty huffed. "Run!"

But he kept his pace slow. He appeared suspicious enough already without running. At all events, he could hardly just barrel through this crowd of bustling merchants, sailors, financiers, and gawpers.

He found the third ship down—the *Willing Mind*. Men moved about the decks, shouting orders and pointing. They all seemed big enough and ugly enough, but the biggest stood head and shoulders above the rest. He was directing trunks and barrels off-ship.

Customs officers, according to Rose, had free reign aboard merchantmen. If a thief like Tug could impersonate one, then likely Will could do the same.

He hesitated.

No, the trick here would be to make a grand entrance.

Overhead, exposed ratlines webbed the ship's three masts. Plenty of footholds there.

He backed up to gain a measure of momentum, then jumped across the expanse of water and caught the gunwale. Straight-away, before he could attract any attention from either shore or boat, he hauled himself over and leapt straight up to grasp the nearest of the taut ropes. Immediately, his hands burned, even calloused as they were. For two very long seconds, he kicked about until finally gaining a foothold on the ratline just beneath. At last, he swung about to face the other direction, bounced the ball of his foot off another of the ropes and shot to the adjacent ratline. He repeated the motion, in the other direc-tion—back and forth, up and up, until he reached the yardarm's furled sail.

As he crouched, he let himself grin. Dear angels in their heavens, had he really done that? He gripped the yardarm to either side of his feet. The wind feathered past his face, ruffling his hair. It still smelt of dead fish, but also now of gravy and spice. His stomach growled.

A man's voice floated up: "Delightful repast! Captain Win-slow, you dine better than I imagined."

More voices murmured. The dinner party emerged on deck.

A woman laughed. "I have sailed with him. Believe me, there are days when rations grow sparse indeed."

Will's heart seized up. If these people surfaced, they could not help but see what was about to transpire.

But why shouldn't they see? They were the ones he was pro-tecting. They must witness his good deed if they were to be inspired to munificence.

Below, Tug's gang were hustling their goods off ship—aided, it seemed, by one of the ship's own company.

The sight of it all swirled a little. Sickness infiltrated the back of his brain. Of an instant, he felt as if he were toppling back-wards. He grasped spasmodically for the yardarm, even though he'd never released it.

Not now! This accursed dizziness. Where had it sprung from? What was the good of standing atop the world if he couldn't open his eyes?

Again, his stomach growled. He should have demanded more to eat than the tea and rye bread Rose had thrust upon him as they left.

Teeth gritted, he tilted his chin up before opening his eyes. After a few blinks, the pinkish sky held steady. But then he glanced west—and the sunset seared his vision. Pain gripped him. What *was* this?

He blinked again and looked down to find Tug and his men exiting at the gangplank.

Time for his entrance then. He flicked back his greatcoat, and he leapt. Vertigo roared through his head. The sky and the sea and the ship warped all about him. He flailed.

A woman cried out.

He struck the deck hard with both feet beneath him, but he tilted too far forward and toppled. Pain shot up through his knees. Slamming his hands to the holy-stoned planks in front of him, he stopped his fall bare inches from cracking his nose.

Heat pricked his neck.

Pushing hard against the deck, he spun to take in the scene. The heat spread to his cheeks, mercifully covered by the up-raised coat collar. At least the swirling coat presented a nice effect.

A short man with small eyes and soft jowls stomped forward. "I say, sirrah! What are you about?" To judge from his blue coat and piqued expression, this was Captain Winslow.

Behind, an officer gasped and pointed. "Sir! We are being . . . robbed!"

Good. Now everyone knew the cut of the cloth.

Will glanced back.

At the gangplank, Tug guarded the rear of his retreating men. With one hand, he helped another man carry a small chest. With the other, he loosed a dagger from his waistband.

He grinned, teeth shockingly white in his mangy beard. "Hold yourselves there, ladies and ignorant sailors that you be!"

Will looked at the captain. "Have no anxiety, sir. I've come to aid you."

"Indeed!" Captain Winslow fumbled for his gilt-handled sword. He pointed, not at Tug, but at Will. "Clap that man in irons!"

Whistles pierced the air. The few ship's men still aboard swarmed from below decks.

Oh, seize it. Fighting villains was one thing. Fighting a whole ship's company was another.

Will whirled to face the outlaws.

Halfway down the gangplank, Tug laughed at him.

Fine. Let him. He wouldn't laugh long.

Before Tug could take even one step, Will stood before him. He snatched the man's wrist in one hand and squeezed—hard. With his other hand, he caught the knife's short crosspiece and wrenched it loose.

Tug's grin disappeared. His eyes widened. "What devil's spawn are you?"

"One you've never seen the like of."

The words sounded pompous, even to him. But what else did a non-villain say? At all events, it was gospel.

He tried to strike a reasonable tone. "You need have no concern with me, if only you'll hand over what you've stolen."

Behind, more whistles and shouts punctuated the slap of running feet against the deck.

From the bottom of the gangplank, Tug's men beckoned. "Come on, then! The bloody Thames police is here!"

Farther out, men with bludgeons shoved through the crowd.

Tug wrenched free of Will's grasp and dragged his partner down the plank with him. They ran quickly despite the weight of the chest between them.

Not quickly enough, of course.

Will rushed past Tug and skidded to a halt not two feet in front of him.

Tug recoiled. "Cor! How you doing that?"

"Matters not." Will scarcely refrained from adding "my good fellow" to the end. "Hand over the chest, if you please."

That was when Tug punched him squarely in the side of the head.

The world flashed white. Will staggered, then tripped and smashed onto the gangplank, flat on his back and only a whisper from the edge.

He'd always had good instincts in a fight: find your feet even before you fully know you've been hit. As a boy, he'd needed those instincts, since he'd been smaller than the rest of the village lads.

Now, thanks to his new reflexes, he surged upright before the pain in his head even registered. He looked about to find Tug—and then the pain registered, well and truly, with a resounding thump in his molars and jawbone.

What sort of daft idiot was he? He had stepped in so close, he'd all but beseeched Tug to knock him flat. He could hold his own in a fight, of a certainty, but not against the likes of that hulking ogre. Speed and surprise—those were his allies now, and he'd cast them both into the wind.

The Thames police—not quite Runners judging from their plain waistcoats—met Tug's gang at the bottom of the plank. Some of the thieves joined the mill, swinging anything to hand, including their plunder. Others ran back up the gangplank, choosing instead to face the ship's company.

Beneath Will's feet, the plank shifted.

A sailor yelped. "They've loosed her moorings, the fools!"

Indeed, the thick rope securing the ship was slipping off the dock cleat. The prow nosed from land, and the gangplank began to scrape away from the gunwale.

Will lunged for the chest and clamped his hand over Tug's on the handle. Turning, he powered back onto the ship, dragging Tug, his partner, and the chest after him. He cleared the gunwale, and Tug thumped onto the deck behind him just as the plank gave away with a tortured screech. Shrieking, Tug's partner plummeted over the edge. His weight yanked against Will's arm socket.

Yelling, Will heaved himself forward, hauling at the chest with all his strength. The thief's weight gave way, and his shout ended in a splash. With any luck, the poor devil could swim.

Will, Tug, and the chest landed in a pile on the deck. Will's pistol slipped from his waistband and skittered across the deck to bump into a pair of polished boots.

"That is quite enough!" Captain Winslow seized the pistol.

One hand still claiming the chest, Will clutched his throbbing shoulder. Wheezing, he faced the captain. "Sir. When I learned these men were robbing you, I came to assist you."

A flush mottled the captain's cheeks. "You amaze me!" He was nearly sputtering.

He *did* appear rather befuddled—and embarrassed. After all, he'd allowed his ship to be burgled under his nose.

At the captain's back, half a dozen ladies stared in fright and bewilderment.

The foremost woman, in her fifth decade but still bright-eyed with auburn tendrils framing her face, smiled in delight. She clapped white-gloved hands. "Bravo, I say. Bravo, young man! Quite the *élan!*"

Captain Winslow reared back, pressing his chin deeper into his sagging jowls. "You are under arrest the same as all this wretched lot!"

Will gained his feet. "Sir, you misunderstand—"

Captain Winslow tracked him with the pistol. He stood very straight, as if trying to reclaim his dignity.

He wasn't the only one.

Behind Will, Tug chuckled.

This was not a'tall how this was supposed to go.

So Will did what he was starting to do best: he dodged.

He crossed the deck in a flash, putting himself between the captain and the continuing struggle of thieves and sailors.

*Speed and surprise.* He caught up a belaying pin.

One after the other, he rapped the thieves upon their heads, felling most of them instantly.

As he reached the last, he spun, and the full glare of the sun pierced his eyes. It burned with an unholy fire, smearing everything to white.

What *was* that? Had this morning's foul fog irritated his eyes so badly?

He blinked furiously and turned from the sun, the belaying pin still outstretched. A shadow moved before him, and he struck.

The man fell at his feet.

He blinked his way back to sight.

The man was a sailor, not a thief.

But 'twas an honest mistake, surely.

Without slowing, he whirled back across the deck and finished by rapping an open-mouthed Tug into unconsciousness as well.

Neatly, he halted before the captain and let the belaying pin clatter to the deck. He met the captain's eyes with what he hoped was a stony gaze. "As I said, sir, I am here to assist you."

The captain's mouth worked, open and shut.

And how was it Robin Hood went about turning his magnanimity to daily bread?

Will cleared his throat. "Donations are very welcome."

Now *that* didn't sound like begging a'tall, did it? The soles of his feet itched to bound away. But what good would that do Tom? He *had* saved the ship's chest from being stolen. Surely, that must be worth something.

Back on the dock, the police had beaten their way through the escaping thieves. Half a dozen stood at the water's edge, brandishing their sticks and shouting. Others struggled through the crowd to snatch the last of the rope before it slipped entirely free of the anchoring cleat.

Captain Winslow's watery eyes wavered. He obviously had no idea what he had witnessed, much less what he had escaped. His hands trembled around the outstretched pistol.

Perspiration sprang up at Will's hairline.

A ship's officer, sword in hand, stepped up behind Captain Winslow and inclined his head to his commander's ear. "Sir, I think perhaps this man speaks truly. Might it be prudent to . . . humor him?" He lowered his voice. "Until the police can reach us."

Underfoot, the deck lurched. The prow glided back towards the dock.

The bright-eyed woman approached the captain. "My dear, he has told you no lies. And he is most interesting. Indeed, I am thoroughly charmed by the entire experience." She flashed Will a smile, both matronly and friendly. "From where do you hail?"

Will opened his mouth, almost told her the truth, then cleared his throat. "Ah, from . . . quite some distance, ma'am."

"I see. A wayfarer then." She turned to the captain and put her hand upon the pistol, easing it down. "Humor me, husband. Give him a token. For the daring of it."

Captain Winslow finally looked away from Will. "My dear, *really*. What has the man caused here but chaos?"

She touched her fan to her lips and nodded encouragement.

Captain Winslow sighed, then gestured to his officer.

After a brief hesitation, the man produced a small purse and proffered it to Will.

"Now, then," Captain Winslow said. "No sudden movements, yes?"

The ship bumped the dock.

Will swallowed. "My pistol too. If you please, sir." His voice sounded steady, almost like a man of the world.

With a scowl, the captain reversed the pistol and held it out.

Behind Will, a new plank thumped into place against the gunwale.

His time here was running out. But what was all this if not a bit of theater? He gave himself a few precious extra seconds to pocket both purse and pistol. Then he swirled back the long coattails and inclined his upper body in the courtliest bow he could manage.

The captain's wife laughed, appreciating the show if no one else did.

As he bent, the glare of the sinking sun once more caught the corner of his eye. His brain turned to fire.

Footsteps hammered up the plank. "Stay where you are, brigand!"

That marked the end of the show. Without his sight, he'd be lucky to escape with his life.

Rising, he turned towards the mainmast. He started moving his feet, merely walking at first—casually, as if he cared not about the police—but the motion only stoked the fire in his head.

He blinked hard and fast. A rivulet of sweat slipped into the corner of his eye and burned all the harder. But at least it cleared a speck of his sight.

Ahead, the dark shadow of the mainmast loomed. Behind, the policemen tromped nearer. Almost, he could feel their breath upon his neck.

"Not one more step!" one shouted.

But one more step was all he needed.

He gathered himself, and he ran. In a great bound, he made it three-quarters of the way up the shrouds. With the sun now at his back, his vision began to return to color and detail.

For one last bit of show, he swung around to salute the lady below. But that only dredged up the dizziness.

God have mercy! Was there *any* part of his head that worked?

Before the nausea could swarm him, he leapt again, up to the main yard.

This time, he did not slow, and he did *not* look down. He kept moving, up to the topsail yard, across to the mizzen, down to the poop deck.

From both ship and shore, gasps assailed him.

He dared not look, lest either the sun or the earth assail him. Both seemed determined to kill him.

He jumped to shore, landed roughly, and started running. Already, his weary muscles burned. The very air desiccated his lungs. But run he must, or he would never escape these gawkers.

He rounded the corner, and faces flashed past.

"Hoy!" Lifty's hail blurred in his ears.

But it was too difficult to halt now. If once he halted, he might never accelerate again. He rounded the building and circled back to the alley behind Lifty and Rose. His legs fell from beneath him. He gasped for air, but none would enter his rasping throat. Perspiration drenched him, and his vision danced, burning white at the edges.

Rose caught at his elbow. "My eye! You really did it!"

Lifty frowned. "Not dying, are you?"

If Will could have managed a nod before collapsing, he would have.

# CHAPTER 16

WILL LAY IN an alley north of the East India Docks and fought to keep from choking on every breath. Even behind closed eyelids, the darkness spun 'round and 'round.

What had Dr. Silas *done* to him? Impressive powers, that was one thing. Running faster than e'er man had run, that was fine. Jumping over rooftops and mainmasts until it felt nigh unto flying, that was fine *and* prime.

But of what eternal good was it if it killed him?

His vitals burned, and the cool draughts he drew through nose and mouth only fanned inner flames. His limbs trembled. Sweat soaked his clothing. Every joint throbbed.

Small hands loosened the buttons of his greatcoat and freed his face from the high collar.

"You're all right, you are." The voice was Rose's. She sounded uncertain.

Lifty grunted. "Ain't never seen a man what looked like that what wasn't dying."

"Ain't never seen a man what did what he just did either, did you?"

Larger hands tugged at Will's coat pockets. The weight of the captain's purse jingled.

"'Ey!" Rose said. "That's his, ain't it? And you know whose else's."

"Ah, blimey, girl, I'm just peepin', ain't I?"

Rose snorted. "And you can't be doing naught of use?"

Will managed a groan, just to inform them he was still conscious—in some measure. He couldn't get any words up his throat. Great shivers wracked his body.

Measured footsteps scraped lightly in the alley dirt.

He managed a squint.

Through the twilit shadows, Mr. Monarch approached, the bulk of his upper body swathed in the patched green shawl. In one hand, he flicked an ebony walking stick back and forth. In the other, he twirled an extended spyglass. He hummed a snatch of tune.

Will clamped shut his eyes and chomped at his lower lip.

"Well, my children. What has happened?"

"Dying, I reckon," Lifty said.

Rose scrabbled to her feet. "I'll fetch water."

Mr. Monarch's stick prodded Will's ribs.

A dull ache raced up to his heart, and he managed to bat away the stick.

"We must do something for this," Mr. Monarch said. "We are much impressed, are we not? This is better than what you spoke of to me."

"Aye." Lifty said. "Fast as Blue-Eyed Jem's fingers, didn't I tell you?"

Mr. Monarch grunted. "And we shall see. Perhaps he will be a Jem for us yet."

From the susurration of cloth and the rattle of harder objects, it sounded as if Lifty were rummaging his own pockets this time. A cork whumped free, and a sharp smell, of turpentine and juniper, shot up Will's nostrils. It pierced unto his very brain.

His eyelids popped open. What little breath he'd managed exploded in a violent cough.

Glaring at Lifty, he rasped, "That's the foulest thing I've ever had whiff of."

Lifty sat back on his heels. He held a rectangular bottle of clear liquid. "Better than aromatic vinegar, I say." He regarded the bottle with contentment, then tilted it to his mouth.

The fumes lingered, and another cough scraped Will's throat. He lay back against the ground and closed his eyes.

Small footsteps trotted up, and a great wash of tepid water overwhelmed his face.

He flung himself over onto his stomach. Water ran from his nose and mouth. He turned to see Rose holding one of her great shoes upside down, water bleeding through its eyelets.

She reached for Lifty's bottle. "Here now, he's the one should be drinking that, ain't he?"

Lifty raised the bottle and pushed her away. "Leave off. Didn't come from his pocket, did it?"

With his cane, Mr. Monarch thumped Lifty in the back of the head.

Lifty went from sitting on his heels to kneeling in the street. His shovel hat fell forward off his head and knocked the bottle from his hand. "Hey, that's the fourteen penny!" He scrambled to rescue the bottle, then sat down and nursed the back of his head. "*Fourteen* penny."

Mr. Monarch pointed his stick at Lifty's nose. He clucked. "You won't give to the boy a drop? Hasn't he more need?"

Lifty compressed his face in further pain. He offered the bottle.

Will shook his head. "Quite revived, thank you."

"Have it, my boy," Mr. Monarch said. "You have need of strengthening." It did not sound a request.

Tentatively, Will took Lifty's bottle. His hand tremored, and he found he had to drag his other arm around to support his wrist. Nose wrinkled and absolutely *not* breathing, he managed half a sip. It tasted as it smelt and seared all through his chest. He swallowed twice afterward to keep from coughing and still had to clear his throat.

Mr. Monarch watched him. "Tell me, are you always accustomed to so much suffering after you perform these most amazing of feats?"

He shook his head. "I overdid myself."

Beside him, Rose knelt. "He ran all the way from the country yesterday. Ain't had no decent belly timber since, I'll warrant."

"Ah, but you should have said so, my boy, you should have said so."

May God be pleased, the lack of sleep and food was *all* that was causing this.

Never before had he experienced this fire in his head whenever he looked at the sun. But the dizziness—there *had* been that spell at the ball when he'd knocked into the footman carrying champagne.

A skein of fear coursed through him, nearly turning his stomach. He had thought his transformation complete. He thought he'd survived the plague, no true harm done. But what if that were false? He knew naught of what had happened to him. For all he could tell, these symptoms were only a dark beginning.

Curse Dr. Silas and his suicidal urges! Where was he now when Will actually needed him?

Where, for that matter, was his golden goddess? She might not know all Dr. Silas's secrets. But she knew *something*. He must find her. Somehow, he *must* track her down and learn what he might.

The gin, for all its unpleasantness, did seem to have reviving properties. His head stopped swimming and contented itself with merely pounding. He was able to draw up his knees and link his arms around them to keep from falling back over into the street.

Mr. Monarch watched, lips pursed.

Will firmed his jaw. At least, he had more than proven his abilities. Back at the ship, he had bowled them all off their feet. He *could* do this long enough to save Tom.

He reached for the leathern purse. It weighed heavy in his trembling hand.

"Ah now, and there is the *beauté*." Mr. Monarch angled his stick down and hooked the drawstrings.

"That's Will's!" Rose blurted.

"Quite so, quite so." Mr. Monarch clamped the stick between elbow and ribs and emptied the purse from one hand to the other. His eyes twinkled. "Well, now."

Will held his breath.

Mr. Monarch trickled just over half the coins back into the pouch. Then he tipped the bag out of his palm and caught it by the drawstrings, letting its weight snug it tight. He pocketed the remaining coins and, with a bow, returned the purse to Will.

"Now. A future of *possibilités* most great awaits us. The *rumeurs* will spread. We will help them to spread." Mr. Monarch pointed to Lifty. "And in no large time, all London will know their persons will be protected, their *monnaie* salvaged." He grinned, flashing the crooked eyetooth. "For a price, of course."

Will released his breath. His throat burned. The trembling in his limbs worsened.

For all intents, Mr. Monarch had accepted the deal.

Now what remained was for Will himself to commit. That was easy enough. Indeed, that was all but done.

But wasn't *quite* done. He could still take today's coins and flee this devil's bargain. Surely, there must be a different way, a different man to provide him the aid he needed.

Mr. Monarch could not be trusted, that much had been clear from the moment Will set foot in filthy Seven Dials. But Will *needed* a guide to the underworld. He wasn't joining hands with Mr. Monarch. He wasn't becoming party to the man's crimes. Indeed, he was subverting some of them.

It was the logic of desperation, of course. But God have mercy, he *was* desperate. Great risk, great gain—that was how this larger world functioned, wasn't it?

Mr. Monarch clapped his hands. "We will start you with a crew of your own, my boy."

Lifty looked a bit offended. "And him just arrived?"

Will shook his head. "No." The word came out too quickly by half.

Utilizing Mr. Monarch's intelligence and paying him for it was one thing. But he'd be hanged before he'd take responsibility for half a dozen reprobates.

"I don't need a crew. I work alone."

"With a partner he means," Lifty said.

Mr. Monarch shrugged. "Ah well, as you wish. Whatever is having the most effect." He grinned. "They could not be keeping pace with you anyway, I think." He turned on his heel and shouldered the stick. "Come, come now. We must bring you to rest and to *nourriture*."

Will pocketed the purse and set both palms to the ground. With a great heave, he pushed up. His limbs were weak as watered broth. He made it one step.

Rose clamped her arm around his waist. "'Ere now. Best not rattle your brains any more tonight."

Lifty knocked back another lengthy draught of gin, then groped in the dirt for the cork and slapped it in place. "She's right. Ain't she always the right'n, though?" He pocketed the bottle and stood to sling Will's arm over his shoulders.

Together, they followed Mr. Monarch into the growing shadows.

———————

The winding streets of Seven Dials were surprisingly alight. Fires spotted the darkness from behind dirty, broken windows. Some of the dwellers walked purposefully past, heads tucked. Others filled the narrow paths with guffaws and shoving that seemed, mostly, in good nature. Dogs barked. More than a few parties huddled at the corners, passing around a bottle like Lifty's.

Should any of these chaps have the wrong notion about Will tonight, he wouldn't be able to face them. The skin down his spine shrank. He tightened his grip on Lifty's shoulder and prayed heaven they couldn't hear the clinking purse in his pocket.

His feet were holding him better than they had in the alley. But the wobble in his knees still felt as if he'd run fifty miles. Which, in all truth, he might have.

Some forty feet ahead, Mr. Monarch opened his door. Weak light streamed into the muddy street, followed by laughter and raucous voices. He clamped his bulk between his elbows, seeming to gather himself, then heaved himself up the step and inside.

Will regarded the stream of light. This wasn't sunlight. But would that make a difference? He thought his body had sweated itself dry, but a few more drops dampened his temples. He slowed.

Lifty tugged. "What's a matter? Ain't you ready to put your bones on a bed and pour something hot down to your belly?"

"Wait." He pulled free and stood on his own legs. He closed his eyes and tottered into the doorway. Then he squinted one eye.

A rim of light appeared . . . but no fire, no pain. His dulled brain took a moment to process that. He opened the eye all the way, and then the other.

That was something at least. It was quite a bit, as a matter of fact.

Lifty spread both hands. "What was that?"

Rose cocked her head, brows knit.

"Come on then." Lifty stomped through the mud to take Will's arm. "It's victuals I'm about." He dragged Will up the step and into the entry.

The rooms that had been empty earlier now held dozens of people: Bull and a few other men, at least a dozen women, and perhaps as many as a score of boys ranging in age between Arthur and littler ones as young as five. They swarmed the front room, perching at windowsills and sprawling on the floor with wooden bowls beneath their chins. In the corner, two were pummeling each other.

Mr. Monarch drifted past the opened curtain into the room beyond, where more boys packed the benches at the table. Three women—glassy-eyed Peggy among them—stood warming their backs at the hearth. Few glanced at Mr. Monarch, but every single boy swept off his ratty hat and stowed it under his seat.

Lifty hauled Will under the arch between rooms and over to a narrow stairwell that hugged the wall across from the hearth.

More than a few stares followed them.

"Who's the new lad then?"

"Almost an old man, ain't he though?

"What'd you do, Lifty—bring his whole pocket home?"

Mr. Monarch paused in unwrapping his shawl. "Peace, my children. At this time, we find Master William Hardy one of us." He handed the shawl to Peggy, then took up a short, sputtering candle and met Will at the stair. "Straight up with you then? You need to be at rest." He handed Lifty the candle, then leant in nearer and lowered his voice. "I must tell you with frankness, I have never been so amazed as I am being this afternoon." For the first time, he sounded in full earnest. "You have the gifts of angels themselves. I will have great *honneur* to be part of what you do."

Not to mention the money he would also have the great honor of taking.

He extended his hand. "We do this together?"

Will's head was all a-swirl, not with the light, and not with the dizziness. But with—all *this*.

Mr. Monarch was correct: he was either a part of this, or he wasn't. After today, it seemed he already was. He'd been deceiving himself. There was no decision left to be made here. He'd made it this morning when he'd run from the Marshalsea. He'd made it this afternoon when he'd allowed Lifty and Rose to bring him to Seven Dials.

Or perhaps he hadn't made the decision at all. Perhaps it had been made for him—when Lord Carstone cast Tom into prison, when Dr. Silas blew up his barn and himself along with it, when that faithless warrant officer accused him of murder.

In the eyes of the law, Will Hardy was a murderer. Will Hardy belonged with these criminals. Will Hardy was as bad as the worst of them.

So why not begin here—at the very bottom of the world? He could only climb upwards. He would *not* be like the others here. He would stay for one purpose only, and as soon as he was able, he would have the strength of character to pull himself free and never look back.

He withdrew his arm from Lifty's shoulders and leant upon the splintery banister. Slowly, he slid his other hand into Mr. Monarch's. "Allow me another day to recover. Then find me the next job." The sooner he began, the sooner he could leave.

Mr. Monarch closed his eyes and inclined his head. "Indeed."

Rose bustled up behind Mr. Monarch. "Here then. We're so late, this was all but the last of it." She balanced two wooden bowls of transparent broth—specked with onions and bullseyed by a thick crust of rye bread, already soddening.

"The last of it?" Lifty said. "What about me?"

"What about you? You can shift for your own self, can't you?"

Mr. Monarch stepped back to allow her to mount the stairs. He looked up at Will, eyes tranquil. "Oh, yes, I almost forget. This Fitzroy you say you know—he is, mmm, having these powers too, is he?"

"Ah." The question's unexpectedness clobbered Will's worn-out brain. "I don't know."

Why would Mr. Monarch care? Mr. Fitzroy would never deign to sell himself to Mr. Monarch.

Mr. Monarch blinked sleepily. "Hmm, if it is so, it is . . . *intéressant*. You are a boy. You have much knowledge to learn yet." He pointed to his temple. "And I will teach you. You will get your worth of our deal, have no *anxiété*. But Mr. Fitzroy is a man of cleverness. Also a man of great ardent ambition. He has a great need to prove himself, yes? I know this."

Will shrugged.

Mr. Monarch smiled. "You have maybe heard him in his speeches? When he is standing for the great *Parlement*? I tell you, you have never told a lie until you have told it with the skill he has. One thing I learn from watching him, and that is a lie is not hiding the truth. It is making the lie *into* truth."

Mr. Monarch was observing Mr. Fitzroy. But why? Politics were a rich man's game, certainly not for the likes of Mr. Monarch. Will's weary brain swam circles around his thoughts, struggling to find a sensible angle.

He shook his head. "Mr. Fitzroy has naught to do with me, I assure you." Not any longer. Even if he could have hoped for Mr. Fitzroy's aid before joining hands with Mr. Monarch, certainly he could hope for it no longer.

Mr. Monarch smiled. "We shall see." He motioned them up the stairs.

When they reached the second floor, Lifty's candle showed only the planks at their feet. The gusting draughts and the scrabbling of an animal in a corner gave the impression of a great open floor. Will tripped over heaps of damp-smelling straw, ragged blankets, and wadded newspapers.

"This is where you sleep?"

"Not you, my matey. You're in with me." Lifty kicked open a door. "On account of we're partners, see? Even though you're beginning to seem rather a perilous investment, what with all this staggering about."

The candle illumined a rack of double bunks nailed against the wall.

Will let Lifty tumble him into the bottom one. It smelt more than slightly of gin, amongst other things, and was padded with a newspaper-stuffed tick. Right now, it felt almost as grand as goose feathers. He settled onto his back.

Rose perched beside him and balanced one of the bowls on his chest.

The thin smell of broth churned his stomach into something between hunger and sickness. Already, sleep reached to claim his eyelids.

She guided his hand to the bowl. "Eat the bread at least, and pick out the herrings. Ain't every night we got meat."

Lifty snorted on his way back to the door. "You're perilous *and* you're taking the soup from me mouth." He left the candle on the floor.

Rose pulled her knees to her chest and set her bowl atop them so she could tilt the edge to her mouth.

After a few slurps, she licked her lips, contemplatively. "It's the light, ain't it? That's what bothered you out there, eh?"

He blinked against the encroaching fog, then managed a nod. She might as well know. If it happened again, she wouldn't be the only one to make it out.

He pinched the bread and forced his hand to his mouth. Two bites, chew, swallow. Two more bites, and it was done.

She drained the last of her soup. "Maybe we could rig up a shade for your eyes."

The words faded in and out of his head. Some vague part of his brain registered the soup bowl sliding from his hands.

"Hey now!" She caught the bowl. "Ah, well. You can afford your own meat soon enough."

The weight of the bowl lifted from his chest. He faded away to the sound of her renewed slurping.

———

He slept the sleep of the dreamless, with only one interruption, deep into the night when the candle had long gone out.

Something scraped the floor beneath his bunk, and he jerked awake.

From under the bed, a small hand reached up and patted his arm. "Go back to sleep, won't you?"

In the upper bunk, Lifty flopped over. "Corblimey, Rose. What you think you're doing in here?"

Her snort echoed from under the bed. "Somebody's got to protect him from that lot out there, and it ain't hardly going to be you, now is it?" She sounded brave enough. Maybe a touch *too* brave.

"Oh, blimey." Lifty rolled back over.

Will dragged himself far enough into wakefulness to make his mouth form words. "You can stay if you want to."

This time, her whisper sounded much smaller. "Thanky."

# CHAPTER 17

IN THE LONG shadow of the Marshalsea wall, Will waited for Lifty. That wasn't surprising, since Lifty was proving wonderfully clever at being waited upon. What wasn't quite so predictable was what Will found staring back at him from that same wall: the very image of himself.

It wasn't a particularly *good* image. Lifty had daubed it on the handbills Mr. Monarch insisted on disseminating throughout the streets—to spread the good word about the services Will offered. The idea was that, this way, he'd look legitimate, like a proper businessman instead of a mere highwayman.

Beneath the crude sketch of a man in a tricorn hat and a blowing greatcoat, the handbill offered the promise of

*Stolen goods Returned!*
*Noble persons Protected!*
*Fear the Streets no more!*

He grinned. One week's time, five robberies prevented, five rewards earned—and already he was renowned. Not, of course, that anyone knew his name. And not that anyone would recognize him as the man in the handbill.

But it *was* him.

He shifted the canvas bag at his shoulder and pulled the bill from the wall. Wait until Tom saw this. He'd think it the yarn of the century. Likely, he was in need of a laugh about now.

At this rate, Tom would be at liberty sooner than even Will's best speculations. But first, Will must discover the exact amount of the debt.

He squinted at the iron spikes atop the wall.

No fog this morn. Only sunshine. Beautiful, barbarous, burning sunshine.

Just walking here had proven torturous. He'd kept his head bent and his hand shading his eyes the entire time, but an ache still thrummed his temples.

That was Lifty's fault too.

Will looked back.

No Lifty. Instead, Rose ran towards him in her great, clomping shoes.

She beamed. Rare expression that it was, it lit up her whole face. She threw a skip into her stride.

"Why are you here?" he asked. "Lifty was to bring the eye shields." Lifty had been promising for the past week to collect the needed glass for the lenses. Will had prepared the metal frames the very first day after his job at the East India Dock.

For all Lifty's great talk of being his partner, he wasn't proving much dedicated. Instead, Rose was the one who followed Will to his jobs. Mattered not how many times he told her to remain behind, she still spied out positions for him and awaited him with a meat pie or some like. He was always ravenous afterwards.

Still grinning, she thrust her hand into her shawl. "Lifty had to go on a job. Soldiers parading everywhere, haven't you heard? And ain't they the easy marks when the morts is all waving their pocket-handkerchiefs? So I brung 'em instead."

She raised the eye-shields to her face: wide-lensed spectacles of smoked glass. Half-inch tin awnings jutted from their upper rims to provide direct shade. Will's best notion had been the opaque shields that slid in from the outer edges to cover the lenses in part or in whole, depending on how desperately he needed darkness.

He took them from her, slid the shields back and forth over the lenses a few times, then unfolded the earpieces and settled the contraption over his eyes. Even with the shields open, the burning dissipated. He slid them halfway shut, like blinkers on a jarvey horse. It halved his vision, but he could yet see around the corners—and, heaven be blessed, it also halved the fire in his head.

He grinned at Rose and flicked one of the shields in and out, like a cheeky wink. "This plan is working out splendidly."

Her own grin faded. "Well. That all depends. After Lifty left, there Mr. Monarch was, going out on *important business*. And it wasn't to see his solicitor, if you know me meaning."

Will shrugged his bag to the ground and withdrew his uniform: greatcoat with its collar upturned, black leathern tricorn, and sturdy leathern gloves—off which he'd cut the fingers to protect his palms and give him a better grip when jumping about.

"Why shouldn't he have important business? He's in charge, isn't he?"

"Oh, yes, he's in charge. He can't do any of the things you can do, but he's in charge, he is."

Will pulled on his coat. "Don't fret about me. I can outrun him, remember?"

She scowled. "Can't outrun everything."

He straightened his high collar, then chucked her chin. "Any man on legs, I can."

She failed to look much impressed. "And when somebody catches you standing still? Then what're you going to do?"

"Jump." And jump he did.

All week, he'd practiced jumping flatfooted. Usually, he could get twelve feet off the ground—which meant his outstretched hands were now able to catch one of the windowsills halfway up the Marshalsea wall. Grasping an iron bar, he crouched upon the sill. He didn't look down—dizziness lay therein—but he flicked Rose a salute.

"Can I come?" she said.

In spite of himself, he darted her a glance. "What? Up here?" His head spun, and he closed his eyes. He might be able to outrun Mr. Monarch's fat legs in their fine stockings, but heaven help him if the man tried to out-climb him.

"They'll let me in at the Lodge," she said. "Since *I'm* not wanted for murder. I'll pretend I know someone inside. Find where your mate is and show you where to jump. You can't march about the bloody quod-house looking for him in that costume, can you?"

He shook his head. "I work alone."

"What about Lifty?"

"Lifty doesn't *work* with me, if you haven't noticed."

"Please."

She sounded so plaintive, he couldn't help but open his eyes. The dizziness swarmed again, so he released the bar and dropped to the street. A glance back and forth showed no one who might have seen.

She bit her lip, eyebrows up, trying to appear normal. But she wasn't normal, quite.

The image of the gutted rat rolled through his mind. "What's wrong? Did Mr. Monarch do something?"

She shook her head. "But I'll give my oath he's got some plan under that hat of his. Ever since you turned up, he goes around singing."

"Why shouldn't he, I'd like to know? He's earning an unholy share of my rewards."

"It's more'n that. I tell you there's scheming afoot." She shifted her weight. "I know the feel of it."

He dropped to one knee and pulled the eye shields down the bridge of his nose so he could see over them. Sunlight trickled past his hat brim, but he ignored the burn.

"Mr. Monarch will not harm you. He has no reason to." It was a tremendous lie, and it tasted like one. He swallowed.

He had no desire for a partner—not Lifty, and certainly not Rose. If he was to escape this place with his own honor yet intact, he must work fast and travel light. And yet . . . she was but a child. Surely, she couldn't quite help it if she'd been born into this life and abandoned to Mr. Monarch's clutches.

He sighed. "All right, then. You can come, but only this once. Wave through a window when you find Tom Colville's room."

Her grin flashed. She clucked her tongue and ran around the corner to the Lodge.

Hat under his elbow, spectacles in his pocket, and collar folded down, Will strolled around the prison. He circled it once and a half before two small hands beckoned from an upper window.

With his costume back in place, he found a likely spot at the nearest corner of the spike-topped wall. At twenty feet, it was too tall to reach flatfooted, so he tipped his hat to a passing lady, then gave himself a running start across the road—and jumped. He caught a handhold at one of the barred windows and pushed his booted foot off the wall to bounce the rest of the way up. Carefully, he stepped over the spikes, then dropped down the other side.

Not one of the souls meandering in the yard took notice.

An open door in the nearest row of barracks stood open and seemed as if it should lead to Rose's upper window.

He turned the corner of the door—and plowed into a rickety duffer who smelt of dust and beans.

The man yelped, and Will snatched him back upright before he could topple.

He was an oldish man—white bristles all over his head and face. He took in Will's appearance and opened his mouth in another squawk. "Saints preserve—"

Will clapped a hand to the man's mouth. "Be silent." He deepened his voice to match his appearance. Even still, the first word squeaked a bit. He cleared his throat and tried again. "I come on a mission of mercy. Speak of this to no one. Or . . ."

When you were a crusader of righteousness, what did that leave you to threaten innocent people with?

"Or," he managed, "'twill be upon your own head."

Oh, splendid. His ears burned.

The man scrabbled backwards, nodding vehemently, then ran from the stairwell into the yard.

Almost immediately, his voice drifted back. "There's a highwayman in there! A genuine highwayman goin' up to see Sergeant Colville!"

Seize it. Unless the man's word was as disreputable as his appearance, that ended any chance of a leisurely conversation with Tom.

Will bounded up the steps, five at a time.

At the first landing, Rose waited before a closed door. "Bleedin' great burglar, you'd make."

"Well, I'm *not* a burglar, am I? And neither am I a highwayman."

"Nay, you're a wanted murderer, you are."

"A charge *you* told me you didn't believe."

She tossed her head. "And still I don't. For all your dashing about, you're the greatest clod ever I've seen. If you'd done the deed, you'd never have got away."

"I get away every time I do a job, don't I?"

"You run away just beautiful." She leant one hand against the door and swung it inward. "It's the getting inside you're needing help with."

Tom stood before the fire, poker in hand. He looked around at Will and started visibly. And then, with a great shout, he swung the poker.

Will yanked Rose back, caught the door, and slammed it shut. The poker cracked wood.

"What devil are you?" Tom shouted.

"Tom! It's me!"

"Quieten," Rose hissed. "You want every turnkey to hear?"

Will clamped his hand upon the latch to keep it closed. "Tom, it's me! Don't be daft. Let me in whilst we've the time to talk."

Silence from within. Then: "Will Hardy? I thought you'd plunged from the face of the earth."

It felt like that sometimes.

Will eased open the door.

Tom stood with one hand at the door's inside latch and the poker cocked over his shoulder. He looked Will up and down. "What are you supposed to be?"

Behind him, Rose sniffed. "Long tale, that is."

Tom glanced at her. "And who are you?"

"Rose Gray."

"Who's Rose Gray?"

She cocked her head. "You're the one what used to keep an eye on Will?"

"I am."

"Well, now I'm the one."

Will pushed her into the room. "Why not put that eye to use at the window, hmm?"

She didn't break stride across the room. "And that's where I'm going, ain't it?"

Will removed his hat and eye-shields and unbuttoned his collar to reveal his face.

Tom eyed the procedure. "Good Lord, Will. What's this guise then? The devil's undertaker?"

"'Tis a costume."

"That I can see."

Tom appeared as he always did, if a bit pinched about the mouth. He seemed weary. He was a man of the sun and the soil. Never had he spent an entire day within the confines of walls, not even that winter when he was down with the dropsy.

But his eyes were keen as ever. The duffer down the stairs had called him Sergeant Colville, so evidently he was already making a good name for himself. Of course, he was. Respectability and honor fair shone out of him. He was the kind of man other men wanted to follow, even perhaps when there was nowhere to follow him *to*.

Will wet his lips. "I'm sorry I didn't come sooner."

Tom regarded him. "Well, I'd've enjoyed a friendly face now and again, I'll admit. But you were at the forge last I knew."

"Yes, well. Actually, I've been in London all along. I tried to gain entrance the first day, but they wouldn't allow me."

A certain wariness clouded Tom's face. "We're allowed visitors."

Will took a breath. "They think I killed Dr. Silas."

"What?" Tom recoiled. "Has the whole world gone mad? *Why?*"

"I don't know. That daft little warrant officer—Hale—he came staggering about like he was drunk, or sick, or something, and shouted I'd killed him."

"Hale? The short fellow with the side whiskers?" Tom frowned. "Couldn't have been him. He was with me in the cart the whole time."

A chill raised the hairs on Will's arms.

Tom had a memory like treacle. He wasn't the sort to mistake something like that. Then again, a man shouting *murderer!* was decidedly harder to misremember than one sitting beside you in a cart.

Will shook his head. "No, it *was* him, even though there's no sense a'tall in why he would want to spread the lie. He couldn't have been trying to cover his own guilt, because he wasn't there when it happened."

Tom knit his brow. "'Tisn't the only thing making no sense. I've had plenty of time to think, believe me, and all I keep thinking is that the arrest warrant couldn't have happened rightly. Lord Carstone only just promised me the extension, you recall? I've written several times, but no response. I'm not sure but that my letters aren't getting through."

Will snorted. "If 'tis Lord Carstone waffling on his word, that's not so strange by any measure. At all events, matters not. I'm not here about him. I'm here about you—getting you free."

Rose crouched in the window-seat, looking out. "If he's in here because someone wants him in here, buying him out might be a hard trick."

Poker still in hand, Tom folded his thick arms. "And how is it you plan to buy me out?"

"I need to know the exact amount you owe."

"One hundred seventeen pounds four."

That was near on to what Will had estimated. One or two more large jobs, and he might be finished with all this.

Tom raised an eyebrow. "Been granted a legacy since last I saw you?

Will grinned. "Bit of truth to that."

Tom eyed him. "That rich fellow came through for you then? I saw his coach there in Affery."

"No. It's more I've a specialized job now."

Tom looked over Will's costume. Then he glanced at ragamuffin Rose on the window-seat. His face straightened out. "What sort of job?"

Will couldn't help a pinch of affront. "You think I'm out there robbing coaches?"

"No, that's not what I'm thinking. My brain is empty of such thoughts." Tom's jaw tensed. "Why don't you tell me what kind of thoughts I should be filling it with instead?"

Rose jumped to her feet, hands still at the sill. "Best make 'em fast thoughts, 'cause there's an old cuff giving this window attention enough to shine it right up."

Already? Heaven only knew when Will might be able to make another visit.

He buttoned his collar. "There's things I'm capable of now,

Tom. Things you won't credit until I can show you. What I do is find the thieves and stop them."

"And you earn from this how?"

"Rewards. I earn rewards."

Tom gestured to Rose. "What's her role?"

She clomped across the room. "I help him because he works for me master and gives him half."

Will steered her to the door. "Why don't you help me now by getting clear, so I don't have to break my back jumping both of us over that wall."

"Doing *what?*" Tom said.

Rose opened the door. "You don't know what he can do?" She clucked and grinned. "Ah, you're in for a joyous sight, you are." She trotted away.

Will settled his hat and put his eye-shields back on. He looked at Tom. "*She* may be a thief, but I'm not, I promise you."

Tom hesitated a bare second. "I believe you."

Will turned to go.

"But that doesn't make what you're doing right."

Will looked back. "Helping people?"

"Extorting people."

Again, he felt the pinch. What right had Tom to disapprove of this? He had no idea how it worked. Not really.

"Maybe," Will said, "they reward me out of gratitude."

The voices outside neared—almost to the ground-level door.

"Maybe they do." Tom unfolded his arms and stepped forward. "I realize there's a deal you're not telling me. You're your own man and you make your own choices. You made that clear enough when you left with that Mr. Fitzroy without so much as a word."

Straight to the heart with that one. Will clenched his teeth.

"But what about the girl?" Tom asked.

"What about her? Rose goes no way but her own, and that's a fact."

"I might have said the same of you at her age." Tom drew back. The weariness in his eyes pulled harder. "You're telling me you can do great things, Will. All right then. Do them for great reasons."

Will firmed his jaw. "My reason is good enough. Once you're

free of this place, we'll escape, start over somewhere. You never belonged here to begin with."

Tom held the silence. "Didn't I?"

"No, you didn't." Will glared. "Do you want to rot in here with the fees and the interest eating up what money you've left? Do you want me to sit upon my hands and do naught? Because I give you my oath, what I'm doing now—'tis the only choice I have. You think I'd be amongst these people if I had any choice at all? I thought you'd be pleased to know you'd soon be free."

Tom's mouth relaxed, slightly. "That's so, Will." He extended his hand. "And I do thank you for what you intend—with all my heart."

Will gripped his hand. "You're not going to stay in here." A great desperate emotion welled in him. "My oath on it, Tom. I will pay the debt and get you out. I owe you that—and more."

A faint smile raised Tom's mouth. "You don't owe me aught. Save maybe . . . to do this the right way. Because there is one thing I know." Still gripping Will's hand, he looked him straight in the eye. "I won't be bought out with money wrongly earned."

Muffled voices echoed from the yard below.

Doubt suffused Will. He shook his head. "Do you know how many robberies I've stopped?"

"And yet you pay rent to thieves." Tom released Will. "Think on that."

Tom could have no idea how much Will had already thought on it.

"I *will* get you out of here. After that, my association with these people will be finished forever."

Tom grunted. "Sometimes 'finished' gets tricky once it's begun."

Footsteps clomped up the stairs.

Too late for Will to take that exit.

He stood there one moment longer. The need for a last word hung heavy in the air between them.

He raised his collar. "I'll return in a few weeks to pay you out."

Then he crossed to the window and flung open the pane. Neatly, he dropped the score of feet to the prison yard.

This time, folks took notice. A few gasped and pointed. One woman squealed.

At the ground-floor door, the old duffer pointed. "There! I said it, didn't I? Didn't old Trabb *just?*"

Will glanced back to the window to see Tom standing there, forehead knit with confusion. Then Will wheeled about, gained a running start at the wall, and leapt to catch the iron spikes.

He sidled through the barbs and dropped into the street at the other side.

But not before he heard a child murmur from inside: "'Tis him, isn't it? He's the one! Has he come to save us?"

# CHAPTER 18

BY THE TIME Rose realized someone was following them, they had trudged across the river from the Marshalsea, almost all the way back to St. Giles.

Will looked back through the crowded streets. "I see no one."

"I ain't seen him, exactly. Just a smoky cove's shadow out my catty-eye." She looked over her shoulder, fidgeting. "But he's there, mark me. I can feel him breathing at us—and it smells a horney's breath."

Will tightened his grip on the sack holding his costume. "A Runner, you mean?"

"Exactly that."

He chewed his lip. "Is there a long way back to Mr. Monarch's? Some way we might be able to lose him?"

"Sure. We'll wander up to Oxford Street, eh? We can get lost in the excitement there today."

"What excitement?"

"You'll see." She clomped alongside for several paces. "So—your friend seems the gent, don't he?"

Will grunted. "What he is is stubborn. He desires miracles, not practicalities. The way he asks for this to be accomplished would have him stopping there until he was a stooped old man. If he has no liking for how I earn the money, then I'll drag him over the wall myself come time."

"I thought you couldn't carry *me* over the wall?"

"He doesn't like that I have to hide behind a mask? Well, neither do I!"

Rose grunted.

"But we live in the world as 'tis. The rules are against us, you and I. The rules say there's no decent way to earn enough honest wages to do us any good. And yet you can't change the rules unless you *have* the money, now can you?"

The words tasted familiar in his mouth: rather like Mr. Fitzroy's vision for revolutionizing poverty.

Well, and Mr. Fitzroy hadn't been so far wrong.

Will looked up. They'd passed Seven Dials and re-entered the neighborhoods with the finer residences, a few streets away from Soho Square.

It made him wonder how Mr. Fitzroy had fared this past week. If he died of the plague, word was hardly likely to reach Will. And if he hadn't died, what *had* happened? Had he been gifted with this same inhuman speed? Did the sun burn his eyes, and the bare height of a single story submerge him in dizziness?

What did he plan to do with his powers? Great things, no doubt. He would have the means and opportunities to do all those things Tom wanted of Will.

So many questions. And nary an answer.

The golden goddess might know. He desperately needed to find her. But where? Henry had been deep enough in his cups to call her Isabella. But Will couldn't walk about the environs of Grosvenor Square, knocking upon doors and inquiring if the young lady of the house was passing fair, Christian name of Isabella, rather disinterested in marriage prospects, but all *too* interested in such radical notions as natural science and superior men.

More to the point, he was hardly the Duke of Veneering anymore. What would she think of a lad who dressed as a highwayman and paid half his earnings to such as Mr. Monarch?

The push of the crowds brought him to a halt. He looked at Rose. "Consider this a hypothetical question."

"Don't ask me. I ain't no physician, am I?"

"What do you think Mr. Monarch would do if I said I'd my fill of the bargain?"

She raised her eyebrows. "Ah, and that'd be why you're wanting a doctor, eh?"

He sighed. "I can't work for him forever."

Even if he didn't resign on the instant, as Tom wanted, he would soon have no need of the partnership.

"What do men like Lifty and Bull do when they want to work for someone else?"

"They don't." She glanced nervously over her shoulder. "Folks like us, they don't get out of working for folks like him—not unless they gain a windfall. And then they're as likely to get their throats cut over it, you know? Like Blue-Eyed Jem, remember?"

The crowd around them had grown. Excited, jostling people packed the pavements.

Two score soldiers, decked in scarlet livery and gold braid, paraded the street. They marched to no fife or drum. In fact, over the happy buzz of the crowd, they marched in an almost eerie silence.

Will tugged Rose's shawl. "Come along."

"Where to? We're past Oxford now. We can double on back. I ain't seen our horney for a long while."

"Let us walk through Soho."

"What for?"

"I should like to see Mr. Fitzroy's house."

They passed the soldiers into the next street, only to find another strangely silent military display—and another in the next street. Finally, they reached Soho, which held the dispersing remnants of yet another crowd watching the same spectacle.

Will stopped and gazed halfway down the street to where Mr. Fitzroy's yellow house gleamed, unperturbed. Few enough answers to be gleaned from a house front, and it wasn't likely Tite would answer were Will to knock again.

Rose caught his wrist. "Hey, and there's Lifty!"

Lifty pushed through the waning crowd, waving a slip of paper. "And look at this, will you? It's the dawning light of a new day, I tell you."

Rose hung her hands at her hips. "What are you on about?"

"It's flush, I am!" He waved his paper again. "Flush enough for daffy all around at any rate."

"And where you getting it?"

"You seen all the soldier coves? Word is there ain't nothing Majestic to them, if you know my meaning. Word is they're paid private-like."

Will frowned. "You mean some nob is hiring a guard for the whole of the East End?"

Lifty shrugged. "Won't work o' course." He flapped his paper. "But the opportunities are very slap whilst they're lasting."

So many things here failed to feel correct in any measure. The skin at the back of Will's neck crawled.

But perhaps that was the way of the city. Perhaps this sort of thing happened all the time. How was a country lad to know?

A carriage rumbled past. The team of blacks looked like Mr. Fitzroy's.

Will jerked forward a step, eager, then halted.

*No.* It did not matter whether or not Mr. Fitzroy was out here under the same sky as him. Walking by the man's house in curiosity was one thing. But Will would not go begging again, hat in hand. That day was ended.

Still, he *was* curious.

He tapped Rose's shoulder as he passed her. "Stop here a minute."

"Hey," Lifty said. "Stick close if you want any gin. Heartfelt generosity only lasts so long."

All Will needed was a glimpse of Mr. Fitzroy—anything to show him the man's appearance in the wake of Dr. Silas's plague. If Mr. Fitzroy looked well, then there was yet hope for Will's own symptoms.

He crossed the still-crowded street and leapt at a lamppost. He caught the glass globe and hung off it, one foot propped against the pole.

A few people glanced at him in surprise, but the feat wasn't so far beyond the abilities of any fit lad.

Down the street, Mr. Fitzroy's team halted at his door, hooves a loud dance against the cobblestones. From the far side of the carriage, Mr. Fitzroy emerged. He mounted the steps to the front door, strides long and sure.

Did that mean he'd survived the plague with none of these wretched side effects? Or did it mean he'd never contracted it after all? Of course, Will himself looked no different now either—save grimier.

If Mr. Fitzroy appeared anything a'tall, he appeared . . . disturbed. Every line in his body cut a hard edge beneath his clothes. A servant opened the door, and he disappeared inside the house without a backwards glance.

Will's lungs burned, and he realized he'd been holding his breath. He looked down at the street, and the cobblestones swirled beneath him. Balance compromised, he released the lamppost and dropped to the ground.

Lifty and Rose approached.

"What was that?" Lifty asked.

Lifty likely hadn't any notion this was Mr. Fitzroy's home.

Will shook his head. "Nothing. Thought I saw an answer to a question I've been asking."

They started down the road, headed for Oxford Street.

"As I was saying," Lifty said, "daffy all around to celebrate a day of easy pickings." He kissed his paper. "Got this off'n the lead soldier boy. If these private guards get paid so handsome, might be I'll buy meself a commission. Ten shillings into my hand all at once, I tell you."

Head still spinning with the dizziness, Will glanced at the paper. Even with the banks all printing their own tender these days, this looked like no bank note he'd ever seen.

"How is it you figure to buy gin with that?"

"Same as any man. Put my note on the counter and keep me finger on the corner 'til I gets my change."

"'Tis blank."

Lifty looked sideways at Rose.

She shrugged.

"We put too much smoke on those spectacles of his," Lifty said. "He's not seeing two feet from your face."

Rose grabbed the paper and turned it over. She squinted at Will. "You dizzy again?"

He frowned. "Never mind." He'd yet to conceive a practical way to solve the dizziness, as he had the burning in his eyes.

Lifty snagged back the paper. "Well, we'll take this by the ol' blessed gin-house and see how blank they think 'tis."

They rounded the corner and nearly collided with Mr. Monarch. His face was flushed, lips pulled back in a snarl. As he recognized them, the snarl scarcely dissipated. *"You.* You are here for what all, is it?"

Both Lifty and Rose stopped short. Lifty's note disappeared up his sleeve.

Will's momentum carried him one more step, leaving him to face Mr. Monarch. "Ah—we took the long way home. Heard about the military parades."

*"Gorm."* Mr. Monarch looked them over petulantly. "I should whip you all, every one of you. You are having rest and *célébration.* You are not at work."

"Ah now," Lifty said. "I wouldn't say that . . . exactly." Slowly, he withdrew the paper.

Mr. Monarch took it between thumb and forefinger and secreted it within his waistcoat. If he noticed it was blank, he gave no sign. "That is most *déplorable.* You must find more. You must go out, you must labor for your living for the rest of today."

He looked at Will. His upper lip bulged as he rubbed his tongue over his crooked eyetooth.

This was the first Will had seen Mr. Monarch disturbed. Everything the man did, he did with precision and calculation—just as he had gutted the rat on the first day. He punished his children and his girls sometimes, but always calmly, almost . . . lovingly. He was always superior, always in control. Mostly because he *was* in control.

What brought him to Soho? Surely, he hadn't been daft enough to seek Mr. Fitzroy.

But if he had, that might explain Mr. Fitzroy's displeasure.

"So much for gin," Rose muttered.

Mr. Monarch slapped her, not hard, just enough to make a startling *thwat* sound.

She jerked back.

"You too, you lazy, worthless side-slip." He indicated Will. "You think following this one around is job enough for you? You go with Lifty. You pick the *poches.* You work like you're supposed to."

She gritted her teeth and nodded.

Will fought to keep from fisting his hands. What was he to do, really? Mr. Monarch was her caretaker. It was a shame and a sin, but the man *did* give her a roof, a bed, and at least a daily meal. That was far more than she would have were Will's interference to cast her asunder.

Still.

He faced Mr. Monarch. "So you've finally met the vaunted Mr. Fitzroy? No doubt, he's honored by your acquaintance, pleased to do whatever would be most helpful to you."

Mr. Monarch's hand trembled—as if he might slap Will too.

They both knew how that would end.

Mr. Monarch cocked his hat. He straightened his expression into, if not quite carelessness, at least composure. "So this is where he lives? I had no knowledge. Perhaps I will leave my card."

Will smiled. "You move in exulted circles, sir. I'd no idea."

Mr. Monarch's mouth shifted once more, then he ironed it all straight. "Let us not have *absurdité*. Let us speak of *sérieux* subjects. I have just procured for you your next job. The biggest job yet."

Will's heart jumped. If it were big enough, it might be the last job he'd need. Then he and Tom could flee this place.

Assuming Tom could be made to see the money was honest.

Also assuming "the biggest job" *was* honest. Mr. Monarch had already attempted to slip him into situations that were more than strictly protection roles.

Will kept his stance loose. "What's the job?"

For an instant, something almost like reluctance diluted Mr. Monarch's pettishness. He pursed his lips. "It is so very big I am at first having uncertainty you possess *compétence* enough."

If he was uncertain about thrusting Will into danger, 'twould be the first time.

Will frowned. "Tell me what it is, and I'll tell you if I can do it."

Mr. Monarch started down the street. "Word has come to me. There is a most ambitious geezer—they call him Gamp."

"Oh, bloody," Lifty muttered, walking behind. "Gamp the Tramp, is it?"

"Who's he?"

"He's a rouster. He'll crack your crag clean, he will."

Mr. Monarch patted Will's arm. "Have no *anxiété* from him. He takes too much more to bite than this time he can chew."

*That* comment seemed more akin to Mr. Monarch's usual approach: hurl Will into the maw, trust he'd survive on the merit of his extraordinary abilities, and if he didn't . . . oh well.

"What's he planning?"

"There will be a great *assemblée* tonight. Many great people, many *riche* people. And Gamp has plan to take them all hostage in their carriages. He will render unconsciousness to their drivers, and he will put his men in their places to spirit them away to a quiet street where he can have from them all their valuables. *That* is a highwayman, yes?" He smacked his lips approvingly. "Like never you have seen."

"But Gamp ain't never seen Will neither," Rose put in.

Will chewed his lip.

It did sound an exciting challenge. One last true adventure before he hung up his greatcoat.

And . . . mightn't it put him in the way of finding a clue to his golden goddess's whereabouts? If he could recognize even one of the fancy people as someone from that ball in Grosvenor Square—that would put him nearer her then he'd been yet. Wouldn't be much, but it would be *something*.

As for this Gamp, Will had learned his lesson with Tug at the East India Dock: speed and surprise were his best tactics. Gamp would have no clue what was happening to him when Will arrived in the dark.

Still, more than one carriage—much less a small fleet— might hold too many fancy folk for him to quickly convince of his goodwill. If they turned on him, he'd never stand a chance of aiding them.

And then there was Tom. Even locked in the Marshalsea, he might hear word of an event as spectacular as this was likely to be. What good would any of this do if Tom decided to play stubborn and refused to accept Will's payment on the debt?

"Maybe," he said, "several smaller jobs would be wiser. Rather than one big one."

Mr. Monarch stared down at the tip of his cane swishing

back and forth. He actually looked torn, almost as if he had lost a little of his iron-clad grip upon the situation, and resented it.

There was something about this job—something he didn't want Will to know. The question was—was it something that would endanger Will or something that would endanger Mr. Monarch?

If it was the latter—if Will could discover something to hold against him—it might provide the opportunity to leave things better than he had found them for Rose and the others.

He looked over his shoulder.

Behind, Lifty shambled along, fingers in his armpits, sulking over his lost shillings. Rose followed, her face screwed up as suspiciously as ever.

He turned back. "Tell me where it is to occur. If I arrive and dislike the looks of it, I can always return."

Mr. Monarch nodded contemplatively. Then, of a sudden, he huffed a resolute breath. "Yes. We let *destinée* decide." He smiled at Will. "Did you think the world much struck with your feats at the shipyards? Not so. Not yet. One job like this, and you will be famous in all *histoire* to come." He gestured expansively. "Gentlemen will see you in the street, and I tell you they will bow to you in awe."

Will nodded back, slowly. He couldn't quite call the thought an unpleasant one. If ever he *could* gain even a measure of fame such as that, he might yet become a man who would have it in his power to change the rules. *Then* he could do great things for great reasons.

Tom would respect that.

# CHAPTER 19

 AFFERY LAD THOUGH he might be, even Will could see something off-color about the fleet of carriages outside the great assembly hall.

The fancy folk, however, hadn't a clue.

The carriages were lined up pert as you please in the center of the cobblestone street, rather than nearer the steps. Even within the vague flicker of gaslight, their drivers all looked shockingly rumpled.

The hour was late, and the assembly guests descended the stairs in a swirl of colors and gems. They must have been too agog with their own splendor to remark what was amiss with their carriages. Aided by footmen, they entered the coaches just as on any other night.

At the corner across the street, Will kept back of the gaslight, where his suspicious appearance might pass unnoticed. His hands trembled, always with the fire to run, run, run. He stood alone. Rose and Lifty hadn't returned from their day of picking pockets in time to accompany him, or even show him the way. He'd got lost twice, but found the place in the end.

He tried on a little grin, but it felt forced.

Mr. Monarch had been correct enough about this being the biggest job yet.

Certainly Mr. Monarch's own nerves had continued throughout the afternoon. The man had spent the day pacing before the hearth, looking a little sick—and angry. Before he left on an errand with Bull, he frowned at Will. "I wish you the God's speed." Then he stomped out into the gloaming.

*Probably* it had naught to do with Will or this job.

But something felt amiss.

He rejected the feeling. He must. Focusing on aught but the job would kill him faster than any of Mr. Monarch's schemes. He might not trust Mr. Monarch's fidelity, but he *did* trust the man's greed. Mr. Monarch benefited from their partnership as much as did Will.

Perhaps Will shouldn't attempt it a'tall. But now that he was here, actually watching these fine fools stick their heads in the noose, was he to simply stand by as their horses were lashed away to God knew where?

He drew a deep breath.

*Speed and surprise. Speed and surprise.* That was the key. He could best twenty confused drivers in the dark. Most definitely.

Sweat beaded his hairline, and he slipped his hand into his pocket for the iron knuckles Lifty had given him. Sheathed low at his thigh was a cutlass pistol, and strapped to his upper arm, over the top of the coat, a twisted rod of iron passed as a dagger. God willing, he would need neither.

Far away up the street, hooves clopped the stones. Wheels rattled. The foremost carriages lurched into motion. All in a row, they followed one after the other, rolling away.

Time to perform.

He settled his tricorn upon his head and flared his coat behind him. If this were his last job, best make it a striking one.

He bounced on the balls of his feet, then started forward. He didn't sprint—something he'd been learning he needn't always do. Rather, he gathered speed one stride at a time. He pumped his arms, each step firm. The power of it surged through him, and, even under the circumstances, he couldn't help a laugh. How did this become more wonderful every time?

In the center of the street, he reached the rearmost coach.

Framed in the assembly's lighted doorways, guests gasped at his speed.

The rearmost driver—one of Gamp's men, of course— looked back. In the gaslight, his eyes glared white. His mouth gaped to a round hole, and he turned to raise his whip to the horses.

Too late. Will had momentum enough now. He leapt and landed on the roof. The carriage jarred against its springs. Within, passengers cried out, as did the people behind.

He dared one look over his shoulder.

The drivers who remained behind, still waiting for their masters, gawked at him, hands slack at their reins. They looked entirely respectable and in no haste to follow.

Perfect.

In the golden glare of the assembly's lights, a woman's equally golden hair gleamed.

He couldn't believe it.

'Twas her. 'Twas actually the golden goddess herself.

Isabella.

But how was he supposed to return and detain her for a very important interview just now?

She stared at him, open-mouthed. She would not have recognized his face, shadowed by his hat. But she might indeed recognize that his incredible abilities were far from natural. She alone amongst all these people might be able to understand *why*.

More guests thronged behind her, forcing her forward. And there was Lord Carstone looming above the crowd, shouting and gesturing. For all his money and power, he could do naught for his abducted friends. He must leave such to Will.

That, at least, offered more than a small measure of satisfaction.

Then something cracked against the side of his neck with stinging force. The driver's whip.

The carriage careened, and he nearly lost his balance.

Oh, fah. If he got himself killed trying to impress the goddess, that would hardly be effective, now would it? Greater things were now at stake, including the wellbeing of every person in these runaway carriages.

He righted himself in a rush, snapping out a hand to catch the next strike of the whip. The lash cracked into his gloved palm. Twice, he twisted its length around his wrist, then ripped it away.

Shouting into the wind, the driver searched his pockets for some weapon.

Ahead, the train of carriages thundered down the streets. Pedestrians scattered. The horses thrashed around corners. Gaslights disappeared, leaving only the full moon for light.

Will took one step back to the rear edge of the carriage. This time, he *did* sprint. In three strides, he covered the length of the roof.

Below, the team of four horses ran hard, crowding the next carriage up.

Will launched off the driver's seat and landed on the rump of the nearest horse. Before the animal reacted, he jumped again, to the near lead horse's broad expanse of haunch—then one more great surge towards the carriage ahead.

It was a tricky thing jumping off a moving animal. His feet found nothing but air. He stretched his arms to their utmost, and his fingers slapped the carriage's roof. The vehicle slewed 'round another corner, scuffing him against a wall.

He kicked hard and found a toehold on the empty footman's step. Then with a great heave, he pulled himself up.

For a moment, he crouched, panting. That was another thing he had learned: his body needed ridiculous, lung-heaving amounts of air.

The shouts of his previous driver roused the attention of this new one. As soon as the man looked about, Will rose and ran and jumped.

All the way down the row of twenty carriages, he repeated the process—with varying amounts of grace.

When finally he reached the foremost carriage, he skidded across the roof.

The driver looked back, and his mouth opened in the familiar expression of shock.

*That's* what speed and surprise could do for a man!

Hardly slowing, Will landed a kick to the driver's chin.

The man's eyes rolled to white. He cartwheeled off the coach, taking the reins with him.

Will tumbled into the seat and caught at the trailing lines. He came up with a handful that felt smaller than it should have, and he leant back, hauling at the horses' mouths. They fought and stumbled, grunting volubly.

The road was narrowing. The skeleton of a great old church loomed above the street, silhouetted in silver-green moonlight. Around a corner, the light of three bonfires exploded into view, revealing a dozen dark forms.

Oh, splendid. Twenty confused drivers were one thing. A dozen more waiting brutes was something else altogether.

Will dragged at the reins. "Whoa! Whoa!"

Four of the waiting men ran forward, arms waving.

Will tucked his chin beneath his cocked hat. Perhaps they'd believe him one of them.

If they wanted to halt the carriages, that was fine. The tricky part for now was to block the rearmost carriage's potential egress, so the other drivers couldn't flee with their captives once they comprehended what was afoot.

The horses fought and bucked, kicking over the traces and dragging the carriage crosswise in the street. Some twelve feet over Will's head, the eaves of the church jutted.

He threw down the reins and jumped. Catching the eaves with both hands, he used his upward motion to leapfrog his legs up under him.

The church's third story was under repair, the entire front wall knocked out and open to the night. A load of bricks and sawn planks lay piled about. He dodged them both and raced back across the length of the room to where moonlight cast its river across the swelling rooftops.

Without slowing to acknowledge a rivulet of dizziness, he leapt down to the nearest roof and scrambled across the houses.

Scaffolding hugged most of the buildings, including the big one at the end—just where the last of the carriages was rounding the corner.

He put on one more burst of speed and jumped with his feet angled before him. He hit hard against the edge of the scaffolding. The entire structure gave a satisfying creak—and then shattered, taking half a newly set brick wall with it.

Not exactly a public service, but perhaps saving these nobs would even the scales.

Mercifully, the street wasn't cobbled. Still, it rose up to meet him with an astounding thwack of pain. He rolled once more, then forced himself to his feet and turned back up the street.

Not far ahead, the rearmost carriage swerved, the driver shouting to frightened horses. Within the shower of dust, rubble now filled more than half the street. The horses wouldn't be able to pull the carriages back over it.

That would do.

Two long strides and a step off a windowsill got him back to the roofs.

Less than a minute later, he returned to the church's open-air third story.

From below, shrieking and cursing echoed up, along with the stamping of hooves.

With any luck, that was a good sign. If the banditti didn't know what had happened, they might not stop to question their ability to overwhelm him.

He produced his eye-shields. They weren't necessary in the absence of sunlight—rather counter-productive actually. But when his eyes were gleaming dark pits in the night, it added a nice effect.

A thick beam, supporting a pulley system for the construction, protruded across the street. He balanced his way to the beam's end and crouched. Dizziness swarmed up from the ground, engulfing his brain. He squinted out the corner of his eye, which helped some.

Horses still stamped about, heads up, eyes white-edged. Both the drivers and the waiting thieves were running down the row of carriages, dragging out shrieking ladies and protesting gentlemen.

In the firelight, the elegant victims appeared grievously pale. Some of the women wept, and down the line, one or two seemed in a swoon. A few gentlemen emerged with canes or fists at the ready, but the banditti thrust them all against the coaches and abused them into submission.

Just beneath Will, silhouetted against the bonfires, a thickset man with a mop of ragged black whiskers waved a pistol. "Stop your jaws, the lot of you!"

Gamp the Tramp no doubt.

A gold tooth glinted in his upper jaw. "Now. You've all had

the bleedin' adventure of your tony lives, haven't you? Ain't no great harm coming to any of you—if you play with us sensible-like. All I wants is your fancies. Your jewels, your purses, anything what gleams, down to the gilt on the doors." He laughed, deep and throaty and, almost, with genuine humor.

Then the grin went out like a candle. "Create difficulties and I might find more use in the ransoming of you, understand? We've trouble enough already with you lot stampeding the horses. I find the cause of that and I'll beat his toffy nose in."

One of the drivers shook his head. "'Twas some great big, dark cove runnin' atop the carriages, flying over the horses."

Gamp frowned. "And are you daft now?" He shoved the driver aside.

"'Twas like a great black winged devil, I tell you!"

A gust of wind swirled through the bonfires. It shot sparks up into the air beneath Will and gusted his coat out behind him.

A woman from the lead carriage gasped. "Look!"

The realization of his presence rushed through the crowd like a wave.

"It *is* the bloody devil!"

"He is one of these brutes!"

"'Tis him! The Wayfarer!"

Pandemonium erupted. The drivers scrambled back. As many as half never stopped—they turned and they ran. Horses shied frantically, and Gamp's remaining men struggled to hold them. This time, a woman did faint.

The Wayfarer? When had he gained that name? His heart thundered in his chest.

It was working. The madness of the runaway carriages, his strange appearance, and perhaps the legend Mr. Monarch was trying to create—it was all working.

That was splendid. But it meant this *must* succeed. He *must* save them. If any were held for ransom, or, God help him, shot by a frightened thief, he would bear the burden.

He stood. Since the beam was only two feet wide, he couldn't broaden his stance. But he squared his shoulders and faced the wind so his coat swirled even more impressively.

"Gamp the Tramp." He deepened his voice until it scraped

into gravel. "I oppose you. Release these people, their goods, their horses, and their carriages."

The nobs gasped.

Gamp propped his pistol not so casually against his shoulder. "What is it you're going to do all by your own self?"

It was a reasonable question.

Will reached for the cutlass-pistol sheathed at his thigh. His voice still as deep as he could make it, he bellowed, "Destroy you!"

Gamp guffawed, but this time he sounded not so amused. "From your own mouth, friend." He raised the pistol.

No surprise there. Will dropped to his knees, even as smoke puffed from the barrel. The *thwat* of displaced air sounded over his shoulder. If it were possible, his heart beat even faster.

In bayonet fashion, a stout eight-inch blade was fastened underneath his own pistol barrel. He slammed its keen edge onto the ropes securing the pulley system. The pallet of bricks hanging beneath him hurtled into the street, directly under the noses of the lead team.

The horses exploded, lunging between the bonfires and dragging away yet another of Gamp's men.

Will leapt off the beam, arms wide. He landed with so much momentum he had to somersault again. He came up covered in dust from the fallen bricks, but with far too much energy coursing through him to know if he'd injured aught of importance. His muscles burned.

He dragged air into his lungs and choked on the brick dust. He fired his pistol at another pallet, this one hanging above the central bonfire.

Thanks to Tom's training and more than a bit of luck, the shot sliced rope. The pallet plummeted into the fire, dousing it to darkness. Enough of its load scattered to put out one of the adjacent fires and strew the embers of the other.

The street blinked from light to a swirl of black shadows.

These days, shadows kept company with speed and surprise quite nicely.

With the pistol's unique brass hand guard over one fist and the iron knuckles over the other, Will rushed through the disseminating sparks. To Gamp's men, he would be a dark blur. To him, *they* were standing targets.

He swept low and knocked one man's feet from under him, then landed him a blow to the side of the head.

It was almost a dance. He had to think about his steps, about the placement of his feet and his hands, lest his body run away with him. One step more, turn, turn, coat flaring about him. Then he struck with all his speed roaring up through his arm and hammering down through his fist. The iron on his knuckles bit into his bones, cracking sharp pain through even his excitement and energy.

Two dark shapes loomed. He caught each man by his outside shoulder and flung them together behind him so their heads cracked each against his fellow's. He let them fall and pirouetted forward, still dancing.

A big man with a pistol faced him. Gamp, of course.

He unfurled his speed and blasted past, all the way back to the church. He ran four steps up the wall, then pushed off. Arms stretched wide and cutlass blade gleaming in one hand, he spun like a corkscrew back through the air, directly towards Gamp. With one arm, he caught the man across the throat and flung him to the ground. He landed beside the rogue, one knee on his chest and the cutlass to his neck.

Gamp's eyes were wide. "Who are you?"

"A shadow dweller." Will forgot to deepen his voice.

Gamp frowned. "You—you're a lad—"

"Not tonight." Will seized Gamp's hair and thwacked his head against the ground until his eyes rolled back in his skull.

Then slowly, he rose, breathing hard.

He stood alone before the sputtering bonfires. Gamp's remaining men had fled, as he had hoped.

Lanterns lit the carriages in a long row. Their owners stood in silence, staring at him.

He shifted, his stomach suddenly clenching.

This was the worst part.

Half the time, those he rescued thought him one of the villains. Those who didn't were either too curious or too flabbergasted to consider a reward.

But this was part of the show too. It was all theater to these people. They'd no notion what had really just occurred—and they never would. After tonight, the cloaked, masked Robin Hood of the shadows would fade forever into legend.

He cleared his throat and bowed deeply. Then he straightened. His tongue was numb.

Slowly, someone in the back began to applaud. One pair of hands took it up, then another, until the sound filled the entire street.

At least they weren't going to attack him.

Neither would they run from him and force him to chase them through the dangerous streets and return them to the safety of their carriages.

This time, they thought him a hero.

A grin slipped free.

He sheathed the pistol. Pain filtered into his consciousness: hip and shoulder, the knuckles on both hands, the welt on his neck where the whip had caught him. He resisted the urge to limp. Biggest job indeed. If ever he faced a bigger one, he'd end up dead in the street.

He met the owner of the first carriage: a polite-faced gentleman with a plump, eager wife and a flushed daughter who watched Will from beneath dark lashes.

The man offered his hand. "My good sir! How can we thank you? We are in your debt."

Will inclined his head graciously. "Gratified to serve." He remembered to deepen his voice. "If you will clear the street behind you and turn the carriages about, I will guide you to your own safe neighborhoods." He cleared his throat. This next part never sounded quite right—even though it was the point entire. "As for how you can . . . thank me, well—" He tilted his head in what he hoped was a meaningful but delicate expression of the obvious.

The man raised his eyebrows to astounding heights. "But of course!" He patted his waistcoat to find a small purse, from which he withdrew two coins. They glinted gold in the firelight. "Thank you, sir. Thank you." He hastened over the words, perhaps fearing Will might yet have a change of mind. Then he turned to his fellow fancies lined up behind. "The Wayfarer—he has been our salvation tonight! He will return us to safety. Don't spare your pockets, friends! He merits our thanks!"

Will nodded as regally as possible, then started down the line.

The doe-eyed daughter brushed his sleeve. "Wait." She yanked at the clasp on her festoon necklace. Without lowering her gaze from his, she pressed her lips upon the gems, then handed it over.

Beneath his high collar, the back of his neck grew hot. He opened his mouth, closed it, then offered another nod. That seemed safest.

He strode the line, head up, pretending rather convincingly his whole body wasn't throbbing. At almost every carriage, someone touched his arm, shook his hand, or offered him coins or jewelry. They all watched him—some suspiciously, but most with outright admiration. Few seemed to begrudge the reward.

And why not? He *had* saved them.

These people respected him. They couldn't see his face. They didn't know his name. But they found him worthy of their money. Were he to continue in this line of work, his reputation might grow so impressive, he wouldn't even need to hint at payment.

Would that make Tom approve more or less?

Halfway down the line, he paused to respond to a dowager's curtsy. He was growing quite proficient with this bowing. In the unlikely event of his ever attending another ball, he'd be more than prepared.

The lady, however, reacted with a shriek. "They have returned!"

He swiveled.

The dark end of a club smashed towards his head.

He dodged without thought and caught only the bare end against his cheekbone. The blow wasn't enough to break anything, but it was more than enough to knock him off balance into the street.

Chaos erupted. The gentlemen and ladies were screaming, trying to clamber back into their carriages. Gamp's men scrambled amongst them, grabbing at those whose purses had been at the ready on Will's account.

The bandits must have met in the outer streets and reorganized both their numbers and their courage. Of course they had.

He gained his feet.

Most of them converged on Will. He dodged one easily, but another smashed him bodily against a carriage wheel. He slammed down his elbow into the man's exposed back: once, twice. Something might have cracked on the second blow.

The man yelped like a piglet, but clung the harder. Perhaps he and his mates had realized their only chance was to obstruct Will's mobility.

This time he'd have to beat them all into injury or unconsciousness. If he left any, they would harm these people who now trusted in *him*.

Well, then.

Lights flickered in the connecting streets. *More* of them?

At the corner, a man halted and surveyed the pandemonium. He hadn't quite the appearance of a criminal. From his starched and squared red waistcoat, he had more the appearance of a Bow Street Runner. In point of fact, he had exactly the appearance of Constable Pish.

"In the name of His Majesty, I place you under arrest!" Pish looked straight at Will. "The lot of you!"

# CHAPTER 20

WAS IT POSSIBLE for this situation to grow any worse? Fortunately, Constable Pish's arrival didn't complicate the solution. At least, Will could now leave the fancy folk to the protection of the Runners.

One of the bandits headed in to help his partner, who had trapped Will against the carriage wheel. Will, in turn, had the man in a headlock. With a shout, he lunged against his captor's shoulder, enough to gain a few inches from the carriage. Then he slammed back against it, letting the man's head take the brunt of the blow. Then he did it again.

The man moaned. His grip slackened just a bit, which was just enough.

Will hammered his knee up into the man's stomach and flung him aside.

The other bandit advanced, teeth bared, eyes intent but wary.

Will rushed him and slammed the heel of his hand against the man's chin. The man went sprawling.

Beyond, Runners swarmed the street, singling out Gamp's men. Pish strode toward Will, drawing his pistol as he came.

Will didn't slow.

Had Pish deduced that this newly notorious cove in the coat and dark spectacles was one and the same with the equally swift Will Hardy of his previous acquaintance?

Pish leveled his pistol. "You there!"

That didn't slow Will either. He dared a grin and touched his hat. After all, the whole show *was* more than a little impressive. "Fare thee well, Constable."

Ahead, one of the teams staggered into a swerving gallop, urged on by a wide-eyed gentleman in the driver's box.

Will grasped the edge of the roof and swung aboard. The carriage grazed the wall of the church, and Will leapt. He caught the jutting beam above his head and hauled himself up into the church's half-finished third story.

The night was his. Barely—but it *was* his.

In his coat pockets, his reward money clanked.

Thin moonlight filtered through the sparse rafters. Piles of bricks and planks and workman's tools cluttered the room, leaving only one narrow path to the back. He could climb down on the far side of the building, then disappear in the streets.

He was as lost as lost could be, of course, but if he couldn't find his bearings by morning, someone would then be able to direct him to Seven Dials. He'd hand Mr. Monarch his share of tonight's reward, and by tomorrow evening, Tom's debt would be paid and they could both be on their way from the cursed experience London had turned out to be. Surely, someone somewhere would know aught of the strange happenings in his body. Someone could help him cure his symptoms before they worsened.

For no reason a'tall, Rose's waif-like face flashed through his mind. He frowned. He and Tom couldn't take her with them. The Runners would still be pursuing Will for Dr. Silas's murder. Two men might have a difficult enough time escaping, much less with a girl child along. She'd be no worse off when he left than before he'd come. He'd give her a goodly handful of coins.

In the corner of his vision, something wobbled, like a reflection in water.

He whipped about, but saw merely another haphazard pile of bricks.

He sidestepped a brick that obstructed the narrow walkway. Instantly, his foot plunged into nothing—as if the floor were naught but air. Flailing, he caught a canvas cast over one of the piles above him. It gave way but shifted his fall sideways. His outstretched arm slammed into solid flooring, and his armpit collided with the jagged ends of shivered planks.

For one interminable second, he hung in a hole in the floor:

one arm and one leg dangling into nothing, the other arm scrabbling against the floor, the top of the other foot wedged, sole up, on the edge behind him.

The canvas and several bricks fell past him into silence, then clattered distantly against the floor beneath. In the dark gape below, the nave seemed all of two stories high.

His breath rasped. What had just happened?

His bracing arm was slipping, slipping. Fingernails in the wood, he scraped another painful inch.

He raised his head to the level of his arm—the level of the hole—and looked about the room in which he'd been walking seconds earlier. In the moon-streaked darkness, it was hard to tell what surrounded him. But what *wasn't* there was any sign of a hole.

The floor planks surrounded his body—all of them uniform and whole. Where he could feel the rough ends of broken planks digging into his armpit, he could *see* only smooth boards melding to his floundering body.

This made no sense a'tall. He was seeing things in the dark. He was dizzy.

His fingernails scraped another two inches.

Gingerly, he lowered his head to see into the room below. With his free hand, he dared pull his eye-shields from his face and allow himself the greatest possible amount of light.

Of course if he couldn't see how far he was from the ground, at least he wouldn't grow dizzy. Small blessings.

From the smell of sawdust, this great room was also under construction. The ceiling was clerestory. Amidst the overall darkness, its great looping rafters were naught but darker shadows. If he could gain a handhold there, he could at least hang on long enough to order his mind. But the nearest support was some five feet distant.

His hand slipped, slipped, slipped—skidded.

He looked frantically in the other direction.

An immense canvas hung from the ceiling, dividing the room and protecting the already finished half of the church from the ongoing construction. It was almost within reach.

Just now, *almost* would have to do.

With a grunt, he heaved his weight to the left, released the floor above and unhooked his trapped foot.

Gravity pulled at him harder than his own thrust. He fell twelve feet more before smacking into the hanging canvas. He scrabbled desperately for a grip, found it, and dared to exhale.

With a prodigious rip, the canvas tore free of the first of its moorings in the ceiling.

He fell again, still clinging to the canvas. His weight hit the second of the fastenings, and it wrenched free as well. In a great chain reaction, the canvas ripped loose all the way across the room.

He couldn't help but yell. The far wall rushed up at him, and he smacked into it. Of their own accord, his hands decided to release the canvas, and he tumbled the remaining five feet to the ground.

He sat in the dust and regained his breath in time to cough.

And *he* was the man who owned the rooftops?

Outside, people were still shouting and running. A gunshot popped.

What had just happened?

He squinted at the ceiling. Every part of his neck and spine ached. He coughed again.

From here, the hole was clearly visible, its circumference awash in moonlight.

He could hardly have failed to see *that*, could he? And yet someone had disguised it so cleverly it hadn't been visible even after he'd fallen into it.

But why? Why cover a hole in the middle of the night in the upper floor of a church that just happened to be the destination of ambitious highwaymen?

His heart tripped. Surely, that trap hadn't been set for him. And yet, who else but him would be in the highest building on the entire street?

*How* had the trap been set—and by whom?

Mr. Monarch? However strangely he may have acted this afternoon, he'd no reason to kill Will. Indeed, he had seemed almost reluctant to suggest the job. But hadn't he also said something about letting destiny decide?

To Will's left, double doors exploded inward and thumped the walls. Constable Pish entered, a lantern in one hand. With admirable promptness, he leveled his small knock-me-down pistol. "Well. Master Hardy, I believe? Or is it 'Wayfarer' you prefer these blessed days?"

Will tried to scramble upright. His feet caught in the twisted canvas, and he thunked back down.

He extended both hands, placatingly. "I know it may fail to be immediately apparent, but I am not the villain here." He pointed up. "And if you need proof, go upstairs. Someone set a trap for me, tried to kill me."

Pish tsked. "No doubt, no doubt. The majority of murders in our vast city result from rows between villain and *villain*."

"I'm no part of that lot out there. I was here to aid those people. Ask them."

"Protestations of good deeds, yet again. As I recall, that's what you told me when first we met."

"And 'tis as true now as then! That's a double witness for you."

Pish picked his way through the rubble. He never wavered in the aim of his pistol. "When once you've fought the criminal element so long as have I, you will realize coincidences are rather less convincing and rather more suspicious." He leant forward and extended the lantern. "You must admit, young friend, you're suspicious all the way around."

Will jutted his chin. "I'm no thief. I stop thieves—same as you."

"Oh, not quite the same."

"True. This is twice now I've had cause to do your job for you."

Pish raised his heavy brows. "Well, blow me down. Quite the cheeky one, aren't we? But it ain't thieving I've the warrant for. Wanted for murder, aren't you? Keen on telling me that's a coincidence too?"

"If a coincidence is what you call a man lying about me for no reason a'tall."

"There's always a reason. Always, always. The world's a sensible place. The pieces always fit in the end, if not the beginning." Pish cocked his head. "I will admit you're a piece of a color I've never seen."

"And never will again, I warrant." Will couldn't help the huff in his voice.

"Yes, well." Pish straightened. "There be other strange things happening of late. You're the cause of them all, are you?"

"Such as?"

"Oh, all these military chaps marching about, for one. For two, the fact not a soul knows where they're coming from or who's keeping them."

Will scowled. "You're the policeman. You can't figure it out?"

"Ah, and that's the point, ain't it?"

Outside, men shouted. They sounded professional—and triumphant. The Runners must have secured the street.

Pish gestured with the pistol. "Let's be on our feet. And none of your tricks now. Believe me, my dear finger is tight as topsails on this trigger. You twitch, and off it goes. Even you couldn't dodge a ball, eh?"

It might be a near thing at that. The first step was always the slowest, and Will wasn't exactly feeling his swiftest right now.

Cautiously, he untangled himself from the canvas. He eased up, using the wall for support. Then he faced Pish, feet squared, hands at his sides. He'd lost his hat in the fall. In the lantern light, his eye-shields glinted on the floor, a few yards off.

Another Runner entered. "Ready to escort the carriages back to Covent Garden, Mr. Pish."

Pish kept his eyes on Will. "Look through the church here first. Our lad says there's a trap at the upper floor, so watch yourself."

"'Tis a hole," Will said, "and you'll see naught of it. It's disguised to appear like the rest of the floor."

The Runner grinned as he passed. He stooped to retrieve Will's eye-shields and toss them to him. "I, for one, see better when me eyes aren't all covered up. I have doubts about any trap looking pristine after the likes of you went tumbling through."

Will folded up his eye-shields—miraculously unbroken—and slipped them into his pocket.

Pish stepped nearer. "How about politics, laddie?" He lowered his voice. "Know aught about that?"

Will frowned. "I'm for the king, if that's what you mean."

Pish joggled the lantern, dismissively. "I mean the doings in

Parliament. They called for a new election, did you hear?"

Will shrugged. "I heard there was to be one."

"I'm no political animal myself." Pish peered at Will, as if awaiting a clue. "But something fails to smell right here. The king and his company have been strangely silent on the whole— about the general election, the private army, all of it."

Politics were for the politicians. Will Hardy had no say in any of that.

Even still—the hairs of his neck rose.

Coincidences. He had little belief in them himself. If all these things started happening just when Dr. Silas discovered the plague, there might be a plausible connection.

But certainly it had nothing to do with *him*.

The other Runner reached the far end of the nave and disappeared around a corner. He clomped up the stairs.

Will shook his head. "I give you my oath. I know naught about any of these things."

"You knew where this grand robbery was to be taking place tonight."

"I heard rumors. I . . . seek information about crimes to be committed."

"Did your information tell you the little *soiree* from which all these fine folks were departing was a political one? All in favor of the man about to be our next PM. As I recall, he's friendly with you. Mr. James Fitzroy?"

Seemed Mr. Fitzroy must not have been greatly incapacitated by his brush with the plague after all. At all events, if he, too, had gained the ability for physical speed, that would hardly aid him in the political arena.

"See here," Will said, "even if I knew aught about this, where's the crime?"

Pish cocked his head. "I've been doing some discreet investigating into your friend Fitzroy. Hardly a trail to be found. Tell me, from what burrow does a gentlemen emerge—fully formed and ready to rule?"

"No crime to that either. A man doesn't *have* to be born to a great name."

Overhead, the other Runner stamped about in the attic.

Pish merely grunted. He twitched the pistol, beckoning. "Come along. Time to be leaving."

Will tromped through the fallen bricks. He halted obediently in front of Pish, an arm's span between his chest and the pistol. With his reflexes already dulled by the night's adventures, he wasn't about to risk a gunshot wound on the *chance* he might be able to dodge faster than Pish could pull the trigger.

However, unless he was mistaken, that buffle-head upstairs was about to provide an excellent distraction. Of course, the man would probably get himself killed in the process.

Pish nodded towards the open door. "Trot along then."

Will took a breath. "Would you happen to be fond of that fellow you sent upstairs?"

Pish frowned. "Why?"

"Because he's about to fall through that hole and break his neck."

Pish still didn't look away from Will. Instead, he raised his voice: "Duff! Anything to wrongs up there?"

"Nary a thing!" The man's steps neared the hole.

"You can hear he's almost there," Will said. "Look! You can see the hole, you can see his shadow!"

Pish moved his head slightly, reflexively almost—but still he kept his eyes on Will. "Duff, look closer! I can hear you too clearly—there must be a hole. Remember, he said it appeared the same as the rest of the floor."

"It must, to be sure, because I see nothing *but* floor!"

Two more steps, at most, and the man would tumble through. Unlike Will, he wouldn't be fast enough to catch himself. Even if he were, he would have no hanging canvas to grasp during his descent. He'd fall a score of feet and break his back against one of the pews.

Pish gestured with the pistol. "Come, come."

Will shouted up, "Kick a brick! Kick a brick ahead of you, man! You're almost to the hole!"

The footsteps hesitated, halted. One second later, a brick skidded across the floor. It plummeted through the hole, crashed against the pews, and exploded into fragments.

That, at last, broke Pish's fervent concentration. He flinched around, only a little, only a look from the corner of his eye.

Will slapped the pistol in one direction, even as he lunged in the other.

The shot cracked, flaring momentary light through the church. Pish had not lied about his grip on the trigger.

"God have mercy!" Duff shouted. More bricks rained through. "He spoke true! I still can't see the forsaken hole!"

Will sprinted to the exit. In the doorway, he looked back.

Pish seemed no longer able to resist throwing a full look over his shoulder. He turned to Will, open-mouthed.

Will knew precisely how he felt. "Perhaps you should think on who it is that would want to kill *me*."

Perhaps they both should.

# CHAPTER 21

OR A CHANGE, Will took the streets home instead of the rooftops. After a few false starts, he found his way with surprising ease.

In part, he chose the streets because the very thought of having to leap or run made his bruises ache. The other part was that maybe, just maybe, if he managed to walk his way back to the starting point of tonight's adventures, he might find a sign of the Lady Isabella.

It was a futile hope. She would have been dispatched straight home, away from danger. But perhaps there would yet be a hint of her whereabouts. It seemed an injustice to get within sight of her, purely by chance, and come away without a single clue.

He took a long stride to avoid a sodden pile of waste and limped the next two steps on his throbbing hips. No bones broken, but still they pained him.

At all events, thinking on Isabella was pleasanter than thinking on whoever wanted to kill him.

Who had aught to gain by his death?

Only Mr. Monarch and Mrs. Fitzroy even knew he was in London.

Of course that was *he* as in *Will Hardy*. Over the last week, he'd made certain the whole city knew of his exploits as the nameless preventer of thefts.

Could someone be after *that* persona?

But why? There was no reward out on him, as yet. Had there been, Pish would have known.

The trap in the church could have been a mistake—an accident—a coincidence. Despite Pish's insistence, coincidences *did* happen. Every day, they happened.

Perhaps the greater question was how someone had been able to conceal the hole so ingeniously. The illusion of the floor over the hole had been flawless—and had endured even after he had fallen through.

That seemed . . . witchcraft almost.

Maybe it was. Certainly, there were strange enough things happening. He was proof of that.

He stepped hard into a low spot. His whole body gave a prodigious protesting twinge, and the coins in his pocket jingled.

At least, the night hadn't been a waste. In point of fact, it had been entirely successful.

He let slip a little grin.

Chasing bandits and protecting innocents, then exchanging bows with fancy gentlemen and all but getting bussed by their pretty daughters. *That* was adventure!

Almost a pity this must be the last time.

He stared up at the patchy moon.

No, the sooner he was free of Mr. Monarch and Seven Dials, the better—especially if someone wanted to murder him. He shivered and rounded the corner.

Several streets ahead, the dim glow of gaslights blinked. Across from him, a white carriage was parked to the side of the road. The horses stood with heads low and ears lazily cocked, as if they had been standing for some time.

A driver in green livery and a tall hat shot Will a nervous glance and tightened the reins. At the rear, an equally fidgety footman stood with one hand clamped to his handhold—ready to jump aboard as soon as the carriage so much as twitched.

They were none of Will's business. Probably it was naught but some scandalous rendezvous.

Yet, after everything that had happened here tonight, it seemed unlikely this carriage's lonely presence was, well . . . coincidental.

He crossed over and cleared his throat—it was rough after all his growling earlier. "Do you require assistance—"

The door opened, and a woman hastened forth. She wore a dark, shimmering gown with an even darker silk shawl thrown over her bare arms. In the moonlight, her upswept hair burned gold.

Isabella.

His mouth fell open. "You—? What are you doing here?"

"You." She gave the word back to him. "You're that boy from Affery!" She seized his hand and pulled him back across the street into the shadows. Standing very near, she turned and raised her face to his.

She was here! She remembered him? She had . . . waited for him?

Whatever breath remained in his weary body vanished. He managed not to choke.

Suddenly overcome with the rash idea of kissing her, he lowered his head. "Isabella . . ."

The flush of her cheeks shone even in the semi-darkness. She flung his hand from her. "You!"

He recalled himself and flinched back. "Um . . ."

She stood there, panting and glaring, but her eyes charted his face eagerly.

Then she gave her head a sharp shake and raised her chin higher. "How dare you call me Isabella? Your impertinence is beyond bounds!"

"I know no other name." The words tumbled out, stupidly. "I never did hear it at the ball."

"The ball!" She whirled to pace two steps, then came back. "The Duke of Veneering indeed. I cannot *believe* I supposed you the son of a duke. There *is* no Veneering. I knew that then, and I know it now—and I have truly no idea why I failed to recognize it."

He jutted his chin. "Perhaps you were too enraptured to notice."

"Oh, you are brazen! Did you follow me to London? Is that why you were at the ball? That day at the forge, I asked you to respect my privacy—to *protect* my privacy. Is this the ungentlemanly manner in which you respond?"

"And I was beginning to think the village lad from the village forge was too far beneath the notice of a high *lady* for her to even remember his face."

"Of course, I remembered you."

"Not until tonight. You saw me atop that carriage. That's when you remembered."

For the first time, her gaze darted away. "Yes."

"You saw what I could do and you knew the only place that could happen to someone was Affery."

She looked back, and again eagerness fired her eyes. "Yes, exactly."

A breath he hadn't known he'd been holding—a breath that felt as if it had been trapped since Dr. Silas's death—poured from him. Some of his pique went with it.

No longer was he alone. No longer was he walking in a void of strangeness and impossibility, with no hope of enlightenment.

"I knew you'd know," he said. "I've been . . . on the watch for you. There are so many things I want to know about what's happened to me."

As quickly as that, a brilliant smile illumined her face. "As do I! I want to know how it feels? Of what are you now capable? How far have you explored your limitations?"

"I don't know that I've yet reached them. What I can do is what you've already seen—run faster and jump higher than any man I've ever heard of. But how does it work? And . . . there are untoward effects as well." The words tumbled from him, almost desperately now that he finally had someone to tell them to. "Dizziness, and light hurts my eyes."

She laughed, the sound gentle, elated. "That is *fascinating!*" A damp gleam softened her eyes.

She was crying?

She laughed again, then closed her eyes. "Right, then." She drew a breath, as if organizing herself, then opened her eyes. "So tell me. How it happened. Dr. Silas told me he was not yet ready to perform trials upon a man. He was going to take the ferret—the one you were not intended to see—to London to show the Royal Society and the Royal College what he could do. He was going to show the world, perhaps find a patron. And

then—" Her face clouded. "He. . ." She drew her brows. "You—
" She stepped back. "He was murdered—in a fire. It was a village boy—Will Hardy." Another step back. She pointed. "You
are Will Hardy?"

He nearly groaned. Would it be *this* for the rest of his life?

"I didn't murder him. I pulled him *out*. He was dead already—
long dead, I assure you."

"And what of tonight's horrible events?" she demanded.
"You use your newfound talents to prey upon the innocent?"

"What do *you* think?" The words came out more wounded
than he'd hoped.

*This* was the goddess he'd been chasing? More like a harpy.
And he'd thought to kiss her two minutes ago.

Now it was his turn to step back. "You believe yourself a daring lady scientist, is that it? You want to make grand discoveries
about the *facts*? Well, I know nothing of natural science, but
I know you can't rightly make discoveries if you're convinced
already you know the answers."

Her wince said he'd struck home. Still, she haughtily flung
her shawl over her shoulder. "Your protestation of innocence,
by itself, hardly constitutes a fact, does it?"

Merciful heavens, but she was the most stubborn, conceited,
overbearing, know-all, little *toff* he'd ever met. It was as well he'd
done all this to save Tom and not to impress her. Else it would
seem a wonderful waste about now.

"You need have no concern for whatever I do," he said. "My
business is now complete, and on my oath, there's *nothing* to
hold me in Seven Dials."

Across the street, the driver loudly cleared his throat. "If you
please, my lady, I must insist! We need to return to Carstone
House. Your grandfather ordered you home after he departed
to speak with the magistrate—and that has been hours past."

Realization hit Will like a lightning bolt.

"You're Lord Carstone's granddaughter."

Could he have been any greater a fool?

He found himself overcome with the urgent need to strike
something. He turned away. "I should have known."

"You must wait, Dodson," she called. "I have not finished."

Will turned back. "Oh, yes, you have. You believe I'm a thief and a murderer and have no use for me? That's well. Because if you ask me *why* I'm here now, tonight, like this, then I would tell you it is because of your grandfather."

"Pray, do not be ridiculous. My grandfather knows naught of Dr. Silas's work—or your capabilities."

"Right, yes—because he's too intent on finding some great well-inlaid nobleman husband who's deserving of you." He stepped up to her, almost toe to toe. "Or could it be he is too much occupied in casting good tenants off his land? Into the workhouse? Into the Marshalsea!"

She held her ground. "He is a good landlord—the best of them."

"Then why is my master in debtor's prison?"

She tossed her head. "Perhaps because he did not pay a debt." But her voice no longer held the same edge.

"A debt he owed your grandfather, and which he *was* paying, and which your grandfather promised him time to fulfill. Promised him!"

His heart was pounding with the old rage—with the old grief. Some strange part of him wanted to weep.

His chest heaved. "Do you even understand what that means? A *promise*? Do any of your lot?"

"I have no idea where you came by this notion, but I promise *you*, you are wrong. My grandfather is the fairest of men. If your master is imprisoned for debt, that seems indicative where the fault lies, do you not think?"

She understood nothing about who was at fault. Of course, she didn't.

"My master is not the sort who takes on a debt, not even if he's starving. He shouldn't ever have come to this. He's there because of *me*." The grief ripped raw inside of him. "Do you know why he took me in?"

She shook her head, hesitantly.

No, of course, she had no knowledge. She was interested in natural science and escaping her fate, not the lives of those who lived and worked and died in her grandfather's parish.

"He took me in"—his voice cracked the tiniest bit—"because

your grandfather sent my parents and my little sisters and my baby brother to their deaths in the workhouse. Tom could save only one—and that was me—and even then he had to have the debt so *I* wouldn't starve."

She drew her brows in a frown, uncertain.

He struck out with the truth as hard as he could. "Now your grandfather lies to Tom and breaks his promise with no explanation. I have no respect for that."

Her indignation flamed back to life. "And I have no respect for your presumption! I tell you my grandfather never broke a promise in his life." She looked at him, critically. "You speak of *respect*. But there is not one ounce of respect in your whole person, is there?"

He caught her elbow and shepherded her across the street. "Why not ask the same question of yourself?"

She jerked free. "I have respect. For my grandfather."

"Do you?" He strode ahead and opened the carriage door.

The driver and the footman shrank back.

Will turned to her. "Then why do you run about behind his back? Why do you lie about your work with Dr. Silas? Why do you disobey him by endangering yourself and your servants?"

Her cheeks burned. "That is hardly your concern!"

"And neither am I yours. You thought I was your little experiment, a strange pet you could observe and ask questions of? Well, I'm not. What has happened to me is mine alone. It's nothing to you."

He propelled her into the carriage. "Go home to your righteous grandfather. Marry a man just like him." He huffed. "And to think I might have spent the rest of my life pining for you."

Her eyes flashed wide. "What? Indeed." She thumped onto the velvet seat and dragged her shawl about her. "You have no right to pine after an . . . an engaged woman."

In spite of himself, he was thunderstruck. "Engaged? Since when?"

She wouldn't meet his eye as she continued organizing her garments. "Long since."

"To whom?" The words kept burbling from him.

Finally, she gave him a baleful look. "To Mr. Henry Fitzroy, if you must know."

"That cub? He's a drunken dandy! He hasn't so much as a spark of either sense or ambition!" Nonsensically, he felt like pulling her back from the carriage and hiding her away where this farce could not proceed.

Not, of course, that she deserved to be rescued.

He leant into the carriage. "Is this what your good, kind, wise grandfather would lock you into for the rest of your life?"

The heat on her cheeks concentrated into two tight spots. "I am fond of Henry. I have always been fond of him. We grew up together."

"He's an idiot."

"Well, so are you, come to that." She raised her chin and faced forward. "We are a fine couple. Which, if you *were* the Duke of Veneering's son, you might have the benefit of witnessing tomorrow at my grandfather's masque ball."

"To announce the engagement?"

"It is a political gathering."

"Another one?"

"Tonight's was an anticipatory celebration. Tomorrow's will be an announcement—about the Prime Ministry, no doubt."

"Daughter to the Prime Minister. Congratulations."

The words were bitter on his tongue. So much for dreams. In the last few weeks, everything he'd spent his boyhood believing had crumbled to dust. Was the golden world he'd aspired to nothing but gilt? A sheen to hide the lead beneath?

Even *her*. She was unlike anyone he had ever met—and not because she was the granddaughter of an earl. Hers was a runaway mind, as was his, desiring a life she would never gain.

But even that could not save her from being insufferable. If Will *had* been the Duke of Veneering, it might all have been different. But they were each trapped where life had borne them.

He wouldn't pine after her. He would *not*. He knew her hardly at all. For the past two weeks, she'd been a mirage, a dream he'd concocted of a world that didn't exist.

His own world was different now. His world was about escaping the Runners and saving Tom. Everything else could go to the devil.

He reached to touch the cocked brim of his hat, only to

remember it lay back in that church. Instead, he pulled his fore-lock—like the plow-boy she obviously still thought him.

"Goodbye, lady."

He turned to go, strides long and sure. At least he could retain some modicum of dignity.

"Wait. . ." She sounded none too dignified herself. "I should—I should report you. To the magistrate."

He halted mid-street.

She didn't sound as if she meant it. But she knew about Tom now, and if Pish were to gain that knowledge before tomorrow, it could create dire complications.

More to the point, he *wasn't* a murderer, and she really shouldn't spend the rest of her life thinking that about him.

Assuming, of course, she did think about him.

He looked back. "If you want to know what happened to Dr. Silas, ask your future father-in-law. He was there. He might have seen."

Through the open carriage door, her expression was a muddle: perhaps surprised at the reference to Mr. Fitzroy, but mostly conflicted, and maybe even a little remorseful.

Well—he, too.

But he left it at that. They'd already shown each other the worst of their tempers. What else was there?

He'd lost the dream of his goddess; she'd lost the ideal of her superior man.

Grand.

He ducked into an alley, to get out of her sight, and continued his trudge back to Seven Dials.

Aye, she was as lovely as ever. But she was deluded. She seemed so positive her grandfather wouldn't have called the warrant officers on Tom—and yet there they'd been. The Marshalsea wouldn't have inducted Tom had the papers not all been in order.

Would they?

There was *something* here—some little niggle—that failed to fit.

In point of fact, more than a few things didn't fit—the trap in the church, the hole that didn't look a hole, Tom's abrupt imprisonment, perhaps even the occurrences in Parliament.

Didn't matter. It would take him far too long to puzzle it out, and he'd likely get nabbed by the Runners in the process.

He reached Mr. Monarch's—alight even at this late hour—and ducked around to the back. He could wait to split the reward on the morrow. Tonight, Mr. Monarch could sit up in anxiety for Will's fate—should he be so inclined.

He climbed onto a windowsill, then jumped to the narrow bridge extending across the alley from the upper story. From there, it was a simple matter to gain the eaves. He wrenched up Lifty's gable window and slid into the room.

On the floor, a flame guttered in a lump of wax. Someone was breathing the raspy breath of sleep.

At the sight of his bed, his muscles softened, threatening to slide right off his bones. Tonight would be the last night he would sleep here, and God willing, he'd sleep so sound he wouldn't even notice where he was. He retained his coat. Best to sleep in it tonight, with his money safely beneath his painful hip.

He scraped up what was left of the candle and pinched its hot softness between thumb and forefinger.

Lifty's top bunk was empty.

In Will's lower bunk, Rose was curled into a hard knot around his blanket.

Seize it. Sleeping under the bed was one thing. But she was moving right in, wasn't she?

He reached to wake her. Then he stopped.

She had her two little fists clenched under her chin. Her cheeks shone red, and her breathing shuddered, as if she'd been crying.

Ah, well.

His heart smote him. What a life she led here. What a sad, solitary, relentless life. To such as her, Affery would have been heaven.

She believed he was going to save her. It beamed from her eyes every time she looked at him.

But he wasn't going to save her. He . . . couldn't. Wasn't he having difficulties enough saving himself?

He withdrew his hand. Slowly, he eased to his knees, puffed

out the candle before it burned his fingers, then dropped to his side. He slid under the bed—the stale pallet a hand's span above his face—and lay with aching bones against the damp floorboards.

He closed his eyes.

He would leave the puzzles of politics to the toffs and the mysteries of murders to the police. His only concern was Tom. He jangled his heavy pocket once. Tomorrow, that pocket would be empty and Tom would be free, and he need not be anxious about aught else until after that.

# CHAPTER 22

BY THE TIME Will awoke, the bunks above were empty and sunlight was thick on the begrimed floor. Reflexively, he checked his pocket. Still heavy.

Time to end this. What would Mr. Monarch say to that?

He met Rose halfway down the narrow stairs.

She hurled herself at him, arms about his waist. "Gawn! And me thinking you were dead!"

He tried to pry her off. "Loads of faith *you* have."

She squeezed harder. "There was more'n a little stink stirring around here. And I didn't see you come back in, that's sure."

"I slept under the bunk."

"Oh." She pulled back. "Well."

One of her cheeks was filthy dark.

Below stairs, Mr. Monarch roared. "You *mal* bunters! Where's the bread?" He sounded cup-shot. If so, it would be the first time in their acquaintance that Will had known him to imbibe overmuch.

Would that make Will's declaration the easier or the harder?

"Tell Lifty I need him at the Marshalsea today." He started to push past Rose.

But something stopped him. He leant in for a better look in the stairway's bad light.

The spot on her cheek wasn't filth. It was a bruise, green-black in its center, swelling out to a faint rim of purple and red.

"What is that?"

But he knew.

In his chest, fury blossomed.

He gripped her shoulder. "What was it for?"

She pulled back with a shrug. Her face went blank, eyes wary. "And why's it matter? He was in a foul mood, that's enough."

"Oh, yes, that's always enough." He breathed in and out, hard. "What exactly *was* afoot here last night?"

Another shrug.

God in heaven, but he'd had his belly full of this man. He couldn't leave this place fast enough—couldn't stop putting money in this animal's hands with enough speed.

He descended the stairs three steps at a time, bracing his hands against the walls.

She clattered behind. "Hey now, don't go making a tussle. You don't want to be rousing him, know what I mean?"

What he *knew* was that last night he'd given a pasting to a dozen of Gamp's men and then escaped half as many Runners. Perhaps it was time to cease considering Mr. Monarch a threat. Perhaps instead of regretting the inevitability of Mr. Monarch's laying his hand to Rose again, it was time to make certain he never did.

At the gleam of sunlight halfway down the stairs, he ducked under the jut of the ceiling and swung over the wobbly banister.

Mr. Monarch sat near the hearth, eyes half closed. He leant his jowl against one hand and motioned impatiently for Peggy to transfer toasted and greased pieces of rye bread to his plate.

Will landed with a thump and didn't break stride.

Mr. Monarch reared up, veined eyes wide. "My—boy. My boy, you are safe!"

He sounded too surprised by far. Was the trap in the church his after all? He had surely murdered many a man before this. But *why* kill Will? Especially since he had no notion as yet that Will would be leaving him today.

Will thrust his hand into his coat pocket. He didn't count the coins and jewels; he withdrew a handful and flung it across the table.

"There. Success." He tried to steady his breathing. "Have you another job for me?"

"I—" Mr. Monarch opened his mouth and closed it. He pushed up from the table. "I— No, not yet, my boy. These things require time. You know this."

"No, I don't."

Mr. Monarch *always* had a plan. If he had none today, was it because he was too intoxicated to think straight? Or because he had thought never again to need a plan for Will Hardy?

Will could reveal his suspicions now. Demand an answer. He could *beat* the answer from Mr. Monarch.

His hands trembled, ready to summon his speed.

But, no. Tom remained his first concern. He would not endanger everything he'd done before the goal was accomplished.

"Where's Lifty?" he demanded.

"I—don't—" Mr. Monarch spread his hands. His gaze shifted as footsteps sounded behind Will.

Will turned.

Mouth open, Lifty stood in the wide entrance, twitching his gaze from Will to Mr. Monarch.

Rose stood beside him at the bottom of the stairs.

Will turned back to Mr. Monarch. "I'll discover my own job for the day."

"My dear, I sense you are having a disturbance in your mind. But you must tell me, you must let me unburden you. You—"

Will stalked from the room. He grabbed Lifty's coat as he passed and dragged him across the broad entrance room to the door.

"Hey, now, what's this?" Lifty asked.

"I need your help."

"Now, I don't know—"

"I'll pay you."

Lifty straightened. "Well, and I'm your man, aren't I?"

Rose ran ahead and opened the door.

Will glanced at her as he passed. "You remain until I return—and you keep off from Mr. Monarch, hear me?"

She nodded. Her eyes were dark with concern, mouth pinched.

---

In all truth, Will had no idea how to go about paying a man's debts. After arriving at the Marshalsea, it occurred to him that one likely paid the *creditor*, not the prison. But his mood hardly allowed for delay.

He and Lifty entered as visitors. The turnkey Postelwaite was on duty again, so Will raised his coat collar and kept his eyes down. Back at Mr. Monarch's, he had picked up another tri-corner hat, which offered some aid. The wretched sun was blaring at full brightness, so he was forced to squint anyway.

Lifty had buttoned up his ragged coat, found a walking stick to clamp under his arm, and produced a foggy monocle. "Thank you, sir," he addressed Postelwaite. "I thank you. And now I'm gratified to say I'm here to pay the debt against that dear friend of mine—the honorable Mr. Tim Conville."

"Tom," Will muttered. He elbowed Lifty and pointed to the yard. "There he is."

Tom stood in the sunlight, in the midst of a crowd. He spoke with his brows drawn, an old familiar expression on his face that said he was in deathly earnest. His listeners were rapt, nodding, looking like they were waiting on him for the great answers of life.

At Tom's elbow, nodding away harder than any of them, was the same old duffer with whom Will had collided at his last visit. Trabb, the fellow's name was.

"Oh, yes," Lifty proceeded. "My friend Tom." He gestured with his stick—more at Trabb than at Tom. "And there he is. Dear old Thomas. What a sweet surprise this'll be for him, what? So if you'll direct me to the head clerk, or whoever 'tis I need to be having words with?"

Postelwaite twirled his large keyring over his forefinger. "Always happy to discharge a prisoner. You wouldn't want another as well, would you?" He chuckled. "Proper influx these days. Never seen the like, have I. This week only, we're stuffed to the gills. Costs a man two shillings a week to get a bed just now."

Lifty sniffed. "Outrage, I say. Pikin' outrage."

Postelwaite pulled a long face as he led them to the chief clerk's office. "And yet there's not a single personage amongst them. One day, I'm going to get me in a real specimen. Like this here Wayfarer fellow there's all this talk of. There's them say he can fly, would you credit that? They're saying he rescued a whole fleet of rich folk yesternight—thrashed an army of ruffians."

210 – K.M. WEILAND

Lifty coughed. *"A-maz-ing,* sir. And I wish you all the luck with that, I do." He looked back at Will and tapped his finger to his nose. His monocle fell out, and he hastened to reinsert it as he entered with Postelwaite.

Will stopped outside the door. Mostly, he watched the ground at his feet and tried to ignore the burn of sunlight trickling in at the corners of his vision. Still, he managed to cast another glance into the prison yard.

The place *was* more crowded than before. People sat on the ground, backs to the walls, with still more packing the midst of the sunny yard. Those who stood roved restlessly. They were louder than before, too; the buzz was angry, frustrated.

That'd be what Tom was tutoring them on then. Peace and patience and all that like.

Tom looked even thinner than before. Beneath a growth of black whiskers, the lines of his cheeks were fiercer than ever. Little wonder. If beds were two shillings, what might victuals be?

From inside the room, Lifty raised his voice. "And what's this? Tryin' to bilk me!"

Another voice murmured.

"Now, look." That was Postelwaite. "Usually, I can tell you the figures on any man here. If you was to ask me the sum of your friend's debt, I would be telling you 'tis one hundred seventeen pounds four."

"Just as it should be, sirrah!"

"But figures can't lie, now can they? The books don't lie."

What the devil? Will pushed up from leaning against the wall. Tom had confirmed 117.4 was the sum of his debt. By how much had these sharps raised the price? Could they even do that? A chill shrank his skin, and he reached into his coat pocket. He had a few coins more, but not many.

Lifty rumbled. "Examine it again, my good man."

"It's right here," Postelwaite said.

"Ah, I . . . see." He sounded as if he really did see.

Casting aside caution, Will entered the room. At the desk sat a scruffy, middle-aged man with lank gray hair come loose from his queue and hanging down either side of his face.

Before the desk, Lifty and Postelwaite each held the edge of a great leathern ledger.

"Allow me." Will took the book from their hands.

The pages were divided into narrow columns, recording all pertinent information about the collegians: name of debtor, name of creditor, and amount of debt. Tom's name stood out halfway down the page—and beside it, Lord Carstone's.

Will ran his blackened fingernail under the names and across the page to Amnt. of Debt.

*509l. 3s. 0d.*

His finger kept on sliding by.

Because that *couldn't* be the correct amount. That hadn't been the amount when Tom was arrested, and it wasn't even close to the amount Tom originally owed Lord Carstone.

"What is this?" His heartbeat pounded in his ears. "This is wrong. This is a downright lie—and you know it!"

"Well." Postelwaite looked confused. "It ain't what I'm remembering, and you'll forgive the boast, but my memory"—he snapped his fingers beside his head—"like that, it is."

Will turned to the official at the desk. "This is wrong. I've come to pay the debt, and I have the full amount, and this isn't it."

The man shrugged. "Seems odd, I'll warrant, but there it is."

"Perhaps someone tampered with it."

"Certainly not. Any tampering would be immediately evident."

Was *this* English justice? His heart pounded on.

He spun to Lifty. "Did you give him the money?"

Lifty nodded.

"All of it?"

Lifty's hand moved to his waistcoat pocket. "Well . . ."

"Give it to him! All of it."

With a sigh, Lifty pulled out a last farthing and dropped it into the pile of coins upon the desk.

"There," Will said. "The debt is paid. Release him."

"Hold your heat," the official said. "The book don't lie."

"Except it is lying!" Will ripped out the page.

Postelwaite choked.

The official shot to his feet. "Now! There can be none of that. You'll join your friend in here if you do not cease this impudence!"

Lifty held out both hands. "We surely don't want to be impudent, do we, Will? Quod's crowded already, did you hear?"

Will shoved the book into Postelwaite's reaching hands and dodged him easily. He crossed to the desk and seized the single candle that guttered over the official's paperwork.

He clenched the paper over the flame. "Cross out the debt and release Tom Colville, or I'll burn it! It's a fraud. It deserves to be destroyed!"

"Cease this!" Still behind the desk, the official pointed at Postelwaite. "Fetch the guards, man!"

"Now, wait, just wait." Lifty snatched Postelwaite's elbow. "We don't need no guards. We're leavin'. Ain't we, Will? We'll come on back once we got the five hundred pounds. Satisfactory all 'round, yes?"

"I will never return here. And neither will this record!"

In the wash of heat above the flame, the paper wavered. A thin trail of smoke curled about it. Tom's name stood out, bold as bold could be. The sum beside it read: *117l. 4s. 0d.*

Will jerked and dropped the candle.

With a yelp, Postelwaite pulled free of Lifty and dove to rescue the flame from the floorboards.

This was impossible. They couldn't all have misread it.

Will pulled the paper up close to his face.

But, no...

Once more it read:

*Thomas Colville*
*Cyrus Barbary, Earl of Carstone*
*509l. 3s. 0d.*

How could this be? Had his eyes fooled him? In the flash of the candlelight, had he seen only what he wanted to?

Or was the higher figure somehow a trick?

A trick like the disguised trap in the church. That, too, had been impossible.

Grimly, Postelwaite regained his feet, the candle sputtering in one hand. With the other, he gripped Will's elbow. "Now, I'm going to have to put you under guard, I am."

"Wait." Will faced him. "It changed. It showed the true figure. This other is a lie, it's a trick somehow. I've seen this sort of thing before—I give you my oath."

"Summon the guards," the clerk demanded of Postelwaite. Then he looked at Will and Lifty, with whom he was about to be left alone. "Err, rather, I'll fetch them." He pushed away from the desk.

Will bore down on Postelwaite. "All these people who have been admitted. You said it was singular."

"If you think we can be letting your friend go on account of overcrowding—" Postelwaite laughed, high-pitched. "You mistake the dignity of this institution."

Will shook Postelwaite's arm. "You've all these people coming in. But how many have got out in the last week? How many debts have been paid off?"

Postelwaite drew his brows. "None—as I can remember."

Will's mouth was dry. "And today isn't the first time someone has been mistaken about the amount of his debt, is it?"

Realization dawned in Postelwaite's eyes—although he didn't seem quite sure as yet *what* he was realizing.

Will pushed him away. He stalked past Lifty out of the office.

In the Lodge, another of the turnkeys was unlocking the door to admit a sanctioned visitor. Will shoved past.

"Hie, there—"

Will kept going, headed for Tom's group in the center of the yard. Everywhere, heads turned.

Tom recognized Will despite the upturned collar. Hope lit his eyes, but only for a second. He would also recognize Will's anger, his frustration. He unfolded his arms and came forward. "What's happened?"

"They've changed the amount of the debt."

"What?"

"It's over five hundred pounds now."

Tom leant back. "Have they then?" He didn't sound surprised.

A bald man clenched and unclenched his hands, heavy muscles jumping in his arms. "It's as we were saying. Somethin' ain't right here. What they're doing to us—even in here—it ain't right."

214 – K.M. WEILAND

"Maybe." Tom's eyes darkened. "But hold yourself, Mr. Claypole. I tell you the time isn't right for rashness."

"And when is it then?" Claypole was missing a molar, and he ran his tongue back and forth through the hole, crooking his whole jaw to accomplish the feat.

"When the time is right for anything, you always know it, and there ain't no question a'tall."

Claypole didn't seem to like that much. It took him a long moment to finally nod. But he did.

At Tom's side, Trabb peered at Will through watery eyes. "You look like that fellow who 'bout took me life t'other day."

Will turned on him. "Come with me."

"Wha? I ain't coming with you." He laughed, somewhere in between bemusement and wariness. "I knows the devil when I sees him."

Will grasped his arm and dragged him towards the gate.

"Will—" Tom strode after. The crowd parted for him. "Stop this. What is it you think you're about?"

"Freeing him—and you too."

"Free." Trabb stopped dragging his feet and trotted alongside. "And how's that?"

"How much is your debt?"

"Thirty-four and nine—and a very little one, ain't it though?"

Will halted at the gate. Postelwaite and his fellow turnkey had locked it upon him. They watched him through the door, nervously.

Beyond them, Lifty remonstrated with the official. He looked ready to grab his coattails and flee.

Will thrust Trabb before him. "Look up his debt."

"Why?" Postelwaite frowned. "He ain't got the money."

"Look up more than his." Will turned to the watching collegians. "Some of you, come here! Tell the man your debts."

For an instant, no one moved. They glanced from Will, who no doubt looked a madman, to Tom, who was one of their own.

Tom hesitated, watching Will, obviously seeing a bit of the madman too. Finally, he nodded.

A handful of collegians came forward and called out the figures.

Will faced Postelwaite. "You wanted something singular to happen on your watch? Well, 'tis happening. Look up the figures."

# CHAPTER 23

WILL LOOKED THROUGH the barred window of the door that detained him within the Marshalsea prison yard.

At the other side, Postelwaite hesitated.

"Look up their debts," Will said again. "It will require but five minutes. If I'm correct, every single debt is a figure higher than it should be."

Postelwaite frowned, but he took one step back, slowly. Then, as if suddenly it was his own notion, he turned and jogged to the office, keyring clanking.

The idea was only a hunch. Less than a hunch: an instinct.

But it was also the truth. Will knew it without Postelwaite's having to look. It was the turnkey himself who needed to see.

Beside Will, Tom lowered his voice. "What are you about?" He didn't sound much impressed—more disapproving. "Raise these people's hopes and what good comes of it?"

And how would *he* free Will were the roles reversed?

"Something wrong is occurring here," Will said.

Pish was correct: none of it was a coincidence, not even Will's getting infected by Dr. Silas's plague. Somehow it all tied together.

He looked at Tom. "All these people—all the new arrivals in the last sennight—why are they here?"

"Debt, mostly. And you're not wrong—there *is* something that ain't right and plain, and we all know it. There's too many of us, and all of a sudden."

"Then why resist this? Maybe I can free more than you, maybe I can free them all."

Tom shook his head, slowly. It was an old expression that said he was deciding: throw in with Will or not? Act the brother—or the father?

That was a choice Tom had never seemed quite able to make for as long as Will had known him. Might be nice if he decided on the brother for the time. If once Will got him out of here, they'd be more equals than ever they had been.

Tom sighed. "There have been whispers."

"What kind of whispers?"

"Other prisons are overfull too—Whitecross-street, Fleet, King's Bench."

A chill touched Will's neck. "What kind of sense does that make?"

"Will—" Tom's expression changed, suddenly earnest. "Tell me the truth. I saw full well what you did the last time. You wanted me to see it. But *what*? What has happened to you?"

Will faced him. "The Affery plague, that's what happened to me. 'Tisn't something any of us ever understood."

A wary light entered Tom's eyes. "Fever, was it?"

"I'm hardly mad! If that's what you think."

"I have no notion you're mad. But you haven't acted straight since first you ran off to London."

Will tried to keep a level tone. "Perhaps I've been too occupied freeing you from this wretched place."

In the office doorway, Postelwaite appeared with the ledger. He beckoned the official and pointed out entries. His eyes were wide—in either concern or excitement. Maybe both.

"How'd you earn the money to attempt this today?" Tom asked quietly.

"I didn't beg for it, and I didn't steal it. That should be enough." Will risked the sunlight to shoot Tom a glare. "Once I pay the debt, you *are* coming."

At that, Tom's jaw hardened. When it came to a battle of resolve, his was as strong as Will's. Stronger perhaps. In times past, Will usually let him win, if only out of his great regard. But if it came down to respecting Tom's wishes or freeing him from prison—that didn't even deserve to be named a choice.

Tom stepped nearer. "Mark me, Will, ends do not always justify means. You said yourself there's more happening here than you and me. Even if you free me, you think we're going to walk away?"

"You're the one who taught me to walk away from arguments I couldn't win."

"What I thought I taught you was to walk away from arguments not *worth* the winning."

Will held steady. "Well, and I'm not walking away from you."

Postelwaite approached, the ledger still in his hands. "It's true! It's extraordinary, but it's the truth. All these debts have increased—and significantly!"

Will closed his eyes against the sun. Then he wasn't mad—and he *did* have enough to pay the debt.

In spite of everything, a grin found his mouth. He looked at Tom. "If you've any things, best gather them."

Tom only raised an eyebrow.

Will turned back to Postelwaite. "You'll let me out now?"

"I daresay that depends on whether we've your word you won't be destroying anything more."

"You have it."

Postelwaite tucked the ledger under one arm and unlocked the door. "Because this discovery here can make no difference to Mr. Colville."

"What?"

Postelwaite opened the door. "The book says what the book says, you know? Long as it says your friend's debt is one thing, that's what must be paid."

Will stood rooted. "But that's daft! We proved the book wrong!"

"All we know is the book doesn't say what we thought."

"'Tis a trick! The correct figure is there on the page. It's hidden somehow!"

"Now, now." Postelwaite moved the ledger behind his back. With his other hand, he gripped the edge of the door.

Will gave him no chance to slam it. He dodged through and stalked to the office.

"Will—" Tom called. "Stop a minute!"

Will entered the office and seized the candle from the desk. The torn paper with Tom's debt had remained in his fist all this time. Now, he raised it above the candle once more.

Postelwaite scrambled after him. "Wait! You promised me!"

"It happened once, it will happen again. You need to see it happen!"

Above the flame, the page wavered. The inky figures remained unchanged.

They *had* changed. He hadn't dreamt it. Something about the candle—its light, its heat—had dispelled the trick.

Postelwaite advanced upon him.

Nothing, still nothing.

Will held the paper closer, almost into the flame. The bottom edge began to blacken, to smoke.

Postelwaite grabbed Will's shoulder. "No, you don't!"

Thin smoke wisped up, across the surface of the page.

The *509l. 3s. 0d.* disappeared; the *117l. 4s. 0d.* appeared.

Will spun, holding out the paper. "Look! It shows it again!"

It read as it should:

*Thomas Colville*
*James Fitzroy*
*117l. 4s. 0d.*

He froze.

*James Fitzroy.*

The true paper did not list Lord Carstone as the creditor. It listed Mr. Fitzroy.

But . . . how? *Why?*

The bottom of the page caught fire.

Postelwaite snatched it from Will's numb fingers. He dashed it to the floor and stamped upon it.

Then he glared at Will. "Good gracious, boy. What ails you?"

Will could draw no air.

Mr. Fitzroy had bought the debt from Lord Carstone? From his *good friend* Lord Carstone? And then called it in?

All this time, it had been Mr. Fitzroy.

But why, why?

To gain Tom's land? To gain the barn and the trackway on which it sat?

Mr. Fitzroy might simply have *purchased* the barn. He hadn't even attempted it. He'd called in the debt without a second thought. Likely, he'd called it in even before he'd cast Will from his house. How else could the warrant officers have preceded them to Affery?

Had Mr. Fitzroy ever been Will's friend? Or had it all been a masquerade?

He felt as if he had been struck in the stomach.

Postelwaite retrieved the slightly charred page from the floor. "You must stop this blessed nonsense. Give your friend a bit of coin." He gestured to the piled monies at the desk. "To keep him in bedding and victuals. Then you go earn some more."

Hot wax slipped down the length of the candle and puddled at the base of Will's thumb. He shook his head. "This is wrong. It's an . . . artifice. I know not how or what, but it is."

Then again, perhaps he did know.

Mr. Fitzroy *must* have been infected with the plague on the day the barn caught fire. He hadn't been given Will's speed; he'd been given something else. Will stared at the page. Something that allowed him to do *this*.

He thought back to the ten-shilling note Lifty had stolen from those soldiers yesterday. It had been blank too—but only to Will. Somehow he had seen through it when the others had not.

Did that mean the soldiers were Mr. Fitzroy's—and he was paying them with false notes?

And the trap yestere'en in the church? Had that been Mr. Fitzroy's doing too?

Mr. Monarch *had* sent Will there to die—but not because he desired Will's death. For whatever insane reason, Mr. Monarch had thought he could get away with visiting Mr. Fitzroy earlier that day. Afterwards, he'd been distraught beyond measure. Why? Quite simple, really: because the great Mr. Fitzroy had somehow twisted Mr. Monarch's arm and demanded he eliminate his new money-maker.

Will's vitals churned.

But what cause would Mr. Fitzroy have to wish him dead? Casting him off was one thing. But setting a trap to *kill* him?

Was it because Mr. Monarch had found his way to Mr. Fitzroy *through* Will—just as Pish had come to Mr. Fitzroy because of Will? Or was it because Will was the only other living man altered by the plague?

Did that make him a threat? He couldn't be trusted as an ally, so he became a foe?

In a roundabout way, Mr. Fitzroy *had* warned Will not to make an enemy of him.

It all made a horrible sort of sense. And yet . . . it didn't.

The packed prisons, the strange guards in the street, even these political happenings Pish talked about—they all tied together. Somehow. For some reason.

Heaven only knew what Mr. Fitzroy wished to accomplish. His grand social revolution seemed pointless when the prisons were bursting with the people he claimed he wanted to save.

Will thrust the candle into Postelwaite's hand.

"Hie there, wait a minute! What of your money?"

"Mark it in the ledger. When I return, you'll see the debt's been paid."

"When you . . . return?" Postelwaite sounded appalled.

Will stalked into the Lodge.

By this time, Lifty had inched significantly nearer the exit.

Tom still stood at the window in the door, the crowd of prisoners ever more restless behind him. "Will, what are you doing? Where are you going?"

Will passed him without halting. "I'll return later. Don't worry."

Tom shook the bars. "I *am* worried!"

"Don't be. I know what I must do to free you."

He would speak with Mr. Fitzroy. It was long past time they sorted their differences once for all.

But first... there was one other man whose sins he must address.

————————

The afternoon grew late by the time Will crossed the river to Seven Dials.

He slammed through Mr. Monarch's front door.

In her chair beside the entrance, Peggy raised her face from her skirt. Her eyes were brighter than usual—positively glittering.

She seized his arm. "Thank God, thank God."

He tried to pull free. "Let go."

"Listen to me. It's little Rose, you hear me? It's Rose!"

He stopped. "What do you mean?"

In the dining room, beyond the drawn curtain, voices murmured.

"He's got her." Phlegm rattled in her throat. "He's been in a fume all the day. He's takin' it out on her, I tell you!"

Not only on Rose to judge by the welt on Peggy's cheek.

Behind Will, Lifty puffed through the door. "What's this now?"

Will left him to attend to Peggy.

He crossed the room and pushed aside the curtain.

At the hearth, Mr. Monarch sat with one hand dipping into a pot of lard. In the other, he held a live rat.

Before him, Rose stood stiff and straight, arms locked at her sides.

"Now," Mr. Monarch said. "Why should you have *anxiété*? You who are liking the rats, yes?" He dabbed the lard on her face, on her arms.

Already, she glistened with the stuff.

He held out the rat. "Have no *anxiété*. You see now," he purred, "the rats they are liking you too." He released the rat against her grease-coated neck.

The animal clung there. It started sniffing, licking—in another moment, it would be chewing.

Rose stared ahead, breaths choked. She reached to pull away the rat.

"No." Mr. Monarch trapped both her wrists in his hand. "You like the rat, yes? You let the rat to be having his *dîner*. Then he will like you too." Without looking, he groped at the table for more lard.

Will moved so fast he had hardly time to think about any of it. He charged across the room, vision blurring. He pulled from within his coat the iron rod Lifty had given him to use as a dagger. Sharpened at one end and twisted into a spiral along its length, it was easy to conceal and more than effective.

He slammed its point into Mr. Monarch's outstretched hand. The rod punctured all the way through and bit deep into the table.

Mr. Monarch screamed, deep, primal, and entirely astonished. Will seized the rat and flung it against the wall.

Rose huffed one great breath, then ran after the rat and kicked it, once, twice, heaving its limp body into the corner. She squatted and flung her skirt over her lard-covered head, scrubbing, scrubbing, scrubbing.

Will faced Mr. Monarch. His chest heaved. "You villain."

Mr. Monarch screamed on in staccato bursts. With his free hand, he scrabbled inside his coat and withdrew a tiny pistol.

Will smacked the pistol aside. It clattered against the hearth's andirons. His blood pumped all through him, hot and fierce. He wanted to lash out, wanted something in his hands he could punish for the disappointments of today.

God in heaven, he wanted to punish *this* man. Was there scum any fouler upon the face of the earth?

"You—" But he had no words. With one hand, he snatched up Mr. Monarch by his coat. He dragged him closer, wrenching the pinned hand and eliciting another wail. He crashed his fist into Mr. Monarch's fleshy jowl—once, and then again.

He could do it again and again and again. He could drop this scum to the ground and kick his brain to putty. The blood raged in his head. He had it in him to do it.

And God in heaven, that frightened him.

He cast Mr. Monarch from him.

The man crashed off the bench, yanking his blood-slicked hand once more against the rod staking it to the table.

Will stood over him. His breath quavered in his throat, so hot and fast.

"You, you—" Mr. Monarch whimpered. He pulled himself up at the table's edge and reached for the rod. "For what do you do this?"

Will fisted the rod, holding it in place. What was there to say?

What words were there? What condemnation would make any difference?

Mr. Monarch's eyes darted about. "But, but we are friends! We are—yes?" Blood vessels in his cheek had broken where Will hit him. "You come to my house of *hospitalité* and you do this thing to me?" His voice rose at the end.

There was only one question Will needed answered.

He leant in nearer. "Mr. Fitzroy laid a trap for me last night."

It wasn't a question after all. He already knew the answer. Perhaps he'd only needed to hear the words.

Some of the panic left Mr. Monarch's eyes. He focused, and a fragment of the old detachment arose. "I am not the one who is your *ennemi*."

In the corner, Rose scoffed. She had wiped most of the lard from her face and arms. Now, she stood with clenched hands. "You bloody devil spawn, I'll show you who's the enemy. You touch me again, and I'll bloody kill you!"

The panic and the groveling had left Mr. Monarch's face. He nodded, as if he now understood something.

"*Ennemi*, what is that?" he asked Will. "Every man has *ennemi* in every other man. We all are *traitres* to others in order to be helpful to ourselves. I am not your *ennemi*." He gestured to his wrecked hand. "Even after you do this thing to me, I am not your *ennemi*. I have *le pardon* for you."

"I desire no pardon."

He shrugged. "But you desire what Mr. Fitzroy can do for you, yes? He can do great things. He does do great things. If we act now with intelligence, maybe he takes us with him as he rises up, up, up to renown and to *gloire* and to *richesse*."

"All I wish from him is what I'm owed."

Mr. Monarch's eyelid flickered. He was growing pale. "You want something from me too, I think? You want me to help you to be like my *Bleu*-Eyed Jem? Better, yes? To take your God-given skills and to *do* something with them."

Will tightened his grip on the rod. "What I *will* want, if ever I see your face again, is to kill you. Whoever Jem was, his greatest feat was getting shed of you and leaving this place behind."

"No one leaves Seven Dials, my boy, whatever you think."

Will yanked the rod free.

Mr. Monarch wailed.

Will stepped back. Gore dripped on the floor. "I'm leaving."

In the corner, Rose jerked forward.

"And I'm taking Rose with me."

She inhaled sharply.

Mr. Monarch's pale eyes flashed cold. "She is not yours to have, I think."

Will looked at her. "Gather your things."

She needed to be told only the once. She thundered up the stairs in her oversized shoes.

Mr. Monarch cradled his hand against his chest. He sucked air through his teeth, looking not a little like the rat. "Then she is yours, yes? I give her to you, as my gift. We have been good *partenaires*." He choked on a laugh "Until today, I think. You remember what I say. You want what our Mr. Fitzroy has? You come to me. We will get it—because I am knowing how."

Will turned and left him.

He crossed back into the other room, where Peggy stood near to the door.

"Where's Lifty?" he asked.

"He hiked off." She licked her lips. She had tremendously big eyes—indigo like the night sky. In her careworn face, they seemed out of place. "You ain't won this, you know. Mr. Monarch won't let you walk away. Won't let little Rose walk away."

Rose clattered back down.

She was right. But what else was he to do?

He opened the door and stepped into the growing shadows. "He'll have to catch me." He glanced back. "Be careful of yourself."

Peggy shrugged. She searched her pocket and came out with a small amber bottle. Laudanum maybe. She grinned without humor, wide enough to show the missing molars in back. "Oh, yes, and I've so much to be careful of, me."

Something like guilt stabbed him.

Hadn't he told Tom he couldn't save them all? Rose was going to be a liability as it was, and no doubt Mr. Monarch *would* come after them. Will couldn't take Peggy too. He couldn't take any of the other women or boys from this miserable place. Not a single one of them.

Rose rounded the corner of the stairs, a good-sized bundle wrapped up under her arm. She cast one furtive look to where Mr. Monarch hunched at the fireside, binding his hand.

Then she ran across the room to Will. Her eyes were alight, her grin tremendous. "Blimey, but ain't you the one."

That look—as if she believed he could do about anything, as if she'd lie on the floor and kiss his feet if he so much as glanced down.

Rose bowed her head for no one. She'd never bowed it for Mr. Monarch, that was certain.

But she'd do it for him right now.

A fierce protectiveness rose within him. She was all alone—truly all alone now. Save for him.

If she lived or she died, it was on his shoulders. If Mr. Monarch trapped her back into this life, if she ended up consumptive and addicted like Peggy—it was all in the power of *his* hand to allow or prevent.

And dashed if that wasn't the most frightening thought amidst all the many disturbing thoughts in his head just now.

He swallowed, nearly choked, and had to clear his throat. "Come."

She slipped neatly from under Peggy's reaching hand. "Goodbye, Peg."

Will nodded to Peggy. "God bless." It was all he had to offer.

He and Rose emerged into the twilit street, and he closed the door.

A grin hinted at the corner of her mouth. "And didn't I know from the first you'd be turning out a hero?"

"Well." He tried to clear his brain. "Look, this here—you and me, I mean—this isn't permanent. Once I free Tom, we'll have to figure something to do with you—someplace safe and pleasant where you can live. Tonight, I have to see about clearing up his papers."

She didn't seem daunted. "Well, then?"

He squared his shoulders. "We have a masque ball to attend."

# CHAPTER 24

AS IT TURNED out, it was a fortunate thing Rose came along.

They arrived in the full darkness of perhaps half past eight. Lord Carstone's grand new villa in Regent's Park was a-glitter with lights. Behind the gates, the half-circle drive was packed with carriages, footmen, and dismounting ladies and gentlemen.

Bow Street Runners guarded the entrance. Gilt-topped batons under their elbows, they tipped their hats to the entering guests.

Pish might be among them. Will squinted. Difficult to tell in the flickering shadows.

One thing was certain: there was no chance a'tall of his gaining entrance through the front door. If he were to have any opportunity of finding Mr. Fitzroy, confronting him, and—somehow—forcing him to free Tom, he must first find a way to sneak in unremarked.

Rose shrugged. "Cor. You get me to a door—any door—and I'll get you in."

He hadn't planned to take her any farther than this. But if she could remain inconspicuous, she might run afoul of less trouble inside the gates than outside.

"Fine."

She grinned.

He loaded her and her bundle onto his back, obtained a running start on a quiet corner of the fence, and cleared it with a decided lack of grace. They crossed the fancy parterre garden in a blur, and he jumped them up to the portico roof, then to a balcony.

She slid off his back to land with a thump and giggled. "That was lovely, wasn't it though?"

He glared. "Glad you were impressed—because it's considerably more difficult when someone's *wiggling* on your back."

Tsking, she squatted to open her bundle. She withdrew two metal pins and went to work at the latch.

Will dug through his coat pockets for his eye-shields. "You've attempted this before?"

In answer, the lock clicked, and she flicked the doors inward.

The clamor of music and voices rose.

He had rather expected this much of the plan to require the better part of the evening. Now the more difficult half stared him in the face all the sooner.

He bent low and scooted onto the inner landing. Through the railing, golden lights glimmered. The smells—of floor wax, of perfume, of savory meats, of wine—wafted up.

His stomach growled. Rose's echoed.

He crept close enough to the railing to see into the grand room below.

Several hundred people laughed and flirted behind elaborate masks. A dais had been raised at the far end, with a number of plush chairs, but it sat empty for now. Judging by the near-deafening music, the orchestra must be positioned beneath this landing.

"Well," Rose said. "And I ain't never seen the bloody like."

He was high enough that the corners of his vision swam with dizziness. He squinted hard and scanned the crowd.

No Mr. Fitzroy.

But there was *Henry* Fitzroy—in a dapper coat of green velvet, its sleeves elaborately puffed.

And beside him . . .

Lady Isabella held a gold mask adorned with a great red feather. The colors matched her sparkling gown, and the sparkling of the gown matched the jewels at her throat. She gestured and smiled in conversation.

Henry toasted her with his wine glass.

Will scowled. "Now there's a pretentious fop for you."

"How can you tell? They all look the same."

He stood. "I can tell because he's the one standing beside the most beautiful woman in the room."

Rose mirrored his scowl. "Who's this?" She peered through the banister. "Thought you was here to find this Fitzroy cove, not some rum mort."

He turned up his coat collar and slipped on his eye-shields. He'd blend in nicely with the masked guests. "I'm going down now. You stay—"

From within the bundle, Rose produced a knee-length wool coat—blackened with coal dust—and a black neck-handkerchief with two holes cut in the center. She tied the scarf over her face like a mask and grinned up at him.

"Rose—"

She withdrew a sling and a handful of large stones. "I've got this too."

"Rose, you can't come."

She frowned. "Why not? I've got a mask too, don't I?" The eye holes were half an inch too wide, rendering her left eye only partially visible. "God knows you need plenty of help." She pointed. "Don't you go denyin' that."

He opened his mouth—and found, in all good conscience, he *couldn't* deny it. He knelt. "I need you to remain here and be my sentry. Can you do that? I can't stay up here long, or I'll become dizzy. But you can. Because that's the special talent you have that I don't." He patted her arm.

She looked at him flatly. "And you're really thinking I'm going to credit that?"

He huffed. "Just do it."

"Fine." She faced away and piled the rest of her stones at her knees. "Don't trip over your feet when you get to your fancy lady, eh?"

"If you move from this spot, I give my oath, I will . . . take you back to Seven Dials."

"Pfft. Think I can't hear the empty in that? You would never." She stared up at him through her crooked mask. "And *that's* why I'm gonna do what you want."

That would have to be victory enough for now.

He held out both palms in a staying gesture, then turned and descended.

The first stairway was empty. Lord willing, none of the guests would take it upon themselves to explore Rose's upper landing.

He encountered toffs on the main staircase and began his bowing routine. Most bowed back. A few stared, but not with suspicion so much as interest. The rest ignored him, too deep in their pleasures to notice his singular costume.

At the foot of the stairs, he scanned the room. Now that he was back on solid ground, his vision returned to blessed stillness.

Everything glittered. The entire room seemed golden, same as at the Grosvenor Square ball he had attended with the Fitzroys. The guests swirled about him: rouged, corseted, padded, pinned, intoxicated. Above the raucity of the orchestra, voices grated, their laughter rising and rising, more hysterical than happy.

He worked through the crush to Lady Isabella.

She saw him and recognized him with a twitch. Straightening, she raised her chin.

He halted shoulder to shoulder with Henry and bowed to her. "What a fine couple."

She pasted on a smile. "Your sincerity is so very much appreciated, sir."

"I say." Henry scanned him. "Who's this then?"

"A . . . friend," she said.

"Friend with a name?" Henry asked.

"It is not a night for introductions. It is a masque, yes?" She fidgeted with the gold tassel at her gown's high waist. "Will you fetch some refreshment? I find I am parched."

Henry tossed back the last of his wine. "As you wish, my own." He touched his elbow to Will's side. "My betrothed, you know?"

Will gritted his teeth. "I know."

Henry looked at him sidelong. "I say, have I met you?"

"Have you met the Duke of Veneering?" Will asked.

"I . . ." Henry glanced at Isabella for guidance, then back. "I . . . naturally."

"Well, then."

Henry grinned, without appearing any the wiser. "I'll fetch you something too. Then we can—reacquaint ourselves." He sauntered off.

Will looked at Lady Isabella through the smoked glass of his eye-shields.

She looked back at him, haughty as ever.

She hadn't called for the Runners. Perhaps that was worth more than a little something.

He took a breath. "I apologize."

She raised an eyebrow above the edge of her gay mask. "Only one apology? Rather a paltry beginning."

He swallowed a growl. "Do you wish to know *what* I've decided to apologize for?"

"I perish of anxiety."

"Your grandfather—I was wrong in what I said of him. It wasn't him who imprisoned my master."

"Well . . ." She sounded genuinely taken aback.

He drew breath and hastened on. "I found it out only today. But the man *is* someone near to you."

She hesitated. "Mr. Fitzroy?"

"You know?"

"I . . . intuited it." She cocked her mask away from her face. "I appreciate your apology. And, um, I believe perhaps I might have been hasty in some of the accusations I offered as well. I will not say I believe you are *not* at fault in some way for Dr. Silas's death, but—"

"Death?" His heart leapt, and he came forward, so barely a foot separated them. "You do not say murder? Why? Have you asked Mr. Fitzroy?"

At the far end of the room, the orchestra completed a song and fell silent.

"No . . ." She glanced over her shoulder, then leant in closer still and lowered her voice. "I felt such a question imprudent as yet. I . . . received something. I hardly call it a missive. It was no more than a clipping from a newspaper—French or Belgian, I am not quite certain which."

Will shrugged, not understanding.

"It spoke of unprecedented doings, rumors really. Curious effects upon man and beast, in the aftermath of a strange—"

Will's heartbeat thundered. "Plague."

"Indeed."

"Then—there's more than just me?"

A smile touched her mouth. "Why should there not be? Did you think your trackway the only one upon the earth?"

"But that's—" He wasn't yet sure *what*. At all events, it meant he mightn't be alone. Would there be others who could help him discover how to deal with the negative effects?

He looked at her again. "The clipping—who sent it?"

She touched the corner of the mask to her mouth. "That is the question, is it not?"

"An associate who knew of Dr. Silas's work, and of you?" The latter seemed just as unlikely as the first.

She shook her head. "I am aware of no such person on the Continent just now. But leave that for the moment. There is more. You are correct—*something* untoward is occurring here in London, and you may be correct in considering Mr. Fitzroy at its heart."

Will glanced at the empty dais. His throat went dry—although he was uncertain whether it was because *she* agreed with him, or because she *agreed* with him.

"Mr. Fitzroy has . . ." He swallowed. "He too has been infected with the plague."

A fierce spark of interest lit her face, but she immediately sobered. "He possesses superiorities?"

"But different from mine. Somehow he makes people see falsities—and believe them to be truths."

Her eyes flickered in thought. Then she looked up. "But that makes much sense! The effects have always manifested differently, from subject to subject, even among the surviving animals. Mr. Fitzroy is altered of late. Even Henry has observed. And it is more than just what is occurring in Parliament."

"He's to be Prime Minister, then?"

"Indeed, and it is unprecedented how quickly the thing has transpired. Even the newspapers are saying Parliament behaved as if a single puppet master were pulling the strings."

He snorted. "But, naturally, it was all done correctly. Just as was Tom's debt."

The orchestra began an entrance march.

"I will tell you this as well," she said. "My engagement to Henry? Although Mr. Fitzroy has discussed it with my grandfather for years, it is also of a sudden, I assure you. I feel it is because he wants to secure me. I think he knows—about my work with Dr. Silas."

Beneath his fingerless gloves, Will's palms began to sweat. "I know he does."

Her mouth fell open. "You *told* him?"

"No! He knew already. It was how I came to be infected. Mr. Fitzroy wanted me to discover what was happening, and to ensure Dr. Silas wasn't using you ill."

She uttered a laugh. "That is ridiculous. Dr. Silas was harmless."

"Dr. Silas was mad."

"He was brilliant."

Something small and hard thwacked the back of Will's neck. "Ow." He slapped a hand over it and looked around.

High above, Rose thrust her face behind the balcony posts. She jabbed a finger towards the dais, then ducked back into the shadows.

Will faced forward.

Lady Isabella frowned. "Pray, what ails you now?"

The orchestra was indeed playing an introduction.

Half a dozen people of quality marched from the adjoining room and mounted the dais. Mr. Fitzroy fronted them.

Will's heart pounded harder.

Mr. Fitzroy was dressed simply, but elegantly: starched cravat, snowy waistcoat, clocked stockings, gleaming shoes. He seemed the same as ever. Quite as handsome, quite as serene. And yet *different*.

"He looks . . . younger."

His face seemed unlined by his two score years, his hair almost as golden as Isabella's. He looked in no way affected by the rigors of recovering from and adjusting to the plague.

Isabella darted a gloved hand to her mouth. "My goodness— it is the king!"

234 – K.M. WEILAND

"What?" Will scanned the line of Mr. Fitzroy's honored guests upon the dais.

The entire crowd was a-murmur.

Prinny, as they'd called him only last year when he'd yet been the Prince of Wales and regent for his mad father, was a vast man in a vast waistcoat with vast stockings upon his vast calves. He was eminently stylish, and yet eminently farcical in the confines of a dandy's clothes.

He nodded graciously to the crowd, and the whole lot dropped bows and curtsies.

Will ducked in time to keep from sticking straight up.

"Mr. Fitzroy knows the king?" he hissed.

"Well, he is Prime Minister." She straightened. "And the king loves a good ball."

In Will's head, Pish's voice screamed: *No coincidences!*

His back crawled. "This is not right."

Mr. Fitzroy stepped to the edge of the dais and raised his hands. He flashed the same old smile—a hint of teeth, eyes crinkling jovially—as if everyone were in on a jest.

But the jest was Mr. Fitzroy's alone. It always had been. The jest was that he made everyone believe they were his friends, his confidantes, his respected peers—whilst he worked behind their backs.

Will clenched and unclenched his hands. His leathern gloves squeaked.

"My friends. Thank you for joining me in this night of celebration."

Genteel applause.

"It is not, however, merely a celebration of my own new position as the leader of your government—of which I sincerely hope to prove worthy."

Will choked.

"Indeed, this is a celebration of what I predict is the beginning of a new age in the history of our mighty kingdom—and one I have asked you here tonight to ascertain whether you will support me in or not."

More than a few hoisted glasses in toast.

"What I see before us is an opportunity to raise our country to greater heights."

Here it was. His grand plan to eliminate social injustice—by doing what? Falsely imprisoning people?

Energy buzzed through Will until he could hardly keep still.

"We will wipe out the poverty and the suffering surrounding us." Mr. Fitzroy raised a fist. "If England is ever to secure her power and her wealth for all future generations, we must have the courage to cast off the shackles that bind the lower classes."

All around Will, the high and the rich called back, "Hear, hear!"

Did Mr. Fitzroy believe in his own righteousness?

Will stepped forward. Why not reveal himself, after all? This was why he had come. He would ask the man himself and let these people hear whatever lie Mr. Fitzroy would spin in response.

"This is why," Mr. Fitzroy continued, "I tell you our past efforts to save this dying part of our society—no matter how well-intentioned—have been in vain. We must begin again. We must look to a new order." He glanced at the king.

The man stepped forward.

He took cues from Mr. Fitzroy? Surely that wasn't how etiquette worked.

Again, Mr. Fitzroy faced the crowd. "I promise we can and we must and we will cut off this tumorous inequality in our society. We must kill it at its heart so we may rebuild upon it a new order—in which there will be no cause for any man ever to bear scorn for low or illegitimate birth or vulgar past."

For an instant, Will held Mr. Fitzroy's words in his head, hearing them over again. *Cutting off? Killing?* Those were aggressive metaphors for . . . what?

Will's blood began to pound, painfully.

Mr. Fitzroy continued. "I reach to you in fellowship, because I know your golden hearts all support me in this great vision."

Murmuring filled the hall.

At Will's side, Lady Isabella's mouth was open. "It makes no sense," she whispered. "It sounds like— But it cannot be, can it?"

Will had no answer. He looked about.

These people appeared as uncertain as he felt. Their smiles

slipped. They glanced at each other haltingly, wondering if they too hadn't misheard.

Even as the murmurs grew, their expressions suddenly calmed. Smiles returned, eyes lit up, heads nodded. As others saw their fellows agreeing with Mr. Fitzroy, they too turned and stopped murmuring.

Was Mr. Fitzroy causing this? Was he casting some sort of spell over these people to make them accept this bizarre proposal? Why should these people have any interest a'tall in the radical equality he was proposing?

The world couldn't run on equality.

The truth wrenched up from within him. If everyone were the same, the machine of society would . . . end. There would be nothing to strive for. Nothing for boys like him to dream of.

This wasn't what he'd had in mind *at all*. Wipe out the *injustice*, yes, that was one thing. But after all, wasn't *inequality* something else altogether?

Not all the murmurs ceased. Some grew louder.

At the edge of the room, an elderly gentleman raised his voice. "Certainly His *Majesty* cannot be in support of this radical rubbish?"

His Majesty said nothing. He smiled beneficently, extended a be-ringed hand towards Mr. Fitzroy, and bowed—as if in sanction.

Will whipped his gaze back to the elderly dissenter.

The man was... gone. Where he had stood, there were now only calm and nodding guests.

"Where did he go?" Will caught Lady Isabella's elbow. "Did you see where he went?"

Her face was frozen. "I think . . ." The pinch of her eyebrows spoke to an emotion between confusion and concern. "For an instant, I thought I saw someone pull him away."

"For an instant . . ."

At the dais, Mr. Fitzroy stood serenely, hands clasped before him as he conversed quietly with the king.

But his eyes were not on the king. He watched the room, every corner of it. He was not merely observing the effects of his speech. He was *monitoring* it.

His face appeared not so young as it had when he entered. Lines strained his eyes. His jaw and neck were hard—almost as if he were laboring under some tremendous physical tension.

His Majesty chattered on, smiling in a congratulatory manner. He seemed not to notice Mr. Fitzroy's distraction.

"Shouldn't the king be speaking to us?" Will asked.

Lady Isabella frowned. "It does seem rather strange for him to attend and *not* speak."

In fact, the king did not even look at his people. Hands behind his back, he rocked on his heels. He seemed deaf to the uncertain rumbling that edged a room full of smiling, agreeable faces.

Will breathed out sharply. "He's not real."

"What?"

He started forward. "It's not really the king. He's not really here." He'd no firm idea how he knew, but he *did*.

She used her mask to hook his arm. "What in heaven's name are you talking about?"

"Somehow Mr. Fitzroy is conjuring this. He can make people see things that aren't there."

She shook her head, not exactly disbelieving, more as if she didn't quite want to believe.

"Watch," he said.

He pushed through the crowd, slowly at first, to avoid notice.

Twenty feet from the dais, he breathed in deeply and shouted, "That is not the king!"

Bursting into speed, he bounded onto the dais. There, he slowed enough for guests to clearly see what he was about to do.

Mr. Fitzroy's eyes widened, then hardened, all in the same second.

Will lunged at the false king. *And please allow it to* be *a false king*.

The assembly gasped. Of all the strange things they had witnessed, certainly the ghastliest yet would be someone brawling with their sovereign.

Will spread his arms wide enough to catch the man's bulk, should there be any.

There wasn't.

He passed through the king. The air fragmented into golden

and rainbow-hued light. In the corner of his vision, the image of the king remained as it had been: standing serenely, rocking on its heels.

God save them all. He scarcely put his hands before his face in time to catch his fall.

He hit hard and immediately pushed off and rolled over.

The first thing he saw was Mr. Fitzroy's face, shocked, angry—but not panicked.

The second thing he saw was the body of the king sprawled on the dais beside him.

Will was swift. But so was Mr. Fitzroy. In the flash of a thought, the man had already changed the illusion to support what had happened.

That was calamitous.

Mr. Fitzroy stared at Will a moment longer. Then he looked up. "Guards!"

That, for some reason, finally made everyone start screaming.

# CHAPTER 25

FOR AN INSTANT, Will forgot how to make his speed work.

As he lay on the dais, Mr. Fitzroy bent to minister to the fallen king. At this proximity, the illusion was not quite so perfect. Or perhaps it was due to the haste with which it had been recreated in its supine position. It frayed at the edges, golden light showing through, clearly not a real person.

No one else seem to recognize the incongruity. Ladies were shrieking. Men were shouting. Running footsteps stamped.

True, Will had assaulted the king. Possibly it was the worst thing any Englishman could do. But it was hardly worth all *that* fuss.

He levered an elbow under his body.

Below, the people were trampling over one another, fleeing for their lives. A dozen men had appeared in their midst.

These men wore long black highway coats, cocked hats, and eye-shields.

These men were all Will Hardy.

Will scrambled to his feet and faced Mr. Fitzroy.

Mr. Fitzroy rose slowly. His eyes were hard, intent. The strained expression Will had noted previously seemed all the greater. Mr. Fitzroy appeared as a man pressed down by a great physical weight on his shoulders.

"What are you about?" Will demanded.

Mr. Fitzroy pointed at Will. "You *dare* attack the King of England!" He raised his voice for all to hear. "You dare attack his loyal and peaceable subjects!"

There could be no answer to that.

Will spun to the crowd. "The king is not real! 'Tis an illusion, I tell you! I passed through him!"

That failed to calm them in any measure.

Throughout the hall, Will's mirror images drew cutlass-pistols. They spoke naught. They *could* speak naught. They were only air.

The people shuddered together into clumps. Whether or not they realized all the figures were the same person, they clearly *did* realize they were being threatened.

"Is it the Wayfarer?" someone said.

"But he saves people!"

Will stepped to the edge of the dais. "'Tis not real! They are not me!"

Mr. Fitzroy placed himself between Will and the king, protectively. "What do you want from us, sir?"

A man from the floor shouted, "Do you think you can make hostages of us all?"

Again, Mr. Fitzroy pointed at Will. "Your reputation as a brutal highwayman precedes you!"

Will stared. His *reputation* was anything but brutal.

Mr. Fitzroy raised his voice in indignation. "You plunder and steal and murder in the darkness of night, and you evade recompense. But not here, sir! Not here!"

"That is not true—"

"You think to assassinate our sovereign?"

Will flinched back. "What?"

"You think you possess the power to halt in its very cradle the new movement that would forever end the depredations of you and your kind? No, sir." Mr. Fitzroy met Will's gaze, fiercely. He was playing the game to the hilt here, and he knew he was winning.

The crowd believed what they *saw*. Even when it made no sense, that's what they would believe.

Fitzroy raised his chin. "Kill me where I stand, but I say, *no sir.*"

"It's not me. It's him—it's Mr. James Fitzroy. He is creating these illusions. Touch them, pull their coattails, you will see!"

No one in the crowd moved.

Then Lady Isabella reached out, tentatively, to touch one of the highwaymen. The illusion fragmented to gold around her fingertips. She cast a shocked look up to Will.

A shot rang out.

She snatched back her hand. People whirled about. In the back of the room, men and women scrambled and shouted.

"He is murdered! The highwaymen have shot him!"

Through the swarm of people, Will caught one glimpse of the old gentleman who had first raised his voice in dissent. He lay in a puddle of blood.

What in heaven's name—? Will's heart crammed into his throat. This had escalated to an entirely new level. Mr. Fitzroy was *killing* those who opposed him? And somehow using his illusions to do it? They were real? They could fire a pistol?

Or was everyone only meant to think so?

But, no. The stinging odor of powder and smoke drifted on the air.

Guards in red and gold livery burst into the room. These men were real enough, judging by the way they flung the doors inward hard enough to strike the walls.

A dozen swarmed the dais in pursuit of Will.

He spun back and snatched Mr. Fitzroy's arm, even as he pulled his iron knuckles from his coat pocket. He would strike Mr. Fitzroy unconscious. That must end the illusions.

But Mr. Fitzroy still possessed his own swift reflexes. And he was strong. He might not have Will's forge-hardened muscles, but he was taller by almost a span and at least two stone heavier.

He ripped free. His eyes glittered, hard and determined. "Do what it is you do best, Will my boy. Run whilst you may."

He was correct. Will could not trap Mr. Fitzroy *and* run from the guards.

He hesitated between choices one second too long.

The guards engulfed him. "You are under arrest in the name of His Majesty!"

Mr. Fitzroy knelt beside the image of the king and appeared to help him to his feet. The king limped along, with Mr. Fitzroy extending an arm behind his back as though supporting him.

Will bucked against the guards.

"Your thieving days have ended," one growled.

If Will could free one hand, he could spin fast enough to gain momentum and free the other. Of course, he might well wrench his shoulder from its socket, but that would be a problem to deal with later.

Unfortunately, two guards apiece held each arm. They dragged him backwards, and he scrabbled his boots against the dais. If he could gain purchase, perhaps he could run off swiftly enough to drag them all with him.

But, alas. They hauled him down the steps onto the floor.

Beyond the dais, Mr. Fitzroy and the king stopped before a door. Mr. Fitzroy glanced back, only once.

At the other end of the room, the Runners clambered in, followed by still more guards.

Pish fronted them, brandishing a pistol. "Hold fast, every man of you!"

Thank God for that. Pish would try to arrest Will's doubles—and his hand would pass through them. He would see the truth, and he would tell these people Will was not their enemy.

Pish strode up behind one of the doubles and clamped a hand upon its shoulder.

His hand did not pass through air. It thudded against flesh and bone.

The double twisted from under Pish's hand and threw a punch that dashed the constable off his feet.

But—they weren't *real*. The king hadn't been real. Will had dived directly through his midst. And the double Lady Isabella touched—

He found her in the crowd.

She stood fast in the midst of the tumult and shook her head at him, eyes wide.

At the rear of the room, something flew from Rose's shadowed balcony.

A stone.

It hurtled into one of the illusions—and passed through in a glitter of light shards.

Will started breathing again.

Some of them were illusions then. For a wonder, *that* was the sanest fact of the night.

And Rose . . . Rose was his only advantage.

He surrendered to the guards and let them haul him across the room, towards the doors, towards Rose's balcony. He even hastened his steps until he was almost dragging them.

"Hie, laddie—in haste for a Norway neckcloth?"

Let Rose see him. Let her know it was truly *him*, so she didn't end up clouting him in the head. And let her realize what he needed her to do.

Behind the balcony railing, she stood in her black coat. Her white eyes stared from the crooked mask. She raised an arm and swung the sling.

With a snap of her wrist, the stone flew free. It arched over Will's head and cracked into the forehead of a guard at his left.

With a howl, the man slapped both hands to his bleeding forehead. "Ow! Me head! I'm shot—am I shot?"

*Thank you, Rose.*

Will wrenched his left arm free. He pirouetted into the guards on his right, twisting too fast for them to recover their balance. He ripped free—with his shoulder still intact, thank the Lord.

Then he gathered himself, and he ran. He passed Pish—still sprawled on the floor—and gave him one backward glance.

Something shifted in Pish's face. It was recognition almost, as if he saw the difference between Will and the doubles.

Pish groped for his fallen pistol. "Hie there!"

Will kept running. He must reach Mr. Fitzroy. That was the only way to end this. Only Mr. Fitzroy could prove the truth of what was happening here tonight. Only Mr. Fitzroy could free Tom.

"Aren't you going to stop these fellows?" Pish hollered.

But . . . Will could hardly leave these frightened, clamoring, *dying* people to their fates.

Of course, if he went darting amongst the illusions, the guards would likely shoot him. And then Mr. Fitzroy would surely escape.

Still, he was nearly the only person who knew what was happening here. Certainly, he was the only one with a chance of standing against the doubles.

With a groan, he brought his speed back under control and slowed. He scanned the pandemonium.

Perhaps as many as two dozen doubles now thrashed through the crowd, wielding cutlass pistols and daggers. Difficult to tell which were nothing but light and air and which were meat and muscle.

In the far corner, nearing the door, a cutlass flashed and blood spurted. That was real enough. Another dissenter cut down? Or was it all random, senseless chaos?

He blasted across the room, scarcely dodging innocent people.

Pish hollered again, words lost in the wind.

Will leapt the body of his double's fallen victim.

The double looked up in time to see Will coming.

Will extended his arms, half expecting to catch nothing but air as he had with the king. But what his arms closed about this time was substantial enough.

Air left the double's body in a great *whoof*. He struck the polished wood floor all the harder for Will's weight atop him. Above the mashed collar, his mouth—Will's mouth—opened in a gasp before the jolt of the floor clacked his teeth together.

Will smashed his iron knuckles into the double's face.

The double's face contorted. But the skin of his cheek changed not a jot. No mark of the blow. No blood. No bruising.

Will grasped at the man's eye-shields. He would rip them away and see if this monster's eyes were his own staring back at him.

His fingers found nothing. They passed through the image of the shields and collided with the softness of eyeballs.

Dazedly, the man yelped and reached for Will's hand.

Will hit him again, and the double's head lolled.

Will scrambled back.

Angels in heaven. Some of the doubles were illusions cast upon the bodies of real men. It was just as the paper at the Marshalsea had been real enough in its substance, but entirely false in its appearance.

He rose and surveyed the room.

People were dying. They were dying because Mr. Fitzroy desired it so—to remove his opponents, to cement his cause, *something*. But they were dying by *Will's* hand.

In the midst of it all, a double descended upon Lady Isabella. She reached to pass her hand through the illusion.

But this one was not light and air. It seized her gloved arm and dragged her forward.

Pish stood not too afar. He shouted at the double, then returned his attention to reloading his pistol.

Will gathered himself on his toes. He could reach her before Pish could fire. On the journey in between here and there, he would eliminate as many of these wretches as possible.

A whistle pierced overhead.

He looked up.

Rose snapped her sling, then with scarcely a glance at him, bent to reload.

He turned back. Her stone passed through a double that was entirely an illusion: it exploded a golden hole through its midst. The hole instantly healed over.

A second stone sailed over his head. This one smacked into the back of a double's neck, and the man slapped at the wound.

That was all Will needed.

He surged forward. Following the guidance of Rose's stones, he blasted straight through the pure illusions. They scattered as prismatic sparks. Doubtless, they promptly re-coalesced behind him, but the show of lights elicited people's gasps.

Where Rose's stones did not penetrate, he adjusted his balance and swept low. Arms outstretched, he swiped the imposters' feet from under them. The Runners could deal with them in his wake.

He erupted past Pish and thrust aside the man's extended pistol. "Stay! You might wound her!"

He reached Lady Isabella before her captor could turn. He leapt. From the advantage of the added height, he hammered his iron-clad fist into the double's temple. The man reeled two steps back, then collapsed, pulling her halfway down with him.

She stripped his hand from her arm. Her color was high, and she breathed ferociously.

Pish shoved over to them. He worked his mouth like an astonished fish. "What is happening here?"

"'Tis . . . hard to explain," Will said.

"Well . . ." Pish raised his pistol. "You're under arrest."

Frustration rolled over him. "You know I'm not one of them!"

Pish's eye twitched. "Yes. But still wanted for murder, I believe?"

"I'm hardly the one killing people tonight, am I?"

Lady Isabella caught at Will's coat. "My grandfather!"

What happened to *thank you*?

"Some of these *things* took him into the back hall!" She pointed towards the door through which Mr. Fitzroy and the "king" had disappeared.

Will's heart stuttered. "Did he dissent?"

"What?"

"Did he disagree with Fitzroy? Or wait—they're friends, yes?" The old anger rumbled.

She clutched his sleeve. "Please!"

Haste churned within him. He shook his head. "I must go. I must find Mr. Fitzroy before he escapes."

"But—" She firmed her jaw and snatched Will's pistol. "Then I shall do it!"

Pish kept his own pistol trained upon Will. "Steady on, my lady."

Will breathed hard, trying to clear his head. Perhaps Lord Carstone was in danger, perhaps not. Either way . . .

He extended his hand to Isabella. "I'll find him."

She closed her eyes and returned the pistol. "Thank you."

Pish shook his head. "You're going nowhere, Master Hardy."

Will turned to him. "I can thrust aside your arm before you can pull the trigger. If you *do* pull it, you'll risk injuring someone else. So *don't* pull it." He held Pish's gaze for one long second—long enough that Pish *could* have shot him had he truly desired.

Lady Isabella laid a hand on Pish's sleeve. "Please, allow him to leave this time—"

Pish scowled. "Well. Way things are going, certainly seems there should be a next time." He lowered the pistol.

Will gave him a nod. "Thank you. Keep her in safety."

Then he ran.

By the time he reached the far end of the room, he had gathered speed enough to clear the dais. He landed at the other side and skidded on the waxed floor. He smacked into the wall and pushed off, running down its length to gain the door through which Mr. Fitzroy had disappeared.

It was ajar. He pushed through and entered the comparative shadows of a broad hallway that continued for at least fifty feet, lit by genuine gas lamps.

To the right, a red-carpeted staircase curved upwards. Halfway up, two copies of himself escorted a tall, silver-headed man—and Mr. Fitzroy. The image of the king was nowhere to be seen.

The elder man, Lord Carstone, protested volubly. "Ruffians, does your impudence know no bounds? An attack upon the king is an act of war! You shall be drawn and quartered as traitors!"

"God have mercy," one double spoke. "Does he never shut his great gob?" He raised his pistol above Lord Carstone's head.

Will darted forward. "Wait!" He leapt at the curve halfway up the stairs. One hand on the banister, he swung up and over.

The doubles staggered back against the opposite banister. "How're you doin' that then?"

One raised his chin. "It's him. The real one! Ain't you?"

Will drew his pistol. "Ain't I though?"

Of a sudden, he wished he weren't. What in heaven's name was he doing here—a gun in hand? A mask on his face? And protecting Lord Carstone, of all men?

He'd started out to earn some money, save Tom, and rescue a few folk from robbers along the way.

Now, before the sun rose tomorrow, the entire city would think him the ruthless leader of the most vile bandit gang ever known.

Mr. Fitzroy looked back at him, face firm, eyes hard. He held no pistol, no obvious weapon. A double gripped his arm, as if he were also a prisoner.

Or perhaps just putting on a show for Lord Carstone?

Will grasped Lord Carstone's elbow. "Sir—"

Lord Carstone wrenched free. "How dare you lay hands on me?"

Never before had Will been so near to the man.

248 – K.M. WEILAND

He was massive. Even past seventy, he filled the broad shoulders of his fine dark coat. His head was a griffin's—never handsome, but always resolute, always noble. His fine gray hair receded from an impressive expanse of forehead. Within the flat creases of his jowls, his jaw remained adamant.

His only resemblance to his granddaughter was in the smoke blue of his eyes—which, like hers, saw what they *wished* to see.

"Lord Carstone—you must accompany me."

The man looked down his patrician nose. "From your voice, you are a Surrey lad. More the shame to you."

Will couldn't help himself. "Not all of Surrey is so proud to claim you either."

Lord Carstone reared back. "Insolent pup!"

Mr. Fitzroy remained still, watching Will, waiting for him to make a move.

What was *Fitzroy's* move here?

He couldn't defeat Will physically. But these two doubles answered to him, and they were armed.

"Come on then, matey," one said to Will. "You're outnumbered, you see? Why not move out of the way. We haven't all night here." He twitched his pistol.

It had been a bit of a ruse when Will told Pish he could thrust the pistol aside before it could be fired. If the man's finger closed upon the trigger before Will moved, Will would have nary a chance. But if he moved *before* the trigger were pulled . . .

He leapt forward and pushed with both hands, thrusting the two pistols wide of his body. One exploded. He surged up two steps, ripped away the pistols, and cast them behind him. Before the men regained balance, he dragged both Lord Carstone and Mr. Fitzroy back and toppled them down the stairs.

Directly between the doubles now, he caught each by the shoulder and shoved hard. Yelping, they toppled over the banister, one by the force of the push alone, the other with the added aid of Will's boot. They smashed to the oaken floor and were still.

Will spun back.

Both Lord Carstone and Mr. Fitzroy had landed at the bottom of the stairs. Mr. Fitzroy had already rolled to his knees and was assisting Lord Carstone.

The earl's hair was mussed now. His cravat had started to unwind. Leaning heavily upon Mr. Fitzroy, he gained his knees. "My lord, are you injured?" Mr. Fitzroy watched Will steadily. He appeared wary—as he should. But something in his face hinted at amusement, as if a jest were in play and he awaited its effect.

"I will be *fine*, sir," Lord Carstone responded. "No thanks to this cad. What are you about, sirrah?"

Pistol still in hand, Will started down the stairs. "My lord, you're in danger. Mr. Fitzroy is no friend to you, believe me. He knows not even what the word means."

Lord Carstone guffawed. It sounded a bit shaky. He narrowed his eyes. "Pray, do not speak of what you can have no possible knowledge."

Will descended another step. "My lord, you must return to your granddaughter and your guests, and you must leave this man to me. Everything occurring tonight—"

"My lord, have a care!" With impressive quickness, Mr. Fitzroy snatched up the double's emptied pistol, lying on the floor, and smashed its butt against the base of Lord Carstone's skull.

Will lunged. "No!"

The old man's eyes rolled up. He crumpled.

Mr. Fitzroy caught Lord Carstone and lowered him to the floor. He looked up at Will, his eyes alight. A little smile pressed his mouth.

Will roared his frustration. Give him two seconds more and he would have this man in his grasp.

Unfortunately, it required only a single second for the world around him to explode—into shards of light and impossible visions.

# CHAPTER 26

IN FRONT OF Will, the stairway disappeared. Where a second before, lush red carpet covered the steps, now a massive pit gaped.

It was an illusion. Nothing but a grand illusion.

He *knew* that.

Still, he teetered at the maw's edge. The depth of the drop swirled his vision, and the old dizziness clawed his stomach.

That was enough to make the image falter. It stuttered like a reflection in a troubled pool.

He blinked hard.

Beyond the pit, Mr. Fitzroy stood beside an unconscious Lord Carstone. He had reclaimed the other pistol—the one still containing its load of powder and lead.

"Master Will Hardy. I hear they are calling you the Wayfarer." He smiled the polished smile of a consummate actor. "Colorful."

Will's own pistol hung heavy in his hand. Could he raise it before Mr. Fitzroy pulled off a shot? Sweat slicked his palm. Never had he dreamt he would have cause to pull the trigger at a man.

"I hear they're calling *you* Prime Minister—as you predicted."

Mr. Fitzroy inclined his head. "Indeed."

"Had your new abilities aught to do with that?"

"Every man uses the gifts he has been given."

"Were you given them? Or did you steal them from Dr. Silas?"

"No more than you. I had no wish for his death. How many more secrets might he have uncovered?"

Will studied the gaping hole in the stairway. He needed only to walk through it. But what if it *weren't* a mere illusion? What if it had substance, as did some of the doubles?

He swallowed, mouth parched. "You—were infected by the plague?"

"Infected?" Mr. Fitzroy's ready smile flashed. "You call this infection? It is magic, it is a miracle. The world is ours to rule, guide, and care for."

"*Care* for? People died tonight. You've killed them!" His pulse hammered in his temples. "And why?"

"They were obstacles."

"Simply that?"

Mr. Fitzroy tempered his smile. "You are very young, Will Hardy. You have not the experience to know the regard of men is not something you earn. It is something you take." He tilted his head. "Or perhaps you do know? Your rumored exploits *are* impressive."

"That's different. I am aiding people."

"And I am not?"

"What you said tonight—your great plan to save the poor? You're not going to save them." Suspicion congealed into full-blown realization. "You're going to destroy them. But . . . why? Why should you even care?"

Now Mr. Fitzroy's smile disappeared. "When first I spoke to you about this, you thought *you* were amongst the poor I spoke of."

Will held his silence.

"Well, you were not. You had yet no idea, did you? Now, you do. I know you have dwelt among them. You have seen. Are they poor only in their pockets? Or is it in their very souls?" He raised an eyebrow. "Which is it?"

A chill—like the skittering of rats—crossed Will's skin. "They're not all of them criminals." Not all the poor lived within the wretched confines of St. Giles. And even within Seven Dials, there were innocents. "Some are children, with no choice."

Children like Rose. Children like . . . Blue-Eyed Jem.

He shivered.

Mr. Fitzroy snorted. "Do not blind yourself with the convenient lies of society. There are *always* choices."

"Yes—live or die."

"Yet it is still a choice, is it not?" His eyes burned. "Just as it is a choice to wallow in the wretchedness into which one is born—or to fight and claw for respect. A man who remains in the same fallow bed in which he is born is a man without regard even for himself. You have seen these men. I know you have."

Will breathed out, hard. "So you would come to power to slaughter them—for their lack of ambition? For their lack of opportunity? Because they are held back by ignorance and fear?"

The strain on Mr. Fitzroy seemed greater now. His eyes—his blue, blue eyes—were those of an old man. But they remained unrelenting for all that.

"I am not on this earth to save them. I am on this earth to create a place in which their world does not even exist. There *is* no saving it. I will cut it out. I will obliterate it."

"Why?" The word ripped up from Will's very center. "Because you care so much about society? About England? Or . . ." And suddenly Will knew. Suddenly, it all came together. "Or because you would wipe out every remnant of your own dark past?"

Mr. Fitzroy's face stilled.

Could it be? The great Mr. James Fitzroy—Prime Minister of England—the man from nowhere—could it be where he was really from was Seven Dials?

He was Mr. Monarch's vaunted Blue-Eyed Jem, so clever and fast with his fingers he'd found a way out—and not just *out*, but all the way to the very top of society.

"*You* tried to kill me," Will said. "You set that trap for me. Why? Am I such a threat to you? Because I know Mr. Monarch? That's it, isn't it?"

Mr. Fitzroy's face grew darker yet. "What I have seen, I have seen. What I will do, I will do."

Will struggled to give it all meaning. That Mr. Fitzroy had risen so high from so low—did it make him the less admirable or the more? Or *had* he indeed risen so very far after all?

A tremendous rush of disappointment flooded Will. The what-could-have-beens seemed the greatest waste of all.

He shook his head. "I thought you a great man. I almost followed you."

"Follow me yet." Mr. Fitzroy's studied mask of composure slid back in place. "My war is not with you. It never has been. Whether you will be a casualty or not may be your own choice. It is an age of miracles, Will. You and I alone, we are the stewards of a great power." He took half a step forward. "Will you join me? We are the only two of our kind. You should be at my side."

Even now, the man's words were golden.

And even now, part of Will's heart yearned towards him. Join him, follow him, do something that had never been done, be part of something that had never been seen. They could write their names in monuments of gold and granite.

"You want the world to bow at your feet?" Fitzroy gestured to Lord Carstone's fallen body. "You want him to bow? Their deference—their adoration even—it is ours now. We need not even take it. We need only . . . show them."

He was correct, in a way. Hadn't Will already experienced that these past days? The name of the Wayfarer was in every man's mouth. Soon enough, they'd fling their daughters and their dowries at his feet.

But why? Because they thought he was doing some great deed? Because the drama of it all impressed them?

He shook his head. "It's not real. It's not respect. It's . . ." He looked about. "An illusion."

Fitzroy laughed. "Of course. What is *life* if not an illusion? Power exists only when people believe in it."

The truth of his words assaulted Will. Had everything Will believed in been a lie? Everything Tom had taught him?

If the world's adulation could be gained by a man like Fitzroy, doing what he was doing here tonight, then what was it but a tawdry trick? A chunk of lead glinting in the sunlight?

If *that* were the path to success, what was the point in honor, in dignity, in rectitude? What was the point of walking this rocky road in his bare feet, when at its end it proved nothing *but* endless road?

He shook his head. "The people won't believe in you." But

they *would*. He half believed himself.

Fitzroy spread his hands. "You want this life, Will."

From both palms, incredible visions blossomed. In swirling sparks of gold and scarlet, images rose: impossible wealth, impossible beauty. They were clouds—insubstantial and fleeting: beautiful women in silk gowns—fine horses and finer carriages—lush and winding gardens—rooms paved in gilt.

"I know you want it," Fitzroy said. "But if ever you plan to claim it, you must first find the honesty to acknowledge what it is." He flicked his fingers. "It is a lie, like all the rest."

The images sped outward from him and grew to full size within the room, solidifying into its opulent reality.

"The lie of it matters not," Fitzroy said. "*We* recognize it, and we use it."

Will shook his head. "You'll never evade notice. People will see."

"Precisely. And what they see is what they will believe."

From beyond the doors, the sounds of chaos filtered back. Footsteps still thundered. People were still screaming. A gunshot cracked.

Time was running out—one way or the other. If the soldiers and doubles in the other room triumphed, it would be only minutes before they arrived to bolster their master.

Even if they were defeated, the Runners would still be coming for Will.

Perhaps Fitzroy did possess some slight reason to want Will at his side. But it was clear, after everything he had done tonight, he certainly wouldn't balk at eliminating Will the instant he became a greater threat than he was a benefit.

Where, then, did that leave them?

It left them each with a loaded pistol in hand.

Will raised his pistol—in a blur—and pointed it at Fitzroy's forehead.

The man flinched, but only just. He kept his own firearm at his side. "Well, then."

"My master, Tom Colville." Will spoke quickly, nearly choking in his haste. "You purchased his debt from Lord Carstone."

Surprise flickered over Fitzroy's face.

"I read your name within the ledger. But others cannot see it."
Fitzroy frowned. "Indeed?"

"Remove the illusion on the prison's books. Release Tom.
You will receive precisely the sum you are owed."

Fitzroy cocked his head. "Or the alternative? You will . . . shoot
me?" His smile surfaced. "If you do that, you will never be able
to reveal the truth of the illusion to your master's guards."

If Fitzroy should die, would the illusions be destroyed? Or
would they remain forever?

Will tightened his finger on the trigger. He did not pull it.

"I will reveal the truth of your past." The words rushed from
him instinctively.

Fitzroy's smile vanished. His face darkened. "No, you will
not."

"Do you think people will embrace you once they know what
you were?" Will leant into the full power of this new weapon.
"Do you think they will not then see the truth of what you are
doing?"

A flush rose on Fitzroy's cheeks. The cords in his neck bulged.

This truth had *always* been Will's weapon to wield, if only he
had known it. This was the reason Fitzroy had cast him aside
after Will's first encounter with Rose and Lifty and the Runners. Perhaps, too, this reason—as much as the threat of Will's
abilities—had caused Fitzroy to force Will into his trap at the
church.

Will was dangerous, not only because he was powerful, but
because he was far too close to this great dark secret that haunt-
ed Fitzroy.

"So." Will planted his foot within the illusion of the pit separating them. With a golden glimmer, his boot passed through
and found solid footing. "Release Tom."

Fitzroy held his ground. "No." The emotion drained from
his face. The tension in his neck disappeared. "No. Attempt
that gambit and you remove any possible remaining choice but
for me to destroy you. Tom Colville will remain as he is. He
is *my* prisoner. His life is in my hand. If you raise your voice
against me, I will destroy him as well. Do you understand that,
Will Hardy?"

The words were a fist in his belly—because they were the truest thing Fitzroy had said all night. Of *course* Fitzroy could control Tom's presence in the Marshalsea.

After tonight, what couldn't he control? The entire city would see what he wanted them to see, do what he wanted them to do.

After tonight, there would be no halting him.

Will must shoot the man, but not kill him. He could not risk Fitzroy's death. He would wound him. He would rush upon him, and he would pound him into reason and submission.

Fitzroy's eye twitched.

Will clenched his finger upon the trigger.

The room erupted. Dozens upon dozens of men sprouted up from the stairway, every single one of them either Fitzroy or himself.

In the corner of Will's vision, Fitzroy appeared at the step beside him. He swung his pistol hard at Will's head.

# CHAPTER 27

WILL DUCKED.

Fitzroy's pistol passed over his face and washed his vision in glittering light.

An illusion. Of course it was not real. Will knew it was not real—and yet still he reacted to it.

He spun back and fired at where Fitzroy stood at the foot of the stairs. Against his palm, the pistol recoiled in a burst of spark and smoke.

The pistol's ball smashed through Fitzroy's chest—but in a spew of light, not blood.

Even before his mind completed its recognition of what had happened, Will threw himself down onto the steps. He skidded through the illusions—all of them staring at him with either Fitzroy's face or his own. Rainbows dazzled him.

A shot ripped a golden path up the crowded stairs.

His already engaged momentum gave him extra speed enough to dodge it—most of it. The ball nicked the heavy twist of the makeshift dagger strapped to his upper arm. Pain smashed against the bone, and he choked on a cry.

He regained his feet and leapt down the remaining half of the stairs.

As one, the illusions followed. They reached for him. They clawed at his face, at his pained arm, at his clothing. He passed through them as if through whispers of air, but the visual sensation bore upon his brain, as if he were in the midst of a true crush. He gritted his teeth and pressed on.

Fitzroy—the real Fitzroy—had been standing at the bottom of the stairs beside Lord Carstone. That had been but a second past. However swift Fitzroy's illusions, the man himself could not have moved far.

Will rounded the newel post.

Before him, Fitzroy stood, half turned away, reloading the pistol.

Will rushed him. With the iron upon his knuckles, he hammered his fist at Fitzroy's head.

His hand met nothing but air. Balance compromised, he pitched forward. Before he hit the floor, he hurled his weight back and spun.

Even as he turned, Fitzroy threw his fist against his jaw—and this time it was a true blow of weight and reality.

Will staggered back through more illusions. Lights danced before him, from within his brain as much as from without. The curving banister smashed into him from behind.

He shook his head hard to clear his thoughts. He spun back.

Fitzroy stood before him. A hidden smile lit the corner of his mouth.

Again, Will rushed him. Again, his hand passed through nothing.

But this time, a movement whispered behind him.

Will spun.

One of his doubles clipped his chin and sent him sprawling again.

Was it one of the two doubles whom he had knocked over the banister when first he found Fitzroy with Lord Carstone? Or was it Fitzroy under the disguise?

The double struck him again, with the pistol butt.

Will lunged forward, tried to catch an arm or a leg—anything solid.

The double caught Will's ankle with his toe. He upended Will upon the floor and pounded a kick under Will's ribs.

The lights faded to black. Will curled up and started rolling. He bumped the base of the stairway and dragged himself to his feet.

Every breath detonated pain in his chest. He groped behind

for the banister and kept it at his back. Fitzroy might still be able to clout him from the stairs above, but it narrowed the possibilities for attack.

He dragged the now-bent rod from its sheath on his aching arm. His vision swam, the dizziness as blinding as when atop a high building.

All about him, the illusions were milling, grinning, laughing. But they seemed less permanent than before. They flickered, the colors swirling, like wasted paint down a rivulet in the street.

Nearby, a ramrod scraped a pistol barrel.

Through the flickering illusions, Will glimpsed Fitzroy.

The man stood near the fallen body of one of the doubles Will had cast over the banister. The image of Will's costume disguising both men stuttered—revealing Fitzroy's fine party clothes and the double's broadcloth and gaiters.

Will shook his head, hard.

The dizziness cleared, and the illusions sprang back, full force.

In a battle of speed and strength, he could best Fitzroy. But not like this. Not when he couldn't see his opponent. Not unarmed against a man with a pistol.

Sweat trickled down his neck.

Fitzroy would be able to see *him*. He would know which of the doubles were illusions and which was Will. In another moment, he would shoot Will, and that would be the end.

Fitzroy would not even be wasting his opportunity to personify Will as the enemy in his new campaign. All he needed for that was the *image* of Will. He had that in legions.

Will's one chance was to move—and continue moving.

He pushed away from the banister and rushed through the illusions, disintegrating them briefly into shards of light.

If he only could strike upon Fitzroy's substance, he'd have him. He swiped both hands before his face, as if clearing cobwebs. His ears must serve him where his eyes could not. At best, he would have but a single chance. He strained to listen.

Then he heard it: a sole scuffed the polished floor. Cloth whispered. The hammer of a pistol locked.

He spun right.

Within two seconds, he covered ten feet. He smashed into bone and flesh. The shot exploded beside his head, the glare of sparks inches from his eye-shields.

He collided with what looked to be himself—Fitzroy still in disguise. They tumbled to the floor.

Fitzroy's breath whoofed a deep exhale. The pistol clattered away.

Will rolled to his knees and planted one hand upon Fitzroy's chest. With the other, he stabbed down hard with the twisted metal rod.

Fitzroy jerked away, not fast enough. The rod's point caught him above the collarbone and passed through flesh. He roared.

All through the room, white light surged. Every single one of the illusions blinked into nothing, as if devoured in a blast of white heat.

The light seared Will's eyes, blinding him even behind his eye-shields.

Beneath him, Fitzroy bucked, and out of the white light, a blow smashed into Will's jaw.

He sprawled sideways, loosing the rod. Scrambling, he tried to get his feet under him.

Once more dizziness swirled amidst the pain, and he opened his eyes to find Fitzroy fleeing across the room: empty pistol in one hand, the other clamped to the flesh wound in his shoulder.

Will gathered himself, and he ran.

He was yet halfway across the room when Fitzroy reached a door in the far wall. Fitzroy glanced back once, blood streaking from eyes and nose. He disappeared behind the door.

Will's dizziness cleared.

The illusions surged back into place. Now, they were *all* Will.

He collided with the door and wrenched at the latch. Locked, naturally.

Fitzroy could hide anywhere. He could disguise himself as anyone, paint himself into any invisible corner. He would escape this night, and Will would not find him.

By tomorrow, *Will* would be the one hunted.

He and Tom, both.

The far door smashed open. Soldiers and Runners alike

stopped short at the army of Wills filling the room. Then they charged, hacking and slashing.

Will sidled along the wall. He'd sneak out behind them. If once they found him, he would be well and truly dead.

At the rear of the crowd, Pish's angular face—flushed with battle—appeared. Will growled. Pish was supposed to have remained with Lady Isabella.

*Lady Isabella—Lord Carstone . . .*

He looked back at the base of the stairs. Let the soldiers and the Runners find the earl. Lord Carstone would be safe with them.

Provided, of course, they did not trample him ere they noticed him.

A small, insistent part of his brain said: *So be it.* Will owed naught to Lord Carstone. The man had sided with Fitzroy.

Still, he hesitated.

From within the swarm of pure illusions, one of the original doubles—identifiable by his uncertain movements—staggered upright. With his disguise back in place, he appeared identical to Will. It was like peering into a mirror.

Not-Will took one look at the chaos, and he turned and he ran. A Runner caught his arm, and the double spat at the man's face before shoving him off and escaping into the main room.

On the morrow, everyone would believe *that* man was Will.

God help him, he was *not* that man.

Gathering his remaining speed, he ran to the stairs. He leapt and managed to get his aching arm high enough to catch the banister, halfway up. He swung himself over, then blasted down to the bottom of the stairway.

Lord Carstone had risen to hands and knees. A mat of blood darkened the back of his head. Unsteadily, he stared at the swarm of violence.

Will caught him under both arms and hoisted him up. The earl was almost a foot taller than he, and his weight felt that of a yearling bullock.

Lord Carstone had yet only wits enough to stammer. "What—how dare you—who are you—?"

"I'm not your enemy!" Will had to shout above the clamor. "I'm taking you to safety!"

A score of feet away, Pish saw Lord Carstone and jerked his pistol to bear on Will. Then he looked again and scowled.

As fast as he dared, Will sped across the room, dragging Lord Carstone along. Before him, the illusions scattered. A red-coated soldier struck at him with a cutlass, and he barely dodged.

He thrust Lord Carstone into Pish's arms. "See him to his granddaughter. Tell her I fulfilled my promise."

"Heaven be gracious!" Pish staggered under Lord Carstone's weight. "Where are all these fellows coming from? Who's doing this? Are you doing this?"

"What do you think?"

Pish shifted his mouth back and forth. He'd dearly love to cast the blame all on Will.

Will gripped Pish's shoulder. "You were correct about the politics."

Pish tipped back his head. A new light entered his eyes. "Ah."

Will gave Lord Carstone a little push. "Now get him out of here."

From behind, a shouting soldier charged Will.

Once more, energy buzzed through his weary muscles. He ran for the stairs and swung over the banister, coat flapping. At the top, he blasted through the doors—mercifully unlocked—and slammed them behind him.

The near silence engulfed him so surely he almost lost his balance.

Ahead stretched a dark hallway, lit at the end by an open doorway. Pain and exhaustion battered him as he started jogging.

There would be no pursuing Fitzroy tonight. All that remained was to collect Rose and race to the Marshalsea. Fitzroy knew Will's weakness now.

He swung around the corner onto an open gallery that spanned the length of the great ballroom.

Below, guests still fled, trampling over and around one another. Ladies' skirts were torn. Gentlemen's chapeaux-bras had been cast aside. Two dozen bodies scattered the floor. Most were doubles. A few of the fallen guests were obviously swooning and not dead. Even still, the chaos was catastrophic.

Doubles filled the room, but the majority seemed illusions only now. In their haste, the guests failed to recognize the difference. They ran shrieking from the illusions as frantically as they had the actual murderers.

Ahead of him, in the balcony above the foyer, Rose crouched in the shadows, watching from behind her crooked mask. She must have exhausted her pile of stones.

She saw him and shot to her feet, beckoning urgently.

To his left, a shadow detached from the wall.

He flinched around, reflexes firing.

But it wasn't Fitzroy. It wasn't a disguised double.

It was a woman in a gown of aubergine.

Mrs. Fitzroy.

He sidestepped.

Her eyes were bloodshot. "My husband."

"This is his doing." His voice came out a dry croak.

She glided forward, gown whispering against the floor. "There is something you should know." The corners of her mouth pinched. "My husband's power? It is an idea. *You* cannot combat an idea."

Tonight had done nothing to disprove that.

He swallowed. "He has *murdered* people. You support him in this?"

She smiled, but only with her mouth; her eyes were unchanging, unflinching. The contrast was startling, even frightening. "I support him." The smile faded, and then there was *only* obdurate cold. "That is enough."

He had no words for her. Even had she any influence with her husband, what could he say that would shake her?

He took a step away, still watching her—then another step and another.

He'd no time for words with her.

He ran to the end of the gallery.

Around the corner, Rose gestured from her balcony. "C'mon!"

He gathered speed enough to jump up and land a foot at the railing at the gallery's end. He launched off and flew across the dozen or so feet to catch hold of her balcony.

As he clambered over the railing, she threw her things into her bag. "Near scared me from my thinking, didn't you?" She glanced at his bedraggled appearance. "Get him?"

"Not quite." He opened the double glass doors to the outside. "We must leave. Tom's in danger."

Below, the long drive was frenzied with fleeing carriages.

He bounced onto the railing and crouched there, one hand hooked under the banister for support.

Dizziness swirled, but not before he caught sight of Lady Isabella's golden hair.

She and Pish escorted her towering grandfather down the drive to a waiting carriage. Not their own, probably, since this was their house and they'd no transportation awaiting them like the others.

He breathed out.

She was safe, and would remain safe as long as Fitzroy had reason to want her for Henry's wife.

Seeming to sense his eyes upon her, she looked up. He would be only a silhouette at the railing—a gargoyle in a flapping coat. But she raised a hand. It was difficult to tell in the flickering light, but it seemed almost as if she might have kissed it first.

For that one instant, his pains blinked from existence.

Rose peered over the railing. "Hmp. Ladies like that—always needing rescuing."

He refrained from pointing out he'd rescued *her* this afternoon.

Instead, he grabbed her arm and swung her onto his aching back. "Come along. This night isn't over."

# CHAPTER 28

THE MARSHALSEA WAS strangely alight. From within the walls, too many voices echoed. A vague glow emanated above the yard. Most of the barred windows flickered with rushlights.

Battered though he was, Will had pushed himself all the way across the river from Regent's Park. His heart felt like a young hare thumping in his chest. At the end of every beat, his vision threatened blackness.

Gasping, he halted beneath the wall and let Rose slide from his back. She'd doubled in weight since the beginning of the evening, even without her parcel of rocks.

He leant against his knees, heaving air in and out of his burning chest.

"Here now." She used her mask to wipe sweat from his forehead. "Don't fall over on me. Nobody could've got here faster'n you, eh?"

He had no breath to explain Fitzroy's alarming new capabilities.

She looked at him critically. "What *was* all that back there? Never seen the like."

"Me either," he rasped.

Except, of course, for the Marshalsea ledger. And Lifty's ten-shilling note from the other day. And . . . the warrant officer Hale on the day of Dr. Silas's death.

He stood quickly enough for the street to wobble. "I don't believe it."

"What?"

He should have realized before. The man staggering about

outside Dr. Silas's barn *hadn't* been Hale. It had been Fitzroy, instinctively using his new abilities. No wonder the ridiculous charges had stuck. If Fitzroy, as a gentleman, had subsequently pulled weight with the magistrate, of *course* they had stuck.

He clenched his fists. "Fitzroy is the reason I'm wanted for murder."

"What do you mean?"

"Doesn't matter now."

"'Course it does."

"I think . . . I think he's Blue-Eyed Jem."

"What?" Her eyes popped wide, then narrowed thoughtfully. "So Fitzroy—he's like you, isn't he? Only . . ." She screwed up her face.

Will said it for her. "He's better."

Unlike Will, Fitzroy had sought this. He might not have known precisely what would happen to him or how his abilities would manifest. But he hadn't been caught with his feet flat upon the ground as Will had.

More than that, the Affery plague had manifested within Fitzroy rather more usefully than it had in Will.

He looked down at his hands—still trembling from the long run. "Wait here."

She snatched his sleeve. "You're not leaving me." Her voice cracked at the last word.

The thought of jumping her up the wall rolled pain through his bones. But if something happened to her down here . . .? Better to keep everyone he needed to protect all in one place.

"Come on then."

He didn't give her time to tie her mask in place. He swung her onto his back, her calves over his hipbones and her arms about his neck. He backed up to gain the running start he'd need.

He made it up, scarcely, and crouched at the top amidst the spikes.

The voices were clearer now. People thronged the yard, shouting their discontent. There were now far more of them than should be contained within this one prison. The numbers had only grown since this afternoon.

Turnkeys and guards lurked at the crowd's perimeter, too few to manage the influx.

In the torchlight, Postelwaite stood near to the Lodge door, hands raised. "Now, now, this is but a momentary tribulation. 'Twill all be sorted by morning."

"I should not even be here!" a man shouted.

"Yes!" a woman added. "I have no debt, I've committed no crime!"

In the flickering light, Postelwaite swallowed hard. "Well . . ."

"Green about the gills, ain't he?" Rose whispered.

"Well," Postelwaite went on. "And 'tis quite singular and interesting, if you think on it. Something to tell your grandchildren, yes?"

"And where's Tom Colville? What've you done with him?"

Will stiffened, scanning the crowd to find the speaker—the heavyset bald chap named Claypole.

"And he's just fine, he is." Postelwaite sounded still more nervous. "Snug in his room. But we can't be having no ringleaders, you know—not on a night like this."

The crowd shifted, milling and murmuring, somewhere between fear and anger. The whole place was a powder keg waiting for a spark—which was probably as Fitzroy intended.

"Best check his room," Rose said.

Will nodded, his heart pounding.

As it developed, getting Rose down from the wall was a more difficult proposition than getting her up. The drop of thirty feet was one he could manage well enough on his own. But with her added weight, his ankles felt near to breaking when he hit the ground.

He pitched forward, almost landing on his face. Thanks to the darkness beneath the wall, the crowd paid no heed.

When they got there, Tom's room was locked.

Will leant his back against the corridor's opposite wall, ready to kick the latch with both feet.

"Have a care." Rose pushed him aside. "Don't bring the whole building down." She withdrew her lock picks and, in two breaths, clicked the latch. Before swinging the door open, she cupped both hands around the keyhole. "Hey," she whispershouted. "You in there, cully? It's Rose from t'other day—and your mate, Will."

Will snatched her back. Oh, perfect. Why *not* announce his arrival to whoever was in that room torturing Tom?

More panic surged, and he tamped it down.

He was being illogical—and hysterical. But why not? He was on the brink of collapse, he'd been beaten by an army of mirages, a madman was about to vilify him to all of London—and everything he'd done to help Tom might end in destruction.

Footsteps crossed the room and halted before the door. "Will—that you?"

The door opened. Silhouetted in the faint glow from the window, Tom stood with the fire iron in one hand and his pipe in the other.

The ball of fear that had been growing within Will's chest exploded into relief.

He seized Tom's shoulders hard enough to nearly topple him. "Thank God."

"Will— What is this? What's the matter?" Tom squinted. "Have you been brawling?"

Rose grunted. "You could say so." She pushed Will forward with both hands, then entered and closed the door.

Will kept one hand upon Tom's shoulder. "Everything's come to naught. Things have happened I didn't even know were possible—and I know more than most."

Tom shook his head. "Well, 'tis a sight more than I know—"

"I was right about your debt, everything—it is *all* irregular. You were bait, Tom, a pawn, insurance—I don't know what to call it—"

Tom's frown deepened. "Insurance—for what?"

"For . . . me, I think. So Fitzroy could control me should I cause problems."

"And guess what?" Rose said. "He went and caused problems."

"Fitzroy?" Tom said. "Mr. Fitzroy, your London friend?"

"He's not my friend. He never was. All this—all that's been happening, 'tis part of something he's been planning since before I met him. He's Prime Minister now."

"Prime Minister?" Tom blinked. "Heaven have mercy, Will, what are you involved in?"

"He's dangerous, Tom."

Tom pulled back. He wore his loose shirt untucked from his trousers, braces down. He closed his eyes, thinking. "But you're dangerous too, lad. Or so I hear?" He opened his eyes.

Rose grinned on her way to the window. "Ain't he though?"

"Not like Fitzroy," Will said. "What I can do? I can run swiftly, I can jump up the wall out there. But him? He can make people see things—anything he wants. A man can't fight that. Believe me, I tried." His whole body gave a great resounding throb.

"You didn't do so bad," Rose said.

"You didn't *see* the bad part."

Tom nudged Will's chin into the poor light. Likely, there was a sizable bruise or two for him to see. His eyes stilled, mouth shifting a little.

He released Will's face. "Not often I've known you to get the worst of a row."

That wasn't strictly true. Will had been thrashed many a time. Tom's meaning was more Will always gave as good as he got.

That hadn't happened tonight. Will had stabbed Fitzroy, of course. But it had ended as a mere flesh wound.

Yes, he admitted it: he was frightened. Before this, he had never been frightened of much. Angry, of course. But not frightened.

He was flailing in cold water over his head, just as Tom had warned. Will could have no proper place near Fitzroy—not as his protégé and certainly not as his opponent.

Fitzroy wanted to rain brimstone upon this wretched city? If he did or he didn't, it wasn't a question of Will's allowing it or not allowing it. It was beyond him. Best to concentrate on the things he *could* control.

He tried to calm the frantic edge in his voice. "Fitzroy promised he would kill you if I don't steer out of his way."

"And is that your plan?"

Will breathed in. "I know you disapprove of how I earned the money to pay your debt. But it is earned, and it is paid, down to the last farthing. That's true even if the guards won't believe it. I can get you out of here tonight. We'll escape—and Fitzroy won't be able to find us. It will be the end of it."

At the window, Rose flashed him a questing glance.

She'd have to come along for the time being—until he found a farmwife to take her in, so he and Tom could go on the run in earnest.

Arms crossed, Tom stared at the floor. He grunted. It took him a fair bit to process ideas sometimes. But Affery man though he might be, he was a soldier underneath it all.

Will had grown up on Tom's stories of the war on the Continent against the degenerate Frenchies. His tales were all swash and swagger. The twinkle in back of his eyes said he enjoyed impressing young Will. But there'd been darkness too. Sadness and regret peered from behind the tales.

Tom was a good-natured man, but he knew how to be serious. Deathly serious when need be.

He looked at Will. "What does Fitzroy want?"

"To wipe out poverty, he says. But he's not talking about setting it right. He's talking about killing it."

"Killing it *how*?"

"I don't know, killing people! People died tonight, Tom. How can I make you understand? And you're next. He has named you!" He took Tom's elbow, wanting to drag him away. "Please. It is my fault you're here a'tall. Fitzroy did this because of me—because I took up with him, because I was too blind to see what he was, because I preferred his lies to the truths you have always told me."

Tom took in a deep breath. He let it out. Then for the first time since the warrant officers had taken him, he smiled. "'Tis not your fault, Will."

"What?"

"'Tis not your fault." With his cold pipe clamped between his teeth, he shrugged his braces back up over his shoulders. "You're not the one doing wrong here, so don't go taking on responsibility for another man."

Will eyed him. "Why are you so cheerful?"

"Because." Tom swiped his coat off the bed. His mouth straightened, but in his eyes, a spark remained. "I no longer must sit in this wretched place with naught to do, wondering why the spin of the world dished me here."

Relief exploded from Will so intensely he felt as if he had been punched. "I'll have you out of here in two snaps."

Tom crossed the room to stand before him. "I'm not leaving."

Will felt another punch. "What?"

"We're going to stop this man."

"No, we're not! Have you not been listening? I can't stop him!"

The corner of Tom's grin tweaked back into view. It was the same expression whenever he was telling the old campaigning stories: jollity and sobriety all at once.

"You can stop him, Will. And I'm going to help you."

"Confound it, Tom. My abilities are paltry beside his! His are respectable. They're . . . impressive. People believe everything he tells them."

"I don't." Rose nodded towards Tom. "He don't." Then she gestured down to the packed courtyard. "Don't reckon those folks will be too keen on him what put 'em here, think?"

She had a point. This great influx of prisoners was no coincidence. If Fitzroy packed all his undesirables into prison, he could dispense with them the easier—and with more legitimacy.

"None of this is about me," Tom said.

That was true enough. Strictly speaking, Fitzroy had no real care at all for Will and Tom. He cared about his grand mission, his legacy, the adulation of the world for his great deeds in revolutionizing a society. He had larger concerns than just one man.

Will, however, couldn't afford that luxury.

"The only person I care about saving is you."

Tom looked at him steadily. "That's not true."

Will could see Fitzroy's plan unwinding before him: he would be imprisoning debtors, dissidents, anyone who looked suspicious. That would eliminate any threat from a tremendous portion of the city's lowest levels all at once.

But despite whatever he preached, he wouldn't begin with men who deserved punishment—men like Mr. Monarch. They were too dangerous, ensconced in the warrens of Seven Dials. It would take months to lay siege to the dens of iniquity Fitzroy truly burned to destroy.

In the meantime, innocents would suffer. People like Tom. People like Rose. People like old Trabb down in the yard.

Will stood very still. Even his heart stopped. "If I do aught to help these people, Fitzroy will know. He'll know it was me—and he will destroy you." Frustration balled inside him. "If you won't come with me, then all that remains is to kill Fitzroy."

"Will." Tom extended a tentative hand, as if Will were a skittish horse.

In an outburst of speed, he dashed aside Tom's arm.

Tom leant back, eyebrows lifted. He had no idea yet what Will could do. He'd seen him jump from a window and scale a wall. That was all.

"Don't be doing anything rash," Tom said. "Opposing this man? 'Tis one thing. But killing him? What do you know about killing?"

Will exhaled, hard, and looked Tom in the eye. "That I can do it."

He had wondered earlier tonight. But now he knew. Fitzroy had loosed this impossible energy within him—this frustration, this anger, this desperate need to *do* something. It was a whirlwind Fitzroy would reap.

But Tom was right. He forced himself to take a breath. Not now. Not in haste. Not in foolishness. However much he wished to have done with this battle, he *couldn't* fight Fitzroy face to face as they had tonight. Speed wouldn't win that battle.

What, then, did that leave for tonight but despair? Fitzroy had Tom in this box—and Tom, like a great oaf, refused to leave.

"What would *you* have me do?"

"You want to free me?"

"*Yes.*"

"Then free everyone."

"What? That would be . . . treason, probably."

"You said yourself half these people are here falsely. If you can do what you say you can—if the rumors about this Wayfarer are true—"

Will shifted.

"Then you can open those doors and set these people free."

Rose turned from the window. "If you let 'em go, they've a chance to fight."

"You're at the heart of this, Will. And if you are, so am I. Whatever's afoot here, 'tis bad, and from the sounds, there aren't many who even realize yet, much less many with the power to end it."

Will swallowed. Leaving London had been his goal all along. To remain now made it all seem a waste.

So much had changed so quickly.

In truth, he *didn't* want to walk away from Fitzroy. The man was as dangerous as he was seductive. With the power he held, he could lay waste to the city—to the country. After that, would he reach farther yet? Would he make Old Boney seem nothing but a bundle of feathers in a rigged cockfight?

Will desired Tom's safety. He desired to get shed of this city forever. But he did *not* desire victory for Mr. James Fitzroy.

"You want us to start a rebellion."

"Wouldn't say that necessarily," Tom said. "There's much yet to be learned before any drastic move is made."

Will grunted. As for himself, he'd always been more partial to learning as he went. He stalked to the window seat where Rose knelt.

Tom followed. "What will you do?"

"I won't free them. Fitzroy would only put them back." He glanced over his shoulder. "But if a prison can keep men in, why can't it keep others out?"

Rose's eyes lit up. "I grasp it. It's a quod, eh? Where in all the world seems more mauled than this? Even Fitzroy, with all his fancy brains, ain't going to think it's the birthin' place of a rebellion." She grinned. "Right?"

He reached past her to open both windows and admit the rumblings of the crowd. "Right."

# CHAPTER 29

ILL STOOD ON the window seat and peered into the courtyard below.

Amidst the flicker of torches and lanterns, the prisoners packed one against another in the yard. Their anger remained, a formidable buzz, heightened liberally with fear.

And whyever not? They were imprisoned.

Near the Lodge, Postelwaite and some of his brother turn-keys pressed back against the door. Postelwaite fumbled with his great keyring. "Everything will be well. Always looks better in the morning."

Will would have but one chance at this.

Tom approached from behind. "What are you about?" he asked doubtfully.

"I'm going to give them a reason to believe in impossible things." At least, he was going to try.

He was going to make Tom believe too.

Will would aid these people *if* they would allow him. Perhaps they could even assist him in stopping Fitzroy somehow. But most importantly, if he transformed this prison into a fortress and the prisoners in it into a resistance, however small—then Fitzroy's intended death trap for Tom might become the safest place in the city.

Before that could become even a possibility though, Will must first make the grandest entrance of his career.

He crouched on the windowsill and withdrew his eye-shields from his coat pocket.

"Got a hat?" Rose asked Tom.

"What?"

"He lost his hat. Part of his disguise, you know?"

Tom grunted and went to rummage out his wide-brimmed felt hat.

Will lowered the brim over his face and raised his collar.

"Now what?" Tom asked.

"You watch, that's what." Rose's grin was audible. She sounded a plump mother, rather than a skinny urchin.

For some reason, her pride pumped courage into Will's bones.

She wanted a show? He'd give her a show.

He stood to his full height on the sill, shoulders leaning beyond the top frame. This was the uppermost level in the building, the rafters jutting just above him. Without looking into the dizziness below, he gripped the eaves with one hand—the one that hurt the less—and swung out. He twisted and caught the eaves with his other hand.

On a different night, it might have been a graceful demonstration. As it was, his full weight hit the thunderous ache where Fitzroy's shot had glanced the iron rod strapped to his arm. He gasped and nearly slipped.

Falling just now, screaming in pain, would probably fail to inspire these good people. Heroically, he managed to keep the scream down to a modest grunt and hauled himself onto the roof. Once up, he looked studiously to the sky whilst gathering his limbs and catching his breath. Getting dizzy right off and falling—this time, screaming in exasperation—would also fail to improve his cause.

As soon as his body ceased protesting, he stood. He drew his pistol. He'd never reloaded it after his shot at Fitzroy, but he had no plans to shoot anyone.

A glance below showed the shifting crowd. They'd little room to move, and their restrained jostling undulated like breakers in the sea.

"Now, now." Postelwaite's voice grew hoarse. "This is what I can do for you. No one pays for his bed tonight. I'll see to it, for the occasion. That's memorable, isn't it? Never happened in the Marshalsea before!" His laugh was forced.

The people quietened.

Another turnkey turned to Postelwaite, his voice carrying: "Ah, blimey, they're prisoners, ain't they?"

That was as good a cue as Will would receive.

He released his pent breath: "No! They are not!"

His height, far above the crowd, gave his voice resonance. It boomed down into the yard, echoing.

His heart started pounding. He must be careful. He hadn't energy for much tonight.

People swiveled, searching for him.

All he needed was for one to see. He waited.

Someone pointed. "Look!"

An exhalation passed through the crowd. They turned, staring. The turnkeys and guards spun to face him.

"*Wayfarer.*"

The name floated as a whisper, mouth to mouth.

Their recognition was almost more frightening than anything else that had happened tonight.

Words balled in his throat. Oh well. It was always easier to *show* people.

He ran to the eaves, spread his arms, and jumped. His coat swirled gratifyingly around him, and, Lord be praised, Tom's hat didn't fall off.

He hit the ground lightly, like a cat, which meant it didn't hurt *much*. He dropped to one knee, head down. Slowly, he rose, lifting his chin to see beyond the hat brim.

Across the yard, Postelwaite stood beneath a lantern. His mouth was open, eyes round as wheels. "I—I—I—" he stuttered.

Well, he *had* desired a specimen.

He looked to the guard nearest. "I— seize him." His voice cracked.

Before the guard turned, Will moved.

Around the perimeter, the guards stood at such distant intervals that they hadn't a chance of joining forces. If Will did this correctly, it might well save him from facing them again. Considering how sludgy his muscles felt, that was the best he could hope for.

He'd make theater of it—just a little. For Tom as much as any of them.

He rushed the nearest and was upon him before the man took two steps. Once there, Will slowed so the people might see him clearly. He stilled long enough for the guard to strike at him—and then he caught the man's fist in midair.

The guard gaped. He attempted another punch, even slower than before.

Will blocked it easily. He spun the guard about by his fist, used his toe to catch the man's ankle, and upended him.

Then he blurred forward again. He tripped the other dozen guards in even less time. Six more stared from across the yard and began backing away.

Thank God for that. His lungs were burning again, and he'd no wish to humiliate these men. On the morrow, they must be allies.

He put on a last blast of speed, rushing through the crowd, dodging people, to reach the Lodge door.

Postelwaite scrabbled for the truncheon at his belt.

Will batted away his hand. He faced Postelwaite, but not too close, lest the man's height dwarf him.

He pitched his voice low. "I'm not your enemy, Postelwaite."

"You—" Postelwaite ducked and peered beneath Will's hat brim. "You were here before—yesterday morning—you—you—that was you?"

Yesterday's desperate impatience might not have been the best introduction. "Yes, well—"

Postelwaite gripped the truncheon, no longer fumbling. He looked dazed. "I had the Wayfarer in my Lodge, and I knew it not." His forehead creased. "But you tore our ledger! I thought you a ruffian!"

"Well, I'm not." He tried not to sound defensive. He deepened his voice. "You had no belief in my words then, Mr. Postelwaite. What do you believe now?"

"I—" Postelwaite scanned his courtyard.

A full dozen of his men were picking themselves up from Will's onslaught.

"The things you do—they're true!"

Will exhaled carefully. "They are."

Thank heaven that, as yet, he was the most impressive thing these people had ever seen. Were Fitzroy to appear just now, they might cease to be awed by such as him.

He pulled his eye-shields down his nose and looked Postel-waite in the eye. "Are you going to stop me? Or are you going to hear what I've to say?"

"I—" In Postelwaite's face, duty warred with fascination, and fascination won. He nodded—barely, but it was enough.

Slowly, Will turned to face the prisoners. He might not have voice enough left to make them hear him—much less impress them.

They stared, silent, waiting. Expectant.

*They* didn't know he was naught but a forge apprentice from Surrey, ignorant of their city ways. They didn't know he had been soundly basted tonight. They didn't know Fitzroy was by far the more impressive specimen.

All they knew was he had just shown them something they had never seen. He was the one the rumors spoke of as saving people. He was the one who silenced their captors.

"You know who I am." The words wobbled, but he pulled them up. "You know what I do."

For a moment, there was stillness.

Then Claypole pushed forward. "Aye, we know what you do. You save toffs. You're sold to the money, same as the Runners."

"Ah—" Will's grand speech stopped up his throat. "No, that's not true—"

At the far end of the yard, Tom and Rose stood beyond the wall's shadow, watching.

Will steadied his voice. "I am here tonight to aid *you*, not the toffs."

"To free us?" a young voice piped.

Behind Will, Postelwaite fidgeted.

An uncomfortable heat crawled up his neck. "Not exactly."

"You said we weren't prisoners."

"Well, and that depends on you, doesn't it?"

He didn't need them to be free. He needed them to stay here and man the place—to protect Tom. But how to explain that? These people were in fear of their lives.

Claypole spat. "Hah." He glared at Will, challenging. "For aught we know, you're a minion straight from hell. How do you do what you do? Don't look like salvation to me!"

At his elbow, Trabb sniffed. "And when is it you became a churcher?"

Claypole ignored him. He jutted his chin, not so much angry as adamant. He pointed at Will. "Don't be coming in here like Revelation on a white horse. Can't profit off them what's already had everything stolen."

Will lost his breath, same as if he'd been struck in the stomach. Part of him felt battered by the injustice. True, he had helped those who could afford to reward him—but he *had* helped them.

Another part felt justly rebuked.

Claypole's words weren't the whole of the truth, but they weren't false either.

Even though Mr. Monarch had made him a one month's legend, the Wayfarer was no hero, not truly. He was an opportunistic, well-meaning lad who faced evil only where convenient.

Across the yard, Tom stood with his arms over his chest, face unreadable.

What would he say if he and Will were in opposite positions, with Will in prison and Tom trying to save him?

Maybe he'd already said it.

Will looked at the prisoners. They looked like Affery folk. They looked like him and Tom.

He could turn his back on them. He could dazzle them with his powers and use them to serve his ends. But then how was he better than those toffs at the party, trampling one another to save themselves?

How was he better than Lord Carstone, who had evicted Will's parents?

How was he better than Fitzroy, in pursuit of some twisted ideal?

He had wanted adventure, hadn't he? He'd wanted glory? He'd wanted the respect of men?

Well, then.

He squared his shoulders. "I *am* here to aid you—if you will accept it."

They stared back at him. They had no reason to believe him, no reason to trust him. To them, he was a freakish spectacle. For all any of them knew, he *might* be the devil's own work.

Certainly, he was no leader of men.

Footsteps crunched through the rustling silence. "The lad speaks true." Tom crossed the yard in long strides. His face was hard, eyes afire.

The people turned to him. He was one of them. They would recognize him, maybe even heed him.

"He has my trust, all of it." His voice carried across the courtyard and echoed back. He looked Will in the eye. "This . . . Wayfarer."

Rose remained behind, eyes shining in her dirty face.

The crowd parted for them, allowing Tom to join Will.

Postelwaite forced a chuckle. "Piffle. He can't free you."

"Yes, he can." Tom turned. "And so can you."

Postelwaite leant back. "What's this?"

"You're a guard."

"I'm a turnkey."

Tom waved aside the distinction. "You maintain the separation between honest folk and knaves."

Will caught on. "You're skilled at it."

"Well, don't know as it requires much skill. Merely wakefulness—"

Will faced him, voice low. "When first I met you, you wanted something famous to occur in the Marshalsea. Well, it's about to. But you can do more than watch. You can take part."

"I don't know—"

"You think me a specimen? You think what I do worth something? Then help us."

Postelwaite's eyelid flickered. He licked his lips. "How?"

Tom turned to the crowd. "Why are you here?"

Claypole held his silence, studying with hooded eyes.

"My debt was called in!" said one.

"The soldiers came today!" from another.

"I know not!" That one sounded almost a weeping.

"Those reasons are only what you were meant to believe," Tom said. "I've only just learned the truth. As of tonight, whether this city realizes it or not, it is at war. And you"—he pointed—"are its first casualties."

Fear murmured through their ranks.

Claypole stared on, like the rest. But he, at least, opened his eyes all the way.

"We needn't lie down like kicked dogs in the street," Tom said.

Behind Claypole and Trabb, a short man raised his voice above the disturbed clamor. "We're in prison, ain't we? What are *we* to do about it?"

"Yes, rather," Postelwaite murmured.

"Rise up," Tom said. "Fight back."

Will wanted to cheer.

Never had he heard Tom like this. He might shout out his views in the alehouse, back in Affery, but that was never for greater stakes than seeing a starving neighbor fed through the winter.

These people wanted a leader? Tom was their man. Will was naught but a figurehead, a sideshow to make them open their eyes and pay attention. He knew it—and likely they did too.

Claypole snorted. "Fight, you say? Nay. Open them doors, and you won't see naught but the back of me."

Will gathered his energy. He blasted through the crowd to stand at the man's nose.

To his credit, Claypole recoiled only an instant before holding his ground.

"If you leave, you validate the man who put you here." Will raised his voice. "Your new Prime Minister, Mr. James Fitzroy."

Claypole narrowed his eyes. "What kind of treasonous jabber is that?"

"Do you deserve to be here?"

Claypole hesitated, then shook his head.

"It is not treason to resist injustice." Will looked to other faces. "Fitzroy has no respect for such as you—or me. Tonight, I heard him declare a war within this city. You'll never read it in the newspapers. You'll never hear it from Parliament or from the king." He stepped back, trying not to limp. "But you'll feel it. You'll see it."

Tom joined him. "We've all heard the rumors. More prisons

than this are overflowing. Before long, we'll tear ourselves apart."

Will's empty stomach rolled over on itself. "Fitzroy depends upon your lack of regard for one another, your lack of regard for yourselves.

A muscle in Tom's cheek jumped. "I, for one, will not accept this as my fate."

"We're in prison." Trabb laughed thinly. "We can't fight anything."

"This battle will be one of subterfuge." Tom walked forward, milling amongst them. Subtly, he beckoned with his fingertips for Will to follow. "Why do you think you have been brought here, silently, supposedly with legality?"

The people turned to follow their movements. Whether their logic sided with Claypole or not, they *wanted* to believe in Tom—and maybe in the Wayfarer as well. It was Tom they listened to, but it was Will they were watching, half with wariness, half with outright hope.

Perhaps if they had not been imprisoned without explanation, they might have scoffed. But these people shared the same desperation Will had carried under his heart these past weeks.

In the midst of the yard, Tom stepped onto a scuffed bench, the better to face them. He looked down at Will as if waiting on him. Waiting on him for what? *Tom* was the leader here; Tom was the one with the words to sway these people. The things Will could do had naught to do with standing out in the open and leading—as Tom seemed to want him to do. They had all to do with skulking in the shadows where people could see him only out of the corner of their eyes.

But what Tom wished him to do was come forward, make a pact, become a surety for these people.

That wasn't a'tall what he intended when he jumped from Tom's window. He wouldn't promise these people what he might not be able to fulfill. He was here to save Tom; that came before them all.

Tom waited, eyes steady.

But neither could he let Tom down. Tom wanted him to be a hero. But as Tom should well know in this moment, the trouble with heroes was they tended to leave their own backs exposed.

If Tom wouldn't protect himself, then Will was still going to have to do it for him.

He stepped up beside Tom. His coat flapped in the breeze that blew through the prison, all the way up from the Surrey hills of home.

"I *will* open these doors." The words croaked from his hoarse throat. At least, the gravel in his voice made him sound older. "You will have the freedom to return to your homes—if you wish."

They exhaled, murmured.

Across the yard, Postelwaite chewed his lip.

Again, Will raised his voice. "But I tell you truly, this prison is the safest place you or your families could be just now. If you return home, Fitzroy will know. His soldiers will come again, and they will imprison you in worse places by far." If they did not simply kill them.

"Tell me, *Wayfarer*." Claypole dropped beefy arms to his sides. "Why should I hide in a prison?"

Silence filled the yard; only the clatter of wheels from the streets beyond filtered in on the night air.

"Because," Will found the breath to say. "It is a prison no longer. It is a fortress."

A tremendous look of approval overtook Tom's face. He clapped his hand to Will's aching shoulder and looked out over the prisoners. "It is *our* fortress. We will fortify it so Fitzroy can only wish he'd the foresight to send you anywhere but here."

The energy buzzing amongst the crowd was palpable.

Will looked to Claypole.

His would be the voice that would decide the night.

But Claypole was not the first to speak.

From the back of the crowd, a clank sounded as Postelwaite threw down his keyring. "Ah, devil take me." He lofted his truncheon. "I'll follow the Wayfarer! To the grave, old boy!"

Not the best of declarations. But it proved no check to the others. Almost as one, they began to nod, chins tucked in determination.

Behind Claypole, Trabb shrugged. "Got no plans for dying

in here." He shambled forward. "But as long as there's victuals about, I can stay for the time."

At last, Claypole stepped forward. "All right, then. *Him*, I'll follow." He looked at Will, but he pointed at Tom.

That was fine. Relief flooded Will. If they let Tom lead them, then they would esteem him. If they esteemed him, they'd protect him.

The people pressed in around them. They raised their voices, some of them arguing yet, but most of them celebrating in a sudden rush of relief and hope.

Rose ran across the yard, shoving through jostling bodies. She clambered onto the bench beside them and leant against Will's leg, grinning up at him.

Tom turned. The look in his eyes was far more approving than it should be. "Well done, lad."

"Saints and martyrs, Tom." He felt near to collapsing.

"Hold fast there." Tom's voice was serious, but there was a spark of joy to it. Pride maybe? "You've done a good thing here. You've done something most men couldn't do even if they'd the spirit for it."

"They're *your* army, Tom."

"This must be only the beginning. Other prisons are just as crowded. Their people will be as confused, as desperate, as *angry* as here. They'll listen. We may yet gain a force to reckon with."

All Will's gathered energy drained away. He could fall over and sleep right here. "By tomorrow, everyone beyond this prison is going to believe me the greatest villain they've ever heard of." *And by week's end, Fitzroy will own the city.* But he held that thought back.

"You want men who'll fight?" Rose asked. "St. Giles'll fight. Horneys and soldiers come prodding into their business? Ain't a one of them wouldn't fight any day of the week."

It was true St. Giles *must* fight. They were at the heart of this if only because they were at the heart of Fitzroy's wretched past.

Will started to shake his head. Let them fight. Let them fall. Fitzroy was not wrong in wanting to destroy such as Mr. Monarch. Perhaps it would be the only good to come of this godforsaken business.

And yet . . . Lifty's face and Peggy's flashed before his eyes.

The last thing in this world he wished was to return to Seven Dials—but at least a few of them needed to be warned. They deserved many a fate, but not Fitzroy's indiscriminate warfare.

And the truth of it was: Seven Dials knew the *true* Fitzroy. Perhaps they were the only ones in all the city who possessed the clues to defeating him.

Tomorrow, first thing, he must visit Lifty.

Rose faced the crowd and shook clasped hands above her head. "Ain't he the Wayfarer—come to save us all? Ain't he *just?*"

In back of the crowd, someone shouted, "Wayfarer!"

One voice at a time, the crowd took it up:

*"Wayfarer Wayfarer Wayfarer"*

A moment ago, Will had been the toffs' man. Now, of a sudden, he was theirs.

His heart beat a tattoo in his ears. From deep within, a new energy jittered.

"We'll organize," Tom said. "Have no anxiety. Just you hold fast. All that falls to you is making sure you go on being worthy of the respect these people are giving you."

Turned out their *respect* was just about the most frightening thing he had faced all night.

# CHAPTER 30

"I'M GOING. *YOU* are not." Will tried to maintain a level tone.

He stood within the Lodge, waiting to exit the Marshalsea.

At the far door, Postelwaite jingled his key ring. He glanced from Will to Rose to Tom to Claypole and back again, waiting for the signal to discharge one or all of them.

'Twould only be one so far as Will was concerned. Slipping into Seven Dials to warn Lifty—and perhaps learning more of Fitzroy's past—was something he could do best without Rose, or even Tom, at his side.

"Blimey." Rose glared. "And now you know your way all about Seven Dials? How many times you get lost the first week?"

From behind his eye-shields, Will glared back.

He was her guardian now—in some measure. She'd made the choice as much as he, and she must learn to heed him.

"You aren't to return. That's—an order."

Her expression darkened, but she clamped her mouth.

Postelwaite unlocked the door.

Across the room, Tom waited, arms folded. "I'm coming with you."

"No." Will said it too quickly. "Who's to see to things here if we all go?"

Rose sulked. "Guess that'd be me."

Will ignored her. "Remain here, Tom. It's safer."

A spark flashed in Tom's eye. He came forward, face to face with Will, and lowered his voice. "You want others to follow you?"

"Nay." He lowered his voice. "I want them to follow *you*."

Tom went on. "First, you must show them that people already follow. Last night was the hardest step. People *will* come 'round us now, if we give them the chance."

"Not from Seven Dials, they won't."

"I've gathered twenty men to accompany us."

"You think dancing out the front gate won't attract attention all down the street?"

"The street'll be on your side," Postelwaite piped in. "Half the families hereabouts have members imprisoned. Rumors is already flying about what you did last night."

"*Already?*"

Postelwaite looked apologetic. "'Twas only a matter of time."

Claypole rumbled deep in his chest. "More'n a few will be on your side once they understand the truth of things."

"*If* you can show them an existing force to rally to," Tom insisted. "Until then, you're not going out alone. You've no notion what's to be found out there."

"I've a better notion than you."

Tom's jaw hopped. His eyes were growing dark. He lowered his voice still more. "I respect what you're doing, Will. I appreciate that you're worried for my safety. But I'm coming with you."

Rose hurried forward. "I'm coming too."

"No." Will turned on her. "*You're* not. What was the point of all my vexation in getting you out of Seven Dials if you're going to run back?"

"You can protect me."

"I'm going to be too busy protecting all these totty-heads slowing me down."

Tom looked at Postelwaite and Claypole. "Whilst we're away, you'll investigate King's Bench and speak with the guards and turnkeys there. We must fortify as many prisons as possible."

King's Bench was the nearest prison; it, too, was on this side of the river. After that, there was Whitecross-street, Fleet, Newgate.

Postelwaite fidgeted with his keyring, somewhere between eagerness and nervousness. "I know the turnkeys there."

"If we can find some who are sympathetic, some like you"—

that increased Postelwaite's eagerness—"'twill make it easier to aid the prisoners."

"I've the day's leave, so the Marshal won't know the difference when he finds me gone. I've given the lads orders to keep him well in the dark."

Tom looked at Claypole. "You'll accompany him?"

The big bald man hesitated only a second before nodding.

Tom turned back to Will, waiting.

Will glared. "I'll meet you at the end of the street. Try not to look like prisoners."

---

It required yet the better part of an hour to cross the river from Southwark, then up through Covent Gardens to St. Giles. Had he traveled alone, Will might have gained the farther shore in half the time, but in light of the fact that his entire body felt as if he had tried to swim the Channel last night—perhaps it was as well Tom and his band of Marshalsea collegians were along to slow him.

His every muscle hurt, and his arm bone was a thunderous ache where Fitzroy's shot had glanced off. The day was gray, so at least he'd no need to battle the sun's rays burning through his head. Still, he maintained the eye-shields, along with the rest of his costume.

The mood in the streets was strangely quiet, placid even. But there was fear too, buzzing beneath the surface. People scattered from their path, staring and murmuring.

His stomach rumbled, partly because he'd neglected the buttered thins and small beer Rose had scrounged up—and partly because the expression in these people's eyes was something no one had ever given him.

Alarm and uncertainty.

Anger rose inside him.

How *dare* Fitzroy take a man's name—Will's own name—and turn it falsely into something to be feared? Hated even? Fitzroy had done it all so easily, with a wave and a word.

Despite Will's and Tom's brave speeches to the collegians last night, they'd both be fortunate to escape this misadventure. Will might fight the rest of his life to disprove the lie and never come close to regaining his good name.

Before he even rounded the corner, the stink of Seven Dials slapped him in the face. The roar of shouting voices seemed more raucous than usual.

Speaking of misadventures, here he was again, at Mr. Monarch's doorstep, back in the belly of the beast.

All he needed today was to find Lifty. He needn't confront Mr. Monarch. A kinchin could bring Lifty out. That done, convincing Lifty to accompany them shouldn't be hard. Will touched his pocket where Fitzroy's gold piece yet lay heavy.

Tom raised an eyebrow. He looked neither surprised nor perturbed by the waste and filth in these streets. "You lived here?"

Will nodded.

"I'm sorry for it, Will. You've had a bleaker time than I."

Will opened his mouth, surprised, then closed it. "I doubt that. And . . . it wasn't so dreadful."

Mr. Monarch *was* dreadful. But most of Will's jobs had, in all honesty, been rousing fun.

They rounded the corner onto Mr. Monarch's street.

Will stopped short.

Before them, at least a hundred men packed the narrow lane. Women and children leant from open windows, adding shrill voices to the hubbub.

In an open space, half a dozen men had gathered. Will recognized most of them. They were leaders, men of relative power here in St. Giles. Amongst them was that great dark bear of a man—Gamp the Tramp from the carriage abductions. He'd escaped Pish's hand after all. And there was a still-battered Tug—whom Will had rendered unconscious with a belaying pin during his first job at the docks.

"Saints and martyrs."

"What?" Tom said.

These were not men Will would choose to meet this morning.

Lifty skulked near them, arms over his puffed-out chest.

Mr. Monarch was nowhere to be seen, but Peggy perched in an upper windowsill.

She saw Will, and her expression turned earnest, urgent. She pointed to the center of the street.

Another voice rose from those gathered there: a higher, shriller voice. A woman's voice.

The twist in Will's innards turned to shock, then outright panic.

"God have mercy."

"*What?*" Tom demanded. He tensed his hand about the length of oak he carried.

Behind, the collegians fanned out, nervously but resolutely.

Will registered their confusion and anxiety with a bare part of his consciousness.

The men at the street's center shifted to reveal the woman.

Red in the face, Lady Isabella stood upon a wobbling wooden crate, her sky-blue coat and pink-ribboned bonnet fair blinding amidst the muted muck and misery. Little wonder she'd gathered a crowd.

She faced Gamp, obviously furious, obviously unafraid—or perhaps insensible—of her danger.

As yet, no one seemed to have put his hand to her.

What in the name of heaven was she doing here? Masquerading as a farm girl and assisting Dr. Silas was one thing. But this could end in far worse than her dented reputation.

Will held in a growl. He had intended to slip in and out of Seven Dials like a whisper—grasp Lifty's coattails and *go*. But he could hardly grasp Lady Isabella's bonnet strings and escape with the same invisibility.

Gamp loomed in her face, grinning. "Come with a charity basket, is it, love?" His gold tooth glinted from a nest of black whiskers. "Come to teach Holy Hannah to the poor savages? Come to preach against the evil gin what's rotting away our lives?"

Lady Isabella glowered. "Believe me, I have no care should you rot away your life. From their odor, your teeth have done so already."

Gamp grinned the more.

Will looked at Tom. "Just . . . stay here. Blend in."

Tom nodded, mouth tight.

Will tucked his chin to hide his eye-shields beneath his hat and slipped into the crowd. Perhaps he could accomplish this without exhibiting his speed and revealing his identity.

Ahead, Tug scowled. "She's the baggage of this strange new bird we're having to call our minister. Ain't you?"

She flared her nostrils. "Indeed *not.*"

"And so you are!" a woman from an upper window shouted. "Didn't I see it in the very newspaper I used to buss me blind cheeks? Marryin' James Fitzroy's own baby son, you are!"

Lady Isabella drew herself up. Her face was stony.

Gamp looked her over, a new light in his eyes. "Well now. Pretty face who's worth a pretty pence, I reckon."

The color in her cheeks rose higher yet. "How dare you question me? How dare you believe you could succeed in ransoming me? Or blackmailing me—or whatever you are contemplating. Do you believe you could detain me without the entire city descending upon you in ire?"

Gamp clucked. "Don't you know where you've come to, love?" He spread his arms. "Even Runners don't come here. What sets foot here stays for all time—if we wish it."

Will had almost reached the front of the crowd. He looked about for a likely next move. But there was none.

He settled for glaring at Lifty. Speaking of totty-heads. What was the fool about?

Lifty saw him. He dropped open his mouth, only to clamp it again. Panic crossed his face, and he jerked his head to the side.

Will glanced past him—and *there* was Mr. Monarch.

The man stood in his own doorway, his left hand swathed in a grimy bandage. With his other hand, he toyed with the lank yellow curls at his shoulder. He watched the drama with vigilant eyes—waiting, pondering, calculating.

*He* would know Lady Isabella's identity, and he would be least likely of all to waste this opportunity.

Beneath Will's skin, energy vibrated. He and Isabella were both in this to the neck now. There was no way to escape without revealing his presence.

Tug advanced on her. "Didn't bring no lady's maid, eh? Means you told no one where you was bound, now did you?"

A flinch of concern cracked her anger. But she lifted her chin. "I have come to see the Wayfarer."

A small, irrational part of Will's mind came to attention. She was here to see *him.* Even as the thought clanged within his head, the rest of his brain caught him up.

He gritted his teeth. Of *course* she'd come looking for him. Like a fool, he had told her he slept here.

"Well, the Wayfarer don't live here, do he?" The amusement died from Gamp's face. "No honest thief, he is." He took her wrist. "Come on then. We'd best find something to do with you."

She jerked away with such haste she caught the wide brim of her own bonnet and knocked it askew. "Sir! You forget yourself." Her tone was deep, imperious.

Gamp hesitated. Then he reached for her again.

Even as Gamp moved, so did Will.

The space between them was too short to allow Will to gain speed enough to reach her before Gamp's big paw—its backside a pelt of black hair—clamped her wrist.

But a second later, Will was there, in the narrow space between them. He stood upon the wobbling crate, his back to Isabella, facing Gamp. Brazenly, he laid his hand upon her arm, just above Gamp's hand.

Both Gamp and Isabella gasped.

No more than three feet separated Will from Gamp. Thanks to the crate, he possessed a few inches in advantage, for a change.

He forced down his pounding heart enough to find his voice. "Release the lady."

Behind him, she flinched again—a sharp intake of breath. She curled her other hand, ever so slightly, in the back of his coat.

Emotions flickered in Gamp's eyes—surprise, of course, anger, perhaps a touch of amusement, and then, finally, fear.

He feared Will.

He seemed not to notice Will was but a lad standing upon a crate. He saw whatever it was he'd seen in the fire-lit darkness of the church-side street. He saw the night angel who foiled his plans, thrashed two dozen of his men, and rendered him unconscious.

But he did not release Isabella. He flashed his gold tooth in yet another grin. Like a trapped animal evaluating his options, he never took his eyes from Will's.

"Well." He laughed. "You *do* come out during the day. But only to save delles, I see."

Gamp's fear—and also Isabella's trusting hand upon his back—pumped certitude through Will. He stood straight, shoulders back.

"Release her." He spoke softly, as if offering the suggestion for Gamp's safety.

Gamp laughed. "Now, now, time we sat down, man to man, and argued this bad habit you have of stealing what another man's already stolen."

Will flicked back the length of his coat and snatched his pistol from its holster. Before Gamp could blink, the tip of the pistol's cutlass pricked his nose.

This time Gamp released Isabella with admirable alacrity. He stumbled back, hands raised. He laughed again, without humor. "Well now. A verily convincing argument, I'll grant."

"Hmp," Isabella said. The sound of it was as much relieved as haughty. "Did I not warn you, sir?"

Hand still upon her wrist, Will pushed her off the crate. "If you can possibly manage it, be quiet."

She landed in the mud with a squawk.

Will held Gamp's gaze for five full seconds. He counted them off in his head.

Then he lowered the pistol. He could nip it back into Gamp's face before the man moved—and doubtless Gamp knew it.

But now came the thorny part.

He faced the crowd, knowing his expression would be unreadable behind his eye-shields and raised collar.

They stared at him.

A small bit of silence was fine. It let him hold the weight of the confrontation—let them wonder about him, what he was thinking, what he might do to them. Gamp and Tug wouldn't be the only ones to know of his exploits.

But in a few seconds more, they would realize he was silent mostly because he had no notion what to say. He would lose his element of intimidation, of mystery.

So he opened his mouth and said what was sitting upon his tongue: "I have come to warn you."

It was the last thing they could have expected from him.

"You've heard of me, in these last few weeks. I know you have." He took another breath. "Just as I know you have heard of another." He purposely looked anywhere but at Mr. Monarch. "The one you call hereabouts 'Blue-Eyed Jem'—and the legend of how he escaped this place."

The crowd shifted, frowning.

"Well, I tell you truly"—he raised his voice—"it is no legend."

That elicited murmurs.

Mr. Monarch's green shawl remained perfectly still.

"The one you call Blue-Eyed Jem is one of you no more." Will looked to Lifty. "He is now a 'strange new bird.'" That's what Tug had called Fitzroy a moment ago.

Lifty's eyes popped wide. "I'll be blowed—" He looked to Mr. Monarch.

The crowd shuffled. Some scoffed, but most kept on staring in the kind of disbelief that wasn't so disbelieving after all.

Gamp squinted. "That row last night—that row *you* was at the heart of?" He threw back his head. "Hah! And you thought you were the toffs' man, didn't you? Thought it was the cush life for you—thanks to these *things* you can do." He waved at Will. "And then you goes and gets your hand outplayed by one of our own." He leant forward. "I knows the feeling."

Of course, that would be their next thought. But getting trapped betwixt Fitzroy and Seven Dials was the last thing he could afford.

"What is happening here is not *about* Fitzroy and me. But he is *like* me, you understand?"

All along, Tug had been eyeing Will warily from where he fronted the crowd. He now snorted. "Unholy fast, you mean? Or straight from the devil?"

Will faced him. "Straight from the devil is exactly right. He's not in pursuit of me—he's in pursuit of *you*. Because you know the secret of his past, and he'll do anything to abolish the memory of it."

From the rear, Tom called out, "This man Fitzroy has no right to his office. He's no right to be taking into his hands the lives of folk all over this city. And you can be sure that's what he's doing. But we can yet stop him. His day is young."

Gamp waved dismissively. "We don't fight for nobody. We don't have to. You heard me before—ain't nobody comes into Seven Dials unless we want 'em." He scowled at Will. "How you got in, I ain't sure."

Will looked at him levelly. "Fitzroy will be here and you won't even know it. He'll be amongst you—he'll be your mother and your brother and your mate. And he'll slaughter the lot of you." He faced the crowd again. "He can do things. Things you won't credit, but they're true. He can make you see anything he wants you to."

Tom advanced, trailing his watchful band of collegians. "If we offer a united front, this once, we may yet stand a chance. But if we remain in ignorance and apathy, he *will* cut us apart."

Tug sized him up. "And you've seen what he can do, have you?"

"I've seen strange things. Prisons packed with people who have no business there. Things that have been altered—things no longer what they once were."

"Ain't what I said." Tug advanced a step. "Have *you* seen what this Fitzroy can do?"

"No." Tom pointed with his cudgel at Will. "But he has. And I believe him."

The words held weight enough to silence the crowd for one long breath.

Then Gamp shook his head at Will. "Why the devil should I heed you? You're a bloody thief."

Lady Isabella freed her wrist from Will's grip and stepped back up onto the crate beside him. "He speaks the truth. That is why I am here. To tell him *I* will aid him in this."

"And you're the man's darling daughter-to-be," Gamp said. "You're a spy's what you are."

She tossed her head, nearly dislodging the skewed bonnet. "I assure you, few are in a better position than I to judge the motives and intentions of Mr. James Fitzroy. I tell you truly, I abhor his intentions. I, for one, will do everything in my power to check him. Even if it means joining hands with this . . . high-wayman." She stared ahead, not looking at Will.

One of Tom's collegians spoke up. "He's liberated the Mar-shalsea, he has. Hundreds there will fight this. We're freeing

King's Bench and the other prisons too."

No doubt there was little the people upon this street had not heard or seen. But every word seemed to set them back a bit more upon their heels. Their eyes were wide, faces still. They shook their heads—but more in thought than rejection.

What Postelwaite said about most of Southwark having lost family to imprisonment would be even truer of those in St. Giles.

Will looked about. He needed one person—one person like Claypole had been last night—to touch this off. These people were on the brink of tipping. When he had walked in here, he had thought to warn Lifty and a few others. He had never thought he might walk out with Seven Dials in his coat pocket. But he might—*if* but one person were to speak in his support.

He looked to Lifty. He was the only man here who qualified as friendly.

It took Lifty a moment to realize Will *was* looking at him. When he did, his eyes went wide. He hastened back, hands raised, bumping the woman behind him.

Will stifled a very real urge to stomp down off the crate and punch Lifty squarely in the nose. *Then* Lifty would follow certain enough.

Perhaps he should not have left Rose behind. She might have known how to incite the crowd in his favor. At all events, she would have no qualms in raising her voice.

Peggy might speak for him, were she not too frightened. But her voice was unlikely to sway anyone here.

The crowd began milling, murmuring.

He was losing them.

For a moment, even Gamp had looked contemplative. Now, he shook his head. "You're not one of us after all, are you then? Else you'd know you can't ask Seven Dials to unite with Southwark unless first you ask us to unite ourselves." He advanced. His left hand crossed his body and slipped beneath his coat.

Will tensed, ready to push Lady Isabella off the crate.

Emboldened, Tug took a step. "You think you can get *all* the flash coves, all the kidsmen, all the fences—even just them at this one little godforsaken corner—to pull all together?" He snorted. "You're daft, you are."

As quickly as that, he had lost them.

It was evil luck the two spokesmen here should be men he had personally clouted. Perhaps had he clouted them a bit harder, he might have avoided the problem altogether.

Now the best he could hope was to somehow get everyone safely out of here. How likely was that?

Tom stood at attention, one hand about his cudgel, the other extended, warning the collegians back.

The corner of a grin tilted from beneath Gamp's ragged whiskers. "Well, now, master thief, can you run away from this?"

Will clenched his pistol. If Gamp took one more step—if he drew the knife from his coat—Will would have to shoot him. He'd drop him with a ball to the brains, and he would not think twice about it. But if that happened, he would never get everyone to safety. Gamp would not be the only one to die.

Will looked him in the eye. "I don't care if the devil takes you, and that's the truth of it." Then he raised his voice, so all could hear. "I've warned you Fitzroy is your enemy. But now I tell you truly—if you choose wrongly here today, if you do aught in an attempt to harm me or anyone I wish to protect—then you will have *me* for an enemy as well." He looked at Mr. Monarch. "And I think you know that is something you do not want."

The air seemed devoid of sound, as if everyone stopped breathing long enough to think about the import of his words.

Mr. Monarch cocked his head far enough that his jowls shifted and hung to the side. The pale blue of his eyes was inscrutable, passive.

If Mr. Monarch feared Will's reappearance, he gave no sign. If he was gratified at the prospect of Gamp and Tug tearing Will apart, that too was not to be seen upon his face.

If anything, he seemed to be calculating some deep sum.

In front of Will, Gamp moved. A blade flashed.

So be it. In less than the space of a breath, Will raised the pistol, the barrel aligned with Gamp's head. He tightened his finger upon the trigger.

At the corner of his vision, green flickered. "I will follow the Wayfarer."

The voice was Mr. Monarch's.

# CHAPTER 31

WILL SCARCELY STAYED his finger upon the trigger. Blood thundered in his ears—whether in panic or in relief, he could not say.

Mr. Monarch held his green shawl closed against his spacious chest. He stepped down from his doorway, onto the boards laid atop the mud. He fixed an inscrutable look upon Will. "I will follow him. I have knowledge that what he says is true. He is an . . . honest man. He does not lie to us in this. I will follow him, for my own sake"—he dabbed his nose with the backs of his fingers—"and for the sake of my kinchin."

The entire street froze, as if royalty had spoken.

Will had known Mr. Monarch was feared and respected here. But did he hold more authority than even Gamp or Tug?

"I'll follow the Wayfarer!" Lifty shouted. "'Course, I will!"

Will had not currently the mental powers to spare him an ironic glare.

"Aye!" That was Peggy's reedy voice.

All of Mr. Monarch's vast household—women, boys, men—followed his lead. Their din filled the street.

As swiftly as that, the scales tipped back in Will's favor.

The entire crowd whooped. Half were probably just shouting in dissent, but from where Will stood, it sounded unanimous.

Gamp lowered his blade. Still, he maintained his gaze upon Will, heavy brows drawn. He didn't look convinced, but he wasn't going to go against Mr. Monarch. As long as he refrained from stabbing Will today, that was victory enough.

"Good," Will croaked the word, mostly to make certain he *could* still speak.

He stepped off the crate, pulling Lady Isabella after him. As he sidestepped, he offered Gamp a steely look.

Outside his door, Mr. Monarch waited.

Will kept Isabella at his back. The last place he wanted her was near Mr. Monarch, but neither was he about to let her out of sight.

He faced the man. "What is this?"

A faint smile raised Mr. Monarch's mouth. "Come now. You would not resent this *aide* I am giving you? You are needing it too much, I think."

Will began with the only question that mattered. "Why should you aid me?"

Mr. Monarch glanced meaningfully at the mob.

With her free hand, Lady Isabella tightened her grip on his coat sleeve. To her credit for once, she kept silent.

Will ignored her. "I have no trust for you."

Mr. Monarch offered a regretful shrug. He held his gaze steady.

"And we both know," Will said, "you've no trust for me."

"Ah, but you strike upon it. We have much in *commun*, yes?" Mr. Monarch leant nearer. "You and me—we have been doing business before and doing it well? Now we shall do it again." He spread his hands. "I *désirer* Jem. So do you."

"Right now, I desire to kill him."

Lady Isabella gasped. "Mr. Hardy!"

"Well, destroy him anyway," Will amended. "That is not what you want, I think?"

Mr. Monarch didn't so much as flinch. "What I *désirer* is for myself, my *entreprises*, my dear girls and my kinchin to continue in *sécurité* and in health." His eyelid fluttered. "I am bearing so much *responsabilité* for my children, yes? I am like the father to them, caring for them, sometimes disciplining them."

Will's finger itched against the trigger guard.

Mr. Monarch sighed, elaborately. Still, his eyes held steady. "You are here for something. And it is not, I think, for this." He gestured to the unruly street.

Will hesitated. "I wish to know Fitzroy's history. How does a man leave Seven Dials and become Prime Minister?"

Mr. Monarch smiled, as if Will had finally asked the correct question. "*A* man does not. But he is *singulier*, yes? I knew that at the moment I was first seeing him, as a small child." His gaze flickered. "There he is, brought to my doorway by my bigger boys. He and his dear *maman*—so lovely she is, white and pink and gold, she is. But he is so small, so *pâle*, with no shoes, no coat. They have not eaten well for how many weeks?"

"Just another street waif, then?"

"Yes, but no." Mr. Monarch tapped his temple. "He is clever, so much cleverer than the others." He flashed his crooked eye-tooth in a grin. "Cleverer than me?" He shrugged. "Maybe this is so." Then his eyes darkened. "Clever like your young Rose, yes? And like your young Rose, he is having no father. The *maman*, she has brought him all the way down from Yorkshire, to find his father she tells him. His father, maybe he is *riche*, maybe he is noble." He shrugged. "Maybe not. But there is no father." He offered another beatific smile. "So then I am his father."

A chill ran up Will's back.

If Fitzroy had been even half so clever as Rose—and Will had no doubt of it—he would have seen Mr. Monarch's guardianship for exactly what it was. He would have accepted it, because it was better than starving. But he would have resented that such as Mr. Monarch should take advantage of him and, especially, his mother. God have mercy. Will could only imagine what might have been her end.

"And then he picked pockets for you," he said.

"He had the touch of it in his fingers. And he was *rapide*. Not like you, but *rapide*."

That, Will had seen for himself.

"But there was more. He was"—Mr. Monarch searched for words—"invisible. Even in those years, he was making people to see only what he wanted them to see. The lie and the truth—it is his gift, yes?"

Little wonder Fitzroy knew how to wield his new abilities so effectively.

"And then he escaped?"

Mr. Monarch raised his shoulder. "He moved on, we shall say. He is never content to be the greatest pickpocket I have seen. He wants to make his fortune, to be a *gentilhomme*. So he is picking the pockets and not paying me for the well-being of himself and his *maman*, as he should. He is picking even from my pockets, I think. And then one day—he is of twelve years maybe—he steals a great *somme*—twelve hundred pounds, I think it was, what had been a *récent* great *victoire* for us. And he disappears. He leaves even his poor dear *maman*, though I am hearing her beg him not to go. He is spurning all of us. But I knew he has gone to make his fortune."

Will squinted at Mr. Monarch. "And you never thought he died? You kept his legend alive all these years?"

"Oh, I know he is very much alive. I keep watching over him."

"Ah." Of course. "And now you will make *your* fortune off him?"

Mr. Monarch spread his hands, modestly. "How do you think my Jem is learning to see *opportunités*? I am watching in much admiration all these years, what he does and how he does it—how he climbs, up, up, up, and never lets them know he was once the side-slip who nipped away their pocket-handkerchiefs when they are not looking." He laughed. "It is all most *remarquable*, it is, isn't it?

Will returned his shrewd look. "And now that you've found him?"

"Ah, I admit to you that has not turned out as I was hoping." Something dark and cold backed his eyes. "My kinchin—their care is of the most importance to me, of course. If my Jem is the *ennemi* to you now, he is *ennemi* to all of us also, just as you say."

Will raised an eyebrow. "And that makes us allies?"

Mr. Monarch spread his hands. "I am not a man of past grudges. I am a man of practicalities for the future."

"You tried to kill me."

"Not so much." Mr. Monarch raised his bandaged hand. "But *I* may yet be dying of this that you have given to me."

Infection was always possible from such a wound. But his

fingertips yet looked pink and healthy. More the pity.

Behind Will, Tom had pushed his way to the crate and was arguing with Gamp about the ideas he and Will had worked out with Postelwaite and Claypole.

"Fitzroy's greatest power," Tom was saying, "is his ability to convince people to believe whatsoever he desires. Our greatest defense is spreading, as quickly as possible, the truth about his illusions."

"And in the meantime?" someone shouted. "If he's as keen to snabble us as you say, then what about us? We don't need to be liberating no city. We need to be protecting our own coolers!"

"We must have defenses as well," Tom agreed.

"Barricades." That was Tug. "Barricade the whole of bloody St. Giles. Keep out who we decides we want out!"

"And for spreading the message," Lifty said, "I know all about that. Handbills, you want? I can draw 'em up slick and fast. Done it before, I have."

With any luck, he'd refrain from telling these people he'd done it to spread word about Will at Mr. Monarch's behest.

Like it or not—and Will decidedly *disliked* it—Mr. Monarch's influence was all that held this valuable little alliance together.

He trusted the man not at all. Whatever Mr. Monarch's motives, they were his own, and they would not be for Will's benefit by the end of the match.

But come to that, *Will's* motives were his own too, were they not? This might yet be a long game. Time enough to avoid Mr. Monarch after today, and time enough to see about defeating him after Fitzroy's madness no longer threatened Tom and so many others.

Mr. Monarch blinked slowly. "So we have yet a partnership again?"

"Not a partnership. A truce."

"That is better almost."

Will tightened his grip upon Lady Isabella's wrist, guiding her forward, away from this wretched street. The longer she remained, the more likely rumors of her presence might reach Fitzroy.

"Will you lend me the use of your rooms?" he asked.

The demand caught Mr. Monarch off guard. He opened his mouth. Then, recovering his poise, he bowed towards the open doorway. "With my greatest pleasure." His gaze drifted to Isabella, his expression far too interested to bode well for any of them.

# CHAPTER 32

WILL ALL BUT dragged Lady Isabella through Mr. Monarch's front door.

The great front room was empty. All the children were either upstairs in the windows or out in the street.

Behind the curtain in the far room, a single great shadow lurked.

From the doorway, Mr. Monarch called, "Bull! My dear, you will come out for this bit—and allow our young friend to be *privé* with the lady."

Mr. Monarch's hulking deputy lumbered from behind the curtain. He picked at his teeth with a fingernail and glared at Will on his way out. He never had much to say, and after their clash over the mail coach robbery, Will never had reason to wish him to.

Will marched Isabella to the far room.

Gray light pooled through the tall window to the left. The hearth was cold and black, and the table was strewn with crumbs and grease from the morning meal. Upon the wash line that stretched from mantle to wall corner, the latest array of pocket-handkerchiefs and shawls seemed brighter than normal amidst the squalor. In a corner, a fortunate rat squeaked.

His heart was pounding nearly as hard as when facing down the mob in the street. Whether with nerves or embarrassment or anger, he couldn't yet say.

He released her and pulled the curtain into place, shielding them from the open front door. "What in the name of all that's holy are you doing here?" Mostly anger, it seemed.

She returned the glare. "Correct me if I am mistaken, but I do believe, *sir*, that you of all people have no right to ask me such." She unfastened her skewed bonnet. Her hands trembled.

Good. God willing, she'd have nightmares of this place and never return.

He lowered the hammer on his pistol and sheathed it at his side, then removed his hat and eye-shields. "You must be mad coming here—and alone?"

She raised her chin. "As I said, I was in search of you."

The same ridiculous buzz warmed his chest again. He quashed it and kept a stern tone. "Why?"

Her chin rose higher yet. "To give you aid, of course."

"I—don't require aid. Not from you."

She looked him in the eye. "Mr. Fitzroy is mustering the King's Guard, the Army, the Lancers, the Navy even. All to halt you."

"So he says."

"Indeed." She took a breath. "All of this goes back to Dr. Silas—and to me."

"'Tis hardly your fault."

"Of course not. But as far as I know, I am more informed on this subject than any other person living."

"And so first chance you get, you escape your grandpapa and your maid and run straight into the worst place in all of London?"

A flush rose on her cheeks. "Yes, well . . ."

"Do you know what would have happened to you had I not chanced along?"

She hesitated. A multitude of emotions crossed her face: fear, excitement, relief. Perhaps even admiration. Naturally, she would never admit *that*.

She moistened her lips. "Would you have gained the ear of those men had I not been here?"

She had a point. But still.

"Your pride, my *lady*, is the most impressive beast I've ever seen."

That stoked the heat of her cheeks yet again. "And yours is not?"

"Were I you, I'd know my limits better than to go prancing into Seven Dials."

"Yet here you are."

He opened his mouth, then clamped it. "I've little time to waste—especially now I must escort you home. What have you to tell me?"

For perhaps the first time in their acquaintance, she appeared the smallest bit abashed. She must know her coming had been a foolish venture. She must also know he *had* saved her. Probably she even knew—within some part of her toff brain—that she was being insufferable.

She released a small breath. "I know your secret."

"You know all my secrets." She probably even intuited he'd once had the crackbrained notion of winning her hand.

She lowered her voice. "What I mean is I know not everything about your abilities is superior."

He narrowed his eyes.

"You will recall you told me about your dizziness."

His heart leapt. *This* was what he had wished to learn since first he came to town. "You know about that? Dr. Silas knew about it? Is there aught to be done?"

She gestured to the eye-shields he held. "And these are to protect your eyes from the light?"

"Yes." He drew nearer, casting his own voice low. No need for Mr. Monarch to know any more of his weaknesses. "Heights make me dizzy to the point of sickness, to the point I can hardly see. And the sunlight sets my whole head afire."

She took the eye-shields and held them before her face. "This is clever. It helps?"

"Some. But there's naught for the dizziness—save closing my eyes and waiting for it to pass." It was almost embarrassing to have his abilities proven so flawed. He forced a chuckle. "'Tis an inconvenience, I'll tell you. I can find my way atop a building, but I can't look down once I'm up."

She lowered the eye-shields. Her mouth hinted at a smile. "Perhaps you can." She returned the eye-shields and withdrew from her reticule an amber bottle no bigger than her smallest finger.

He accepted it. "What's this?"

"An experiment."

He dislodged the tiny cork and sniffed.

It smelt like a dog that had sampled its master's gin. His stomach rebelled. But it would be worth it if it worked. If he again faced Fitzroy, any advantage would be important.

"You made this?"

She grinned. "Some of the animals suffered as well. It was my theory that they could be aided by a precise mixture of herbs and other medicinals."

"Dr. Silas let you have theories?" The man might have been madder than he knew.

"Of course he did. That was how we met. I was visiting in the village with a charity basket, and he happened to be attending a man with a strange quaver in his voice. Dr. Silas thought it might be an effect of the trackway, which I deduced through a random comment he made."

"I'm surprised he didn't throw you out for endangering his secret."

"Immediately, his research interested me, of course. It was I who suggested he might access the energetic properties by distilling it from the geographical elements upon the focal point. He allowed I might watch—and make notes, you see. He was much impressed that I could communicate in Latin, which he found necessary for both reasons of science, and, to some smaller degree, secrecy. After a time, he allowed me my own studies." She bit her lip, looking suddenly bereft. "He was terribly open-minded."

That hadn't been Will's experience, but he kept his mouth closed. He looked at the vial. "And it works?"

"It seemed to." Her smile returned. "You will be my first subject capable of communication."

"And you can make more?"

At that, her smile slipped. "I'm afraid I haven't access to the ingredients. Dr. Silas knew a gentleman, here in London, an apothecary with whom he consulted. Some of the rarer ingredients came only from him. Unfortunately, I never met the gentleman nor attended his shop."

Will's heart sank. "You don't know where to find him."

"No, *but*"—she came forward—"Dr. Silas maintained a

thorough diary. I believe he would have recorded at least the address."

That was excellent news. That she looked not more gratified with it was *not* excellent.

"And where are the diaries now?"

She raised an eyebrow, mouth tight.

Will's heart sank. "Fitzroy?"

"He has been retrieving Dr. Silas's belongings—his research, his diaries, everything that survived the fire. I saw the crates when I was with Henry yesterday."

Will passed over the bit about Henry. "They're at his house?"

"Perhaps one or two volumes, which he is reading. He has hidden the others."

Will grunted. "That's easy enough for him to do now."

"Yes. He has not spent the night in idleness. Indeed, I now believe he has not idled away a single moment since his return from Affery."

"He's far ahead of us all, that's sure."

"He has troops—recruits—real men as well as illusions—concealed all about the city. I believe he has safeguarded the bulk of Dr. Silas's things in one of these hidden barracks."

Will's head hurt, and this time he couldn't blame the sunlight. "You don't know where any of these barracks are?"

"Not as yet."

The moment stretched between them.

After such a revelation, what was there yet to say?

"Will you . . . use my physic?" she asked.

"Yes. I will. When next I am giddy." He corked the bottle and secreted it in a coat pocket.

When he looked back up, he found himself awkward in this new, almost amiable silence between them. "I—" He cleared his throat. "If I am afflicted, mightn't Fitzroy be also?"

She hesitated. "It is true he seems fatigued, as if he carries a great weight."

Will snorted. "Guilt?" But he'd seen it too. "Last night, there was blood beneath his eyes and welling in his nostrils. That's as it was in Affery after he was first infected."

"It makes sense that maintaining the illusions would place a great strain upon his mind." She stared into the empty fireplace, calculating. "He is casting vast numbers of false images."

"And there is more than one sort of illusion, as we saw last night."

"Yes, he is able to *attach* some to physical objects."

Absently, Will scratched at a splinter in the tabletop. At times, the illusions that were naught but air had disappeared altogether, as if Fitzroy had lost control over them.

He looked up. "Perhaps in affixing the illusion to something physical, he is able to provide it a degree of permanence. Would that alleviate some of the strain upon him?"

"I do not know. Possibly? As I said, there are soldiers all about today, and I cannot believe they *all* are truly soldiers. But if they are illusions, and he is able to maintain so many so well, the strain must either be unbearable, or—"

Will stopped scratching. "Or he is far more powerful than we credit." His muscles jittered, telling him to *run, do something*—before it was too late.

He paced away.

Outside, the crowd clamored on, shouting oaths and ideas.

Thank God for Tom's handling of that—although from the sound of his own shouts, he was growing impatient too.

Still, it was better than Will could do at the moment. He rammed his fingers through his hair and clutched a handful.

"Perhaps," Lady Isabella said, "there is a way to disperse those illusions he intends to be permanent."

Will spun back. "Of course. Wait there." He crossed to the door.

Mr. Monarch had moved nearer the crate where Tom stood with Gamp and Tug, so Will's way was clear.

He spotted Lifty and gestured him over. "Picked any more soldiers' pockets?"

Lifty's wary, more-than-slightly guilty expression disappeared. "'Course, I have. I'm a responsible working lad, ain't I? I keep occupied."

"Have you any more bank notes?"

The wary look returned. "Maybe."

"Let me have one for a moment."

"Now, mate, you can't be asking a fellow that, can you? Hard-earned bread money, that is."

Gin money, more likely.

"Fine." Will reached into his pocket for the golden sov. "Hold this in assurance of my bringing back the ten bob, yes?"

Lifty's eyes widened. "You ain't been carrying this around the whole time you's in Seven Dials, have you?"

Will took Lifty's note and handed over the sov. "You carry it for me a mite longer."

Probably Lifty would have the whole beautiful thing spent before Will ever got back to him.

Inside, Lady Isabella fingered the silk pocket-handkerchiefs upon the line.

He approached the mantel to rummage for flint and steel. "We need a fire."

"Why?"

"Remember I said I discovered who imprisoned my master?"

"And that he was *not* my grandfather?" Her expression was only slightly scolding.

"Not that you care to hear a defense, but the reason—or one of the reasons—I believed it was your grandfather was because the Marshalsea ledger *said* it was your grandfather."

She frowned. Then realization bloomed. "An illusion?" She frowned again. "And you . . . saw through it?"

"Through a haze of smoke. "

"But that is splendid!"

"If we could repeat the effect, it might prove vastly useful."

She pointed to the ten-shilling note. "And this?"

"Lifty picked one off a 'soldier' the other day. He thought to buy gin with it, but I could see it was blank."

Unfortunately, flint and steel were nowhere to be found amidst the clutter of rushlights, jugs, and cutlery laid out upon the mantle's stained parquetry.

He growled.

"Here." She offered a small gilt pocket mirror. "We can use this."

He selected a short rushlight from the chipped vase upon the mantle and crossed to the window, where sunlight trickled to the floor. Careful to keep the glare from his eyes, he knelt and laid the note to the floor.

Her cunning little mirror doubtless cost more money than he'd see in a year's time. He tilted it to catch the sunlight and redirect it to the tip of the rush.

A wisp of smoke gathered. Another moment and he'd be able to light the half-blackened logs in the hearth.

Behind him, she gasped. "It *is* blank!"

"What?"

The note lay upon the floor, looking as inked and official as ever.

"In the mirror!" She knelt beside him upon the foul floor, unheeding of her already mud-splattered coat and gown. "In the mirror, it appears blank!"

He tilted his head.

Indeed, within the mirror's circle, this note was as blank as the first one.

A grin split his face. "Then he's not infallible."

She laughed, surprisingly deep and throaty. "No, he is not!" For a second, she smiled as if she were really smiling at *him*. Then she darted a hand towards the note. "Oh! Have a care!"

In his distraction, he had allowed the angle of the mirror to dip towards the note. In a hiss of orange, the paper began smoking.

She snatched it up and held it before her face, blowing softly. The sparks spread, chewing through the paper. "The smoke works too!"

"Here, now!" He reached for it. "That cost me a whole pound!"

He dropped it to the floor and patted out the sparks with his gloved palm.

"How did you realize the notes were under an illusion?" She sat back on her heels and regarded him. "You saw them through the smoke also?"

"In point of fact, I didn't."

There had not been even a haze from off the Thames that morning. It had been so bright he'd needed to wear his eye-shields.

He reached to where she still held his shields. He slid them onto his face and plunged the room into shadows.

The bank note remained unchanged.

"This makes no sense." And then he remembered. He pulled off the shields. "I was dizzy."

"What?"

"I had climbed a lamppost—to gain a better perspective of Fitzroy. Even that much height made me giddy."

She cocked her head. "But what of last night? You didn't see through the illusions then."

He frowned. "No—"

*Except* for that once when Fitzroy had struck him. He'd been dizzy then too. All the illusions had flickered out. That's what had allowed him to finally find Fitzroy amidst them.

He stood. "I can see through the illusions." In his hand, the pocket mirror winked at him. "We all can." It was the first cheerful note of the entire week.

He looked down at her and laughed.

She sat there—a lady, an earl's granddaughter—upon a filthy floor in a filthy hovel in a perilous district, where she had risked herself to help *him* in his impossible battle.

The sun gilded the radiant cream complexion of a noble-woman whose skin had rarely seen daylight. And yet—there were *freckles* too, a dusty smattering scarcely visible upon nose and cheeks.

He tried to swallow and found his throat dry.

Clearly, she cared not what people thought of her. She cared only for doing what she believed in—boldly, blindly perhaps, but without regret and without needing the reward of commendation. Not even her grandfather's.

She was not looking at him as if he were the forge boy she'd all but forgot. Neither was she looking at him as if he were the "superior" highwayman who had possibly murdered her mad mentor. She looked at him as if she—well, as if she rather liked him.

What did that mean? Anything? Everything?

Forge apprentices couldn't win earls' granddaughters. That was the way of the world. But the world was changing, and *he* was proof of that. Might she change as well?

He cleared his throat and helped her up. "My lady."

Her smile faded, but she did not remove her hand from his. "I hope you find use for the physic," she said.

"I . . . I cannot repay you."

"It is a gift." She flushed. "Let us say it is recompense, for rescuing me—again."

His neck warmed. "I need no payment for that." But it was pleasant to at last hear her thanks.

Behind him, the curtain ripped aside with a clatter of brass rings and more than a small amount of dust.

Rose stood in the opening. "There you are." She looked at their joined hands. "Well, then."

In spite of himself, the heat on his neck mounted. He released Lady Isabella's hand, and immediately regretted it. Why in heaven's name should he be embarrassed—and before Rose of all people?

"Why are you here?" he demanded.

She tossed her head. "Guess I know when I'm safe coming and going." But her mouth was pinched and her eyes failed to blaze with the same fearlessness as her words. "I'm here with a message." She raised her chin. "Soldiers came to the Marshalsea for Tom."

His entire body cinched tight. "*What?* When?" As soon as the soldiers reported Tom's absence, Fitzroy would know Will was at work against him.

Rose raised both hands. "Don't worry. That old duffer Trabb? He told 'em he was Tom."

Will's heart paused its galloping. "Did they harm him?"

"Just looked him over and told the turnkeys to lock him in a cell. Trabb didn't much like that."

Bless Trabb. Bless that bottle-headed old codger.

"We'll release him on our return." He beckoned Lady Isabella. "We've wasted too much time here as 'tis."

"Haven't you just." Rose gave Isabella a narrow look. "But there's more."

"What's that?"

"One of the collegians came back with word of strange doings nearby Drury Lane. Soldiers everywhere, and somethin's hidden there, something big."

Isabella inhaled sharply. She reached out to him, but did not touch him. "Perhaps it is one of the hidden barracks, where Mr. Fitzroy is collecting Dr. Silas's things."

That was worth pursuing—and soon. He nodded thoughtfully. "We can deface his illusions. Force him to expend more energy to maintain the deception that all is well in the city."

"Certainly, he can bear only so much mental strain. He must exhaust his physical resources before long. What he is doing is not like what you do: he can never truly rest."

Drury Lane wasn't far afield. Perhaps in time the Seven Dials lads might be convinced to put their more dubious talents to use helping him nose about.

He faced Isabella. "I need to investigate, so we can plan a proper offense. Would it be satisfactory if Tom and his collegians saw you to safety?"

She tied her bonnet's pink ribbons. "Of course. You will get word to me if you discover Dr. Silas's diaries?"

"I will, and I thank you." He ducked his head to look her in the eye. "I do mean *thank you*. But never return here, aye?"

She nodded perfunctorily, only slightly chastened. "I agree. But if I should need to get word to you?"

Rose harrumphed.

The corner of Isabella's mouth flickered with annoyance, but she kept her gaze upon Will. "I am your only spy in the enemy camp. We must conceive a way to benefit from my position."

"I don't want you endangered."

"I cannot help but hear, I cannot help but see. Do you think I would withhold valuable intelligence if I could save lives?"

Judging by today's actions, self-preservation was not her best skill.

"Fine. But only if 'tis *unquestionably* vital. And don't come to Seven Dials. Dispatch a maid or something to find me at the Marshalsea. Ask for Postelwaite. And be circumspect. We're all prisoners there, you know?"

"I understand." She started for the door, pausing only to glance at Rose. "Child, you are most fortunate to have a defender to rescue you from this place."

Rose raised both eyebrows. "Ain't the only one, am I now?"

Isabella compressed her lips and walked on.

"My lady," Will called.

She looked back.

"You won't hesitate to—call upon me if ever you feel in danger? I mean, should your betrothed fail to aid you suitably?"

The expression that crossed her face might almost have been amusement. She inclined her head and continued on into the big room.

Will jostled Rose's shoulder. "And what was that? I know you can at least pretend you're civil. She's an earl's granddaughter, you realize that?"

"Oh, yes?" Rose crossed her arms. "Since when are you caring about that? You only fancy her 'cause she's rich and hoity."

"That isn't so, and I don't fancy her, and 'tis none of your concern." At least one of those statements tasted slightly untrue—but it wasn't the last one. How anyone developed a mouth as officious as hers in naught but nine years was miraculous.

She hunched into her shawl.

Of an instant, his irritation softened.

She was jealous. That was all. She'd had no one to care for her in all her life. No one to love her. Now she thought Will was that person. And he *was* in a way, even if things couldn't continue.

He squeezed her shoulder.

She wouldn't look at him, just clutched her shawl tighter. "You'll never win her. Not if you defeat Fitzroy. Not even if you make fifty thousand pounds. That ain't how the world works."

His irritation flashed again. He wheeled her towards the door. "I know that."

She craned a look back at him. "At all events, you're worth ten of her any day, ain't you?"

That shouldn't have warmed him as much as it did.

But it did.

He squeezed her shoulder once more. "Come on. Why don't you see if you can retrieve my sov from Lifty's hot palm."

# CHAPTER 33

GINGERLY, WILL APPROACHED the edge of a crumbling roof. Around him, the world swayed. Already this morning, he had been up and down more than a score of times. The notion was that if he could use the height to trigger his dizziness, he might see past Fitzroy's illusions to find the hidden barracks—and Dr. Silas's diaries.

From the mucky street below, Gamp squinted up, arms crossed. "Well?"

The whole of the Seven Dials crew stood ranged along the street. They looked as inconspicuous as it was possible for a score of sharp-eyed, poorly-dressed, heavily-armed chaps *to* look.

Even still, they were far less conspicuous amid the ruins of Drury Lane than were the equal number of tip-toeing collegians. Tom's crew hailed from the Marshalsea and also from the handful of other gaols and sponging-houses Tom had liberated in the past week.

It had been an industrious sennight. Tom had kept the new recruits busy. Else, he said, they'd scatter. He insisted they needed something to rally to.

That bit wasn't so difficult. Fitzroy was not being subtle. Troops—real ones—were rounding up people all through the poorer yards and mews. If the city's prisons had been full last week, they were now erupting.

Will jumped from the roof to the ground, and found he needed to crouch momentarily. The dizziness was growing worse, not better. He could bear the heights for less and less time.

"Well, what?" he asked Gamp, trying not to growl.

"*Well*," Gamp enunciated, "I was hoping you might be ready to share some clever news about where to find these bloody-backs we was dragged out here to scuffle with—for king and country and our own poor necks, eh?"

Tom looked him in the eye. "And what would you have him do differently?"

Gamp chewed ragged whiskers. "Torch the street. Smoke 'em out. He says that'll clear the ghosties—and to all our eyes, not just *his*."

"That's discretion, is it?" Tom said. "Every barracks in the city would be on us before the smoke cleared." He faced Gamp, just as tall, if not so heavy. "Not to mention, this is a street of innocent homes." He wore a long gray coat and his felt hat. He was one of only a few to retain a pistol in his belt. Gamp and the Seven Dialers preferred daggers and truncheons: less risk of sending themselves to the drop by killing someone.

Gamp grinned. "Innocent, is it? Drury Lane might even be worse than Seven Dials."

Will ignored them. He rose, resisting the urge to lean against the wall. He pulled his eye-shields down his nose—the day was overcast, thank God—and scanned the opposite side of the street.

Everything looked just the same as before he'd leapt to the roof and allowed the dizziness to claim him: tall buildings with nary a cranny between, black smoke chugging from the clustered chimneys, broken panes in almost every window. Faded signs spoke of struggling custom.

All through the morning, they had been in and out of Drury Lane—down to Aldwych and even the Strand—trying to find Fitzroy's disguised warren.

Save for Gamp's rumblings and the men's nervous shuffling, the narrow street was mum as death. Even this close to Lincoln's Inn Fields and the bustle of legal business from Chancery a few streets over, all was still.

Rose clomped up beside him. "That old wife over there? Says soldiers are coming and going all the blessed time. She just don't know where it is they're coming *to*, you see?"

Will clamped his eyes shut. "Are you ever going to heed aught I say?"

"I *can't* stay in back. Mr. Monarch and Bull are there."

"What?" He dared a glance past Tom and Gamp to the back of their dubious party.

Indeed, there stood Mr. Monarch, with his tall beaver hat rakish over one eye and his walking stick beneath his arm. Bull slouched over him, a massive shield, shifting his glare from one side of the street to the other.

Regally, Mr. Monarch inclined his head to Will.

Will growled. "Thought he was staying in Seven Dials. That's why I let *you* come."

Rose scowled. "I'm more useful than that lot over there, ain't I?"

"Not much, telling me what I already know."

"Oh, yes? And you know you're looking at the wrong side of the bloody street, do you?"

He halted mid-scan.

She raised both eyebrows. "The old wife and her soldiers?" She pointed down the near side of the street.

He had, of course, scanned both sides more than once. But this time, instead of crossing the street and looking back, he peered over Rose's head, down the length of the way. His vision still swirled enough to catch the edge of something new: a gap between a falling-down tenement and a third-rate theater. He stepped into the street, turning for a better look.

Already, as his dizziness faded, a haze bloomed over the spot, like a glob of soot in a puddle. Before his eyes, a great building bloomed to fill in the gap between the tenement and the theater. Behind the haze of the new building, he glimpsed spoked iron gates—and beyond them, a dozen infantrymen lounging within a cobbled yard.

Finally. He might have been giddy out of his head and sick to his stomach all the morning, but Fitzroy could only wish for so useful a weakness.

He beckoned the men. Tom, Gamp, and Lifty crossed to join him. Rose tagged after.

At Tom's suggestion, they had divided their growing following into smaller bands, each with its own leader. For better or worse, Lifty, Gamp, Tug, Claypole, and Postelwaite had all been given positions, although each was supposed to answer to Tom. The others were off on their own missions elsewhere in the city today.

Will pushed his eye-shields back up his nose. He pointed. "This side of the theater. There's an iron gate. They'll be able to see us through it, so we must approach swiftly and get over its top. 'Tis an ordinary gate. No spikes, so 'twill be easy to climb."

Tom clapped his shoulder. "Easy for *you* to climb."

Even the slight force of Tom's slap rocked nausea through him. He had pushed too hard this morning.

Gamp peered. "You expect me to run my lads straight at a bloody building?"

"That's what we've been waiting to do all day." Why else had he made himself so wretchedly sick? "Once inside, we'll use smoke to disperse what illusions remain."

Lifty looked from the gate to Will and back again. "Why not use the smoke now?"

Will pushed past and gestured the rest of the men forward. "'Twould waste time and alert them of our presence." He turned back to Gamp. "You've seen me point out illusions all week. Have I yet to guide you wrongly?"

Gamp shifted his mouth back and forth.

The answer was *no*, and they both knew it.

Will turned to Rose. "You get to the rear."

She shook her head hard. "I ain't staying back." She glanced at Mr. Monarch and Bull.

"Well . . . stay behind us anyway." He leant on her shoulder, a bit heavier than he intended. "Once we're through, hide up against the gate, inside the illusion—where you won't be seen from the street."

Concern—for him—flickered across her face, and she touched his hand at her shoulder. But she nodded.

He eased her aside so he could face the gate. Expectant energy swirled through him and stirred his light head.

He reached to his pocket and grasped Isabella's tiny vial.

Countless times this week, he had touched it, only to leave it be. If it worked, it would temporarily eliminate his ability to see through the illusions. But the time had come. He would need a clear head now if ever he did, and for the moment, he too could trust to blind faith in finding his way to the gate.

He thumbed the cork from the vial's neck and tilted it to his mouth. The thick liquid tasted like Lifty's gin mixed with bitter herbs and castor oil. It burned through his chest and struck his stomach in a gout of heat.

He cast aside the vial and ran.

For the first two strides, the street smeared like running paint. At the third stride, he stumbled. By the fourth, his stomach was still burning like a sinner in hell—but his booted sole struck pavement firmly. The remnants of dizziness faded; the world righted itself.

Ahead, the last tell-tale flickers of the illusion vanished. Where a moment ago he had glimpsed the gate, a three-story building loomed. The rearward part of his brain screamed at him. He was running straight for a solid wall. If he leapt at full speed, he would break his every bone.

He kept running.

From behind the illusion, a sudden clatter of alarm erupted.

During his brief glimpse, the gate had looked about ten feet high. He could clear that without touching it. But the men behind needed to be shown the way. He scanned the building, searching out what should be the approximate top of the gate—several feet above the ground-floor lintels. He jumped straight up, hands reaching.

For a heart-halting second, his hands met nothing but air. Then his chest slammed the top of the gate, two feet higher than he had intended. He rammed his hands back down to catch the gate.

Even as he did so, his head penetrated the illusion and entered the courtyard.

Soldiers—most of them half out of uniform—gaped.

These days, Will was instantly recognizable. In a way, Fitzroy had advanced Will's legend. Even Mr. Monarch had only been able to paint him as a solitary lad who occasionally came larking up from the underworld. In vilifying him, Fitzroy's propaganda had transformed him into a fearsome *army* of outlaws.

Will gained a foothold atop the gate and leveraged himself up and over.

In the eyes of the soldiers, he would be flying. Some froze in their scramble for weaponry, too shocked to move. Others scrambled the faster, tripping. Only a few remained cool enough to continue loading their muskets.

He landed inside, dropping into a crouch with one gloved hand braced against the ground and the other raised behind for balance.

The yard was small—no wider than the illusive building that shielded it. Bulls-eyed by a dry fountain, it extended fifty yards back to a three-story brick barracks.

Men and still more men poured from the door. Almost an entire battalion. Some of the soldiers must certainly be illusions. This narrow place couldn't house so many.

Will rose and flowed into the dance that was becoming second nature: burst of speed to reach one opponent, pound his speed into a blow to lay the man aside, then twist about and flow directly to the next opponent.

Behind, the gate clanked. Apparently, Gamp had deigned to follow after all.

Will whirled and rushed another soldier, only to stumble through the man's body. At the corners of his vision, golden dust flickered. He stumbled hard and caught himself with a hand upon the ground.

A young trooper charged, bayonet at the ready, his cry more terrified than terrorizing.

Will flipped over, like a cat, and the blade passed above his chest, inches to spare.

Balance compromised, the soldier stumbled.

Will caught the musket and levered himself to his feet. As the soldier staggered past, he slammed the stock into the man's head.

Then he looked up.

No longer was he the center of the soldiers' attention. The men poured over the gate, yelling like harpies.

"Half are illusions, at least!" Will shouted. "Fetch the smokers!"

"Smokers!" Tom roared, battering aside a soldier.

From within his sleeve, Gamp flung his favored weapon: a two-pound cannon ball encased in a long stocking. He clouted a captain to his knees, then caught his weapon's rebound by the stocking's end and hauled it in for another go.

"Get the gorm smokers in here!" he bellowed.

From his vantage on this side of the illusion, Will could see through to the street beyond where Lifty shouted to half a dozen men. Running bent over, they rolled up the four barrels that had been kept in the rear all morning. Once the barrels were snug against the gates, they scraped flint to steel. Sparks bounced from their knuckles to the lard-soaked rags in the barrels' open tops, which were stuffed with slow-burning, smoky oakum.

With a cheer, they peered not *at* the gate, but through it. Lifty pointed at Will and laughed.

Will released his pent breath. It was working.

The breeze caught the smoke and floated the haze across the courtyard. Those soldiers who were mere illusions flickered to prismatic gold at their edges, then frayed to transparency.

"Will!" Tom shouted. "Behind you!"

Will turned.

Perhaps half the soldiers remained. Their sergeant shouted hoarsely, trying to organize a firing line.

Packed as they were within the confines of the yard, Tom's men would be destroyed by even a single volley.

Will reached the sergeant first, crashing the man to the pavement with an arm across his chest. That left him standing at the end of the firing line, looking down the row of extended muskets.

Without their sergeant to shout the command to fire, the men looked about, wide-eyed.

At the far end, one shrieked, "Ready!"

Will slammed into the first of the extended muskets and knocked it from its owner's hands. He rushed straight through the line of muskets, tearing them free, clattering them to the cobbles. The soldiers reeled, some falling, some squeezing off wild shots.

At the end of the line, Will glanced back to where the soldiers sprawled upon the ground. Already, Tom's men rushed through the growing smoke, shouting and brandishing neddy clubs and blades.

The gates gave way with a mighty clangor. Lifty and Tug and their boys scrambled over, yelling as if they'd been in on the fight from the start.

The day was as good as won.

All that remained was to deface the illusions. Destroying them was no good, since that would only ease the strain upon Fitzroy. Instead, they must create *holes* within them, revealing the truth of them, forcing Fitzroy to expend all the more energy in rectifying them.

Another thing remained: discovering Dr. Silas's diary.

Will ducked into the musty barracks.

The shadowed corridor was empty and strangely silent.

His neck began crawling, as if someone were there with him, watching. Treading carefully, he squeaked open each door to check the tidy rooms. All were empty, all were dark. In no more than a minute, he reached the corridor's end.

The final door already stood open a bare crack.

Laying his palm to the door, he eased it open.

In a rush and clatter, a red-coated sentry sprang up before him, musket raised.

Will lurched back, snatching at his pistol.

The soldier stared past, unseeing.

Saints and martyrs. He breathed out. It was but another illusion.

Had Fitzroy *expected* the barracks to be found and overcome?

Why else plant so many illusions within the walls?

Or perhaps the worth of the treasure merited such effort?

This illusion looked less solid than those in the courtyard: the sentry was faintly transparent.

Will squinted, and the transparency grew—as did the nausea in back of his head.

The physic was wearing off already? He frowned. Well, it had served its purpose. But if a single dose lasted only minutes, he would have to lay by a blessed great stock.

He walked through what remained of the illusion.

This room was different. A tiny window cast gray light across a single pallet and a large desk. Behind the desk, boxes and chests crowded the wall.

*Let it be Dr. Silas's things. Please let it be Dr. Silas's things. And please let there be an address for the apothecary.* The hand gripping his pistol trembled, just a bit.

From outside, victorious shouts filtered in.

He approached the desk.

Worn volumes piled the desk, as if the captain had been cataloging them. They were bound in soft leather and secured with huge padlocks.

*Dr. Silas's, most definitely.*

One of the diaries lay open, its adjacent padlock speared with a small key.

He tilted it towards the murky light.

*Acta hoc est stricte privata. Subsisto lectio, pediculum vobis!*

Latin probably, like Isabella's notes. *Seize it.* He'd have to take the whole lot with him and somehow smuggle them to her before he could discover if there even *was* an address to be had.

From outside, the shouts grew savage—as though the row had reignited.

Nothing for it. He snapped the volume closed, sheathed his pistol, and scooped the other diaries into a tall pile. He pocketed their keys with a jingle.

To his left, something scuffled.

He froze. Once again, the hair lifted at the back of his neck.

A breath rustled, and it was not his own.

# CHAPTER 34

S LOWLY, WILL TURNED his head. He was not alone.

Of course not. How could he have been so heedless? When he had entered the captain's quarters, the illusion of the sentry *clattered*.

He reached for his pistol, low on his thigh.

At the corner of the desk, movement flickered.

He snatched up the pistol.

In the dim light, he had failed to remark a sturdy wooden cage balanced upon the desk's edge. Two feet long and one foot high, its floor was covered in straw. Save for small pewter bowls holding water and an egg yolk, it was empty.

And then, it wasn't. Before his eyes, a sleek white animal appeared.

The ferret.

His breath caught. It was Isabella's disappearing ferret from the day he met her.

He glanced about.

Within the room's shadows, nothing else moved.

Outside, the shouting grew raucous.

Pistol in his hand, he scooped the piled diaries into his arms and returned to where the fading illusion of the soldier still guarded the door. He'd retrieve the ferret when his arms were empty or he could dispatch someone.

In the doorway, he looked back.

The ferret stared at him, black eyes glistening against white fur. It blinked and glanced over its shoulder to the corner of the room where first Will had thought to have heard someone else.

Will peered into the shadows. Was that the flash of an eye? "Will!"

He jerked about.

At the far end of the corridor, Rose stood silhouetted in the doorway. "Get out here!"

With a last glance, he left, the back of his neck crinkling once again.

He jogged down the corridor into the courtyard. The sun still hadn't appeared, but even the contrast of the gray light was enough to make him squint.

The yard was a complete rout. Soldiers were scattered upon the ground. A few were prone and still—perhaps dead. Others raised themselves to positions of dazed defeat. Seven Dialers and more than a few collegians ran about collecting weapons and searching pockets. They weren't the source of the renewed shouting.

That was coming from the streets.

"What's happening?"

Rose compressed her mouth. "Sounds like more troops are coming. Tom went off to investigate. Leaves Gamp to his own devices, don't it?"

"Well, that's prime." Will beckoned a collegian and heaped the diaries into his arms. "Guard these with your life."

The man's eyes widened.

Will glanced at Rose. "You stay here with him." She would safeguard the diaries, and the task would keep her from harm.

She raised an eyebrow, as if she knew exactly what he was about.

"Be good." He left her with the collegian and crossed the yard, pausing to leap the fallen gates.

Without, the street was pandemonium.

The few soldiers who remained had fled haplessly out here. Overcome by victory, the Seven Dialers were bludgeoning them by blunt force. Across the way, a soldier in a torn red coat dangled, wriggling, from a noose suspended over a cobbler's sign.

On Will's side of the street, two of Gamp's men had dragged a bench from within the barracks and were using it to batter a storekeeper's door. For the first time today, a few of the wary street-dwellers surfaced from their homes, pleading for their property.

Gamp was nowhere.

A frisson of something—fear, horror, and, overwhelmingly, responsibility—ran through Will. Oppose Fitzroy's mercenaries, yes. Kill an unavoidable few, no doubt. But this was not how Tom would want to fight this war.

Farther down, Lifty had accepted the sword of a surrendering private. He scrutinized the sword's silver hilt, then laid the point to the soldier's throat.

Will's rage erupted. "Stay that sword!"

The entire street stopped and looked at him. The noosed soldier kicked harder.

Will jabbed a finger at him. "Cut him down! Now!"

After one shared glance, the lads released the rope they'd used to haul him up. The soldier hit pavement, perhaps more dead than alive, but alive yet.

Will stalked down the street, past the fellows trying to batter in the shopkeeper's door. He ripped the bench from their hands and flung it aside. He continued on, straight to Lifty.

Anger trembled through him. He clenched his empty fist to keep from striking Lifty across the face. "What are you doing?" his voice emerged with surprising softness.

Lifty looked from Will to the now-silent men ranged along the street, then to the soldier kneeling before him—and then back to Will. "Well—"

Will extended his hand. "Give here the sword."

Lifty sighed. "Sterling silver, that."

"Give it to me."

Lifty handed it over, sulking. "Weren't going to kill him."

Will flung the sword to the street, with a clang.

He looked about at the men.

They stared back, some ashamed, some defiant, some merely impatient.

He raised his voice. "We must be better men than this." It was not simply a question of morality. "Everything depends upon it."

The people of London were rallying to them. They were

328 – K.M. WEILAND

watching Will and Tom and his men. They were listening. The newspapers could decry them all they liked, but upon the street, the word spoken was a different one from *outlaw*. Fitzroy insisted people believed what they saw, and what they were seeing was the Wayfarer.

Earlier this week, he had helped Tom fight a pitched battle in defense of several families being forcibly admitted to Newgate. Such exploits were spreading faster than even Lifty's handbills. Fully half a dozen public houses had scratched tremendous W's in their doors. It wasn't much, but it *was* a start.

And one day such as today could ruin it all.

Across the street, Gamp emerged from behind a tavern's splintered door. He raised a pewter flagon to his mouth, then swiped a sleeve across damp whiskers.

Will faced him and raised his voice. "Hasn't Tom said surrendering soldiers are to be given quarter? None are to be summarily executed after a battle. And no citizen's property is to be damaged."

Gamp stepped into the street. "And what about blighting the illusions? You want to put the strain on Fitzroy or not?"

"Not like this. This is ineffective."

Gamp guffawed.

Will firmed his jaw. "Fitzroy has no interest in repairing any damage you do to Drury Lane. But that"—he hooked his thumb at the smoking barracks—"that he *must* maintain."

It had been a large illusion—one of the largest yet affixed to a permanent object. Once the smoke dispersed and the illusion reemerged, the broken gates would protrude through the building's façade. The illusion would now be more than ineffective: it was proof it *was* an illusion. Until Fitzroy repaired it, it would stand a silent witness to his deception.

Tom and half a dozen collegians jogged up the street. The great rent in the sleeve of his gray coat and the trickle of blood down his arm slowed him not at all.

His expression was intent, concerned. "Reinforcements are coming. No telling as yet how many are real, but it appears a full company."

Gamp cast aside the flagon. A pillaged musket in the crook

of his elbow, he crossed the street to Will. The amusement that sometimes filled his eyes was gone.

Will held his ground.

"Look here, kinchin. You may strut like you've tail feathers." He stopped toe to toe with Will. "But know one thing."

Will hadn't replaced his eye-shields after leaving the barracks. Without them, he would appear precisely what he was: a downy-faced, callow lad.

He looked Gamp in the eye.

Gamp pointed a finger. "I don't believe in your crowing. I don't believe in you."

Will raised his chin.

Still panting, Tom came up between them. "Now's hardly the time."

"You stay out of it." Gamp glanced at Tom. "*You* I'd believe. You're a man, you're a soldier, you know which end of a musket to hang onto. And if *you* shot me, you'd shoot me straight." He looked back to Will. "But I don't like little lads telling me fairy stories. I don't like little lads telling me anything."

Will couldn't exactly argue that. But he'd faced Gamp down twice now, and twice he'd beaten the man. His youth or his size mattered not: he could do it yet again, and Gamp knew that.

Will unclenched his teeth. "We don't always get what we like from life, do we?"

Gamp leant in closer. "You come to us like a savior. Going to save London—going to save us from the evil prime minister. And now you're going to save all these poor, innocent people from the likes of ol' Gamp the Tramp."

"You're supposed to be saving them too."

"Why? Because Mr. Monarch snaps his fingers and says so?" He shook his head. "You ain't been amongst us long enough if you think Seven Dials is that simple."

"Then why are you here?"

Gamp hesitated, mouth shifting. "Whether it's accidental or not, you *are* right about some things." He took two steps back. "But you're also a bloody chancer. Can't tell me you're not. Taking every advantage of a situation. That's what you were when first I'd misfortune to lay eyes on you—and that's what you are today." He looked to where the pounding double-time of marching feet sounded around the street corner. He whistled to his men. "Come on then!"

Will glanced at Tom, unsure what he would find there.

Tom watched him. Maybe just listening, maybe considering Gamp's words.

Gamp *had* bulls-eyed the whole problem with this mad scheme of theirs. Will hadn't any of Fitzroy's powers of illusion or talents for deception to help him along. At the end of the day, all he had was the truth. And the truth was—he was everything Gamp said.

That was the problem.

He looked back at the fallen gates.

The smoke was dispersing, the illusion once again coalescing into brown mist. The remainder of Tom's men scrambled from the yard, loaded with weapons and plunder.

From their midst, Rose burst forth. Wild-eyed, she scanned the street until she found him. Then she reached back past the illusion and pulled insistently.

The chap with the diaries staggered out behind her.

Will caught her eye and nodded toward Tom, to make sure she saw him. Then he gathered himself onto the balls of his feet. "I'll circle about and draw off the soldiers."

Tom cocked his head, listening to something. "Wait—"

Energy surged through Will. He motioned a petulant Lifty aside and stepped forward. With the reinforcements marching up the western end of the lane, he could dash around the far corner and return up behind them via Russell Street to the southwest. With luck, they'd see him, swallow the bait, and follow him whilst everyone else scattered.

He took one step more and leant into his speed.

Tom grasped his coattail. "Wait!"

His speed hauled Tom forward several feet, then Tom's weight caught him up and jerked him back. He smashed into Lifty, all three of them toppling in a great heap.

"What's this?" Lifty was smashed flat on his belly beneath Will, facing back towards Tom. "I gave you the bloody sword, now didn't I? Wasn't me hanging folks or stabbin' anybody. That ain't Lifty Lefty's racket."

Rose scampered across the street. She reached for Will's elbow to dig him from the pile. "We got to move."

Will craned a look back at Tom. "What was that for?"

Tom had landed on his backside, one leg sprawled atop Lifty. He still gripped Will's coat. "Thought I heard yet more of them."

A few children—street urchins, the lot of them—rounded the corner at top speed, obviously clearing out of the way of trouble.

Had Tom not stopped him, Will would have run into it at top speed. He wouldn't have been able to slow in time. Surrounded by soldiers at both sides, he could well have been overwhelmed and captured.

Seemed he still needed Tom to watch out for him. A spot of heat rose at the back of his neck.

He breathed out hard. "Thanks."

The corner of Tom's mouth rose. His eyes twinkled, ever so slightly. Still, he did Will the dignity of saying nothing.

Will pushed up from the ground. "I'll jump to the rooftops and circle behind this lot. You'll have to scatter through the buildings—get out through the back windows into the side streets."

With a sudden gasp, Rose lurched back towards the barracks. "Will—"

"Wait—" Tom grabbed her skirt and snatched her back too. She sat down hard upon Lifty's shoulders.

Lifty brayed. "Steady on!"

Unheeding, she scrambled onto her knees to face Will. Her eyes were big. "And it's Mr. Monarch, ain't it? He was in there the whole time!"

Will took a precious second to scan the barracks' fast-disappearing entrance, just as Mr. Monarch slipped past the corner. Bull slouched out behind him, carrying something the size of a small trunk, shrouded in a blanket.

Had Mr. Monarch been in the captain's quarters? The skin up Will's spine went cold. What would he seek amongst Dr. Silas's things? Leverage on Fitzroy no doubt. But *what*?

The stamp of approaching footsteps grew thunderous.

Mr. Monarch caught Will's gaze, held it for an eternity, then smiled and inclined his head. Bull only glowered. They both hastened into the public house across the street.

That's where most of the lads were fleeing, so Gamp must have discovered a back way out.

At the moment, Mr. Monarch mattered not. Time enough for riddles later, when everyone was safe.

Will got his knees under him, felt a tug upon his coat, and looked to find Lifty guiltily snatching his hand back from Will's pocket. In pursuit of that sov again no doubt.

Will favored him with a glare, then met Tom's gaze. "Meet you back at the Marshalsea."

Tom gained his feet, already reaching for Rose's elbow. The twinkle in his eye was gone. "I don't like putting all the danger on you, lad."

Will grinned. "Less a danger for me than you, now isn't it?"

A muscle in Tom's jaw hopped. "Soon enough, we'll make a move at Fitzroy himself. Be safe."

Will saluted and gathered his speed for a leap to the nearest first-story window. Half a minute later, he gained the rooftops. Careful not to look down, he raced eastward towards all the oncoming troops Fitzroy obviously thought necessary to oppose him.

---

Four hours later, Will limped into Southwark, eye-shields in his pocket, coat collar turned down. Back in Drury Lane, he had dropped from the sky into the soldiers' rear. They recognized him immediately, of course, and gave chase.

They might have larger numbers—and firearms—and the sanction of the law—but they were surprisingly undisciplined. Members of the "dangerous classes" themselves perhaps. It made a sort of sense that Fitzroy should draw his expendable militia from amongst those he cared for least.

Problem with that was his soldiers were starting to believe in Will's legend as much as any of the others down here. They had scattered into confusion, chasing and firing after him.

For the better part of an hour, he led them a merry chase, before losing them in Cheapside, where he pulled up behind the cover of a tremendous chimney. A tiny, filthy chimney sweep was up there too. They had given each other a start, exchanged stares, and watched together as the soldiers clattered past. Then Will saluted against the brim of his hat. The boy grinned, a flash of white in his midnight face.

Now, back in Southwark, Will turned the corner of Borough High Street and trudged under the cool of the shadow cast by St. George's tall steeple. Ahead, through the growing twilight, a small crowd gathered. Something glittered—a gilt carriage. A team of matched whites tossed their heads.

*Lady Isabella.*

His heart tripped. Resisting the urge to lean into his full speed and attract even more attention to her presence, he broke into a trot and shoved through a dozen murmuring collegians.

Still within the carriage, she saw him. Relief crossed her face.

Relieved he had arrived to rescue her—again? Or relieved he had returned safely?

At her open door, Tom turned and saw him. "Thank God, Will. No trouble?"

"No. What's happened?"

Within the carriage, Dr. Silas's journals were scattered across both benches.

From under her hat's ridiculous feather, Lady Isabella looked up from the volume in her lap. "I have discovered it. The address of Mr. Losborne, the apothecary."

"Never mind that. I could have *sent* you the journals. Why have you come?"

She raised her chin. "I am gratified to see you as well, Mr. Hardy."

Did it mean something that she had progressed from *Master* Hardy?

Tom jostled his arm. "Where's your manners then?"

"Yes." She raised an eyebrow, *almost* teasingly. "It was only sensible for me to peruse the journals on the spot, else I would have had to send you another message."

With an almost physical effort, he quashed his fear. After all, Tom had been here. And for whatever it was worth, this was Southwark not Seven Dials.

"Have you the address?" he asked.

334 – K.M. WEILAND

"I shall write it down for you. Your young ward is fetching ink and paper. The shop is in Blackfriars, across the river."

Rose ran from the Marshalsea, balancing an ink well in one hand. She tromped past Will and offered Isabella a scrap of parchment and a quill. She gave him a small grin—relieved too, no doubt, to have him back of a piece.

He took a breath. "You didn't come for this, Isa—my lady. Why are you here?"

She glanced up from her scribbling. The teasing was gone from her face.

Heaven help them. His heart sped up yet more. "What is it?"

She dashed an underscore beneath the final line of ingredients and gave the paper a swift shake to dry the ink.

She breathed out. "Mr. Fitzroy has secured the physic for himself."

"How? It's yours. You said you created it. How could he have got the receipt?"

"Dr. Silas recorded it—in a different diary, one of later date than these, along with Dr. Losborne's address."

New perspiration rose at Will's hairline. "And?"

"And I believe it is working admirably for him."

For a moment, they all remained in silence.

"Well," Tom said finally. "So what we did to his illusion today—what we've been doing—'tisn't putting the strain on him, as we wished?"

"To my eye, he looks much revived already."

Rose bit her lip. "He's growing stronger?"

Lady Isabella looked to Will. "There is more, I fear."

"'Course there is," Rose said.

But Will knew already. "He has something planned, hasn't he?"

Lady Isabella piled the diaries on the seat beside her. "I was at Fitzroy House earlier today, with Henry."

Will managed not to scowl.

"Mr. Fitzroy was unhappy. Everything you have been doing—it *has* been successful."

Tom snorted. "Meaning we've only prodded him the more."

"We knew that would happen," Will said. "It was a matter of time before he planned a retaliation. But he doesn't know where we are, where we're based." He glanced past the carriage to the Marshalsea. "He's already searched here. This is the last place he'd look again."

"Maybe." Rose chewed her lip. "But Mr. Monarch knows, don't he?" She tilted her thumb towards the carriage. "Knows about her too."

"And Mr. Fitzroy certainly knows Mr. Colville is still here," Lady Isabella said.

Will looked at Tom. Even he must now see it would be daft to keep the room in the Marshalsea any longer.

"We can hide in Seven Dials," Will said. "Lifty'll get us a place. It might actually be the safest spot in all the city."

Tom frowned at Lady Isabella. "What's he planning?"

"I do not know. But it will be public. If he cannot strike at you directly, he *will* strike at your image. You have become popular with the people."

Will shook his head. "He's tried to discredit me. It hasn't worked."

"He *will* try again. It is his greatest weapon against you."

Rose looked at Will. Fear lurked in the depths of her eyes. "And what weapon do we have against him—really?"

"We have him on his heels."

"I wouldn't go quite that far," Tom said.

"Well, maybe we're as yet only a buzzing bee, but we've stung him, haven't we? And he doesn't like it." Will gave a nod. "So we continue stinging him. What is it you're planning for tomorrow? Still Whitecross-street?" It would be the biggest liberation yet.

Tom nodded.

"Well, that's what we do. Keep on as we are."

Lady Isabella gestured to several bulky canvas bundles upon the opposing seat. "I have brought tools. As many mirrors as I could purchase—torches, flint, steel. I am stockpiling more at Carstone House, should you require them."

"Mirrors." Rose eyed the bundles. "How much fortune you pay for all that?"

Will grinned. "Now, that is welcome." Manpower they had; tools were harder to come by.

"I must contribute something, must I not?"

Will looked to Tom. "You'll distribute these to the lads, for tomorrow?"

Tom pursed his lips. "However many are left after Gamp's nonsense."

Will didn't want to think about that. "I'll look up this Dr. Losborne."

Lady Isabella scribbled again, at the back of the parchment scrap, then handed it over. "These are the ingredients. I will send him a note to prepare the way for you. He will be discreet."

Will pocketed it. "I'll see if I can obtain aught for myself— and perhaps halt Fitzroy's supply." He glanced at Tom. "You can manage Whitecross-street without me?"

"I can. But do you even know whereabouts this Blackfriars is?"

Will's familiarity with London might be growing by the day, but in point of fact, he'd yet to visit Blackfriars.

Rose looked up at him and blinked, expectantly.

He sighed. "Want to come?"

Lord help him, he *was* trying to keep her from harm's way.

She shrugged. "Why not? I know the way. And I'm good at distractions, me. Coach approaching or something? I can lie right down there in front of it."

He spared half a glare. "That isn't amusing."

She grinned.

Tom just nodded. "Well, then. That's that." He touched his hat brim to Lady Isabella, then moved to the carriage door to withdraw an armful of the supplies. "You should be off, my lady. And with all due respect, don't return. The risk is too great."

She hesitated, then nodded. "You are correct, I know." She looked at Will. "I just . . . had no one I could send, no one about me I can trust, you know?"

It *would* be difficult: living with the enemy always at her back. And whatever her intentions regarding Henry, he would be no aid a'tall come the hour of emergency.

Moving Isabella to a safer location would be trickier than moving Tom, especially since the lady herself would undoubt- edly resist. Still, some part of her seemed to desire adventure. Perhaps going on the run—provided he could discover a safe place—would be adventure enough to tempt her.

He would have to mull on that. For now, there was wretch- edly little to be done.

"Have a care," he said. "If anyone should see you here, what will you tell Fitzroy—or your grandfather?"

She raised a shoulder. "That I was set upon. By ruffians." A tiny twinkle mitigated the concern in her eyes.

"Ah." He closed her door. "I think you mean gentlemen highwaymen, my lady."

Behind him, Rose huffed. "Oh, yes. Ruffian highwaymen who don't want your money and don't claw you off?"

Will glanced back. "What do you mean?"

She looked from him to Isabella, her expression conflicted. Then she raised her shoulders in a deep sigh.

She squatted to scoop up a double handful of mud and smear it upon the carriage. "It's too clean, eh? If you come from the enemy camp untouched, what's that make you?" With her fingernails, she scraped at the gilt on the door. "None of your gold is touched? Nah." She faced Lady Isabella. "Any of your toff cullies asks you, you tell 'em we took your money, your jewels, eh?"

For the first time, Isabella looked Rose in the eye—truly looked, as if she were seeing a person instead of a filthy little street urchin.

Then she smiled that smile of hers that transformed her face. "Indeed. Thank you, Rose."

Rose was the first to look away. She shrugged and tromped around to the carriage's other side to finish her work.

Will watched her go. He didn't fool himself. What she was doing was in spite of him, not for him. Rose followed her own strange code.

"Here." Isabella handed him the diaries through the window. "I dare not keep these, lest Mr. Fitzroy see them."

Will accepted them, one hand at the bottom of the pile, one hand on top.

She took a breath. "Ruffians it is then. Brazen, presumptuous, daring ruffians." A smile turned up her mouth.

He smiled back. "God bless, my lady. Be safe."

"And you as well, Mr. Hardy."

# CHAPTER 35

LADY ISABELLA'S BLESSING got Will and Rose safely across Blackfriars Bridge on the morrow. They'd difficulty deciphering her handwriting of the apothecary's address, but Rose finally gained her bearings and directed Will into what must be the narrowest lane in the entire city.

She tromped at his side, skipping occasionally to keep pace. She kept looking up at him. "Well?"

He spared a glance from the dangling, dusty signs above the entrances. "Well what?"

The street was as still as tombs, insulated from the clamoring city. They were, however, only a hop from the professional environs of the Temple and Doctors Commons. Fleet Prison wouldn't be too far either. Perhaps they should stop to investigate before returning to meet Tom in their new quarters in St. Giles.

Rose skipped once more. "Well. Ain't it time to be putting on our costumes?"

Ahead, a square sign showed the outline of an apothecary's mortar and pestle. It bore the faded inscription: *Mr. Losborne, Draughts, Lotions, Plasters, Physics, Prescriptions, & Medicines.*

Will stopped. "*Our* costumes?"

She patted the folds of her shawl. "I brung me mask."

Ah, yes, her mask. He opened his mouth to tell her the truth: that her mask was, in point of fact, one of her few misconceived ideas.

She watched him, expectantly.

He closed his mouth, then tried again. "Why the mask? No one else wears one. Tom doesn't wear one."

"They're just cullies. But me—" She pursed her mouth, as if trying for the proper words. "I'm the bulk and you're the file, eh?"

"And what's that mean?"

"You know, like when buzzers is working together. You're the one what gets the job done—what picks the pocket. I'm the one what jostles the mark and keeps 'em distracted. I'm your . . . partner."

"My partner."

"Yes. And I should get a mask, same as you."

"If you mean my eye-shields, they're mostly to keep out the sun." He pointed to his face, bare even of his raised collar today. "And I'm not wearing them for this job." Another beautifully gray day had given him the opportunity to walk about as normal as the next chap.

She sniffed. "You look better with 'em."

"Thanks." He climbed the steps and knocked. "You honestly believe that mask of yours is practical?"

She followed him up. "How's that?"

"The purpose of a mask is disguise. But you blend in. You're invisible."

"But I *am* your partner, ain't I?"

He blew out. "I . . . don't really have a partner."

"And what's Tom then?"

"He's my . . . master. He's my friend." He turned and looked her in the eye. "You're my friend too."

She kept her brows knit. "And her ladyship, what's she? She's your friend then too?"

*That's* what this was about?

He leant down to her level and set a hand upon her shoulder. "You really think this is the time to be having this conversation?" In his opinion, they *never* needed to be having it.

She cocked her mouth, reproachfully. "You like her better than me, don't you?"

"No. I don't. It's . . . different." He was beginning to feel a bit reproachful himself. He could think about the Lady Isabella any way he wanted to think, without it being any concern of a little girl.

Footsteps scraped behind the closed door.

He turned to face it. "Why does her ladyship matter to you?"

The footsteps halted. A pause ensued, and then the latch scratched.

"Well. I just been wondering, you know. What happens to me once all this is over? Once you've beat this Fitzroy cove at his game, yes? You're going to be a hero, go off with Tom, smell madly of April and May whilst saving her ladyship, all that. You're taking me with you, ain't you?"

Unlike him, her mind always seemed to be leaping to the far future. Meanwhile, *his* imagination was busily full of death and despair and the entirely too practical prospect of Fitzroy's tossing them all into Newgate's darkest corners. The present was all he could control, so it was much better to concentrate on that.

He'd rather hoped Rose might be doing the same. But no, of course she wouldn't be. Of course, she would have heard everything he *wasn't* saying. *Couldn't* be saying.

"When the time comes and I must move on with Tom, I will find you a safe place." He looked back. "I will not leave you in danger. I promise you that."

The tension in her face didn't ease. She nodded, as if this were what she'd been resigned to all along.

It wasn't what she wanted, he knew that. But it was all he could legitimately promise.

The door opened a crack, and an eyeball—topped by a long white brow—appeared, followed by the corner of a mouth.

"What do you want?" The man's voice sounded reasonably educated—no Cockney accent despite the proximity to Bow Bells. But it pitched high and alarmed, almost cracking.

"You're the apothecary?"

"Who are you?"

"I'm . . ."

The name *Will Hardy* would mean nothing to this man, and aside from the pretension of the announcement, *Wayfarer* came loaded with problems—especially since Fitzroy had already got to Mr. Losborne first.

Will smiled—friendly in an *I-mean-no-harm* sort of way, but not too friendly in an *I'm-trying-to-put-you-off-your-guard* sort of way.

"The Lady Isabella Barbary was to send a note on my behalf."

The eye stared, blinked. "Well, she didn't."

"She . . . didn't?"

Who knew what went on in her toff brain, but she didn't seem the sort to go back on her word. Unless danger had prevented her.

His heart sped up, firing his body with the now familiar need to run. "Mr. Losborne, I must speak with you. 'Tis urgent."

"Shop's closed." Mr. Losborne moved to slam the door.

Will moved too. He slapped the door, the thrust of the blow shoving it open.

Within, a tiny man, wearing an open waistcoat and dowdy knee breeches, stared through half-spectacles. His cloud of white hair wafted in the breeze of the door.

His eyebrows twitched. "What—? You—? You're one of *them*!" He looked as if he couldn't decide whether to be terrified of Will's speed or fascinated by it.

Will tried to maintain a level voice. "In point of fact, there's only two of 'them'—myself and another."

Mr. Losborne snorted. "You believe that, do you? Anyway, the *other's* already been here. I can't place money on both boxers in the same match, now can I?"

Will crossed the threshold. "I shan't harm you."

Mr. Losborne glanced at Rose. "Well." He eyed Will from under his prodigious eyebrows. "But *he*—the other'n—might. Comes parading in here, all bundled up in a great cloak, thinking I won't know who he is. But I know! I went to Westminster for a glimpse." He tapped his nose. "And then he's showing me old Theobald's diary with that barmy recipe for curing all manner of nastiness he's dredged up with his beloved 'plague.'"

"You know of the Affery plague?"

Rose scooted in to stand beside Will. She peered about the shop with interest.

Mr. Losborne retreated behind a high counter covered with

vials, jars, and packets. The whole room was dark and dusty and smelt of powdered herbs—thyme, saffron, comfrey.

He set his hands firmly upon the counter. "Of course, I know of the confounded plague. I can't cook up something to aid Theobald's poor animals without first knowing what he's done to them." He frowned. "Won't say it's sacrilegious, quite. But it doesn't strike one as responsible, does it?"

"You've obviously realized Fitzroy is dangerous."

"And you're not?"

"Not to you."

"But he is to Fitzroy," Rose put in.

That stopped Mr. Losborne. He pursed his lips.

Will dared another step. "This antidote—or physic—or whatever you want to call it—it worked. It works on me, and 'tis working on Fitzroy."

"Of course, it works."

"Have you any you can give me?"

Mr. Losborne hesitated. "To even the odds, is it?" He glanced to the other end of the cabinet at what looked like a great pile of triangular snuff packets. With a sigh, he walked to the end of the cabinet and gestured to Rose. "Let the child come for it."

Relief flooded Will. Then there was yet hope for conquering the dizziness. Isabella's vial hadn't been a singular solution.

He kept a firm face. "I thank you, sir, but you realize I must do more than merely *even* the odds."

At the counter, Mr. Losborne froze, hand outstretched to give one of the packets to Rose. "Fitzroy's ordered a regular supply, you know. What will I tell him?"

"Don't tell him aught." Reaching gently for the extended packet, Rose nodded to the pile. "Give Will this lot and make another for Fitzroy—but leave somethin' out of it, see? Somethin' important."

"Or," Will said, "you could come to one of our refuges. You'll be safe."

Mr. Losborne's eyes flickered. He was no more a fool than was Fitzroy. He had to know Will *would* force him should he fail to choose rightly of his own will.

Will eased another small step forward. "Her ladyship believes you are trustworthy. I believe *her*."

That did it. The resistance—and a measure of fear—drained from Mr. Losborne's face. "Her ladyship." He snorted. "What she's doing mixed up with Theobald, I'll never know. She should be grateful he moved on, she should." He sighed again, pulled the packet from Rose's grasp, and flicked it back into the pile. He ducked behind the counter.

Rose cast Will a questioning glance.

He raised a hand in a staying gesture.

Mr. Losborne resurfaced with a burlap sack. Hugging the pile of packets to himself, he dumped them all inside.

Rose's outbreath was audible.

Will held his in, but he shared the sentiment.

"Ah well," Mr. Losborne said, "and I'm old, aren't I?" He peered over his spectacles. "And you did ask a mite more civilly than the other."

"Thank you, sir. You may have saved my life."

"Yes, I know, and half the city besides." Mr. Losborne twisted the bag shut and handed it over the counter to Rose. "I'll make up the altered batch for Mr. Fitzroy, and then perhaps I'll travel." He pushed the spectacles up his nose. "London isn't the place to be at the moment. Could be I'll have to join old Theobald."

Will blinked. "Don't do anything . . . rash, sir."

Mr. Losborne pondered. "Well, Paris might be rash at that. Brussels, maybe." He turned to the shelves behind the counter and started removing bottles.

Rose held the bundle with both arms and maneuvered back to Will. "Ready?"

He didn't move. "Paris." His heart pounded an insistent tattoo.

Mr. Losborne looked back, eyebrow raised so high the long hairs quivered in the draft from the door. "That's right, Paris."

"You're saying Dr. Silas is in Paris?"

In response, the other eyebrow rose, clearly sardonic.

"Dr. Silas is in Paris—he's alive? He didn't die in the barn fire? I . . . didn't murder him." He looked at Rose.

She looked suitably impressed. "Blimey. Back from the dead."

"But he died," Will said. "I saw his body. Burnt to a black char."

With a grunt, Mr. Losborne lined his bottles upon the counter. "Heaven knows how old Theobald came by *that*. But you can be sure a man so cagey isn't going to be dying in a fire of his own making. I'd word from him only last week. He's gone abroad to continue his research. If I wasn't now following right after him, I'd say good riddance."

Will found he had to remind himself to keep breathing. He shouldn't be so surprised. The body he pulled from the fire had been already too far burnt to have ignited with the blaze. And the newspaper clipping Isabella had received—it must have been from Dr. Silas, warning her in his own strange way that he was yet alive.

Mr. Losborne squinted, thoughtfully. "You say you know her ladyship?"

Rose snorted. Will nodded.

"Well, then." He withdrew a folded letter, sealed persistently with five globs of red wax. "Seeing I'm headed across the water myself, perhaps you'd be so good as to pass this on to her."

"From the doctor?"

"From himself."

Will came forward to take it. "Thank you, sir. For everything."

Mr. Losborne shrugged. "Theobald thinks he's living in the age of miracles. But I told him I'd prefer the real plague any day. At least a man knew where he stood with that."

"Indeed." Will touched his hat and followed Rose out.

He shut the door and paused upon the step.

She waited at the bottom, arms around the burlap sack. "So what's that all mean? The cove you was supposed to have killed, he done it to himself—only he didn't?"

"It means . . ." He studied the missive. One word was scrawled over its front in great smears of black ink: *Her*. "It means, there's a chance yet for me. For a cure."

He could go to Paris. Take Tom with him. They could put this whole nightmare to their backs. Wheresoever Will might find Dr. Silas, that was where he'd find hope for recovery, for healing. Indeed, it was his only hope. Once more a normal life for him. No more the runaway heartbeat, the burning headaches, or the nauseous dizziness.

He gripped the letter until it crinkled. Then he sucked in a great draft of air and secreted the missive in his coat pocket. He would take it to Isabella tonight. Perhaps it would offer them an address. Perhaps they could leave immediately. Perhaps she might even come with him.

Of course, there was yet the revolution brewing here at home—which he and Tom had helped start.

He chewed his lip.

Far away, past the end of the street, a clamor arose, louder than the customary bustle. It seemed urgent, chaotic, ireful even.

Frowning, he leaned down to open the sack in Rose's arms and withdraw one of the twisted packets.

"You're going to swallow that?" she asked.

The thought of clearing this accursed dizziness from his head, even for a short time, was exhilarating. "'Tis what it's for."

He tore open the packet. Unlike Isabella's vial, this was nothing but powdered herbs. The liquid in hers must have been all gin—little wonder it smelt of a public house.

Still, this smelt as rank. Wrinkling his nose, he poured it into the back of his throat. Dry as it was, it coated his tongue and his throat. He gagged, coughed, swallowed, then coughed again, spastically.

Rose shifted the bundle to her hip so she could whap his back. "And I thought you was all pleased t'other day because being dizzy let you see past Fitzroy's ghosts? 'Tis a special power in itself, I'd say."

He swallowed another cough. The back of his nose burned, and his eyes watered. "Thanks to the smoke, *everyone* can see through the ghosts." He took the sack from her and guided her down the street.

"Ain't always got smoke."

"Nonsense."

Already, his head seemed clearer. The edges of the buildings, the railings, the steps, and the signs all seemed sharper, the dusty colors more vivid. He walked with a lighter step.

Towards the end of the street, the houses tapered nearer, coming together in a solid wooden gate. Beyond, the crowd clamored. Voices shouted angrily.

He halted, pulling Rose to a stop alongside him.

"*We shan't be put upon like this!*" a man cried.

"*Bloody champion, indeed!*"

"*And the papers is true after all, ain't they?*"

The skin up his back went cold.

"Corblimey," Rose muttered.

He scanned the alley. He could jump the gate with ease, but doing so was always guaranteed to draw attention.

Rose knelt where a two foot plank had been broken off the gate's bottom. "Sometimes," she said, "I think you bring me 'cause I'm the only one what's little." She looked at him, knowingly. "Mr. Monarch uses the little'ns too, you know."

He leant back. "You're saying I'm like Mr. Monarch?"

"Don't be barmy." She rolled her eyes. "I'm saying I'm valuable—valuable enough to be a partner."

He glared. "Partners don't sit about having conversations in the midst of a crisis."

With a sniff, she wiggled through the crack.

Beyond, glass shattered.

The voices rose, including a new addition: "*You people had best mark me. You want protection—you want considerations? Then you best stand out of the way of me and my chaps!*"

If that was one of Fitzroy's soldiers claiming to protect anyone, that was a first.

Setting the sack upon the ground, Will reached first into his coat pocket for the iron knuckles and then into his boot for the twisted rod. He hadn't brought his cutlass-pistol—too conspicuous, especially since he hadn't intended to meet with any resistance today.

His heart started pounding.

Rose thrust her head back through the crack. Her eyes were wide, her face white. "Best get out here."

He took three running steps towards the gate and hoisted himself into a crouch atop it.

Below, the street was crowded with costermongers, customers, and passers-by. In front of a moneylenders' shop across the way, traffic had jammed to a halt.

In front of the shop's shattered window, a man stood. And that man was Will.

# CHAPTER 36

WILL'S HEART CLOGGED his throat, but only for an instant.

The man across the street—the man with *his* face—was, of course, another of Fitzroy's infernal doubles.

Up this high, Will should have been able to see through the illusion, but thanks to Mr. Losborne's physic, he wasn't dizzy enough to work that particular magic.

The double wore Will's usual costume—long coat, high collar, eye-shields, cutlass-pistol. He gripped the sleeve of a fat, well-dressed chap—the shop owner, no doubt—and waved his pistol at the crowd. "This ain't between me and you lot, is it now? This is between me and this gent. I've to eat too, haven't I? I've to feed my men, haven't I?"

"Bloody highwayman!" someone shouted.

"Curse me for a fool," said another. "And I'd almost believed the papers were naught but lies!"

"Stop your jaws!" the double shouted. "You should be grateful, you should! The papers *is* lies. Your Prime Minister, he's nothing but a rotting carcass. I'm the one protecting you, ain't I?"

"And who's protecting us from you and your devils, I'd like to know? You're in it for naught but the fame and the money, same as any other outlaw!"

Will had known Fitzroy was trying to discredit him. Up until now, he'd been relying on his own actions to disprove the newspapers' lies and the illusions. This, however, wasn't a mere

348 – K.M. WEILAND

illusion. This was a reality the people could see. It was a reality they would *believe*.

"*Hsst.*" Below, Rose beckoned.

Faces were turning in his direction.

He dropped off the gate and blinked hard. Thoughts blurred through his head.

"What are you going to do?" she asked.

"Stop him. I have to stop him."

"Wait." She grabbed his hand. "You look a common chap today, remember? Nobody'll know 'tis you. They'll still think he's the one."

Seize it. And him leaving half his costume behind today of all days.

He shot her a sharp look. "Where's your mask?"

Her face lit up momentarily, then sobered as she realized his intent. She dug into the voluminous folds of her shawl and came out with the black cloth. "Might not fit."

He tied it about his face. The eye holes that had been too wide for her were a bit close for him. But it would work. He could see well enough.

He turned his collar up over his mouth. "Be ready to flee if things look the least bit foul."

"I could be a distractio—"

"Rose."

She firmed her mouth. "Fine."

He eased into the crowd, slowly. He couldn't risk trampling anyone.

Even still, people peered at him. They saw his mask and the crude dagger in his hand, and they flinched back.

Whispers followed him.

*"Here's another!"*

*"The whole band'll be here, won't it then?"*

*"I ain't standing for this. I don't have to stand for this!"*

Will sought to steady his voice. "Be at peace." But the words came out too softly. He raised his voice, deepening it. "This man is an impostor. He was sent by Fitzroy to confuse you!"

Silence followed—and then, snorts of derision.

He gritted his teeth and continued on, pushing people out of his way.

They, in turn, skittered back from him.

The double had stopped his shouting and was looking straight at Will. Impossible to tell from behind the illusion of the eye-shields, but the rigidity of his posture *might* speak to sudden fear.

That was something, at all events. If the double believed in Will, that would be the surest testimony to Will's authenticity.

Will pointed the twisted rod at the man. "What are you about, sir?" Two steps more and he would be free of the throng and able to rush him. He gathered himself, ready to fly.

A hulking burgher stepped in front of him, a spade cocked over his shoulder. "Devil take your scurvy hide. Who do you think you are?"

Will pulled up short, off balance. "You . . . know who I am."

The burgher's broad, honest cheeks were flushed. "*You're* the bloody Wayfarer?"

From behind Will, someone shouted, "Get on with you, mate! If you're *not* one of them, you'd best clear out, because we ain't standing for this no more." The man raised his voice, directed at the double. "You hear?"

Well, that's what Will got for wearing Rose's crooked mask.

The burgher took a heavy step towards him—as if trying to frighten a stray dog.

Will growled. "I haven't the time for this." He dodged the burgher with all speed and slipped past.

The burgher jerked forward to stop him. He met empty air and lost his balance.

Several people gasped.

"It *is* him!" the burgher shouted.

Good. Will breathed out, relaxing the part of his brain that had been occupied with the crowd. Now he could focus upon the double.

The double was already leaning back, seeming all too ready to flee.

Under other circumstances, Will might have allowed himself a grin. But he was wearied to death of this—of Fitzroy's masquerade, of his scheme for the "greater good" and its wanton destruction of lives.

He halted within three yards of the double. "Give the man to me." From here, Will could snatch away the double's pistol if he so much as twitched it.

For a long moment, the double remained frozen. Then he shouted: "Beware, sir! Behind you!"

He had a partner? Will frowned. But even before he could look over his shoulder, he heard the crowd.

They were roaring—moving forward.

Time stretched around him. For the instant, it felt as if he were slow, so very slow, slower even than before the plague. Perhaps it was because he did not wish to see what he knew he would.

The crowd's fury exploded. They surged forward—towards the double. But also towards Will.

As far as they were concerned, *he* was the double's partner.

He backpedaled, clumsily. "Stop! This man is no associate of mine!"

They kept coming, the burgher at their front. They swarmed both him and the double.

The double laughed, hard and bitter. He must know he had doomed himself, even as he had doomed Will. He fired the cutlass-pistol into the crowd.

A woman screamed in pain, and the crowd's fury rose higher.

Will scrambled back, pushing against them, dodging out of their way. "Wait—"

The burgher swung the shovel at his head.

Will ducked so fast the air whistled in his ears. He came back up, energy buzzing through him.

The crowd overwhelmed the double. He went down, shouting vile curses.

Panic flooded Will's brain.

Fighting these people would only confirm their belief in his antagonism. But if he remained, they would kill him.

Hands reached for him, grasping at his coat, tearing at his mask. Faces leered, flushed, sweating, angry—and just as fearful as he was himself.

"Troops!" A child's high voice—Rose's voice—pierced the length of the street. "They're comin'! Scatter!"

The crowd did *not* scatter. But a good many at least turned to look.

With tremendous effort, Will twisted free. He shoved the burgher and leapt for the near eaves. Flatfooted as he was, he barely caught them with both hands.

Someone swiped at his leg.

He kicked hard and hauled himself to the roof by raw strength.

Across the way, at the gated cross lane, Rose gave him one sharp nod, then wiggled back through her hole.

Amidst the turmoil below, the double had gone down. Cursing, the crowd pounded him with their fists, with their shovels, with whatever came to hand.

Still more men were climbing up the windowsill to gain the roof in pursuit of Will. Their faces were twisted in anger over what *he* was doing to them. They thought him a common thief, a bandit. They thought him no better than a Seven Dialer.

He opened his mouth to tell them the truth.

But of course they would not credit him.

Fitzroy had won this battle. How many battles like it was he winning all across the city?

The bitter aftertaste of Mr. Losborne's powder sharpened within his mouth.

The burgher hauled his head and shoulders over the eaves, and Will stared into his eyes. Let him understand. Let him see Will was not an enemy.

With a roar, the man kept coming. "Here he is, the blighter! I've got 'im!"

Will turned away. He ran.

―――――――――

He would have run to exhaustion, had Rose not finally hailed him.

In a side street off the Strand's bustling thoroughfare of fancy shops, he skidded to a halt. He wheezed, feeling quite as wild as he doubtless appeared.

She frowned over the top of Mr. Losborne's bundle. "Hold up and catch your air. Don't need you swooning again, do I?"

Every breath burned fire through his chest. He had torn a

fingernail in scrambling onto the roof, and dried blood cracked along the back of his hand. Her mask was a damp ball in his sweating fist.

He could not keep still. He stalked on, breath clawing at his chafed throat. "God help us, Rose. What am I to do now?"

She trotted after. "You tried to save the muggy cove, didn't you?"

He spun to face her and slapped his chest. "They think *I* did it. How can they think that? After everything I've tried to do!"

He felt betrayed.

He huffed.

Rose contorted her face, mingling concern and uncertainty. If even *she* had nothing to say, they must be dished indeed.

He snorted. "I knew Fitzroy would do this—*was* doing this. I just thought I was doing it better."

The last of his energy drained from him. He could collapse in the street right here and close his eyes against this wretched world and sleep and sleep and sleep until it was all at an end. And then he and Tom and Isabella could search out Dr. Silas.

"Not everyone believes Fitzroy's rubbish," Rose said.

"Enough do, that's clear."

In the street, hackney coaches and carriages clattered past.

She looked sidelong. "You know it ain't personal? They don't know *you* one way or t'other, so it ain't truly you they're thinking badly of, now is it?"

He was a fool to make it personal in any measure. He needed their regard only to combat Fitzroy's lies. And yet . . . it hurt unduly.

That they should care so little for the risk he and Tom were taking—nay, that they should *despise* him—made it all seem so wasted.

He thrust his hands into his coat pockets.

If they did not want him to champion them, then what in heaven's name was he doing?

Only a few yards ahead, a closed carriage rattled to a stop.

A woman, veiled in dark blue, thrust a gloved hand through the open window and beckoned Will. "You there!"

Rose grabbed at his arm.

"I say." Inside the carriage, a man drawled, "Really, Mother."

The woman raised her veil. Framed within the window, Esther Fitzroy gestured. "Come here immediately."

Will hesitated. But what cause could this woman possibly have for speaking to him?

"Who's that?" Rose hissed.

The driver urged the horses forward, bringing the window alongside Will.

"Come, come." Mrs. Fitzroy gestured to Will. "Afford some haste, can you not? I require you to do me a service—to carry a message. It is most urgent."

Had she gone barmy? She spoke as if he were her servant, not her husband's dire nemesis.

He started to shake his head. And then the truth of it struck.

She spoke as if he were *one of her husband's servants*. She thought him a double, at her beck and call.

She glanced at Rose, then back to Will.

His expression must have revealed his realization, for its mirror image dawned in her own. "You—"

He touched his forehead. "At your service."

Her eyes flashed. "Indeed."

Henry leant forward. "What are you on about now? All this shopping and searching. We're farcically late for Father's grand dinner." He sniffed at Will. "Speak with one of the other chaps once we're home, what?" He knocked his walking stick against the ceiling. "Drive on, Darnay."

Mrs. Fitzroy opened the door. "Stay!" She leapt out, catching Rose by the arm.

With a yelp, Rose kicked at Mrs. Fitzroy's leg, striking only petticoats. The bundle in her arms jostled, and several packets fell to the pavement.

Will seized Rose's other arm. "Release her."

"No. You stand and you listen to me." A flush heated Mrs. Fitzroy's cheeks. She looked overwrought—feverish even, as if this business were burning her up from the inside out.

She glanced to the fallen packets on the pavement. Her gaze darted back to Will's—full of sudden knowing.

His heartbeat ratcheted back up. Would she realize he had

found Losborne thanks to Isabella's guidance?

"What do you want?" He dropped all measure of entreaty from his voice.

Her mouth quivered. "I want, *Will Hardy*"—that drew a start from Henry—"my husband's safety."

He raised an eyebrow. "From me?" Apparently, she had yet to realize the contest was weighted in Fitzroy's favor.

Her mouth twitched in a false little smile. "I despise what he is doing, you understand?"

Rose blew a quavery breath. "Then why not shove off?"

"He is my *husband*."

Will looked her in the eye. "People are suffering, dying. The social revolution he is trying to create—it is monstrous."

She hunched.

He leant forward, pressing the point. "If you go along with him in this—if you aid him—you are complicit."

Dread filled her face, almost as if she expected a blow.

"You are his wife." He poured all the persuasion in his soul into the words. "You, if no one else, have the power to influence him, to halt this."

Her rage reignited. "His *wife*. Pray, do not be imbecilic. I have no power over my husband. I never have." She straightened. "What kind of a man would he be, if I did?"

"If your advice were for him to stay his hand, and if he heeded you, then what he would be, madam, is a far better man than he is today."

Her nostrils flared. "You know nothing of my husband. You know nothing of what he has done, from where he has come."

"I know all about where he's from. I know all about what he has *done*." God blind Fitzroy, with his charm and his daring and his golden, ruthless words. The world fell at his feet, and without hesitation, he trampled it. "Your husband is the worst of brutes, and you, of all people, know it to be so."

"You have no idea at all what was done to him!"

"He does not deserve your loyalty. I do not believe he ever did."

She raised her chin. "It matters not what he does, or who he is. I will stand behind him, I will aid him, and I will protect him."

Once more, she hid her pain and despair behind the cracked mask of faded beauty.

Rose glanced back and forth, anxiously.

Will tightened his grip on her arm. "What do you want of me?"

Mrs. Fitzroy worked her mouth, as if doing difficult sums.

Finally, she raised her shoulders in a determined breath. "There is a man of your acquaintance. I wish you to carry him a very clear message. Inform him he must not attempt to write or meet my husband again. Whatever he thinks he offers, it is worth neither the past nor the present association."

A chill touched Will's neck. "What man?"

"A Mr. Monarch."

Mr. Monarch had been in communication with Fitzroy—*after* throwing his support behind Will?

Why? To bargain for his life? Or to exchange Will—or Tom—for a high position in this new order of things?

"I know you will carry this message," Mrs. Fitzroy said.

"Does it come from Mr. Fitzroy—or from yourself only?"

Her eyelid flickered.

Then it was her desire alone? Fitzroy had, unfathomably, decided *not* to destroy Mr. Monarch?

"You will take this message," she said. It was not a question.

"What I do or do not is my affair."

She frowned. "You will do my bidding, or I will punish, not you, but this child." As suddenly as that, she produced the short gleam of a stiletto blade.

Rose choked and froze. She looked up at Will, panic lighting her eyes.

Without even time for thought, Will seized Mrs. Fitzroy's hand upon her dagger and yanked Rose back.

Both of them yelped faintly. Rose recovered first, scrambling to crouch behind him. One hand upon his coat skirt, she began gathering the fallen packets.

Mrs. Fitzroy glared. She tried to free her hand but had not the strength.

He squeezed her wrist, forcing her to drop the dagger. Then he pushed her away.

She rubbed her wrist. "You are a beast."

"You know enough of that sort to make the judgment, I suppose." He toed the dagger behind him where Rose could reach it, then sidestepped to hold the carriage door.

Mrs. Fitzroy hesitated, visibly gathering herself—and her pride. Scorning Will's offered hand, she reached inside for her son's.

Henry tsked. "Now we shall surely be late. Father won't like it. All those foreign dignitaries come to toast him and all that jolly rot." He looked to Will—really looking now that he recognized this rumpled highwayman as his father's erstwhile house guest. "Well, so you're the Duke of Veneering, are you? I rather wondered."

Ah, yes, another unfortunate connection to Lady Isabella.

Will hid a scowl. "Henry," he returned, shunning any appellation of respect.

Henry slouched against the seat cushion. "I simply can't deduce what all the fuss is about." Despite his pout, he knit his brows almost earnestly. "There didn't need be all this row. Father liked you, you know. And believe me, he doesn't like many chaps."

Mrs. Fitzroy restored her veil. "Darnay!"

As the carriage lurched, Henry leant around his mother. "Why not return? Father might have you, you know." He turned up his nose at Rose. "Leave behind all the dirt and insects. Why not wealth and respectability instead?" He resumed his seat. "You've the talent for it, I warrant, even if some of us haven't."

Mrs. Fitzroy raised the window glass with a sharp crack. Darnay snapped his whip, and the horses trotted on.

"Cor, but she's barmy." Rose tilted her mouth, cogitating for a moment. "I suppose that ain't so good about Mr. Monarch, is it?"

"No. 'Tisn't good a'tall."

He and Tom must take Seven Dials in hand today, even enact Tug's idea of a barricade. Mr. Monarch would appreciate neither, but that was growing more and more beside the point.

He watched the carriage clatter around the corner.

Rose peered at him from over the top of the regathered bundle. "What that buck said—about Fitzroy taking you back—ain't likely to be true. You know that?"

"I know it."

Fitzroy had already played that card, and Will had been right to refuse it. Fitzroy would only have used him—as he used his wife, as he was most certainly using Mr. Monarch.

Still, something within twinged. Had he been able to join Fitzroy, he wouldn't now be fleeing across rooftops. The very people he was aiding wouldn't be spitting after him and casting rubbish.

He'd be attending fancy dinners for foreign dignitaries, perhaps even courting Lady Isabella in earnest. But now, in all reality—cursed, dark, bleak reality—the best he could do for her was to save her from her attempts to aid *him*.

With any amount of fortune, Tom would have returned from the Whitecross-street mission by now. He wasn't going to like the idea of departing for Paris, but even he must now see the necessity. Before the night was out, Isabella might be in greater danger than all of them combined, and Tom himself would most assuredly be next.

He swung Rose onto his back. "Time to go."

# CHAPTER 37

WHEN THEY FINALLY made it back to Seven Dials, Mr. Monarch was nowhere to be found—which made Will only slightly less nervous than it did Rose. Still, it left one less thing to be dealt with tonight.

In the faint glimmer of a rushlight, he dug through Lifty's room, searching out his hat and eye-shields. He would not be without them again.

Tom leant in the doorway, fingers under his armpits. As of today, Lifty begrudgingly shared the room with him as well.

"Once you find her ladyship, you're going to do—what? You can't bring her hither."

Will pulled one of Mr. Losborne's packets from under the bed where Rose had stashed them before she'd run after her tea. "I must."

Tom snorted. "Safety is hardly abundant here either, lad."

Will pushed the bundle back under the bunk and rose. "You and me and Rose and Lady Isabella—we must be ready to leave."

That drew the expected scowl. Tom dropped his arms and came forward. "The Whitecross-street liberation went better even than the Marshalsea's. A full hundred men, at least, are ready to join the cause."

"Until Fitzroy's whispers convince them *I'm* the one thirsty for their blood."

To that, Tom could only close his mouth.

The turning of today's mob was a bad sign, and they both knew it. Rumors flew faster than the fog off the Thames. If the right wind got behind the news, then everything they'd accomplished could blow away in a twinkling.

Tom shook his head. "I've an idea for taking this fight direct to Fitzroy's door. With the aid of the stockpile Lady Isabella is gathering, the foundation's already in place. I tell you we can beard the dog in his dwelling. If we can only keep hold on this a little longer, it's going to become bigger than just us."

"That's good." Will couldn't hold back the bite of irony. "Because we can afford to stay no longer. I'm not jesting this time, Tom. I mean it. And—" He gained a breath. "I believe Dr. Silas may not be dead after all. He's in Paris. He can aid me."

Tom frowned. "Didn't know you were in such need of aid."

"I haven't told you all. But it *is* a plague, Tom. I must find Dr. Silas while I may, before he moves on. He's the only one who knows enough to help, to tell me if the symptoms may yet grow worse, if they may even . . . kill me." He buttoned his coat. "We can take Lady Isabella with us to the coast, Cornwall perhaps, find a ship. She will wish to seek out Dr. Silas too."

Tom's mouth shifted. "You're giving up."

Will glared. "*No*. I still intend what I intended from the start, which is keeping you safe. What's happening here is not our battle, it never was."

"Isn't it?"

Will turned to where his weapons were laid out on the bunk and pocketed them. "We'll find Rose someplace safe along the way. Some family to care for her."

"She won't like that."

"She's a little girl. She doesn't get to make this decision."

Tom snorted, without humor. "Wasn't long past, you were the one too young to be making decisions. And now here we are. Don't even want to listen to your old master, do you?"

Will faced him. "I am listening. But what else am I supposed to do here—within reason? Tell me that."

Tom's brow creased.

Will lowered his voice. "I'm *glad* you've faith in what's happening. But—" The truth sat heavy on his tongue. "All I have faith in now is that sooner or later, everything is going to explode beneath our feet. Am I to exchange your life—or Isabella's—for the wretches who live upon this street? A hundred of them aren't worth one of you, and I refuse to pay that price."

"Will. Listen to me." Tom came forward. "What we're doing, *why* we're doing it—and certainly the things that have happened to you—they're not easy. I know it. But you've been given a chance to do something important."

"And I've *done* it. You said yourself, we've put the wheels in motion. We've shown those who wish to fight how to protect themselves. What happens now depends on factors beyond us."

"You can't tell me you don't understand this is about more than just *stopping* Fitzroy."

"Then what? You tell me."

Tom halved the distance between them to only a few feet. "You can do something here, Will." He pointed at the filthy floor. "*Here.* If we win this—if you save this place and others like it—you'll have a chance, not merely to stop the bad, but to do something good."

Will started shaking his head. Gamp and Tug and Lifty and Mr. Monarch and that mob in Blackfriars today—they'd all clarified the folly of any larger mission.

Fitzroy wasn't wrong about their being reprobates.

Tom leant back, mouth shifting. "You saved Rose, didn't you?"

"Rose is one little girl."

Will huffed. He hadn't the time for this. Who knew what danger Lady Isabella was in even as he spoke. If nothing else, he was growing to know his limitations. Wasn't it better to act to the fullest extent within those limitations, than to get everybody killed trying to exceed them?

He looked Tom in the eye. "Even you weren't able to save more than one—more than me."

Impatience flashed in Tom's face. Slow, methodical debate had never been his strength. "But *you* can! You can save scores more from the likes of Mr. Monarch—*if you stay the course.*"

"You keep saying that! But I didn't ask for this. I don't want this! This—all of this—was *your* idea."

The admission of it—hanging between them for so long—finally knocked Tom back on his heels. The eagerness and impatience faded from his face. In their stead, resignation remained. Resignation—and disappointment.

*That* was a greater burden than Will wanted to bear, but the truth was the truth.

"I don't desire the life of an outlaw. Not to save these people, not to save Rose, not for anybody. I want a proper life. I always have."

Tom knit his brows, wounded perhaps. Certainly, he hadn't been able to give Will that life.

"What I want," Will said, "is to be a man who has a right to court a lady like Isabella." The impossibility of every word was a shard in his heart. He spread his hands. "And yet here I am—a curiosity of nature, running about the city in a highwayman's cloak, aiding criminals and bloodying constables."

"You want to be Fitzroy." Tom's voice was soft, controlled.

"Do I respect where he's risen from?" Will looked about the shabby room. "What he was able to do with his life? Would I like to do the same?"

He let the question hang between them. He'd already spoken the answer aloud in a dozen different ways.

Tom held the silence.

From outside, the first taste of a freeze blew in, all the way from the faraway sea. It whistled through the broken window pane. The whole building creaked. From downstairs, the clatter of plates and the high-pitched voices of Mr. Monarch's illicit brood filtered up.

"One thing I know." Tom's eyes were so very serious. So very disapproving. "And it's that a man can't reach the place where your Mr. Fitzroy stands without walking the same dark road."

Perhaps that was true. Perhaps not.

Will breathed in and out, slowly. "One thing *I* know is I'm not going to see those I care about die for Seven Dials or anyone in it."

Tom's face closed up. The lines around his eyes seemed almost pained.

And that pained Will. Never in a thousand years would he desire to cause Tom offense, or, worse, disappointment. The thought of that hurt worse than all the shouts and stones of today's mob.

But what did Tom expect of him? Will *wasn't* Tom—never

had been, never would be. He was just Will. Despite all Tom had tried to give him, what Will still carried foremost in his heart was the legacy of his father's broken dreams.

Back in the village, Tom said Will was his own man. Well, he *was*. For better or worse.

He crossed to the door. "I'm sorry, Tom."

Tom stayed as he was. "Don't be sorry, lad. You make your choices. You stand by them." But he sounded no less dismayed.

Will left the room.

In the shadows of the stairwell, Rose's white face gleamed up at him.

He halted.

Her eyes were huge, her mouth turned down at the corners, as if fighting tears. But her cheeks were dry. Her chin did not tremble.

He hesitated. "Rose?"

She didn't move, not at all. She only looked at him.

Had she heard?

"That wasn't about you."

"I know." Her voice was scarcely audible.

"When it's time for Tom and I to go, you're coming with us. You know that?"

"Yes."

"I promised I'd find you a safe place. I won't break that promise."

"Yes."

And still she stared at him, wide-eyed, betrayed.

That look, paired with Tom's, was a double blow.

But heaven as his witness, he *hadn't* betrayed her, or Tom. Indeed, they were his to protect, and he'd do that any way he must.

For a second more, he stood there, torn between frustration and the desire to heal her hurt. He could crouch, pull her into his arms, hold her. That's what you did with children, wasn't it? Let them know somebody loved them and was looking out for them.

But Rose wasn't exactly the sort to be embraced. Rose didn't even seem a child half the time. She didn't need his approval or his love. She'd taken care of herself all her life. She'd move past this.

"I need to see to Lady Isabella now." He had delayed too long already.

"I know."

"Why don't you—talk to Tom." He waited for an assent that didn't come, then forced a nod and ran downstairs.

———

Outside Fitzroy House, the street was awash in red—the Royal-livery red of the soldiers and the robin-breast red of the Runners.

Will crouched atop a roof across the way. As soon as he'd passed the barricade Lifty and the lads were constructing roundabout Seven Dials, he had consumed three of Losborne's packets. But now, without his dizziness, it was impossible to recognize how many of the men below were illusions.

The Runners were clumped about the entrance, eyeing the soldiers. In the gaslight, a gilt-topped baton flashed.

Will squinted. Would it be Constable Pish? He still wasn't certain if the man was on his side or Fitzroy's. More likely, neither.

He scanned the house—six floors, all of them gleaming with a scandalously expensive show of lights. Two stories up, shadows flickered behind the windows. A feast for foreign dignitaries, Henry had said. Judging from the parked carriages lining the street, Fitzroy had packed in as many as he could. Solidifying his political alliances, no doubt.

Will crept across the slate to the back of the roof. Once there, he dropped over the eaves and jogged to the end of the street. He crossed all the way over to Fitzroy's side and continued on until he reached the narrow back alley, the mews where the horses were stabled and the servants' privy was found.

Within the stream of light from an unshuttered window, a great, slavering wolfhound paced across the way.

Will froze.

Soldiers he could manage. But a beastie of a dog was something else.

The dog swung its narrow, evil head towards him and glared.

Far away in the darkness behind Will, footsteps clomped.

He took another step back, both hands outstretched. "Ssh."

The dog sullenly swung its head away and paced on, as if blind.

Will released half a breath.

It was an illusion, meant to frighten those who'd no notion of such things.

He huffed. *This* was what came of taking Losborne's powder. Without it, he would have seen through the beast straight off.

Once again, the wolfhound leered at him. Will walked directly through it with the usual fizzle of sparks.

Twenty paces more, and voices reached his ears.

Two soldiers stood above the glow of the kitchen's sunken entry.

He ducked back into the shadows.

"I don't care for it, that's all," said the elder soldier. "Reeks of witchery, you want my opinion."

"Then what are you here for?" The younger soldier was an earnest chap with an unfashionably long queue of dark hair.

The elder sniffed. "There's money, ain't there?"

"Well, I think it's extraordinary, what Mr. Fitzroy's doing."

The elder scratched his whiskered chin. "Too many uncanny things for my liking. Who's Fitzroy's family? Nobody ever heard of him before he comes to London twenty years ago. And now the things we're seeing all about—if he's the one doing them—well, 'tisn't natural."

Then Fitzroy's ability to persuade the people *wasn't* indomitable. If even his soldiers had their doubts, that was encouraging.

The younger soldier scowled. "The Wayfarer ain't natural either, that's sure."

Well, it was *half* encouraging.

Less than three feet in front of Will, a ledge outlined the corner of the first floor.

He jumped to it with a faint clatter and leant in against the stone face, balancing with his fingertips stretched to the windowsill above. He could gain access there, then slip inside to find Isabella.

"Heard the hum going 'round?" the younger soldier asked, below.

The older grunted. "When isn't there a hum these weeks?"

"You know what I mean—'bout her young ladyship what's to marry the young Mr. Fitzroy."

Will froze.

"They're saying she may not be quite the thing. She might even be"—he lowered his voice—"a traitor."

No surprise there, but Will's heart still started pounding.

"Ladies ain't traitors."

"I had it from the kitchen maid when that sour-faced butler weren't about. She said her young ladyship ain't allowed to attend tonight's dinner, even despite her illustrious grandpapa. The both of 'em ain't come down a'tall."

"And how'd you—*or* the kitchen maid—know that? Neither of you even whiffed the dining room."

"She says the young Mr. Fitzroy and the old earl's got her young ladyship upstairs somewheres, trying to reason with her."

Will's fingers cramped against the ledge. Surely Henry hadn't the energy or the inclination to harm her, even should such have been his father's orders. Lord Carstone, whatever his faults, would never allow it.

"Indeed," the older soldier said. "Probably, she has the vapors, like any other lady about to be married. This is all idle chatter, and it's naught to do with either of us, is it?"

"Well, and I was letting the time pass, wasn't I?" The younger sounded affronted.

Will peered up. The dining room would be on the floor directly above his head. If Lady Isabella were "upstairs," that meant she was at least one floor yet above that. There, the windows were dark and silent.

He'd clung to the window too long now; his hands were too cramped to raise himself. Releasing the sill, he dropped back into the shadows with a bare *whump*.

The guards cast him not even a glance. But farther down the alley, beyond the shaft of light where the greyhound paced, the distant footsteps were still approaching.

He backed across the alley, gave himself an unabashed running start through the darkness, and leapt all the way to the grated windows of the dining room floor. Thankfully, it was not the window to the dining room itself, but only a back passage for the servers. No one inside saw him, but with the light streaming all about, he was now in egregiously plain view to those below.

He hauled himself up the grating and gained the darkness of the third set of windows, making rather more of a clatter this time.

Below, the two soldiers spun about. The elder brought his musket up in one clean motion.

The younger fumbled, catching the strap upon his elbow. "Who goes there?"

The footsteps from down the alley hastened into a run, and a third soldier appeared.

The guards lowered their muskets.

"Why aren't you at your post?" the older demanded.

"Saw something." The newcomer's voice was high-pitched—youthful, but certain. "Didn't you hear naught?"

"Naught but *your* plodding about," the younger guard grumbled.

Will spared a small grin.

"I seen a chap," the newcomer said. "By the hound. I was yet a ways down, but he walked on through the blighted thing like he knowed what it was. Mr. Fitzroy said even the Runners weren't to know about such."

And *that* marked the end of any advantage to be had here.

Will fingered the sill, found the bottom of the pane, and pressed hard, praying it would give without squeaking.

It did. Quite as any fancy man's window should, it rose silent as silk. He hoisted his legs inside, then worked his top half through.

From below, the high-pitched voice sounded once again: "And did you hear *that?*"

Seize that new guard for a twitchy fellow. As if Will needed further incentive for haste.

He lowered the window back into place and looked about. He was in another back corridor, one designed for the servants to scuttle through unseen. From the narrow stairway to the left, the clatter and conversation of an active dinner party echoed up.

Directly before him, voices rumbled behind a closed door:

"Saints preserve us, Isabella, this is ridiculous, I tell you. Wantonly ridiculous."

That was Henry, of course.

"Young man"—that was Lord Carstone's deeper voice—"whatever respect in which I hold your father does not, perforce, extend to yourself. I beg you earn a measure of that respect by curbing your natural insolence."

Hand at the latch, Will hesitated. Dealing with Henry alone would have been much the easier. Would Lord Carstone even realize the danger in which his granddaughter found herself?

If Will waited, hidden in the darkness, perhaps Lord Carstone would return to dinner. Perhaps even Henry might. But had he the time? Was it not as likely Fitzroy should dispatch someone more formidable to "reason with" Isabella?

However much it was not his foremost virtue, patience was certainly the wiser course on occasion. But holding his breath in the shadows of his enemy's house—surrounded by dozens of people with the potential to discover him—was that truly wiser? He should charge in and deal with the situation as it stood. His every taut muscle demanded it.

Still, he hesitated.

From the stairway, a young woman's whisper wafted up. "Please, you can't be going up unannounced. What would Mr. Tite say? He'd have our heads on a roasting spit. There's no one up there that shouldn't be."

"But you can't be sure, can you?" It was the high-pitched voice of the twitchy soldier.

"Nobody could get up those stairs without coming through the door. And nobody gets through the door without Mr. Tite's knowing."

A pause. "Well." The soldier sounded determined. "And ain't some of 'em sayin' the Wayfarer can fly?"

Sometimes there was a distinct danger in having one's reputation proceed him.

Will drew his cutlass pistol and opened the door. "Good evening. I'll beg you to keep silent and not move a'tall. Thank you very much."

# CHAPTER 38

NO DOUBT WILL presented a startling spectacle in the doorway of a fine library: face shrouded, hands full of weaponry. But to their credit, the three people within managed absolute stillness for all of five seconds.

Then Lady Isabella bounded off the chaise. She was dressed to have attended the dinner, her gown a blue so dark it was almost black, with a thick span of gold embroidery 'round the bosom and down the centerline to the floor.

She caught at Henry's sleeve. "Do not move." She extended a hand to Lord Carstone. "If you please, sir, do not be disturbed. All is well."

"Indeed." Lord Carstone heaved his great frame from its chair by the hearth. Leaning a hand against the mantel, he turned to glower at Will. "I well recall this ruffian."

He looked the worse for his blow to the head at the grand party these weeks past. Before, he had seemed yet a doughty patrician; now, he hunched and wavered like an old man.

Will lowered the pistol. "Pray, heed your granddaughter. She knows me, and you, I daresay, do not."

Lord Carstone reared back. "Knows you, sir? *Knows* you?"

Henry remained slumped on the chaise. He scowled. "Of course, she knows him. It's all Robin Hood and Marian with them, isn't it though?"

Will looked at Isabella, opened his mouth, then closed it. He colored up even if she did not.

She was too occupied in steadying her grandfather's elbow. "Please, Grandpapa. You already know Mr. Fitzroy is not as we have always believed. He is playing us falsely, and he *will* harm us."

Lord Carstone looked back and forth, from Isabella to Will to Henry, still undecided.

Henry rolled his eyes. "Oh, tut. The governor's not violent."

Will snorted. "How can a man be your father and still you know nothing of him?"

The long-suffering boredom in Henry's face vanished, replaced by first a flash of pain, then by honest anger. He rose. "And how is it, sir, you are brought into the man's very home, as a guest, and you dare return as a burglar?"

"I'm not a burglar." Will felt a bit offended in spite of it all. "I've come to steal nothing."

Henry flushed. "Except my deuced bride!" It was the most energy Will had ever seen him expend.

He aimed the pistol at Henry's chest. "Sit down."

Henry ground his teeth and sat.

Isabella gestured to Will. "Grandpapa, this is Mr. Hardy."

Will's mouth dropped. "Don't tell him that!"

"Whyever not? Even Mr. Fitzroy knows your name."

Lord Carstone straightened his broad shoulders. "Why not instead name him by that dramatic title he has so arrogantly chosen? The *Wayfarer*?"

"I don't call myself that. And at all events, 'tis neither here nor there. What's *here*, sir—"

"Is the rather blatant fact that you perpetrated violent injury upon my person when last we met."

Will breathed out, striving for patience. He could almost hear the *thump, thump, thump* of the guard marching upstairs.

"Sir," he spoke through gritted teeth, "it was not I who struck you, but Mr. Fitzroy."

"It is the truth, Grandpapa," Isabella said. "He rendered you aid *against* Mr. Fitzroy. He did so at my explicit request." Her eyes were imploring. "He guided Constable Pish to you."

Lord Carstone's white eyebrows twitched. Perhaps he caught an edge of memory. Some of the choler left his expression.

Still, he frowned impressively. "And what, pray, does he do here now?"

Isabella took in a deep breath and turned to Will. "I believe he is come to rescue me."

Will strove to steady his voice. For all that this felt like theater, it couldn't possibly be more serious.

"Indeed." He looked at Lord Carstone. "Mr. Fitzroy knows her loyalties do not lie with him."

"He has had me watched ever since I returned from Southwark yesterday." For the first time, fear shadowed her eyes. "Someone must have informed him. A servant or—" She glanced at Henry.

Henry pursed his lips, almost indignant. "Why should I peach on you to the governor?"

"He is your father," Will said.

Henry stood, tugging at the powder blue velvet of his coat. "There's naught in it for me if I peach to him." He pointed at Isabella. "But there'd have been gold in it for any one of the dozens—hundreds, even—who undoubtedly saw your carriage between here and Southwark."

She looked at Will. "When I arrived tonight for the dinner, I was locked directly into this room."

"*Mrs.* Fitzroy?" Will hazarded.

"Perhaps. Grandpapa and Henry have only now come to speak with me."

"And now you are here, sirrah." Lord Carstone eyed him closely, but perhaps not with the same degree of antagonism. "And one wonders of your intentions."

Will looked at the earl squarely. "I've come to take Lady Isabella away, and"—he forced the words—"yourself as well, sir, if you will come. She is in great danger, and her danger is yours."

"Take her away?" Lord Carstone spoke incredulously.

"Where, I should like to know?" Isabella said.

"The Continent—Paris." It was at the tip of his tongue to name Dr. Silas. He glanced at Lord Carstone. But perhaps this was not yet the place. "We can go to Cornwall or Dover, the coast somewhere to gain passage."

"But—" Isabella looked stunned. "You are not leaving. Not now, certainly? Not in the midst of all that is occurring?"

"I will not leave you here to Fitzroy's mercy."

She opened her mouth, visibly taken aback.

From behind him, the *thump, thump, thump* in his imagination became a very real, very audible stamping in the stairwell.

He dashed across the room to grip the door latch.

Outside, there was an undecided shuffling, then a hesitant knock.

His voice clogged his throat. How might a gentleman respond to an unwarranted interruption? And if Will did speak, would the guard recognize his voice?

Again, the soldier knocked. He cleared his throat. "Apologies. This is Corporal Rouncewell from downstairs, and I believe someone might have entered here. Begging your pardon, but I need to have one look, if I might. I know it's what Mr. Fitzroy would want."

"I—" Isabella said, speechless yet.

It was her grandfather who stepped forward. "Indeed, Corporal, you *should* apologize. You have no reason to be in this house, much less disturbing our private meeting. I am the Earl of Carstone, and I assure you there has been nothing untoward in this room for the past half of the hour."

Will had to concentrate to keep from starting.

Lord Carstone looked at Will steadily—not in friendship, never that, but as one might view a necessary, if unsavory, ally. He *would* put his granddaughter's safety first, and bless him for that. His heart couldn't be black entire.

More embarrassed scraping sounded from outside. "Yes, sir, well, I'm sure I'm most sorry, but I really must be investigating. It's at Mr. Fitzroy's orders that all suspicious occurrences be treated with sobriety—and it is his house, after all."

Isabella whirled upon Henry and dragged him forward. "Speak to him," she hissed.

Will frowned. But what other option had they?

Once Henry had shambled near enough, Will caught his sleeve and dragged him the rest of the way. He raised his eyebrows so that his eye-shields slid down his nose far enough for Henry to see his eyes.

"Do it," he whispered.

A muscle in Henry's cheek flexed, hard and fast. Rolling his eyes, he straightened his striped waistcoat and stepped up to the door. "Oh, do be on your way. All this attention to duty. Such an infernal bore. This is Mr. Henry Fitzroy, you know. Can't a fellow spend a few minutes chatting with his betrothed in private"—he glanced back at Lord Carstone—"or semi-private, at all events?"

That garnered a slightly longer hesitation.

Will held his breath.

"Well, yes, sir, if that's as you want it then."

The footsteps tromped away.

Will released his breath.

Now to somehow get Isabella from here sight unseen.

The steps halted. The corporal called once again, "And . . . you're sure you're not saying that under duress or nothing, are you, sir?"

Henry opened his mouth. Then he closed it, looked at Will, and opened it again. "As a matter of fact—yes."

The entire room went still as tombs. Will stared at Henry. Henry stared at the door. And, in the corner of Will's vision, Lady Isabella and Lord Carstone stood frozen.

"Henry," Isabella murmured reproachfully.

To his credit, Corporal Rouncewell demonstrated extreme punctuality in the face of his duty. Without even the warning of a running start, he slammed into the door.

The door rammed open several inches, thrusting Will back against Henry. Will heaved his weight forward and knocked the door again into place, fixing his gloved hand upon the latch to prevent its turning.

Again, the corporal struck the door, harder and with a great grunt. "Hold fast, sir. I'll see you out of there!"

Will glared at Henry. "You filthy turncoat!"

Henry snorted. "Why the devil should I be on your side, I'd like to know?"

"Since when are you on your father's?"

Henry's expression flashed to sudden, and very unlikely, determination. He drew himself up. His muscles tightened.

Will knew the look. It was a look with which he had grown most intimate in the last weeks. Henry was actually going to strike at him. And then there *would* be a brawl—on both sides of the door.

Isabella stepped hastily forward. "Henry—"

Henry freed his sleeve from Will's grip. "Sir." For once in his life, he managed to sound both condescending and dignified. He cocked his fist.

Once more, Corporal Rouncewell slammed into the door.

Will released the latch and stepped away.

The door flung inward. The edge caught Henry's forehead. His eyes rolled to white. Boneless, he crumpled to the rug.

Tripping over Henry, Corporal Rouncewell sprawled upon his face. He was quick enough to grasp his musket and roll onto his back in search of Will. But not quick enough.

Will batted aside the musket and clouted Rouncewell cleanly upon the skull with the iron knuckles.

Unlike Henry, Rouncewell managed to moan. He shook his head dizzily. "You . . . are the—"

Footsteps fled back down the stairs.

"Never mind," Will said. He rushed into the corridor and caught the kitchen maid—Kitty—halfway down the stairs. Hand over her mouth, he dragged her into the library.

She squealed and wriggled, desperately.

"Kitty, please, it's Will Hardy. Don't fight, and I'll release you."

Isabella snatched up her train and crossed the room to stand before the girl. "All is well, Kitty. No one desires to harm you, but you must make no noise."

Slowly—infinitesimally—Kitty ceased struggling and finally nodded.

Will released her mouth. When she did not cry out, he let her go.

She spun and backed to the hearth, staring about wildly.

Lady Isabella and Lord Carstone appeared stunned as well, but Lord Carstone decidedly the more so. Isabella had already seen the face of this fight. She knew what it looked like.

Will returned to the dazed Corporal Rouncewell, rolled him onto his stomach, and used the gold braid Isabella ripped off the back of the chaise to bind his hands, feet, mouth. Then he stuffed him under the chaise.

Will leant over to meet the man's bleary eyes. "You did your duty, Corporal, and I hope you know 'tisn't personal." Then he turned to Kitty.

"*You*'re the Wayfarer?" she said.

"You were kind to me that morning when I needed something to eat, and I wish to be kind to you now. Can I rely on you not to cry out or leave this room until at least half the hour has passed?"

She wrung her hands. "Half the hour? Dear Lord love you, sir. The rest of the guards will be here in half the *minute*."

Seize it. He had been a fool to let down his guard. He cast a look about, but the room was windowless. No escape.

Train still in hand, Lady Isabella hastened to the far corner. "Here." She pulled aside a tapestry to reveal an ornate door.

Ah. Of course, the family wouldn't use the servant's stair.

Will turned to Lord Carstone.

He hadn't counted on rescuing the old man tonight. Honestly, he hadn't given overmuch thought to him a'tall. He could carry Isabella at a pinch, but never Lord Carstone and certainly never the both of them. But Isabella wasn't likely to leave her grandfather, and Lord Carstone *was* likely to face Fitzroy's distrust should he remain.

"Will you accompany us, sir?"

Lord Carstone fetched Rouncewell's musket, handling it with the easy grace of a lifelong hunter. Groping behind him, he found his chair and eased into it. He laid the musket across his knees.

"You go." He looked to Isabella. "I will watch these two and delay the others."

"Grandpapa—" She spoke not so much a dissent, as a caution.

He flicked a long-fingered hand at her. "Hasten, my dear. I may be under suspicion after this night, but naught will happen before I can reunite with you." He looked at Will, without approval but also not quite with derision.

Will was beginning to understand the feeling.

"I entrust her to you this evening, Master Hardy. That is a sacred trust."

"No harm will come to her, sir." Almost without thinking

about it, he removed his hat and inclined his head.

Steady footsteps tromped quietly up the stairs—trying to be circumspect in proximity to the dinner party, no doubt.

Before Isabella could protest further, Will caught her arm and pushed her through the door.

The curtain fell back into place behind them, and he fixed the latch. Turning, he found himself in a comparatively wide, shadowy corridor—smelling of beeswax upon the floor and oil paints in the frames upon the walls. This was the main part of the house where they might meet any one of the household.

Isabella stood quite near, her hair agleam in the faint light from the stairway at the corridor's end.

"God bless you, Will Hardy," she whispered. "I know not what Mr. Fitzroy might have had done to me tonight."

"I wouldn't leave you to him. We're in this together, aren't we?"

"We are." She smiled, softly.

The light of that smile radiated all through him.

"How did you know to come for me?" she asked.

"Mr. Losborne. When he said he'd not had a note from you, I knew something must be amiss."

Her smile widened to a grin. "Clever of you."

"And then there's this." He drew Dr. Silas's missive from his pocket.

She cast one glance upon the scrawled direction and gasped. "Then it is true!" She clutched it to her. "I hoped it was so, but I dared not speak it. Where is he? What do you know?"

"Paris, at the time of this writing. 'Tis all I know. Come." He felt he should hold her hand or at least her arm and guide her down the corridor, but he dasn't go so far. He took one step. "We must make haste."

"Yes." She lowered the letter. "Yes, of course." Then she grasped his elbow. "But—Mr. Fitzroy! He is here. And so are you."

He used her grip on his arm to pull her along several paces. "All the more reason."

A dull knocking sounded from the library's back door. Lord Carstone rumbled a reply.

This time, Will did take her arm and hasten her to the stairs.

"You know what is occurring in the dining room?" she asked.

He peered over the banister. The stairs led downward some dozen steps, then hooked to the left. Faint lights drifted from the second flight. The tinkle of crystal and silver and the undulating hum of conversation wafted up.

"A dinner party," he said. "Foreign dignitaries."

"Indeed." She laid both hands upon his arm. "In essence, the eyes of the entire world are upon Mr. Fitzroy tonight."

He looked back at her. "Ah."

"What is seen here tonight will be remembered always." Her eyes glittered. "The audience is too large—too esteemed, too diverse."

A desperate sort of excitement spread through him. "Fitzroy can't lie about what happens here tonight."

Again, she grinned. "Precisely."

Behind, someone started knocking at the study's walls, looking for the hidden door.

"Come." Boldly, he took her elbow and hurried down the stairs.

"What are you to do?" Her whole face was alight now. "Charge into their midst and declaim him as a villain?"

"No. I shall be subtle." For a change.

She raised her brows. "And how are *you* to do that?"

"I require writing materials."

---

It took them all of fifteen excruciating minutes to gather what they needed, then sneak into the back hall behind the dining room. This corridor was considerably busier, bustling with footmen and kitchen maids.

Will remained in the shadows of the staircase where he could not be seen. For the moment, Isabella sat beside him on the step, her dark gown blending into the shadows.

Every so often, the dining room would open. It glittered with as much light as one could hope for without the sun: at least three chandeliers, a great fireplace, and dozens of expensive beeswax candles all down the table.

The dinner must be well on by now, but the scents wafting out were as rich as ever. Will failed to distinguish all of them, but there were definitely meats and heavy sauces, fish perhaps, and mulled wines.

His stomach pinched. His single meal of the day had been greased "thins"—the flimsy bread pieces on which Seven Dials subsisted.

From this angle, few of the guests were visible. Fitzroy sat at the head of the table, his profile to the door. Standing behind his master, the butler Tite surveyed the dinner with sharp eyes and a blank expression.

Fitzroy seemed much engaged by the guest to his left, a middle-aged gentleman with his auburn hair quiffed elaborately over his temples. He punctuated every word with a wave of his fork, as if conducting an orchestra.

"Monsieur Lagnier," Isabella whispered. "The representative from France."

Whenever Fitzroy spoke, M. Lagnier touched his chest and bowed his head in a gesture of flattered humility. As ever, Fitzroy's charm worked in his favor.

The door swung closed behind a footman bearing in a platter of thickly-sauced meat. The corridor and the staircase plunged once more into the murky shadows of the single candelabrum at the sideboard.

They must wait for the footman to return.

All about them, the house creaked. Footsteps crossed and re-crossed the upper floors. The soldiers were combing it for them—doubtless wanting to be certain their quarry were not upstairs, before daring to interrupt the dinner party.

Sooner or later, they *would* dare—and then Will and Isabella must be ready to leave at the instant.

Every creak touched the back of his neck with a shiver. This was a great risk, and one of which he was none too certain. Charging through that door and plowing into the midst of the party—taking Fitzroy prisoner before the man could realize what was afoot—that was something he could likely accomplish.

But Isabella was correct: he must not waste this singular opportunity. Capturing Fitzroy would not end this war; Fitzroy had made certain the battlefield was much larger than that.

Rather, Will must kill the *idea* of Fitzroy.

Footsteps whispered back across the dining room to the closed door.

He shut his eyes. *Please may it be the footman and not Tite.*

Beside him, Isabella patted her upswept hair and the one long curl over her shoulder. Taking a deep breath, she rose.

He gave her an encouraging nod.

She must necessarily bear the brunt of the initial risk. Unlike him, her appearance would not instantly raise the alarm. If there were trouble, he would be at her side of an instant.

His body's cry for speed ran all through him. He bounced his knees, silently, and flexed and unflexed the little spasms in his hands.

The dining room door opened, the footman exited, and the door swung closed.

Isabella descended the final step. "Pardon me—Abel, is it?"

"My lady—" He sounded surprised. No doubt the entire house had heard rumors of her confinement in the library.

Still, he inclined his wigged head. "Shall I ask Mr. Tite to set you a place?"

She held out the pile of notes she had transcribed, following Will's instructions. "Would you be so good as to deliver these to M. Lagnier, Sir Lawrence, and the others. They arrived by courier only a few minutes ago, and I intercepted them, since the other servants were occupied downstairs."

"But, of course, my lady."

Leaving his serving tray upon the sideboard, Abel pushed back through the door. He neglected to close it all the way behind him.

Now it was time to leave, especially since the footsteps above were fast approaching the stairs. Will rose.

Isabella hastened to him, eyes agleam with adventure.

He reached for her arm and started down the remaining steps. But he couldn't help peering into the dining room.

Abel delivered the notes to Tite, who frowned. Might he recognize Isabella's script? Might he decide to pass the notes to his master before delivering them?

Will's heart hammered.

But, no. Still frowning, Tite moved towards M. Lagnier.

Isabella tugged at Will's elbow. "Come."

Will took one step more, but also one look more—and then he halted.

It seemed Fitzroy had presented M. Lagnier a gift.

Upon the corner of the table sat a handsome mahogany cage. Beside it rested the orange silk shawl that must have covered it. But inside the cage was . . . nothing.

Will's lungs stopped working.

Even as Tite handed the delighted M. Lagnier his note—the man seem to think it *another* gift, how marvelous!—the air inside the cage flickered. The outline of a white ferret appeared and solidified. The animal blinked its black eyes straight at Will.

"I don't believe it," he murmured.

But of course, he did.

*This* was what Mr. Monarch and Bull had taken from the barracks the other day.

Mr. Monarch feared Fitzroy. He had told Will as much. But he also coveted his powers. Of course he would try to redress the past. Of course he would bribe Fitzroy.

"Mr. Hardy . . ." Isabella hissed—and then she, too, gasped. "Surely, not."

Within the dining room, however, the ferret was old news.

M. Lagnier's delight faded. He looked up from re-reading his note. "What is this?"

Fitzroy, unsuspecting, forked a bite of meat into his mouth and glanced over, blandly. Immediately, he frowned at M. Lagnier's incredulous—almost insulted—expression.

Farther down the table, an English voice spoke up: "I say, sir!"

M. Lagnier's eyebrows quivered. "This cannot be true?"

Still calm, Fitzroy touched his serviette to the corner of his mouth. "A troublesome communication?"

M. Lagnier rose from his chair, dropping his own serviette into the seat. "And I have often wondered, *monsieur*, how a man such as you comes from nowhere to do these things that you are doing."

Now, Fitzroy's face darkened. Now, his weak spot had been tweaked.

Upstairs, the soldiers had almost reached the first flight of steps.

Will stood, rooted. He needed to see the outcome, needed to be certain of Fitzroy's downfall, so he could take the victory to Tom and speed them on their way.

Beside him, Isabella gripped his coat sleeve, equally transfixed.

"This is outrageous," said the unseen Englishman. "I, for one, demand an explanation, sir."

"Explanation for what?" That was Mrs. Fitzroy's piping voice.

"For this." M. Lagnier passed Fitzroy the note. "This that says your antecedents are less than honorable. Indeed, they are criminal!"

Fitzroy read it at a glance, and his jaw turned to stone.

The guests had already been primed, just as Will had hoped. They had believed Fitzroy's truth thus far because it was the obvious one, the convenient one. But they would have heard the rumors about this strange man who had come from nowhere only a score of years past. They would have registered the impossible inconsistencies to be found at every side. All this time, they had needed but a push to return their own questions to the forefront of their minds.

"Gentlemen, please," Mrs. Fitzroy said. "Your behavior is most rash. Who has sent you these perjurious notes? Will you not listen to my husband's honest defense to whatever slander they bear?"

For an instant, Will felt a flash of regret. His note told only the truth of Fitzroy's past. But nothing in that past was so very vile that a man who had put it behind him should then be crucified for it. Indeed, Will hoped his own future would be such someday that he could say he overcame as much.

He did not blame Fitzroy for his past. In any other circumstance, he would have been the first to put it aside.

But he *must* blame Fitzroy for his present. And as it turned out, Fitzroy's past was the only rope left with which to strangle him.

Fitzroy did not look at his indignant dinner companions. Nor did he look to his wife. He turned and he looked, as if he knew what he would find, at the half-open door.

He looked straight at Will.

Will stood upon the step with his shoulders back and his head up. He returned Fitzroy's look as an equal.

The ground between them had just been leveled. Indeed, what Will had done tonight might well be the victory entire, depending on how deeply and quickly these gentlemen searched out the truth of Fitzroy's past as a lowborn charlatan.

Even as soldiers tromped down the stairs behind him, Will took the time to bow, low and deliberate.

A flicker of something that might *almost* have been apprehension crossed Fitzroy's face.

Then Fitzroy looked up. "Guards!" He pointed at Will. "Seize this man!"

# CHAPTER 39

FITZROY'S COMMAND MOMENTARILY silenced his unruly dinner party. But Will had no time to observe their response. The guards behind him broke into an outright clatter, all but tripping down the stairs.

He swept Isabella into his arms and threw himself into his speed. That turned out to be considerably more difficult with the addition of her ladyship's weight than it was with Rose's. Nevertheless, he cleared the last flight of steps into the basement kitchen without breaking his ankles. He blasted past the shrieking maids, upending more than one platter.

They emerged in the street, up through the kitchen's front entry and past the Runners.

"Hie!" That sounded like Pish.

Will surged down the empty street.

Footsteps stamped behind him.

"Halt! Stop him! Stop them!"

Some fool cracked off a musket shot. It crashed into the stonework of the far house as Will rounded the corner.

"Don't shoot!" someone ordered. "You'll hit her ladyship!"

Only half a mile more, and Will was forced to set Isabella on her feet. With his arm about her waist, he helped her keep pace. They ran on, dodging 'round corners and more corners yet, into the dark heart of the city.

Finally, they halted outside a church with a great lantern jutting from a beam above its doors.

Isabella's face glistened with perspiration, and the small wisps of hair about her forehead were turning to wayward curls in every direction. Her eyes were wider than ever he had seen them.

Hearing a musket ball glance past your shoulder had a way of doing that.

She breathed out sharply. Then she threw her head back in a great laugh.

He grinned. All his tension burbled into his mouth, and he laughed as well.

They laughed with the sheer idiocy of it all, the luck that they were yet alive *to* laugh. Then they laughed yet more at their laughter.

She spread her gloved arms wide and spun, tracing her gown's train through the dust. "I cannot believe it! I simply cannot believe it." She spun back. "That was marvelous. I have no other word for it. I feel like . . ." She raised her shoulders, searching. "Like . . . I could fly!"

He grinned broader still. He could not fly—not yet—but sometimes he came near enough. He dashed across the street at top speed.

Bordering the opposite side, a twelve-foot stone wall was lined with the vines of a still-blooming sweet autumn clematis. He did not slow when he reached the wall, but ran a semi-circle up the side of it, snatching a white blossom from the top.

She laughed again and clapped.

Back at her side, he swept off hat and eye-shields and bowed extravagantly. He presented her the four-petaled star. "My lady."

Delicately, she pinched its stem and plucked her gown in a deep curtsy.

They held the flower between them for a long second— mock-serious and verging once more on hysteria.

She looked as if, in another moment, she would whirl, dancing all over the empty street. Was it because they had destroyed Fitzroy's reputation for good and all? Or was it merely the excitement and the danger? Was there any chance a'tall his own presence was any sort of factor?

He straightened, still holding the flower, and his amusement sobered.

She straightened with him. Her eyes grew ever so slightly more serious. But her smile deepened.

She looked at him as if he were her equal. As if this wild sharing of life-threatening danger had put their feet upon an even path. She was content, if only perhaps for this night, to walk beside him instead of before him.

He found he desperately wanted to say something. He cleared his throat. "My lady." But he had no words a'tall.

Dozens of footsteps clattered around both ends of the street.

"And you can halt there!" The voice belonged to the elder kitchen guard.

At the instant, Will's pistol was to hand. He snatched the iron rod from his shoulder sheath and dropped into a fighting crouch, his back to Isabella.

How far might their incautious laughter have carried on such a crisp night? What would Tom say had he seen Will making calf's eyes at a great lady and getting the both of them caught unawares?

From both sides, the soldiers swarmed in on them.

The dark-haired younger of the kitchen guards grinned. "Ah, we got you now, mate, don't we?"

"And he's just a lad, ain't he?" said another

Will stifled a growl. He wearied of that response.

The old guard tromped to within a dozen feet and poked his musket towards Will. "You be keepin' feet to the ground, you hear me? We won't have no more runnin' about tonight."

"Stand back," Will said. "I warn you, I will not be taken, and neither will the lady." But he could hardly fight the lot of them *and* protect her.

She touched his elbow. "Might we not leap away?"

From here, he would have to jump flatfooted and try to catch the lantern hook above the church doors. He'd be a fool to try that with even just Rose's weight upon his back.

"You'll forgive me, my lady, but you're too heavy."

"*Indeed.*" She edged out from behind him. "All of you, listen! This gentleman is with me, and he will be leaving *with* me. If you dare lay a hand to him, I will bring every magistrate in the city down upon you, Mr. Fitzroy notwithstanding."

The old soldier hesitated, then shook his head. "Apologies,

my lady, but you're to come as well. I daresay most of us'd like it best if it was all kept pleasant."

"I assure you there will be nothing pleasant about it."

Will's heart crammed into his throat. With Isabella to care for, he was trapped as surely as if he were shackled. After his pistol afforded its single shot, he'd be left to manage a score and four soldiers with only the short cutlass and the iron rod.

For what it was worth, the guards obviously feared that single shot—and *would* fear it until he discharged it. They formed a semi-circle, boxing Will and Isabella into twelve feet of space against the church, but they came no nearer.

"You shall not touch her," Will said. It was bravado as much as anything, and they all likely knew it.

The younger guard grinned, showing a missing tooth. "Who are you to be running off with a lady?"

Sooner than later, they would rush him, probably from the side. His one shot would best be used upon their leader—the old guard?—before he engaged the attackers. Even in close quarters, his speed could serve him. He could shoot and return to face the attackers in but a blink.

The problem was they would *all* be upon him in two blinks more.

Still, he trained the pistol upon the old guard's breastbone. Energy coursed through him, and he fought to steady his hand.

The old guard stiffened and eased backwards.

The young guard paid no heed. "Gentleman highwayman, my own foot. You ain't nothing but a plow-boy, that's what I heard. Parents died in the work'ouse."

Will's ears burned. He swallowed hard and steadied the pistol.

To his left, the troops were shifting, inching nearer. Any second, someone would lunge for him.

"Work'ouse boy." The younger guard leered. "Running away with the earl's daughter. A scandal, ain't it?"

Will couldn't help it. He shifted the pistol from the old guard to the young one. "Be quiet."

The man flinched back.

"The moment one man breaks this circle, at least one of you is going to die." Will looked the young guard in the eye. "Seems it's you."

The guard tightened his grip upon his musket.

The heat upon Will's neck flashed to cold. He *was* rather assuming Fitzroy wanted him alive. What was to stop any one of these chaps from shooting him and taking Isabella?

Heaven help him, he was going to have to do this in cold blood. He tightened his finger upon the trigger. Then they'd all shoot him for certain.

More running footsteps clapped down the street.

"It'll be the king's warrant then, lads! Stand aside!"

Constable Pish.

Will missed a breath. He steadied the pistol, still pointed at the younger guard.

"Principle officers, gentlemen. Make way, make way."

Reluctantly, the soldiers parted to admit Pish and three red-waistcoated Runners.

Pish pointed his small knock-me-down pistol at Will, but his expression didn't seem overly triumphant. "Well, and what's this? Show of violent force?" He clucked.

Every muscle in Will's body was screaming at him to *move*, to flee, to *do* something. He forced himself to remain still.

"Now, now, my boy," Pish said. "I'm afraid your reign of terror has ended."

"Please, Mr. Pish," Isabella said.

He inclined his head to her, civilly but abruptly. "My lady." Then he returned to Will. He was only three strides off now. "I told you I believed in the facts, now, didn't I? And they are quite black, quite black indeed." He raised his eyebrow—meaningfully.

Will frowned. He knew better than anyone that the facts were difficult to see these days. So what was it *Pish* saw?

Was he sympathetic to Will in any measure? Or was this but a ruse to get past Will's defenses?

"Mr. Fitzroy is a blackguard," Will hazarded.

Pish nodded sagely. His great dark eyes watched Will, full of intent. "He's a great man though. And what have you been doing against him tonight?" He raised his free hand and used its thumb to tick off points on his long fingers. "Invaded his house, abducted his son's betrothed, and scandalized his dinner party with your dark tales."

"They're no tales."

Pish leaned nearer, as if imparting a secret. "Half his guests—including that dapper Frenchman—were leaving in high distress. What's a great man like Mr. Fitzroy to do other than dispatch messages of refutation around to all his friends at the *Times* and the *Chronicle*, eh? I'd say you've robbed him of the night's sleep."

Naturally, Fitzroy would exert his every resource to halt Will's gambit. The question was: could his lies outrun the truths that would be told by so many powerful men after this night? And if they couldn't, then what? Fitzroy wouldn't pack his trunks for a midnight flit. He'd remain; he'd resist.

He'd remain if only to punish Will.

Pish squinted out of one eye. It was a sinister expression, but something about the general twitching of his features made it seem confidential. "Lads such as you can't hardly be doing such as this to great men such as him, now can you?" He raised his voice. "I've no choice but to arrest you on the king's warrant." From his coat, he withdrew manacles.

Isabella gasped. "This is outrageous. What reward do you stand to gain from this? I demand to know!"

Pish stepped nearer.

For some reason Will couldn't quite name, he allowed it. He watched Pish's eyes all the way, even as Pish watched his.

"Throw down the weapons," Pish said.

God save Will for a fool, but he trusted Constable Henderson Pish. They mighn't be allies, but Pish was *not* Fitzroy's man. Will would stake his life on it.

He obeyed.

Pish's angular features eased, and he tucked his chin in the smallest of nods. He touched the icy iron to Will's wrist—but he did not lock the cuff.

Loudly, he said, "In the name of the king, William Hardy, I pronounce you under arrest."

The soldiers visibly relaxed.

Behind Will, Isabella tensed, as if she might lunge at Pish and scratch out his eyes.

Will shifted his free arm back to lean against her, warning her to remain still.

Pish gave another little nod. "Well, I'll say this—you grow less the fool every time I see you."

That seemed a bare commendation.

Then Pish lowered his voice. "Take hold of the irons in both hands, as if I've chained you. Walk two steps for'ard with me, until the guards relax—then take her ladyship and do that demonic magic of yours."

"'Tisn't demonic, and she's too heavy."

"Mr. Hardy—*really*," Isabella said.

Pish raised an eyebrow. "Listen, my boy, unlike you, I've no miracles in my waistcoat pocket. Either you find one in yours, or we're both dished."

If Pish weren't being so confounded friendly, Will might have scowled. "Right then."

"That's the spirit." Pish raised his voice: "And no more of your cheek, I'll thank you." He placed the other cuff into Will's hand with a clanking of the chain.

Will held onto both and attempted to appear less alert and more dejected.

Pish turned away, his hand upon the chain. "Now, my bullies, you can see it takes but a few of Bow Street's officers to do what a whole great regiment can't."

The soldiers—especially the old guard—had vanity enough to look disgruntled. Reluctantly, they lowered their muskets and loosened their semi-circle. Sullen now, they backed up. Some even turned.

That was as good as this was likely to get. Another moment, and they'd be falling in around Will and Isabella in a cordon.

Will dropped the manacles, snatched up his pistol, and spun to sweep her into his arms. She clung to his neck, sensibly holding as still as possible.

Jumping for the church eaves was out of the question. Instead, his muscles followed the memory of his actions only a few minutes earlier. He blasted across the street, through the last of the straggling guards. At least one tumbled to the ground.

"'Ey there!" Pish's voice was loudest of all.

In a great clatter, the soldiers whirled about.

"Don't shoot!" Pish thundered. "You risk her ladyship!"

At top speed, Will hastened towards the clematis-covered wall. Five feet away, he jumped as hard as he could. With Isabella's added weight, he couldn't clear it, but he gained enough height to shove her onto the top. With a small yelp, she started to roll off the other side, then caught herself.

He backed up and jumped again. He tangled his foot in the fragrant vines halfway up and slammed his hands down upon the wall's top for balance.

Still hanging off the other side, Isabella scrabbled for a loose stone. "They are coming!" She hoisted herself onto a gloved elbow and flung the stone with surprising force—and accuracy, to judge by the thump and the howl from behind.

He freed his foot and hauled himself up and over.

Before he could turn back to aid her, Isabella dropped into the crackling leaves at the wall's base.

He caught her hand and pulled her into a run. "Come!"

"You see," she found breath to say, "I am not so heavy, am I?"

———————

They made it across the cemetery before the soldiers even clambered over the wall. After that, their escape was a simple matter of disappearing—silently, this time—into the darkness.

When finally they pulled up, they were almost to Hyde Park. They would have to circle back to gain either Regent's Park or Seven Dials. The time must be almost midnight by now, and the general weariness of the day—indeed the month—pulled at Will.

Isabella walked beside him, silent in her own weariness no doubt.

"Still enjoying the adventure of it, then?"

She smiled, slightly. "It *is* still an adventure, isn't it? The true reckoning comes not until tomorrow."

"And you don't fear that?"

"I suppose. But—" She walked on. "At least, there is a purpose to all this. That means something. That is worth a measure of fear."

Silence carried them to the next empty crossing.

He hesitated, weighing words. There was so much he desired to know about her, so many questions. But had he earned the right to answers—or would it still be so much impertinence?

He attempted another topic. "Is there light enough from the moon to read Dr. Silas's letter?" He withdrew it from where she had bid him secrete it in his coat pocket.

She stopped short. "Of course, I forgot." With one motion of her forefinger, she broke all five globular seals. The light was patchy at best, and she tilted the paper several different ways before finding an acceptable angle.

Her flickering gaze seemed to take in the message all at once. She uttered a short laugh, both happy and resigned, then read it again.

When she looked up, tears sheened her eyes. She smiled. "It is true. He says little, but he lives. The body in the barn—it was all a ploy to protect himself. He is in Paris, as you say, though he does not promise to be there much longer. He is on the trail of something, he says—whatever that implies." She lowered the letter, and again she laughed in a short, high burst of relieved emotion. "I am so exceedingly glad you did not kill him."

He grinned. "Me too. I thought . . . For so long there, I thought I would never find answers. There would be no one to help me reverse the negative effects."

"Everything will be well in the end. I am certain of it. Dr. Silas will have ideas. He is not the self-seeker you paint him. He *will* aid you."

"If I can reach him." The moment stretched between them, and he couldn't stop himself asking after all. "Why are you doing all this? I mean, from the beginning, with Dr. Silas. You have risked—well, everything—to be a part of this madness. Why?"

She gave him the respect of at least considering her answer. "Well, I suppose I must admit I am not always very apt in weighing risks."

To that, he could only pull a rueful scowl.

"But do you not see?" She spread her hands. "There is this entire world out here, and there is so much to be discovered, so much to be done. There is purpose." She looked at him. "I crave purpose. I suppose it is what I have desired above all else for as long as I can remember."

He stared, incredulous. "Of course you have purpose to your life. You were born with the world within reach."

"What you mean is I have never wanted for material providence or possession." She huffed. "Social functions and grand carriages are not purpose."

"But think of it. You—and all those in your world, Fitzroy included—have the opportunities and abilities to do so many wonderful things. You needn't spend your time with no greater purpose than scrabbling for existence."

The yearnings of his entire life rose, pulsing within him. He looked about the shadowy street. There were no words for it all.

"Do you know," he asked, "what I would do in your place?"

She waited.

"You can be sure I wouldn't sit about like Henry Fitzroy and his sort. I would *do* something with what I had been given. I would help my tenants, my servants—I would help them to rise, instead of binding them beneath me."

The faint light of the half moon painted her face and neck in alabaster and glinted in the muss of her hair. "I believe you would. Indeed, I do."

His heart still had energy enough to stumble. Heavens above, but she was beautiful—and brave—and shrewder indeed than he. And here she was standing in this empty street beside *him*.

"If I were of your world, I would—" He spoke in spite of himself. "I would go to your grandfather, hat in hand, and I would ask to court you as a gentleman." The words hurt his throat.

She blinked her eyes wide, but not, perhaps, in offense.

He released his pent breath. "But I am not a gentleman. I am not wealthy. I am what those soldiers said." The words felt an admission almost, as if he were finally telling a truth he had kept even from himself. "No better than a village plow-boy. Worse even, now."

She remained frozen, caught in the awkwardness of it all, probably wondering how to respond.

And then she smiled, and it was like the slow dawning of sunlight. "Will." She used his first name, as if she already possessed a right to it, even though they both knew she never would. "I cannot imagine you wealthy."

From anyone else, the words would have been a glove in his face. From her, spoken like that, they sounded almost a commendation.

She moved nearer, her voice soft. "You, of all people, do not require wealth or a great name, in order to be respected, to have purpose."

A sudden warmth spread through him. Still, he had to speak the obvious. "You mean because of what's happened to me, what I can do?"

"*No.*" She tilted her head to look up at him. "Not that at all, no more than it renders Mr. Fitzroy worthy. No, it is that you have taught *me*, for the first time in my life, to see beyond all that."

He shook his head, not sure he understood. She was so near, and his pulse thundered in his ears.

"I see it now," she said. "I think perhaps I always suspected it. But I never understood." Her eyes shone. "All my life, I saw myself as this cog in the wheels. What was I except what I was born to? And I hated it."

Her expression stilled. Perhaps she felt the same energy between them as did he.

She took a breath. "And then I met you."

He reached for her arm and eased her another inch nearer.

And he kissed her.

It was against all of her world's rules. But why not? He had broken the rest already.

She kissed him back, and *his* world began spinning recklessly.

When he pulled away, only a bit, she shuddered out a short breath.

Then, as one, they both stepped back.

Even in the moonlight, her cheeks were pink. She looked down the street, first in one direction, then the other, and finally at the ground between them.

Then she glanced up. "Well, that was—I mean—I suppose—"

Already, his thoughts ran away with him, far away into a host of future impossibilities that were *still* impossible, but somehow not so much as a few minutes ago.

"Do you want me to apologize?" he asked, meaning it.

"No." She rejected the idea almost sharply.

"Come with me," he said, then immediately heard how that sounded. "I mean to Paris, to Dr. Silas, away from London."

She looked to the ground again, then back. "I cannot do . . . anything without my grandfather's consent, you realize that. I am not yet twenty-one—and neither are you, I think."

Once again, the door clanged shut upon the future.

He steeled himself with a deep breath of the chill night and shrugged out of his coat. "Here. I'm sorry I had no thought of it sooner."

She took the heavy coat without protest and ducked her chin beneath its high collar. They walked on for nearly fifty feet more without finding a word to speak.

"Well, then," she said at last. "I suppose we both know Mr. Fitzroy will not accept tonight's events without a counter-move."

"No. But the blow *is* struck. I think the scale has tipped at last, and I think he will know it."

Depending on how successful the blow turned out to be, it might leave Fitzroy with no other counter-move than simple retaliation. Indeed, no matter how successful Will had been tonight, Fitzroy would certainly attempt to strike at him directly. Will had once again proven himself far too great a threat to ignore.

A shiver ran through him. "We've barricaded Seven Dials tonight. But it may not stop him. The illusions allow him to disguise his forces. We won't be able to tell friend from foe."

She looked at him sideways. "Do not leave, Will. Promise me that. I know what it means to you to go to Dr. Silas now—what it may cost you if you miss him. I know all that. And, indeed, I respect your desire to put your master's safety and my own above all else. But you *must* end this. No one else can. The people will follow you. Aid them, and they will aid you."

He shook his head. "Fitzroy's campaign against me has been ruthlessly effective. He has shown me for what I am and worse—an outlaw, unworthy of any man's regard." Bitterness clogged his throat. Perhaps had he been better, faster, smarter, he could have been the symbol of hope Tom wished him to be. But too late. "We're becoming desperately outnumbered."

"That is untrue." She stopped and turned. "Mr. Fitzroy cannot muster more than several hundred hired guards, and they must be spread throughout the city. The rest are naught but illusions. Even if the common citizens are not yet for you, they have no reason to rally to *him*."

He spared a short laugh. "You didn't see them this afternoon."

"Will."

He sobered.

"When the time comes, show them something to rally *to*. They will come to you. I believe it."

He could not share her belief, but he kept his mouth closed.

"Now." She drew a deep breath. "Conduct me home."

"No." He clasped her arm. "Please. Arrange passage for yourself. I will stay, if it means you going."

She reached out of the coat and laid her hand atop his on her elbow. "I cannot leave without my grandfather."

"I fear he's lost to us after tonight."

"No. Mr. Fitzroy *will* allow him to return home. He dare not risk affirming the rumors just yet."

He shook his head. "Fitzroy will only be the more audacious now. He's less to lose than ever before. Let me take you to Seven Dials. Tom's already there. Tonight, it may be the safest place in the city."

She didn't even blink. "Do you trust me?"

"Yes, but doesn't mean I trust your judgment."

She scowled. "Well, and I am sure I do not always trust yours. However, I trust you to understand I *must* do this. If you see me home tonight, I will bring my grandfather to meet you in Seven Dials tomorrow. Fitzroy cannot possibly make a decided move before then."

That was true enough. Nevertheless, he ground his teeth. Perhaps he could remain with her, stand guard over Carstone House through the night. But, no. However much he might owe her, he owed Tom and Rose as much.

"I'll wait until tomorrow evening," he said. "Then I shall come for you."

She smiled. "I expect no less."

# CHAPTER 40

EVEN HASTENING, WILL did not reach the outskirts of St. Giles until long after the half moon had set. He did not run; he could not afford to waste energy.

In this last witching hour of night, the streets were so silent they seemed not even to breathe, as if all their struggling, striving, raucous children had disappeared.

The cold breeze tasted of coming winter. It smelt of soot and waste, with a mere whiff of the putrid river to the south and a burst of sweetness from a pile of spoiling, unsold violet clusters at someone's doorstep.

His brain was a-swirl. He had dealt Fitzroy a true blow tonight. Perhaps *the* blow. Need they deal another, final one? Or was his plan still the better: take Tom, Rose, and the Barbarys and start afresh whilst Fitzroy's plans lay in ruins behind them? It all depended on what, if anything, had happened in Seven Dials in his absence.

And then there was Isabella. He had *kissed* the Earl of Carstone's granddaughter.

And she had kissed him in return—and all but told him he might have courted her had things been different. That alone was enough to bounce him between exultation and despair.

He thrust his cold hands into his coat pockets. So many possibilities pulled at him. What would Rose say?

The thought surprised him. Customarily, he would wonder what Tom would say. But, indeed, Tom had said already what he thought.

Perhaps Rose had too . . . with that wide, hurt look as he left.

Child that she was, *she* had given him her heart far more fully than had Isabella. Though she would never admit it, she was starved for love. What she needed was a family to put that sharp-edged mind of hers to worthy industry before she ended up worse than Peggy.

He thought of his sisters, younger than Rose when last he saw them. His stomach turned with the old grief of missing them, missing the women they would now be.

Even could he yet be a brother to Rose, it wasn't enough. She needed someone who could teach her to be more than a clever hoyden. She might not see it, but the best thing he could possibly do for her was find her a real family.

He rounded the corner.

Before him swelled Lifty and Tug's barricade—barrels and crates and chairs and broken-off doors. Trust the Seven Dials lads to at least care for their own.

He pitched his voice low. "Look out in the barricade!"

Only the rustle of blowing newspapers returned to him.

He frowned. Tom had given explicit orders to mount a guard at all times.

"I'm coming up," he whisper-shouted.

He took two steps back and easily jumped to the top. He scrabbled for balance atop a wobbly board, then crouched.

Naught but shadows crowded the base at the other side.

At the end of the street, some fifty feet distant, shapes moved in the glimmer of a lantern. Voices murmured.

He squinted.

Beneath the swinging wooden sign of a rag-and-bone shop, two men stood in conference. The taller had his back to Will. The shorter wore a tall hat and a green shawl.

Will tensed.

Mr. Monarch's voice drifted down the street. "And I am to be cast out from my home? This is right?" He shook his head. The words were less calculated than usual; they held the sharp edge of earnest anger. "I think it is not."

The other man murmured something. With his face to the lantern, he was only a dark back. Was it Bull? Gamp? Lifty?

It couldn't be Fitzroy. Will's heart raced. Fitzroy would not come here alone, to see Mr. Monarch of all people.

At Mr. Monarch's feet rested several small kegs. Gin . . . or gunpowder?

The men had not yet heard him. But that would not last. He would make a great clatter howsoever he dismounted this treacherous pile.

Speed and surprise it must be then.

He leapt off the barricade and landed, already running. He reached them almost before they could turn.

The lantern flickered against the taller man's face. It was— Tom.

Will drew up, nearly stumbling. "What are you doing?"

Mr. Monarch glanced between them, shocked—stricken even. He clamped his bandaged hand against his chest. "I—"

"All is well," Tom said. But his gaze bore into Will, demanding, angry even. "So you are returned? I had thought you far afield by now."

"Of course I returned. I would never leave without you." He glanced at Mr. Monarch. But what mattered it if the man overheard? Will would lock him up until this all had ended. Perhaps he might even find a way to turn him over to Pish.

Mr. Monarch looked pale, stunned. But already his old satisfaction was creeping back into place.

It made no sense he should complain to Tom. Tom would have even less patience with his treachery than did Will.

Yet here they stood.

Will deepened his frown. He turned back to Tom. "We must speak. Things have happened. I believe Fitzroy is truly on his heels."

Tom watched him steadily, his expression guarded, showing little surprise. "And so you intend to remain in London?"

Wariness began to fill Will. "You don't want me to?"

Tom stepped nearer. "I know already what has occurred tonight. I applaud you for it, indeed I do. It is a blow well struck. But we must not overestimate its effect upon Mr. Fitzroy. Indeed, I believe I have been guilty of *under*estimating the man." He gestured to the barricades. "Our paltry defenses here? They cannot stand once he musters forces directly against us."

Will shook his head, carefully. "This is Seven Dials. 'Twas nearly impenetrable even before the barricades."

The force of Tom's gaze did not leave Will. "I do not wish to see you injured. The man is too strong. He *will* defeat you in the end—if you do not give heed now."

Even the breeze against Will's cheek seemed to falter. He stared at Tom. This could not be merely the outcome of their arguing. Since when had argument ever changed Tom's mind about anything?

Tom clenched his jaw in that old stubborn immovability. His face burned with intensity. In this weird light, his eyes looked almost blue.

Blue like the warrant officer Hale's had been when he accused Will of murder.

Blue like . . . Fitzroy's.

Featherlight footsteps pattered down the corner street.

"Will. You're back." It was Rose's voice, full of relief. Then, just as he knew she would, she gasped. "Cor. How'd you get here ahead of me?"

Already, *Tom* was backing up.

It wouldn't save him. Will's heart beat hard and steady.

Fitzroy was *here*, on Will's ground. His army couldn't save him. The Runners couldn't save him. Even his illusive disguise hadn't saved him. Finally, he was within Will's reach. Face to face, strength against strength—that was the battle Will could win every single time.

"Fetch Tom," he told Rose, "and gather Lifty's men."

She fled back towards Mr. Monarch's a few streets away.

Tom's face compressed in a rueful laugh. Tom's body took another step away, nearly backing into the rag-and-bone shop.

"Well," Fitzroy said, "and you *are* clever tonight."

The illusion floated from his body in a cloud of golden sparks. Above his head, it coalesced. Then it shot straight up into the air, some fifty feet above the buildings. It exploded into a tremendous show of fireworks. Every dark corner of the street lit up like a signal.

Dark spots blotted Will's vision. He blinked hard and lurched forward.

Instead of dispersing, the spots grew—larger and larger. From their roiling, shadowy depths, glaring eyes of pure light rolled up to fix upon Will. Writhing, stretching limbs detached and extended—growing and growing as they reached for him. The monsters' faces split to reveal rows of ragged, gore-ridden fangs.

All about, a veil of darkness fell in a great circle, blocking sight of everything—the rag-and-bone shop, the surrounding streets, even Mr. Monarch.

The back part of his brain panicked. It reacted to what it saw.

But the rest of him knew it to be a lie. Indeed, what he *knew* was that this pitiful attempt at a nightmare was the only remaining card Fitzroy could play.

Strength and speed flowed through him. Before Fitzroy could disappear into the darkness, Will slammed into him. He caught him by the throat. Momentum dashed them both against the rag-and-bone shop's window. Glass shattered, shutters gave way, and they both toppled through.

Darkness filled the musty interior of the shop, but this was a natural darkness—shades of light and dark, dark and light, hinting at piles of crumpled papers, musty clothing, and reeking gin bottles. The lantern in Fitzroy's hand clattered to the floor beside them, but did not break. The flame guttered wildly, shadows thrashing through the room.

Will landed hard on one knee, and a line of fire burned down his leg where he had caught it on a shard in the windowsill. Maintaining his grasp upon Fitzroy's throat, he hauled him to his feet.

He withdrew his pistol. "Now. It *is* over." Everything in him tensed, nerves all afire, ready for Fitzroy's resistance.

But Fitzroy, coughing yet, stood passively. His hands dangled at his sides. He glanced about the shop, then back.

He smiled, that same old charming smile. "I do not flatter myself you have any longer a desire to learn from me. Still, I would teach you one thing more."

Will inched back towards the door. Tom would be here soon, and together, they could overwhelm Fitzroy properly.

Fitzroy did not resist Will tugging him forward. He limped

slightly as if he had tweaked his ankle. "I am here looking for you, Will. I am here to end this."

"Indeed. Then you needn't look for me. If you wish to treat, you must treat with Tom, man to man. I don't speak for these people."

Fitzroy shook his head, his eyes hard and knowing. "I will treat with you, as the only man here who can stand as my equal. I know you no longer wish to admit it, but you and I, Will, we are much alike."

"Stop it." He twitched the pistol into Fitzroy's face. "Enough of your silver words!"

"Why?" Fitzroy looked at him steadily. "Because they are the truth?"

"Because they are lies. You've never spoken aught but a lie. That's all you do! Your abilities—your illusions? What are they but lies?"

"This is no lie: the war we fight is destructive to all."

"You began it."

Fitzroy breathed out hard through his nose. "What you did tonight—" The words seemed to pain him, and yet he laughed. "It was a masterful stroke, as thorough as it was daring. You played the game by *their* rules, and you played it very well. Once, you told me you wished to rise above your birth—yet now you choose not to allow me to rise above mine?"

"And you've risen so very far? You lie and you cheat and you steal. Man or boy, that seems not to have changed."

The lines of Fitzroy's face restricted further. He spoke, but his mouth scarcely moved. "Men do not change. We can only pretend."

"I don't believe that." Will reached behind him and wrenched the latch. He kicked the door open and glanced back.

Even now, the illusion of darkness was total. Footsteps ran through the distant streets. Was it Mr. Monarch fleeing or Tom arriving?

"And how have you changed at all, Will? You wished to transform the world, to salvage young people like yourself from lives of degradation—and I applaud you for it yet. But now you have discovered what I have long known. It is impossible. You cannot change a man from birth. You can only wipe out the filth and start again."

"You *are* mad."

"Am I?" Fitzroy offered no resistance as Will yanked him up to the threshold. "Will you not hear my offer?"

"I am not the man to speak to. It is not my place, whatever you think."

Fitzroy seemed not to hear him. "Give Seven Dials into my hands. It is all I want. It is all I have ever wanted. It is little enough to ask, and now it is yours to give."

The breeze chilled upon Will's neck. "Why would I do that?"

Intensity lit Fitzroy's eyes. He leant forward as much as possible with Will's hand upon him. "Because you despise it as much as I. And because I have orders in place that will yet tear this city apart."

Will shook his head. "I can't."

"Why would you save this filthy, godforsaken, damnable place when you know it for what it is?" Fitzroy's features contorted with raw emotion: desperation, hatred, pain. For an instant, in the glimmer, he looked almost the sweet-faced boy he must have been when first he came here.

Will's hand sweated around his pistol. "You cannot punish everyone for what Mr. Monarch did to you and your mother."

The pain and the hatred merged. Fitzroy barked a laugh that sounded almost a weeping. "It took me not even a twelve-month to know my survival depended upon escaping this place. I scrimped and I saved and I stole, and I took the beatings when it was thought I did not bring home as much as I should. I even watched as they beat my mother—because I believed I would yet free her."

For one blink, tears sheened his eyes, and then they were gone. "But she lost herself—her dignity, her sanity. By the time all was in readiness, she was so far degraded by this place, she betrayed me herself. Even as I hid in the darkness, she called after me, pleading for my return to depravity, threatening the filth she would commit before my very eyes if I would not—so that I might blame myself for it."

He seemed to catch himself. He breathed out, hard. "But I

do not blame myself. I do not believe in blame, only justice. I bent my life to this cause, so that one day this changeless darkness at the heart of society might be obliterated. And now it is in our hands to do so."

Will could only stare. This was the polished gentleman who had tossed him a sovereign? He had no words in response. "This is not the way."

Fitzroy straightened. The pain bled from his face, until there was only the mask of calm. "Is it not?"

"How can you say these things when *you* are tolerating Mr. Monarch's assistance?"

"He wishes to be useful. So I will use him, as he used me, and then I will assuredly destroy him. Do not tell me that brings you no pleasure."

Will had to concentrate to maintain his breathing. He would be a liar indeed were he to deny it. Aye, he despised Seven Dials, as any decent man would. He despised everything it stood for, everything it did.

Would he trade it for the rest of the city—for Tom and Isabella and Rose? A thousand times, yes. Indeed, he had already told Tom as much.

But was this indiscriminate justice his to mete out? Certainly, it was not Fitzroy's, whatever he had suffered.

Fitzroy studied him. "I wish you to do this because it is righteous. But there is more. There is Dr. Silas to consider."

"What?"

"I know he did not die."

Will stared. "All this time you knew?"

"Not until recently. My investigators have discovered his address."

Dread surfaced in Will's stomach. "What is that to do with aught?"

"You did not believe I would come here without insurance, did you?"

The dread clenched into an actual cramp. "You would not harm him?" Not when he was the only clue either of them had to rectifying the ills of the plague, perhaps of surviving it altogether.

"It need not be that," Fitzroy said. "None of this need be as dark as it now seems. The future is ahead of you, Will. Do you even comprehend it, I wonder? You think of this wondrous thing that has happened to us as if it were a curse, when it is the greatest blessing you will ever gain."

"It hasn't treated me so."

"Has it not?" Fitzroy leant forward, nearly forcing Will back. "Everything that has happened to us, *between* us, it need not be but an unfortunate memory. If you choose well this night, you can yet step over it as if it never were. Claim the future you desire. That you deserve."

Will scoffed. "And I suppose you would yet tell me you can gift it to me?"

"Perhaps. If you were to insist upon it as part of our terms." Fitzroy smiled. "The Lady Isabella. She is a singular young lady, is she not? She would marry you, you know, were I to allow it."

Will clenched Fitzroy's collar. He could smell the fine soap the laundress had used, the faint waft of Madeira, the odor of fearful sweat.

"And what of Henry?" The question scraped from his throat.

Real emotion twisted Fitzroy's face. "Henry." He snorted. "Shall I tell you the rest of my story? Of a man who builds an empire from nothing only to find himself bereft of a worthy heir?"

The rawness of the answer was like a detonation between them. Will leant away.

"You," Fitzroy said at last, the word hoarse. "You might have been a worthy heir." The pain faded. The blue of his eyes was open, honest even. "You might yet."

Will couldn't help it: his heartbeat throbbed in his ears.

"Think on that," Fitzroy said. "Let us make a pact of peace between us. I will listen to your demands, even modify my plans. If it must be so, I will allow the degradation of our society to continue. But you *must* give me Seven Dials. I would rather you kill me now than deny me this one justice."

Think. Will had to think straight. He swallowed. Was the man in earnest? End this battle—end the depredations on the innocent poor? Or was it yet another lie?

"You, at least, can begin anew, Will. Marry the Lady Isabella if you wish. Rule England someday. I tell you, it is not beyond your grasp."

The pain of it all was that, for once, it wasn't a lie.

Why would God grant him these abilities if not for such a purpose? Perhaps it was even a sin *not* to take them as far as they could go. Will could yet take them far indeed, perhaps farther than he had so far been capable of imagining.

If Fitzroy were to cease his actions against the poor of the city, then Will could logically have no more reason to oppose him. The battle would be won right there. Such a treaty would lead to greater benefits for everyone than would the rubble and chaos that would remain if the Prime Minister of England simply disappeared.

Will released Fitzroy's collar and grasped his sleeve instead. He kept the pistol trained upon him yet.

Fitzroy watched him. "You have won, Will. All the choices are yours now."

He could release Fitzroy and claim a treaty publicly. Then all the world would know he had won. They would know he was no murderous ruffian, no bloody-minded thief. He could be the hero of not only the poor, but every class. Dr. Silas could survive. Will himself could survive.

He need only sacrifice Seven Dials. 'Twas not so great a sacrifice as all that.

"Will—" The voice was Tom's.

He started and looked past his shoulder.

Tom and Rose had broken past the circle of darkness.

Beyond, the sound of running footsteps and shouting men echoed down the streets. Lifty's men must also be on the approach.

Tom carried a bludgeon. His hair was tufted in back, mussed from sleep. He held Will's gaze, his brows a dark line. His mouth worked, and he shook his head, slowly. His expression was shocked.

No, not shock. It was—disappointment.

He had heard then, what Fitzroy had been saying? More than that, he had seen upon Will's face the truth of his perilous thoughts.

"What are you doing, Will?" By his joyless tone, he knew already.

A burst of shame overwhelmed him. Clarity struck like a blast of Fitzroy's white light—swift and brutal.

Could he have just lost the respect of the only man whose respect had ever truly mattered?

And for what?

Fitzroy was not so wrong. Weren't these people the lowest of the low—lower even than Will himself? Weren't they the scrapings of society, unwanted by anyone, despised by all? Weren't they, after all, as irredeemable as Fitzroy claimed?

He caught himself.

This was, in not so many harsh words, exactly what the likes of Lord Carstone and that young fop Richard Grainger would have to say of Will Hardy. This was what he had struggled all his life to throw off, so that he might prove himself better than the world labeled him.

He had named it wrong when they thought it of him. How was he not as wrong in thinking it of every man, woman, and child in Seven Dials? They were not all Mr. Monarch. They had not all committed his crimes. They were not all worthy of prejudice and purging.

He raised his pistol's sagging barrel to point once more at Fitzroy.

"No," he said.

Fitzroy raised an eyebrow. "No?" But he understood.

"No," Will said.

He would do this rightly, for the right reasons, in the right way. He would not walk away from this night having lost every last measure of his own self-respect.

Fitzroy drew a deep breath. He released it, and he nodded. "I see." He smiled, a bit sadly. "It was worth the asking, I think."

Will dared one glance at Tom.

His rejection of Fitzroy's grand bribes had been too little too late. He knew that. He might not have rejected them a'tall had Tom not arrived when he did.

But he understood now what Tom had tried to teach him all this time. Indeed, what Tom had been teaching him all his life. Would Tom realize at least *that*?

Tom looked only at Fitzroy, his eyes unflinching. Then he lurched forward. "*Will.*"

Will whirled back.

Fitzroy's fist plowed towards his face.

Will jerked away, and the fist grazed the corner of his jaw—in a burst of golden sparks.

He had scarcely time to register the illusion before Fitzroy—with his *real* hand—batted aside Will's pistol. The weapon tore from his grip and tumbled beyond the veil of darkness. Fitzroy spun free, and Will staggered, off balance.

All around, illusions sprang up—a score of Fitzroys.

Will straightened, blinking hard against the disorientation.

He must move immediately, before he lost the true Fitzroy amidst the crowd. He would jump up high, use his dizziness to see through the illusions—but, no. He had downed one of Losborne's packets earlier. He would not be able to see.

Tom was already in motion, hurtling towards the blanket of shadow covering the space where Fitzroy had been standing but a second past.

"Hold fast!" Rose shouted. "Lifty's coming! He's a score o' men with him!"

Lifty's men would make no difference if Will lost Fitzroy in the darkness.

Curse him for a fool.

Tom smashed into the dark space, and from the contortion of his body, it was clear he struck something. He tumbled to the ground, hard.

All around, the illusions blinked. Fitzroy's doubles fizzed into sparks. The shadow monsters dissolved. The encircling veil of darkness dropped.

Fitzroy reappeared, crushed beneath Tom's weight.

Will raced forward. He leapt over Tom and Fitzroy and skidded a few feet through the rag-and-bone shop's open door. He turned and dropped to one knee beside Fitzroy, trapping Fitzroy's arm.

They had him. Will had not breath enough to release in relief. His treacherous hesitation had not lost them the night. Thanks to Tom.

He looked up to meet Tom's eyes.

But Tom was looking into the street beyond, which had been invisible only a moment past.

Torchlight spotted the night afar off. Muskets erupted, but even they were drowned by the clamorous shouts and the clatter of men clashing.

At the crossroads, Rose stared fearfully at the corner of the rag-and-bone shop.

A keg had been positioned there. A black thread of powder led away from it, to the street in front of Will, where it intersected with two more such threads.

A trap. This had all been a trap? His heart thudded. Mr. Monarch had *not* fled. He had worked silently whilst Fitzroy sang his siren song, whilst Will came so close to falling under his spell once again.

Time all but ceased. He raised his gaze, slowly.

In front of him, Tom moved. He leapt away from Fitzroy's body.

Will froze between two actions: following Tom's movement and redoubling his grip upon Fitzroy.

Then he saw what Tom had seen.

At the intersection of the powder trails, Mr. Monarch stepped from the shadows with Will's cutlass pistol extended. He looked at Will, face blank. He pulled the trigger. The spark lit the pistol's breech.

It was aimed at Will's chest. He could not dodge it. He had not seen it in time. The ball would tear into his chest and splay his blood upon the walls and the street and the windows. It would slay him as if he were any ordinary fool—as surely he was.

But Tom had seen it. Tom had moved even before Mr. Monarch pulled the trigger.

He sprang to his feet. He flung himself before Will.

It was Tom's chest into which the ball tore. It was Tom's hot blood that splayed back against Will's face.

# CHAPTER 41

THE SOUND OF the shot exploded through the narrow street. Tom's body jerked, like a Punch doll flung from its stage. He hurtled back against Will, driving them both through the doorway into the rag-and-bone shop.

They smashed against something. Heavy bundles clattered down upon them. Something struck Will's ribcage. His head slammed the dirt floor, and for an instant the stars piercing his vision were all he could think of. Then pressure upon his body, his legs, penetrated his awareness.

The dusty smell of old bones—cattle and sheep and horses—filled his senses. He coughed. His nostrils and the back of his throat burned with the hot coppery smell of fresh blood.

Tom's blood.

*No.* It was the only word in his head. It was a single great exhalation: *No.*

It couldn't be. Tom couldn't be shot. This could not be reality, could not be his life. What he had seen, what had happened, it could not be. The idea that danger could overtake Tom was naught but a fear—a great, impossible, overwhelming fear that had dogged him since the beginning of this misbegotten adventure. It had driven him in everything he had done since Tom's arrest. But it could not be true.

His body knew what his head did not. His heart raced faster than ever it had, even since the plague. It was a dizzying flutter in his chest. Even trapped beneath the bone bundles, his limbs shook.

"Tom." The name worked free.

He attempted to roll over, but the pressure of the shifting bundles trapped him against the floor.

He turned his head. "Tom!"

Beside him on the floor, an arm's span away, Tom sprawled beneath more bundles.

"Will—" The word was a wet splutter. He sounded surprised.

"No." The word in Will's head finally dropped onto his tongue. "No." He scrabbled for a hold on the bundles.

*No*, he wouldn't allow Tom to die.

*No*, Tom could not be hurt so badly as that.

*No*, this could not have happened.

No. No. No. He rejected all of it.

No.

He heaved against the bundles. The topmost one shifted, rolled off. It clumped down and bumped into Tom.

He groaned.

Through the doorway, silhouettes guttered. Mr. Monarch assisted Fitzroy up from the street.

Behind them, the spark of a fallen rushlight glinted on the street. Another shadow shifted.

Rose.

She cast panicked glances at the shop even as she kicked apart the lines of powder.

Beyond her, the clatter of the conflict in the street and the glow of torchlight rushed the barricade.

"Well, now." Relief edged Fitzroy's voice—but also anger, as if piqued Will had forced him into such near straits. "Are you certain you will not treat with me?" He snorted a humorless laugh.

Rage seared Will from the inside out. It blinded him. It built in the pit of his stomach and it surged through his chest.

"I will kill you for this!"

"Blame yourself, Will Hardy." Fitzroy's breath came hard. "You had not the mettle to walk my road."

The rage felt a wild thing within him. He could not think, could not see. He shoved against the bundles, kicking, writhing. They tumbled, falling in every direction. His legs remained trapped, but his chest and his arms came free.

"You've killed him!" he screamed. "That was your mistake—and now you'll pay for it! You've nothing left to hold over me now!"

Fitzroy's posture shifted—stiffened. "Do I not?" He looked to Mr. Monarch.

As swiftly as any rat, Mr. Monarch turned. He scampered to where Rose was destroying his powder lines—as if he had known she was there all along. He caught her arm in his good hand and yanked her around.

She shrieked, clawing. "Get off me, you devil! Get off me!"

He spun her around, trapping her against his chest and pinning her arms to her sides. From within his shawl, he produced the gleam of his tiny dagger and touched it to her throat. He must have cast aside Will's pistol after its one shot.

She froze, eyes a white gleam from across the fire-lit darkness.

The fury in Will's chest dissolved into panic. He kicked harder, an animal scrabbling in a trap.

The bundles gave way to his frenzy. His left leg came free, then the other. He jumped his feet under him and pushed off. He could reach top speed in seconds. He would destroy them both—Fitzroy and Mr. Monarch—kill them where they stood before they felt the breath of his passing against their faces. He would save Rose, and he would, somehow, save Tom.

Before he could take a single step, Fitzroy's trick of blinding light flashed. It smashed into his brain as if 'twere a physical blow. He staggered for only a second.

It was a second too long.

In the space of a single blink, utter darkness overtook the light.

His momentum carried him, but not swiftly enough. Even as the latch clicked shut, he smashed into the closed door. More stars filled the artificial darkness.

Outside, running footsteps swarmed the street. "There he is, mates!" Lifty's voice was flush with battle.

Rose cried again. Abruptly, the sound cut off.

"Where'd the blighter go?" Lifty shouted.

They would not see Fitzroy. Perhaps never again would they

see him. He would disguise himself and Mr. Monarch and Rose—if she yet lived—all the way to safety.

Will pounded the door. "No!"

"Will?" Lifty called.

A new volley of musketfire sounded from farther down the street, and the clash renewed.

He groped for the latch and shook it. He raised a foot and hammered a kick into it. Still nothing. He stood, panting.

The scent of smoke drifted to him.

Outside, the rushlight was still lying in the street. If it touched any of the rubbish out there, it might yet spread to the powder lines Rose had tried to disperse.

He turned back. "Tom?"

The faint rattle of breath reached him.

Fitzroy's illusion of darkness was utterly opaque. It offered no sense of depth, no fluctuation of shadow.

He swiped his hands before his face and stumbled forward. He would trip over Tom before he found him. He dropped to his hands and knees.

To his right, the tiniest glimmer broke the darkness.

Fitzroy's fallen lantern.

He lurched towards it, and his hand bumped the hot glass. He righted it and drew it to him. The sputtering flame, more than half drowned in wax, scarcely penetrated the illusive darkness.

He scraped across the floor.

"Tom."

His master lay upon his back, both hands at his chest, framing the great black hole through his breastbone. With every heaved breath, his back arched. Blood slicked his chin and striped either cheek. He rolled his eyes sideways to see.

Will's throat closed up. "God help me, Tom." Never in his life had he seen such a wound. His hands shook. "I don't know what to do."

"Will—" Tom struggled to raise his hand. It trembled violently.

Will caught it. "Tell me what to do. You've been around wounds, you know what to do. Tell me. Tell me so I can save you."

"I—don't think you—can."

From outside, acrid smoke seeped in. Darkness wavered.

Footsteps raced up and someone smashed into the door.

"Will?" Lifty shouted. "Will, I can't see a bloody thing! Are you in there?"

"'Tis an illusion!" came another voice. "We'll light more fires. Smoke it out!"

"No more fires!" Lifty said. "You blighted fool, there's gunpowder out here, I can smell it! Will, you got to come out of there, you hear me?"

Will gripped Tom's hand in both of his. "I'm sorry, Tom. I'm sorry. Please forgive me—for everything. What I almost did back there—"

"Will—lad." By his expression, Tom wanted to say more but could not manage the words. "I saw. I saw it all."

The tears came, and Will couldn't halt them. "I know."

Tom swallowed hard. The muscle in his cheek churned, as if he were fighting for strength. "I saw it in your eyes. Don't think I didn't."

Will had no words. He shook his head again, harder.

"Don't mistake me. I know what choice you made."

Will's own chest felt as if it had a ball buried within it. He couldn't breathe.

Tom had seen—what? Had he seen that Will *hadn't* taken Fitzroy's bait?

It had been a cursed close thing. Even now . . . if it would bring Tom back, if it would save him, Will would change his mind. Devil take him, but he would.

"I got you killed," he said.

Great drops of sweat beaded Tom's mouth. He worked his head back and forth. "'Tisn't about me. And 'tisn't about you. Never is."

Will should be *doing* something, he should be moving, finding a way out of here, stanching Tom's terrible wound.

But he could do naught. He could only sit and stare and try to drag in one burning breath after another.

"This"—Tom flexed his hand inside both of Will's—"was always about doing the right thing."

In the flickering lantern light, Tom's eyes gleamed white.

But he was not looking at Will. Not anymore.

Will couldn't move.

Tom was dead. Dead.

His teeth rattled. Every beat of his heart slashed fire through him. Every breath of smoke was a hammer to his chest. But he could not move. Emotion filled his body—like a living being, growing and growing and hurting him more and more with every second.

He dropped Tom's hand, and he scrambled back. Somehow he gained his feet.

He stared down at Tom, and he shook his head, harder and harder, and then when the pressure grew too great, he threw back his head and he screamed with the pain and the rage and the impossibility of it all.

Around him, the darkness had changed. Smoke poured in, and the crackle of heat hissed from behind. The smoke chased away Fitzroy's darkness, filling the space with its own thick, undulating shadows.

The streets sounded in chaos. People were running, they were shrieking, shouting. Their words were a senseless smear against the night.

What more had Fitzroy unleashed upon them?

From down the street, an explosion rent the night, so bright it cut through the smoke.

Will didn't move.

Outside, people wailed and ran all the harder.

"Will!" Lifty shouted. "That's done it! The whole shop's gonna blow higher'n Davy's kite! Get out now!"

Will didn't move.

He stared at Tom's open eyes, scarcely visible within the swirl of smoke.

He would stay in this shop. Stay with Tom. Let this whole cursed disaster end. He needn't do a thing. He need only wait.

Except . . . he could not.

That much Tom had made certain of. He had left Will in this bind. He had made certain Will *couldn't* give up, even now when he had nothing left to fight for. Tom had died for this, had died for *him*, no matter what he said. And Will couldn't leave that be. This sacrifice—didn't it have to be worth *something?*

"Curse you, Tom."

Beneath his boots, broken glass gritted.

Of course. The window had broken when he and Fitzroy first tumbled through.

"Will!" Lifty yelped. It sounded a last warning.

Grasping Tom's warm, limp body beneath the arms, he clutched him against his chest and released all the strength and speed left within him. He powered through the smoke, towards the flicker of light, and he hurtled through the window.

The shards in the sill scored his coat, ripping it. New lines of pain opened on his legs and his arms. He tumbled through, hauling Tom with him.

He landed on the ground outside and rolled to his feet.

The street was lit like noonday, fire everywhere. People ran, shouting, hauling goods from their houses, dragging their children.

Just as Mr. Monarch intended and Will feared, the lines of powder had caught. Sparks and smoke crawled towards the kegs at the shop corners.

Roaring, Will hoisted Tom's body into his arms and ran.

From the barricade at the far end of the street, Lifty beckoned.

Will was still running when the keg exploded. Heat and splinters peppered his back. The hairs within his nose burnt away to nothing. He caught his toe and fell, smashing into the street.

There, he stopped.

Behind him, the fire howled and crackled.

People rushed to put it out.

He looked down at Tom, and with an uncertain hand, he closed his master's eyes.

Before him, men gathered.

Beside Tom's body, he crouched, hands on his legs. He looked up at them.

Their faces were streaked with soot. They seemed to hold their breath. Indeed, the whole street had gone impossibly still.

Lifty cast a nervous glance at Tom's body, then up to Will. Blood streaked his arm. "Now what?"

Lifty's men must have dispersed the first round of Fitzroy's soldiers, since the musketfire and most of the fighting had moved farther afield. But a faint clamor still echoed from beyond the barricade.

Peggy ran from a side street, skirt hiked to reveal the great holes in her stockings. "Word's coming in." Her congested lungs rasped. "From all over."

Lifty caught her arm.

Like the rest, she looked to Will. "There's attacks all over—all the prisons we've been using as bases—Whitecross-street, Fleet. Here and Drury Street, the East End, everything this side of the river. Monsters roaming the streets—great, black monsters, eating the children, they're sayin'."

"The Marshalsea?" Lifty demanded.

She shook her head. "North of the river is all I've heard. But word'll take longer to come up from Southwark."

Will stayed as he was. Perhaps Fitzroy had been planning this all along. Or perhaps it had been but a final, furious response, spurred by Will's actions.

It mattered not.

It was done. Fitzroy had struck his blow. Tomorrow's battle would decide their war. They both knew that now.

He took a breath. The smoky air filled his chest and lifted his shoulders. He did not cough on it.

He looked at the expectant faces looming over him.

Lifty. Peggy. People from Seven Dials. Even some up from the Marshalsea. The crowd grew and grew. They were running in from the side streets, even climbing over the barricade. They were coming because they'd nowhere else to turn. They were coming because he was here.

With fear upon their faces, they watched him. But they watched him with steadiness too. These weren't people who had given up on themselves, as Fitzroy insisted. These were the people who would fight to the last breath to protect themselves and their families.

Maybe, as Tom said, Will had helped them find a little of that hope. Maybe not, but *maybe*.

The darkness was fading. The faintest edge of pink glared

through the smoke-soiled sky. Dawn was coming.

"Well." Lifty shifted his weight. "What do you want we should do?"

Strangely, Will found his mouth in a weary, wasted smile.

God help him, but everything he'd been trying to do all this time, it had been futile, hadn't it? He wasn't worthy of respect—not from the squires and earls of the world, not even from these disregarded people.

He'd used them for his own ends right to the brink of leaving them. He had nothing left to give. He had only the one opportunity Tom had left him: to find a way to *earn* something to give.

He nodded to Lifty. "Can you put out the fires?" The words grated in his wrecked throat. He looked at Peggy. "The monsters aren't real. Spread *that* word. Use mirrors and smokers—not fire—to see past them. Tonight, we draw back, across the river. If the Marshalsea yet stands, it is our most defensible position whilst we reorganize."

"Then you're to help us fight 'em?" Lifty said.

Will unbent his aching knees and creaked to his feet. The people drew back, forming a large circle roundabout him and Tom.

"Yes," he said. "I'm going to help you fight them."

# CHAPTER 42

WILL SAT ATOP the Marshalsea's roof, above Tom's room. He sat in his torn and singed trousers and rolled shirtsleeves, without his coat or his hat or his eye-shields. He sat with his elbows against his propped-up knees, hands hanging between them.

"Blind you, woman!" Lifty's voice drifted from the open window. "Watch where you put your hands! Am I wounded or am I not?"

"Shut your great gob," Peggy rasped. "You're the lucky one, aren't you? You're not the one got taken by monsters—like little Rose."

"But they wouldn't harm her." Postelwaite sounded distraught. He had been elated to see them all troop into the Marshalsea at sunrise. Rumors of the night's terrors had reached this far even if the fighting hadn't yet. "Surely," he said, "they've no cause to do aught to her?"

Lifty snorted. "And why'd they need cause, eh? She's spat in Mr. Monarch's eye often enough. He'll bring his wrath even if this Fitzroy cove don't."

"Stop it," Peggy said. "That's no way to be talking. We'll get her back. Something'll be done to get her back."

"Fine, be daft. You don't want to notice the great bloody *war* we got ourselves into, that's prime. That's going to render Rose aid, that is."

Will stared out over the rooftops of Southwark.

He hadn't taken one of Losborne's packets for nearly twenty-four hours. Every once in a while, the corner of his eye would catch the busy swarm of people in the courtyard, and the dizziness would claim him. But if he looked across the city, towards the river, he could keep steady. He could keep watching for Fitzroy's inevitable attack.

Even this early in the afternoon, it was a dark day—dark as night almost. Filthy fog from the river blackened the sky. For hours, news had been coming in. Fitzroy was finally doing it. He was finally taking the city in earnest. Of course, he was. He had no other play left.

Sooner than later, he would come for Will, and somehow Will must stop him. Not for pride and not for fame. But for Tom, and for . . . Rose.

Over and over in his head, she shrieked as she was dragged away. He swallowed a shudder. Hang him for a fool. He'd tried to save her from Mr. Monarch, and where had it got her? Back in the man's own clutches, and in more danger than ever.

She'd have been better off never knowing Will. Surely ending like Peggy wasn't a worse fate than what he had tipped her into.

He scrubbed his gritty face with both hands.

Little Rose. She had trusted and championed him from the start. She'd been his greatest friend in this wretched city, never mind she was but a child.

And he'd taken her for granted every single day. Just as he had Tom.

Now she was lost, and he must find her, and God help him, he had no idea where to begin.

From within came the steady clomp of footsteps up the stairs.

"Say"—it was the old man Trabb—"I went out and got us a prisoner. Tolerable valuable one."

Lifty snorted.

"What's this?" Postelwaite said.

Trabb sniffed. "See for yourself, eh?"

More clomping as someone else entered the room. Everyone gasped.

A chair clattered against the floor. "Gorm horney!" Lifty said.

"Now, now." The voice belonged to Henderson Pish. "We

needn't be too rash in our meeting here." He almost sounded apprehensive.

Will slid to the edge of the roof and swung back through the window to land in a crouch upon the window seat.

Pish held both arms extended straight up above his head. "Well."

From behind, Trabb poked at him with a wooden stake.

Lifty stood before an upended chair, a knife in his blood-streaked hand. Even Peggy had come out with a shard of window glass or something.

"Stay." Will pushed Lifty aside. "He's a friend."

Lifty growled. "No friend of mine."

Will looked at him. "Stand down."

Lifty huffed, but stepped back. "Friends with a bloody horney. And the world ain't up on its head these days?"

Across the room, Pish lowered his arms, stepped away from Trabb, and tugged his red waistcoat.

He nodded to Will, managing to look both grateful and put upon. "Thank you."

Will waited.

"Well." Pish licked his lips. "Well, in point of fact, I have come to tell you I've—resigned."

Will raised an eyebrow. "From the Runners?"

"Indeed." Pish hastened on. "The regrettable circumstances of late cause my principles to dictate that . . . I resign and... join you in outlawry."

Of all Will might have expected, this wasn't anywhere near the head of the list. "Well . . . thank you."

Pish relaxed his face—insomuch as the stern edges would relax. "And I've brought my lads. Quite a few of us see through this Fitzroy cove." Pish actually smiled. "And there's more. I can tell you what's happening in the city."

"We got a fair good idea last night, didn't we?" Lifty said.

Will nodded. "Fires, illusions, people turned out of their homes. It's the 'clearing out' he's been threatening all along."

"That's the truth, and he ain't stopping with clearing out. Bow Street got the word this morning. That's why me and my lads took our leave." Pish lowered his voice. "He's wanting to *purge* the city."

420 – K.M. WEILAND

Will's skin turned cold. This wasn't only about Fitzroy's quashing Will for good and all. This was the last stage of his grand social scheme, all at once.

"And why not?" Will said.

"What do you mean?" Lifty demanded.

A slow heat burned in his belly. It grew, and it spread. It fired new energy through his limbs, warming his arms and legs, his hands and feet, his very brain. His desire to move, to run—always present, but so nearly exhausted after last night—flickered in the back of his head.

He crossed to the corner bed where he had cast his Wayfarer costume.

"It means we've been waiting for Fitzroy to come to us. But he's not coming."

"'Course he is," Lifty said. "You're a wasp in his carriage, and he ain't going to let you keep buzzin' forever. Thought that'd be clear enough after last night."

"Last night was merely to set the bait." Will pulled on his now-ragged coat. His hands trembled, with exhaustion and with anticipation. "He doesn't *have* to come to us."

Pish nodded. He'd understood before ever he'd come here. "Word is he's starting with children—particularly any one of them brought up in the dangerous classes."

Peggy's raspy breath whistled. "Rose."

Likely, Fitzroy had dispatched that word to Bow Street on purpose, knowing Pish would carry it to Will.

In the rooms below, loud voices echoed back and forth—men laying plans, trying to work out what to do. Ultimately, however, what they were doing was waiting for Will.

As long as Rose was being used to lure him in, then Fitzroy had a *purpose* for her. He wouldn't kill her, and he wouldn't hand her over to Mr. Monarch's vengeance. He'd keep her alive, and he'd wait.

That was Will's battle. He was the only one of them who could fight it.

But it wasn't the only battle.

There were hundreds—thousands—in the city who would suffer tonight. Fitzroy would work his plan for its own sake and not only to reel in Will.

And there was Isabella.

She and her grandfather were supposed to have met him in Seven Dials today. Even had he *been* in Seven Dials, they could not have passed through the fighting and the barricades.

He breathed out carefully. He needed a plan—and he had only one—and it depended entirely on others.

"Come." Without waiting, he marched down the stairs to the courtyard.

Directly below Tom's room, the doors to the great room were wide open. The room was packed with men—angry, intent, impatient, frightened. Any one of them could have led a charge to reclaim their homes, but they all remained, waiting.

Will stopped in the doorway.

With his hat in hand and his eye-shields pushed up on his head, he must look the lad he was.

Slowly, the men ceased their clabber and turned. At the back, Gamp and Tug stood with what remained of their crews.

Behind heavy whiskers, Gamp watched Will, eyes hooded.

Will drew breath. "Fitzroy is putting all his eggs into the pudding. If there's to be a chance of besting him, it's now. 'Twill never be another."

The men didn't even nod. They only watched.

"I am not asking any of you to follow me."

Gamp knit heavy brows.

"You followed Tom more than me. I know that. But I am going out there tonight, to fight Fitzroy."

Isabella had told him to rally the city. She said they would come to him. Whether they would or not had to begin here in this room.

Claypole stood near the door, arms crossed. "You've a plan?"

"No. But Tom did. The only way Fitzroy can stifle this city is if the city refuses to fight back. He hasn't forces enough—nor the energy to conjure illusions enough—to halt even a quarter of the citizens. But people must be made to see that. They must not run, they must not hide. They must believe this is a fight they can win. They must rouse themselves. They must believe themselves *worth* fighting for."

Claypole shook his head. "When people are afeared, they don't fight, they run."

"Then we show them." Here was the part he could not do alone. "We show them resistance is possible. We show others how to use the smoke and reflections to see through the illusions—to dispel Fitzroy's lies. And we show them how to fight the soldiers that will remain after the illusions are gone."

In the back, Gamp twitched his mustache. "And Blue-Eyed Jem?"

Will raised his chin. "We start by spreading smoke through all quarters of the city. Dispel the illusions, tax Fitzroy's ability to maintain them, weaken him."

Pish stepped up behind Will's shoulder. "That'll also make our numbers seem all the bigger in the chaos."

Will watched Gamp. The man had called Will a chancer, said he was only in the fight for his own benefit. Well, it had been true enough. Will had no right to expect any of these men to follow him. But he needed them.

"We attack Fitzroy's house," Will said.

Gamp shook his head. "His whole street's a barricade, don't you know? You think the man's going to leave himself open to you?"

"He expects an attack. If we give him that, 'twill be distraction enough to allow *me* to infiltrate the house."

Lifty clucked. "Alone, matey?"

Gamp glanced at Tug, who shrugged.

"I'm the only one who can," Will said. "But first I must gain entrance, and for that I need all of you."

He held his breath. If Gamp joined, the rest would follow. If Gamp could put aside the past, if he could maybe for only this once join a larger fight—then maybe hope remained.

"I know you have little trust for me," Will said. "You would have rathered Tom Colville lead you." His throat throbbed. "Well, so would I. What am I left to do but finish this as he would have?"

In Gamp's face, something shifted. "I won't spend any bit of my day weeping if Fitzroy finds a way to feed you to his shadows." He stepped forward and looked about the room. "But we got ourselves a proper puzzle on our hands this day. And in all dear honesty"—he turned back to Will—"if I have to fight this battle tonight, then I'd as soon have you in it."

Will nearly sagged, but kept his face impassive.

Gamp crossed to stand before him. Finally, the gold flash of his grin glinted behind his whiskers. "I'll tell you something else. If you're volunteering to face this devil Fitzroy all alone, I'm not the one to argue with you."

The beat of Will's heart filled his chest. He gave Gamp a nod, but didn't request too much of fortune by offering his hand.

"We require supplies," he said. "Mirrors, smokers, weaponry. We've a stockpile at Carstone House in Regency Park. I'll travel ahead to secure it." He glanced back. "Mr. Pish and his Runners can follow and aid in dispersing the items."

Pish nodded. "Sensible. My officers can move about the town with less resistance."

"Gamp will have charge of the Seven Dials lads. Claypole will bring up the men from the Marshalsea and organize King's Bench and the other prison bases. Postelwaite's to retain a contingency and guard the prison and the women and children who remain."

Gamp nodded, judiciously, then faced the room. "Here 'tis, me cullies. It's a street-fight, this is, and don't we know more about that than any jumped-up soldiers?"

To a man, they shouted. But they were watching Will, not Gamp.

Some of these men he had come to know. Some he had never yet seen. Some watched him with the eyes of honest workmen. Some were, without doubt, criminals. Some would return to crime, even before the battle was properly joined.

They wanted him to say something. He *needed* to say something.

He licked his lips. "Fitzroy thinks he can play God and decide who deserves to live and who does not. He believes he is striking a blow against darkness—and we are that darkness."

The men shifted, some insulted, others ill at ease, perhaps recognizing the measure of truth in the accusation.

Will squared his stance. "On this night, let us give the lie to his charges. Let us prove we are better men than he would have the world think us."

They did not jostle one another or even shout in agreement. They waited, sober, attentive.

"God is no respecter of persons." His throat cramped around Tom's words of old. "Only of hearts. Let our intent and our actions speak for us tonight. Let us join this fight with honor and justice. Let us prove Fitzroy wrong. What he has given us tonight is the opportunity to become the men we should always have been. So let us do it."

They did not cheer him.

Gamp cocked one corner of his mouth, amused perhaps.

Will turned to go.

In the doorway, Lifty chewed his lip and shifted from foot to foot. Mouth still twitching indecisively, he offered Will a nod.

In the yard, Postelwaite, for one, looked as if he would choose to cheer. Beside him, Peggy clasped her hands beneath her flushed chin, as if stricken. A tear wet her hot cheek.

Pish stood at attention. The gaunt lines of his face were as hard as ever, his eyes narrowed as he studied the exiting crowd. He resolutely did not look at Will.

At least, they were not scoffing.

This was his army now. With them, he would fight. With them, perhaps he would die.

All those years when he had dreamt of coming to London and changing his life . . . this was not a night he could ever have fathomed.

But dreams or no, assuredly here it was. Assuredly, it had *already* changed his life.

"Put out the call," he said. "Anyone willing to stand with us and end this—tell them we are to battle." He settled his eye-shields and put on his hat. "May God be with us tonight and allow we might change our fates."

# CHAPTER 43

PURPLE TWILIGHT ENGULFED the city. It writhed through the streets, watched by fire-orange gaslight eyes. Every so often, the darkness would open its mouth, and it would howl frustration and horror and death.

All the way to the river, Will kept his feet upon the ground. He ran far ahead of his motley army, headed for Isabella's stockpile at Carstone House. His innards twisted. Heaven knew what else he might find there.

He crossed the river, ignoring the toll plate. Tonight, no one cared for pennies.

The Iron Bridge undulated with the exodus from north of the river. They came in droves, pale and sweating, eyes huge and dark. They were beggars and merchants, costers and financiers. Fitzroy might not be striking at them all, but fear knew no class.

Some saw Will and skittered wide. Women shrieked.

"It's him! It's the Wayfarer!"

A pock-faced lad darted from side to side in panic. As Will neared, the lad lunged for the railing. He flung himself over.

Seize it all. Will burst forward and scarcely caught the lad's arm. The boy's great bundle tumbled into the river far below and splashed white in the swirl of the breakers. He swung wildly, scrabbling at Will's hand on his arm.

With a shout and a burn of pain, Will hauled the lad up and over the railing. Leaving him sprawled upon the bridge, he pushed through the fearful crowd without a backwards glance.

So they all thought the Wayfarer was going to kill them? They thought he was a part of this, perhaps even the one summoning the monsters? Isabella had been more mistaken than she knew in her belief he would rally the city.

It mattered not.

Truly—and for the first time—he found it did *not*.

Their opinion of him changed nothing about what was happening here tonight—or about what he must yet do.

At the end of the bridge, the crowd parted as if a cannonball had landed in their midst. They swarmed towards him, screaming, crawling one over the top of the other.

And then Will saw why they feared.

Fitzroy had modified his blob-form shadow monsters of yestere'en. They were still shadows; but now, they were giants.

Two towered over the buildings, so tall their faceless heads disappeared in and out of the low overcast. Blue flames flashed past rough junctures of opaque ribs and up through gashed throats to blaze from the tops of their heads.

They weren't real. And yet even Will's heart froze. He could not tear away his gaze.

No longer was Fitzroy restricting his illusive powers to what might be mistaken for reality. He was fully declaring himself and his abilities.

The giants tromped down the street, silent. At the juncture in the road, they halted and, as one, flinched. Slowly, lines of blue fire dissolved their bodies down their centers.

But they did not fall. They did not die. Each half morphed into an entire giant of its own. Each flinched once more—and lumbered on.

The crowd fled, shrieking, stumbling, trampling each upon his fellow.

"They're not real." Will looked about. "They're not real!"

The steady stamp of marching feet penetrated the pandemonium. Rows of soldiers were visible—their redcoats a ghastly bruised purple by the light of the giants' blue fire. *They* were real enough.

Will could not dispel the monsters without lighting the whole wretched street afire. Had Fitzroy penetrated the secret of the smokers? Clever of him to add light to the illusions. It would discourage people from unwittingly starting fires.

But how great a burden must illusions of this size and complexity place upon Fitzroy? Surely, he could not sustain them—especially if they appeared all across the city. Or had Losborne's antidotes proven even more effective for Fitzroy than for Will?

He shoved off the bridge and broke free of the crowd. He got a running start at the side of a building, gained the second-floor windowsill, and hauled himself to the roof.

Before him, as far as he could see through the violet-black haze, the endless twisting streets were alight. Blue flames flickered imperiously, but also the orange heat of fires, spotting the night like a thousand burning eyes.

A chill touched him. It was a view of destruction.

He ran.

---

Even high above the fleeing mob, it required the better part of an hour to gain Regent's Park. There, where the fine houses were spaced by grand parterres and he could no longer leap from rooftop to rooftop, he dropped back to the ground.

People choked the streets. The canals writhed. Everything was alight. Commoners hurled themselves against fine houses, striking out in the only way they knew. To them, the rich represented Fitzroy—and, indeed, many of the wealthy had cast their lot with him from the beginning.

No shadow giants roamed here, thanks to the fires. But in every street, Fitzroy's red-coated soldiers clashed with the common folk. They were also attacking a select few of the great mansions—those belonging to Fitzroy's dissenters, no doubt.

Will cut across the long stretch of the neighboring estate's gardens. Even before he gained the iron fence roundabout Carstone House's grounds, the glare of flames and shouts of soldiers were evident.

Without slowing, he leapt for the top of the fence, easily caught it, and swung up to crouch.

All across the half-circle drive, people were running. The grand double doors had been thrown open, and soldiers packed the entrance. The rabble was attacking. The whole front hallway seemed filled with carnage. People hurled themselves at the ground windows, heaving torches at the glass higher up.

Isabella was in there yet.

And Fitzroy's men were defending her and Lord Carstone against the mob. Why? A strange new fear struck his innards like lightning. Her loyalties were with *him*. Of course, they were. Even Lord Carstone would not join hands with Fitzroy now. Surely.

Either way, his stockpile was inside, and he needed it before Pish and the Runners arrived.

He kept to the shadows until he reached the drive, then he cleared the line of decorative shrubs and bounded around to the back of the house.

A running start and a calculated push off the wall allowed him to grasp an open shutter.

Immediately, the topmost hinges cracked.

Confound it.

He hurled his weight forward, dragging the shutter around, towards the window. The hinge tore loose in a fine powder of mortar and stone. He smashed into the wall and scarcely managed to slap one hand upon the sill.

As the shutter wrenched completely free, he gained a second handhold and scrabbled his feet against the side of the house. He got a knee up onto the sill, one hand pressing against the top of the frame to keep from falling back out. He drew his twisted iron rod from his shoulder sheath and smashed it against the panes.

The glass shattered, leaving a skeleton of lead panes. He struck several times more, clearing a hole. Then he tumbled through, crashing against the polished floor.

Only a glow of coals lit the hearth to his left.

He pocketed his eye-shields, blinking.

In the shadows, forms took shape. Before him stood the ceiling-high posts of a tester bed.

Leaning a hand against the nearest post, he gained his feet.

Past the bed, light flickered in the narrow gap beneath the chamber door. From the rooms below, shouting and crashing furniture echoed up.

He crossed the room and tried the latch.

Locked.

Why? What in this room was worth protecting?

From the chair beside the hearth, a crystal goblet flashed.

He whirled and snatched his pistol.

From over his sherry, Lord Carstone watched him. His silver hair gleamed in the faint light.

Will looked about. "Lady Isabella?"

The earl shook his head. "She was here. They locked her in too."

His lungs tangled, somewhere between relief and panic.

Then she hadn't betrayed him.

But she *was* in danger.

"Where?" He stepped forward. "What happened?"

"She escaped." Lord Carstone nodded to a second door beside the hearth. "She had a key upon her, for the boudoir."

"She escaped?" Another tangle within his chest. "Where did she go? Why?"

Lord Carstone contemplated his sherry. "I find I am an old man, Mr. Hardy." He blinked up. "It is Mr. Hardy, is it not?"

"I . . ."

"She locked me in, you know. Protecting me, I daresay."

Will's blood pounded. "Where did she go?"

"She spoke of a weapons stockpile." Lord Carstone peered at Will. "I hope she does not intend anything rash. That young fool—Henry Fitzroy. He is here."

The hairs on Will's neck stood.

From below, he could now make out Henry's blustering tones: "I say, my buckos, keep this rabble back, I say!" He sounded strangely and forlornly out of place.

Will turned to the boudoir door. The latch was flimsy enough. Tom would have laughed at the "workmanship" of such a piece.

He backed off enough to kick the panel just beneath it. The whole thing gave with a crumple of splinters.

Lord Carstone stared on, eyebrows raised. Here in this flickering room—with marauders ripping his house apart beneath his feet—he did not seem the great patrician. He seemed an old man—weary, beaten, confused.

"Remain here, my lord. I will dispatch someone to your aid as soon as ever I can."

Lord Carstone looked Will in the eye. It was a strange look: no animosity, no superiority even.

"You young people." His mouth hesitated. "I admire you young people. You were correct about Fitzroy. You knew what to do about this, and you are doing it."

In point of fact, Will hadn't a notion what he was doing, but he left it at that.

"Remain here, sir. I'll do what I can about these rogues, and I *will* find the Lady Isabella."

He left, propping the broken door shut behind him and stumbling through the clutter of a lady's dressing room to gain the far door.

This one opened without resistance.

Bracketed near the ceiling, extravagant gas lamps lit the corridor. The floor was treacherous with the remains of furniture, paintings, and table silver. Halfway down, he began finding pieces of a lady's clothing: a hair comb, a black and silver shawl, a satin shoe. He bent for the shoe. Perhaps it meant nothing. After all, loot was scattered everywhere.

But these seemed all of a piece, as if they might have been worn together.

Shoe in hand, he stood.

The voices below grew louder. At the far end of the corridor, light colored the darkness. There was cheering—more raucous shouting.

"Well done, chaps, well done." That was Henry, trying to sound authoritative.

Will eased a look around the corner of the landing that topped the broad sweep of a red-carpeted staircase.

Past the marble railings, men moved through the entrance hall. Bodies scattered the floor.

The soldiers had triumphed, in spite of Henry's leadership.

"Now," Henry said, "we must see to the rest of that lot outside. And, you there, you see to the prisoners, what?"

"And whyn't you see to 'em? Locked in, ain't they?"

Then Isabella *hadn't* been recaptured.

Will took in a deep breath. He came around the corner fully into the long gallery that joined the landing—and nearly collided with three soldiers.

"'Tis him!"

He struck the speaker across the teeth with the twisted rod and sent him sprawling. His speed allowed him to dodge the grasp of the second, but the firm hand of the third upon his coat yanked him back.

"I say!" Henry called up. "Now what's the row?"

For a long instant, Will windmilled. Then he thrust all his momentum in reverse and smashed into his captor. The soldier crashed into the wall, and Will crashed into him.

His breath exploded from him, and his vision burned white. Growling against the clout of pain, he spun around. Hammering his elbow into the gasping soldier's temple—once, twice—he kicked his feet from under him.

He turned back.

The remaining soldier lunged him, bayonet at the ready.

Stumbling back against the banister, Will lost his feet and toppled down the stairs.

Above, the soldier leveled his musket.

Skidding on his back, head foremost, Will raised his pistol. Supporting his elbow in his other hand, he pulled the trigger.

It caught the soldier high in the shoulder and spun him about in a blur of blood. A fortunate shot.

Will's head cracked into the marble floor at the stair's base. For an instant, he could do naught but stare at the ornate ceiling two stories above. Then he leant his head back and saw—Henry.

He stood alone in the grand entryway, with its tall candelabrums and great bronze lions guarding the stairs. Through the open door, the fires and the clamoring of the mob presented a harsh contrast with the room's opulence. Cold wind ushered in smells of smoke and sweat and blood.

"Well, then." Henry managed not to stare open-mouthed. He even managed to point his pistol down at Will's face. "I told you, didn't I? You could have avoided all this."

"Henry." Will strove for a reasonable tone. He rolled over carefully, never looking away. "Where's Isabella?"

Henry twitched the pistol up to follow his movements. "Oh, yes, you would want to know that, wouldn't you?"

He was as impeccable as ever in a green velvet coat with

puffed sleeves. His flowered waistcoat was improbably decorated across one shoulder with a bandoleer, upon which hung three dueling pistols.

Will couldn't dodge a pistol shot, not at this range, but Henry *would* hesitate before pulling the trigger, and that might give Will time enough.

In the wavering lights, Henry's face was waxen, eyes huge. He kept glancing up the stairs to where the gunshot soldier lay moaning.

The other two were picking themselves up, cursing muzzily.

"Why are you here, Henry?" Will gained his feet and darted a surreptitious glance about the room. "I don't believe this is your idea, not for a moment. You wouldn't harm Isabella. You wouldn't harm anybody." He looked Henry in the eye. "You're better than this."

"Oh, certainly." Henry flushed. "You can take that tone. Who are you? A village lad from nowhere? And my governor—my topping ol' governor—he has one look at you and thinks *you're* worth something. Even when you're trying to kill him!"

"You needn't prove yourself to him. Believe me, *he's* the one unworthy."

Henry raised his chin. "I'm here for myself." He was almost convincing. "I'd say it's past time my affianced was brought to hand."

Will stiffened. "She won't marry you—not after this."

Henry glared. "Well, and she's not going to marry you either, is she?"

In the shadows behind the curve of the stairwell, something clattered.

Henry looked.

Will lunged, ducking low beneath the pistol and reaching to close his arms about Henry.

Beside his head, a shot flashed. But the roar of it hammered no pain through his ear and seared no heat along his cheek.

Instead, the explosion issued from the shadows to the left and hissed over the top of his head.

As he hurtled to the floor, Henry's image transformed into a rainbow of sparks.

A trap.

Of *course*, Fitzroy wouldn't send his witless son without protection.

All in one motion, Will caught himself with both hands against the floor, pushed up, and twisted.

Near the base of the stairs, the real Henry stepped from the shadows. Behind him, a narrow door opened upon another set of descending steps, these much narrower and darker—the servants' stair, no doubt.

He had drawn a new pistol from the bandoleer across his chest. Already, he aimed it at Will. His face wore a sick, surprised, determined expression.

At Will's elbow, the illusion re-coalesced. Though still facing the stairs, it mimicked Henry's every action.

Clever. Instead of covering Henry with the illusion, Fitzroy had *connected* it to him—creating a double even Henry could control.

He shook his head. "Henry—don't."

From the far side of the stairwell, movement flickered again.

"Henry!" Isabella rushed across the room, her hair a tangle of gold down her back and a scarlet coat thrown over her gown. Without a glance, she passed Will. She embraced Henry about the neck. "Henry!"

He staggered under her weight. His pistol twitched towards the ceiling. "I say—Isabella—"

She took his face between her hands, and she kissed him. Enthusiastically. And repeatedly.

Will froze.

Even the soldiers tromping down the stairs faltered.

Henry tottered back. "Well, now, that was—" He blinked. "Well, my girl, you know I'd no idea—"

She set her hands upon his chest. "For shame, Henry." With a great shove, she toppled him down the servants' stairs.

Will felt his mouth come unhinged. His face burned.

She shut the door and locked it. Then she turned and glanced from him to the two soldiers now hastening down the stairs. She glowered at him. "Well?"

His good sense caught him up. "Oh."

He rushed the soldiers just as they reached the base of the stairs. Passing between them, arms outstretched, he caught them both in the centers of their foreheads—one with the side of the iron rod and the other with the butt of the pistol.

Both toppled, and he turned back to deal them each another sound blow.

From outside, the clamor renewed. More soldiers? Or perhaps Pish's arrival. Or perhaps Henry's gunshot had summoned attention.

He crossed the room to grasp Isabella's arm. "Well, make haste!" The words sounded bad-tempered, even to his own ears. He pulled her into a run, back up the stairs.

She caught at her skirts and hopped over the fallen soldiers. "Pray, is this the thanks I receive for rescuing you?"

"And I'm the one who's here to rescue *you*, aren't I? Even though, heaven help me if I was even certain whose side you're on."

"In*deed*. And whose side have I ever been on save yours?"

They gained the top of the stairs and avoided the remaining soldier, who cowered amidst the wet splash of his blood upon the rug.

Will prodded her around the corner. "How am I supposed to tell what goes on in a nob's brain?"

She freed her elbow and snatched her silver slipper from the floor where Will had dropped it at the start of the fight. "You are insufferably patronizing! Has no one ever told you that?"

He groped for a response. "Well—why'd you have to kiss Henry?"

"I would very much like to know how kissing *you* would have got Henry down the stairs."

"Well—"

This time, she was the one to grasp his hand and pull him down the corridor. "Come along. You are here for the mirrors and such, I am certain—since you obviously counted me amongst Mr. Fitzroy's sycophants."

He scowled and dogged along after her. "I merely . . . had a doubt or two."

The look she shot him was decidedly reproachful.

She led him up and up, to a room at nearly the top of the house. Using a key from a chain about her neck, she unlocked the door. "Fetch a light."

He fetched a candelabrum from the table at the end of the corridor and stepped inside.

Light rebounded back at him, reflected in dozens of mirrors. Some were tall pier glasses for hanging between windows. Some were full-length cheval glasses on pivot stands. There were wall mirrors, hand mirrors, pocket mirrors.

*This* was wealth. What would Lifty do were he to stumble upon this hoard?

"Saints and martyrs. You collected all this on such short notice?"

Kneeling, she piled vast swathes of oakum rope into a canvas sack. "I have been purchasing all I could without attracting notice. Grandpapa and I ordered the servants to collect all the house mirrors as well. After last night, you know."

Last night. He struggled to orient himself within the span of time to which she referred. For her, not even twenty-four hours had passed since they had parted—since she had kissed *him* and not Henry.

It seemed a far lifetime ago.

"Last night." The words were ash upon his tongue.

She glanced up at him and frowned.

He didn't want to tell her. Didn't want to have to say the words. During the blind flurry of the last few hours of planning and doing, he had almost forgot.

"Tom's dead. Fitzroy took Rose."

"What?" She stood. "Oh, Will." She looked as if she would reach for him.

He shook his head. "Fitzroy is filling the streets with monsters. People are fleeing in droves. If we don't make haste, no one will remain to oppose him."

She nodded, slowly. "You intend to confront him then. Will." She came forward and gripped his sleeve. "Do not let him kill you."

Outside, men were shouting, louder than ever.

She darted to the window, looking out over the front garden. "Good Lord, there is that Mr. Pish. And a whole fleet of Runners. Doing battle with Fitzroy's soldiers!"

The news was a dash of cold energy through his veins. He grasped another sack, into which he gathered a whole armory of pistols laid out upon a table.

She turned back to her sack of oakum. "If your men can use these supplies to demonstrate the use of the mirrors and the smokers, perhaps others will comprehend the idea. God willing, there will not be a single mirror left on its wall by night's end."

He put his hand over hers. "Thank you for this. You're the only one of us who could have done it. Remain here with your grandfather for the night. I'll tell Pish to guard the place."

She freed her hand and raised one of the sacks. "Not at all. As I said, you require people to explain how this is to work. I am one of the few who know."

He took her elbow. "Please don't force me to lose someone else tonight."

She smiled gently—that radiant smile that lit her entire face. "Bless you, Will Hardy. I shall so endeavor." She leant in, and she lowered her voice. "*But*, sir, I am not yours to lose, I believe." Then she pushed past, headed for the door.

How was he supposed to interpret that? He opened his mouth once, then firmly closed it and followed her with his arms full with three overflowing sacks.

When they reached the main landing, they found Pish and his Runners battling in the entryway.

Soldiers rushed in from other parts of the house.

"Mr. Hardy!" Pish's nose gushed blood and his voice was garbled. But his eyes were alive with the fight as he emptied his knock-me-down into a soldier, then spun to the stairs. "Look lively! Behind you!"

Isabella pushed Will's shoulder. "Will!"

He turned to find the two soldiers he'd left upon the stairs, both of them now conscious. Desperately, he dropped the bags and rummaged them for a pistol. Closing his hand about one, he pulled it free.

Before he could squeeze the trigger, first one shot, then another, cracked from behind.

Lord Carstone paced down the hall, a dueling pistol smoking in one hand, another clamped under his arm. His eyes were bloodshot, probably with sherry as much as excitement. But he reloaded with the assurance of experience.

"Grandpapa!" Isabella said. "We must go!"

"You go, my dear. This is no place for you. It is time I did my bit." He glanced at Will. "As I trust you to do yours."

Will hesitated only a moment.

For now at least, Isabella would be as safe with him as she would be here in the midst of this siege. "Come along."

She nodded, resolute.

Together, they fled downstairs into the shrieking, flaming night.

# CHAPTER 44

SOHO SQUARE WAS under siege.

Will arrived from the north and turned into Soho to find that Fitzroy had barricaded his house to within a hundred feet on either side. Unlike the makeshift barricade at Seven Dials, this was a properly constructed wooden obstacle, fifty feet high and packed with soil.

For once, Will's men had done as they were told. Gamp, Lifty, and Claypole had brought their crews—and hundreds more besides. In front of the barricade, they clashed with neddies and truncheons against musket and bayonet. For a wonder, they held their ground. Scarcely. But they held it.

The big barrel smokers dotting the street were now only trickling smoke into the fire-streaked darkness. They hadn't the strength to dispel more than the nearest illusions.

Indeed, the shadow giants, with their blue-fire souls, roamed the night, stepping over entire buildings, or sometimes walking directly through. The formless blob monsters from last night had reappeared as well, oozing down the gutters, thick blood squeezing between jagged teeth.

There were far more soldiers than could possibly be real. Their red coats and the flash of muskets packed the streets.

Behind Will, the others—Isabella, Pish, and the Runners—staggered to a halt. They gasped at the illusions.

"Dear Lord in heaven preserve us," Pish said. "What are these, straight from the mouth of hell?"

"They're not real." But even knowing the monsters were

nothing but lies etched upon the air, Will felt the gooseflesh rise on his arms.

Pish clamped his jaw. "Yes, of course. Hardly factual."

Eyes wide, Isabella stepped up beside Will, her arms filled with the sack of oakum. "They are marvelous."

Will and Pish both scowled.

She blinked. "I mean, yes, certainly, they are horrifying."

Will's men were valiantly ignoring the monsters, even marching straight through them in flickers of prismatic sparks. It was the soldiers, as always, that were the true danger.

Fifty feet down the street, Lifty ducked a bayonet swipe and lunged to impale his attacker. His dagger passed through without resistance, the soldier's chest flaring temporarily into a golden haze.

From behind, another soldier coolly finished reloading his musket and withdrew the rod from the barrel. He raised the stock to his shoulder and aimed at Lifty's head.

*That* one was real enough, or Will missed his guess.

He dropped the sacks of pistols. Upon his back, he carried a wall mirror, four feet in height. He shrugged it around to hang against his chest. Pistol-cutlass in hand, he charged at full speed.

Lifty had recovered his balance, but another flash of red distracted him. He did not turn to the soldier behind him.

"Lifty!"

Now Lifty jerked about. He looked to the mirror glaring against Will's chest. Within the mirror, the soldier he had been pursuing must have disappeared. His eyes went wide. Then he saw his true danger and threw himself to the ground.

Just as the musket went off, Will plowed into the genuine soldier's shoulder. He rushed past, then spun back.

The soldier teetered and fell.

Lifty, still sprawled on his back, kicked the man's face—once, twice. His eyes were huge. "Corblimey, mate."

Will hauled him to his feet. "Come on." He set himself back to back with Lifty, and together they cleared the near end of the street.

A line of soldiers—two dozen at least—turned and rushed them.

Will set his feet firmly and gritted his teeth. Not all were real. They couldn't be.

Behind him, he could hear Pish and his Runners clattering up.

From the rear, Isabella called to him: "You must erect the mirrors as a perimeter there at the end!"

"God preserve us!" Pish gasped.

Will risked a glance away from the soldiers.

Behind him, the row of glistening mirrors revealed the fire and chaos and clash of the battle. But the monsters were nowhere to be seen, and the bloody-backed soldiers had faded to half their overwhelming numbers. Those charging Will proved naught but air.

He turned back to where the illusions charged on. His body didn't credit the mirrors. His pulse thundered in his head. Perspiration slicked his face. He forced himself to remain still.

"Blimey, blimey, blimey," Lifty muttered.

The charge reached them, met them, and passed them in a blur of displaced light.

Will looked back to Pish with a nod of confidence. "That will answer." His voice wobbled a bit more than he might have wished. "Distribute the hand mirrors."

"And the torches," Isabella called. Through a crack in the cordon of mirrors, Will could see her take a lumpy bag from a Runner and withdraw staves, wrapped all around their ends with oakum.

"Look there!" Lifty said.

Will turned back.

In the firelight, Fitzroy's house was a sickly yellow, its windows dark. Indeed, the place seemed deserted, in strange contrast to the uproar outside. Fitzroy might not even be there. He might have fled, leaving the illusions and the soldiers to convince Will otherwise.

But, no. Will followed Lifty's pointing finger, all the way up to a flicker in the corner window of the fifth floor. Will clawed off his eye-shields and squinted across the distance.

A man stood there, his waistcoat a dark blur over the flowing white of his blouse. His head was bare, his hair a flash of gold in the firelight.

Fitzroy.

His hands moved before him, dreamily, as if conducting an orchestra.

As his hands moved, monsters appeared and soldiers converged. And wheresoever the illusions went, the true soldiers followed. They fell, with sanguine shouts, upon knots of Will's own men.

Fitzroy looked down the street.

He would not be able to see Will in the shadows, but that didn't stop Will's heart from faltering. From this distance, he could scarcely see Fitzroy, much less make out his expression. Still, the man's face seemed disfigured somehow—marred with black down both cheeks to his open collar.

Blood? Was he bleeding again, as he had on the day he was infected in Affery?

Perhaps Losborne's physic hadn't rendered him infallible after all.

Will's heart started up again.

Fitzroy continued to stare—looking at the mirrors, of course.

Beside him, a smaller shadow appeared. Mrs. Fitzroy. She raised a white handkerchief to her husband's face and held a glass to his mouth. The physic no doubt.

Seize it.

She pulled at his arm, guiding him away. He followed, but not before flicking his fingers towards the mirrors.

From out of nothing, a lone soldier appeared. He charged the mirrors, bayonet extended.

It was a signal.

Almost before the illusion reached Will and the Runners, a musket shot cracked from atop the barricade. The central mirror shattered.

Will whirled to the nearest mirror, kicked its stand from under it, caught it, and lowered it to the street. "The mirrors! Protect the mirrors! Everyone, down!"

Without the reflected light, darkness dowsed the end of the street.

He threw himself to the ground beside the mirror, arms over his head.

More shots cracked. A Runner yelped. An upended mirror shattered.

"Well, that's prime, that is." Lifty said, not far from Will. "What bloody good was all this show, I'd like to know!"

"Reignite the smokers." Will peered through the darkness for Pish. "Distribute them down the street. Locate Gamp and Claypole. I must gain entrance to the house as quickly as possible."

In the darkness just ahead, Pish rustled amidst the broken glass. "Right you are."

Lifty growled. "And what you think we've been tryin' to do this whole time? Trust me when I tell you there ain't nowhere into that wretched place."

Will rolled to reach the sack of pistols. "Never mind the barricade. I can manage that."

"I ain't talking of the barricade! I'm talking of every entrance, door and window, locked and chained. He's got iron bars over the whole lot, didn't you see?"

"No, he does not." Isabella's voice sounded a few yards off. Her face was white in the darkness. "I saw but a glance in a mirror, but I think—the bars are false."

"And you want Will to risk his nob on that?"

"Be sensible," she said. "There were no bars yesterevening. Mr. Fitzroy has had no time for such improvements."

Will crouched. "'Tis the truth."

Lifty huffed. "If you get over that barricade and find you can't get through the bleedin' door—you're well and truly wedged, you know that?"

Everything in Will screamed at him to go, to *do it*. But Lifty—for once—was correct. He would have a single chance at this. He must be certain.

"We'd need a mirror to check," Pish said. "But it'd be no less than self-murder to raise one now."

Will had resolutely *not* taken Losborne's physic tonight. Why else, if not for this?

"I don't need a mirror."

He clambered to his feet and ran at the buildings on the opposite side from Fitzroy's. In the vague flicker of the fire, he could see a cornice high up. He bounced off a windowsill to gain the cornice, then hung by his fingertips, foot against the wall.

He took a deep breath, and he looked over his shoulder.

The scene below—monsters and soldiers, fire and blood—smeared into one dirty wash of light and dark. Dizziness swarmed the back of his head. He felt himself falling, and he gripped the cornice tighter. His fingertips burned against the stone, pain exploding in his knuckles.

What good was being able to see through the illusions if he couldn't *see*? He blinked hard. This was worse than ever it had been.

"Do not fall!" Isabella commanded.

Lifty snorted. "If he bloody falls off that bloody wall and breaks his bloody neck after dragging us out here after that Fitzroy cove, I will spit a gob at his bloody corpse. Crook my elbow and may it never come straight." He gave the oath respected by every man of St. Giles.

"*Do* be still," Isabella said.

Will clamped his eyes against the unsteadiness of the world. Then, with a quick breath, he looked directly at Fitzroy's house.

Giddiness overwhelmed him immediately. But not before he caught a glimpse.

He dropped back to the street. His arms shook, and *still* the street heaved beneath his feet. For an instant, he thought it an illusion: Fitzroy had transformed the street into a river. He lost his balance and slammed forward.

Isabella caught his arm and pulled him around before he smashed his face into the pavement.

"It's true." His stomach rolled over and over. He tried not to choke. "There are no bars." He looked for Lifty in the pitch and swell of his vision. "Gather whoever remains of your crew."

No one moved. No one spoke.

Then, from Lifty: "I'll be honest with you, Will my mate, you're looking sick as a horse."

Will gritted his teeth. "'Twill pass." It *was* passing—slowly.

Isabella shook his arm. "Where is the remedy—the physic? Why have you not been administering it?"

"I can't see through the illusions when I do."

"But you must! The reflections achieve that purpose—and

the smoke. You cannot face Fitzroy as you are. Where is the physic?"

He hesitated. But she was not wrong. Better to risk mistaking the illusions than to incapacitate himself. He found a packet in his coat pocket and upended it in his mouth. The bitter powder coated his throat. He had to swallow three times to force it all down.

For one precious minute, he waited, eyes closed, head as still as possible. He could feel the physic burn into his blood. Even behind his closed eyes, the world stabilized.

He looked up.

Her concerned face came into focus. "I wish it were not this way for you."

He got his feet under him and found the ground steady enough. "I need a mirror. Not a hand mirror, but a smallish one."

"What'd you see?" Lifty asked.

"Lady Isabella spoke truly. We can gain entrance."

"*We?*"

"I'll need assistance." He peered through the darkness for Pish. "You'll distribute what the men need?"

Pish nodded.

"And see her ladyship is kept safe." He looked at Isabella, striving for sternness. "If the fighting comes nearer, you're to depart, you hear me?"

She wouldn't, of course. She would be out here all the night, running betwixt musket balls, carrying water and broth to the wounded. Really, her sense of propriety was severely impaired. He must speak to her about that later.

"Be safe," she said. "We are counting upon you to halt this. *I* am certainly counting upon you to return alive." From within her scarlet coat, she withdrew a finger-thin blade—a woman's stiletto, wrought with jewels upon the hilt. "Have this."

"I've defense a-plenty, my lady."

"Have it. In the event you might require it."

He accepted, if only because he'd no more time to argue. Every minute he waited was another minute in which Fitzroy gained ground.

He looked again at Pish. "I'll manage the marksman. Re-establish the mirrors and move them forward as you're able."

Pish raised his pistol, cocked and ready, beside his head. "God speed you, Mr. Hardy."

Will couldn't have spoken apter words.

He slung torch staves into a quiver over his shoulder, tucked a small mirror into the back of his trousers, and gathered his pistols. Then he grasped a sack of oakum and took a firm grip of Lifty's sleeve.

"This is not going to work," Lifty said. "Not in a hundred lucky years." But he stumbled after Will. "You think I ain't seen me share of perilous jobs? You think I don't know when a venture's doomed?"

Will broke into a trot, then a lope, slow enough for Lifty to teeter after him.

He entered the blur of the fray, as blind to the illusions as any of the others. The chaos and the crush of it caved in upon his senses.

He halted only once, dropping the oakum long enough to steady his pistol with both hands. He cracked off a shot, clean and true, and bowled the marksman off the top of the barricade.

Immediately, the mirrors gleamed to life behind him, illuminating the entire street. In them, the monsters disappeared. Half the soldiers disappeared.

The men roared.

Even Lifty started to yell. "Huzzah! Forward, me men!"

"The barricade!" Gamp shouted. "Blow the barricade!"

A great barrel trundled down the cobblestones, wisping smoke. It thumped against the side of the barricade nearest Fitzroy's house. In a hail of earth and splintered wood, it exploded.

Will ran forward.

Shots from above hailed down around him, but he was too swift for the riflemen to track. Only the most unfortunate of balls would find him.

The midst of the barricade remained very much erect. He leapt at it and found a handhold three-quarters of the way up. Scrambling, leaping, never halting, he gained the top and dropped his sack of oakum.

A rifleman looked up from reloading his musket and charged, yelling.

Will met him halfway, caught the musket in both hands, and shoved the stock around to smash the man in the head. He hurled him from the parapet, then jumped down into the comparative darkness on the other side.

A winged skeleton of molten light rushed him.

He ducked.

Once again, they were everywhere: monsters and soldiers.

He struck at a man, and his fist passed through nothing. Another soldier threw a blow that clipped his chin with a crack real enough to rattle his teeth.

Head tucked, Will plowed through the confusion. From his quiver of supplies, he pulled one of Isabella's oakum-wrapped staves. Holding it as a spear, he ran at a gaslight, and he leapt. The oakum end smashed the glass and flared to light against the flame.

Turning back, he caught a true soldier across the face with the torch. He hurled it, end over end, at the top of the barricade.

It landed squarely atop the sack of oakum he had left there. Fire and smoke erupted in equal measures.

At the barricade's ruined end, Lifty and his crew scrambled over the rubble, screaming like Bedlamites.

Will met them at Fitzroy's oaken door.

Lifty skidded beside him. "How we getting through *that* great blinker, I'd like to know? Need a housebreaker's ram, we do."

"'Tisn't the wood we need to break."

The fine ironwork of the latch was as solid as anything he might have crafted under Tom's most scrutinizing approval. The hinges, however, told a different tale.

Behind him, Gamp's men poured in and clashed with the soldiers in the street.

Will jammed the flat end of his pistol's cutlass under the top hinge. He shoved up and out. The whole thing popped like a worn horseshoe coming off a hoof.

"Well," Lifty said, grudgingly.

From behind, a pistol shot cracked.

The man beside Lifty toppled into his arms.

Lifty squeaked and cast aside the limp body.

"Come on then!" Will said.

Together, he and Lifty and half a dozen more threw themselves at the top of the door.

It gave beneath their weight and heaved inward. The bottom hinge cracked free. The door smashed down upon the floor.

What would Tite the butler think of *that* entrance?

Will rolled away from the writhing pile of bodies and gained his feet.

The entry was empty, almost eerie.

He patted himself roundabout, readjusting his remaining weapons. The mirror that was wedged into the back of his trousers seemed yet whole enough. His heart pounded in his ears.

Rose would be here somewhere, surely. Where else would Fitzroy take her? He might have handed her over to Mr. Monarch. But he might also have eliminated Mr. Monarch.

In all truth, Will had no notion what he'd find above.

If he made it that far.

More shots rained in from behind.

"Well?" Lifty shouted at his men. "And shut the door after you, eh? Ain't you rotten lot got no manners?"

A full dozen scrambled to re-erect the fallen door and pile all the available furniture against it.

Smoke seeped past the cracks. That fire Will had started would work to their advantage for only so long before endangering everyone.

He approached the stairs.

Around the corner of the first landing, a lantern gleamed. A great hulking shadow of a man appeared, backed by four more.

More illusions?

The light penetrated the hard angles of the first shadow's slab of a face.

Bull.

He leered down at Will. "You sad little weasel. You clap me in the face all that time back?" He reached into his pocket and came out with iron knuckles. "This day's been writ ever since."

Will broadened his stance. He charted the stairs and the men upon it. There weren't many options save to go *through* them—and they were pounders, every one of them.

He stepped back. "Where's Rose?"

Bull tromped down the stairs. "With Mr. Monarch, ain't she? That Mr. Fitzroy cove, he's got no use for little blowens."

"He'd no use for Mr. Monarch either, last I knew."

Bull bared rotting teeth. "Mr. Monarch's got flash ways of making himself valuable enough, don't you know that?" He was almost to the bottom step.

Will held steady. He must dodge Bull's first blow. Nay, *all* his blows. One clout from that hammer of a fist, and the night would end.

From behind, Lifty shoved Will. "Go on, will you?" he muttered. Then he glared at Bull. "Come on, you great bleedin' ox. I always did want a go at you."

Will couldn't help but stare.

Bull stared too. "You rubbishy little rat-faced leech." Then he lurched forward.

With the admirable reflexes of a pickpocket, Lifty flung a blow into Bull's face.

When the blow connected, Lifty was the one who yelped in pain. But Bull was the one whose great flat nose cracked aloud. Blood gushed.

Lifty dashed back into the protection of his men. In his hand, his blade flashed. He glared at Will. "Well? Go!"

Will burst into his dance of speed. Around him, the world slowed. He stepped up, he dodged Bull. He spun, pirouetting between the men he left behind him. He ran up the stairs four at a time, and then he leapt straight up the stairwell. With both hands, he caught the slanting banister of the next flight. For one precious second, he hung. Then he hauled himself up and over.

Below, Lifty's men clashed with Bull's in a roar of fury and, inevitably, pain.

Will ran, gaining so much momentum he scarcely needed to touch the stairs as he leapt between flights. He clawed his way up and up, all the way to the top—to where he had so briefly seen Fitzroy silhouetted in the window.

Upon the topmost floor, he crouched in the stairwell's mouth. His breath ripped great swathes of fire through his chest.

Before him, darkness shrouded the corridor.

At the far end, a window burned an orange hole through the black. Musketfire, the clash of arms, and the howl of battle floated inside, surprisingly muffled.

For an instant, the strangeness overwhelmed him. How could any of this be? It felt all a dream. His brain tried to grasp at the facts, but only sluggishly.

On the floorboards near the window, a fainter line of light underlined the closed double doors leading to Fitzroy's study—where first he had taught Will to pick his pocket.

Fitzroy was behind those doors now—perhaps unwitting, or perhaps waiting.

At the other end of the corridor, behind Will, a footstep sounded.

Reflexively, he shot to his feet and leapt, shoving off the side of the stairwell. His right shoulder reached the ceiling. He lodged his opposite foot against the opposite wall and found a grip on a jutting board beside his head.

Wedged there, the skirt of his coat hanging about his legs, he held his breath. Perspiration traced icy lines down his temples. For what seemed an interminable second, a drop hung from the tip of his nose. It fell, and in the strange bubble of stillness, it struck the step below, audibly.

Two soldiers strode past, their coats red-black in the weird darkness.

Freeing his feet, Will swung forward. He caught the near soldier in the pit of the back with both boots.

The man gasped in pain.

Before his fellow could turn, Will landed soft as a cat. He grasped the stricken soldier's bandoleer, hauling him backwards and clouting his head against the side of the stairwell, then toppling him down the steps.

By the time the other soldier finished turning, Will had regained his feet. He clamped a hand upon the man's shoulder, yanking him nearer, and hammered his iron-knuckled fist into his head.

The soldier had only time enough to widen his eyes before they rolled up in his head.

Will stared into his lolling face. For all he knew, the man might be dead. God forgive him—and aid him, that this might not be the last man he killed tonight.

Gently, he lowered the soldier to sit in the mouth of the stairwell.

Then he trod the corridor, his footfalls a whisper.

Across from the closed doors, he halted.

Voices murmured.

"And I always am knowing you to be a great man."

Mr. Monarch.

"Look at this," he purred, "look at what you do."

"Be silent." Mrs. Fitzroy's voice was shrill. "You have no right to be here, to speak to my husband. You would drag him back to where he has come from, to all he has overcome. You want naught but to profit off him in his triumph." The direction of her voice shifted. "Why do you tolerate this creature?"

"Now he is *my* creature." Fitzroy sounded weary, but also content. Perhaps he believed he was winning. Probably, he *was*.

Will swallowed hard.

Without doubt, more soldiers would be waiting inside, and as soon as Will entered, Fitzroy would summon illusions aplenty. With Losborne's physic coursing through his veins, Will would not be able to distinguish the falsities from the true threats.

He crossed to the wall opposite the doors. A fortuitous painting hung there. Silently, he removed it and felt for the nail.

He would have but one chance to penetrate Fitzroy's defenses. He must make no mistake between an illusion and a true threat. If he failed in this, not only would Fitzroy live to complete his treachery—but Will would have no chance at all of finding and saving Rose.

And he must save her. He *must*. Rose was his. She had been so from the start. He understood that now. Just as he had been Tom's to save, Rose was his.

He reached beneath his coat and pulled the mirror from his

trousers. A crack webbed one corner, but the remainder was yet intact. He hung it upon the nail.

Then he faced the doors, drawing his pistols. He kicked open the doors, and light flooded his vision.

# CHAPTER 45

EVEN BEFORE THE double doors clashed all the way open and hammered back against the inside walls, Will spun. He turned a full circle on his heel, coat flaring. He slowed only once, with his back to the room. In the mirror across the corridor, he caught one full glimpse of Fitzroy's study.

The great mahogany desk loomed directly across from the door. Fitzroy sat upon the vivid blue of his chair's upholstery. In surprise, he drew a blood-spotted handkerchief away from his nose.

Mrs. Fitzroy and Mr. Monarch flanked the desk: she stirring dark herbs into a crystal goblet; he hunched, half-subservient, half-confidential, hands clasped.

No Rose.

He gained only the one glance into the mirror to mark the presence and positions of a dozen soldiers. Then he completed his revolution. He faced the room and raised both pistols.

Without the filter of the mirror, the room seemed suddenly a-swarm with soldiers. Scores of them—more than he could possibly hope to combat. Fear and hopelessness flooded his brain, even as he rejected the lie of it.

Before the shock of his appearance could finish registering on the faces within, he entered. Holding the mirror's vision firmly in his mind's eye, he found first one, then another of the true soldiers. He fired once and again.

The sound of their falling, the smattering of their blood—*that* was no illusion.

Mrs. Fitzroy shrieked, more in fury than fear.

Fitzroy dropped the handkerchief, and a dark bead of blood welled in one nostril.

As if he had signaled them—and surely he had—every soldier in the room spun about and charged Will. Only half responded in synchronicity. The rest struggled along, a step in their rear.

The stragglers—those would be the flesh-and-blood soldiers.

From within his coat, Will drew a second set of pistols.

Soldiers charged his right side.

In the mirror, that end of the room had been bare. He clenched his teeth and held steady, aiming again at those he *knew* to be real.

His pistol erupted in his hand. The flint sparking the powder flashed heat through his glove. His aim was true. Another soldier fell. How many was that tonight?

He raised the other pistol, aiming again.

At his right side, the illusive soldiers rushed him, inches away.

He held steady, prepared for the glitter of displaced light as they washed past him.

Instead, they struck him with the solid force of true matter. They bowled him off his feet. They hammered him against the polished floor, trapping his legs. His pistols clattered from reach.

God save him. They had not appeared in the mirror. They must have been concealed around the corner, out of sight.

He clawed at the floor, slipping once before gaining purchase. He hauled himself forward, levered one leg free, and battered it back into a soldier's face.

"Enough," Fitzroy said.

A soldier landed a hard punch to Will's back.

Black stars danced in his vision, but he dragged himself forward another few feet. He touched his pistol, closed his fingers upon it and rolled onto his back. Pistol extended in both hands, he pointed it at the nearest guard.

The man jerked back, hands extended, eyes wide with sudden fear.

"Enough," Fitzroy said again.

454 – K.M. WEILAND

Will knew what he must do. He would not waste his final ball on this frightened soldier. With all the quickness he could muster, he gained his feet and turned the pistol on Fitzroy.

But he did not pull the trigger.

Fitzroy had risen from his seat. He had left the bloodied handkerchief and the goblet of physic upon the shining desk. He had crossed to the gun cabinet against the right-hand wall.

The cabinet was an impressive piece. Gold-wrought mahogany to match the desk, it reached almost to the ceiling. The uppermost two-thirds had been designed to display and protect hunting muskets behind doors of filigreed ironwork.

On this night, however, it held no weapons.

On this night, it was a cage.

Within, hunched forward with her face against the ironwork, was Rose.

Pale hair straggled about her shoulders, and a scabbed bald circle showed where a hank had been torn free. Her face was streaked with dirt and dried tears. The corner of her mouth gleamed with blood.

"Will." She breathed his name, her tone caught somewhere between relief and fear.

His heart erupted: tremendous soaring gratitude that she lived—and burning, frightened rage that she should have been hurt yet again by these animals.

Fitzroy held a pistol to her head. "I propose a ceasefire." His eyes were as flat and cold as ever Will had seen them.

Will froze, his pistol aimed at Fitzroy's heart.

He could kill him. Kill him in this room.

But Fitzroy's pistol was too near to Rose's head. Before he could even fall, his death convulsion would blast her brains against the wall.

Will could end the battle, end Fitzroy. That's what he had come for. But he had come also to save Rose. And God help him, he could not sacrifice her for the greater cause. Not now.

"Release her." His voice came out deep, strangled. "Release her, and I will surrender."

Hope flashed in Rose's eyes. Then, immediately, her face darkened. "No." She rattled the ironwork. "He's going to kill you! It's the whole point. He's going to kill you!" Her voice rose, almost hysterical.

Fitzroy inclined his head, graciously awaiting Will's decision. The line of his jaw was hard.

In the corners of Will's vision, soldiers were moving forward. Two carried manacles, for his hands and for his feet. They crowded around him—illusions most of them, pressing upon his senses.

Mrs. Fitzroy and Mr. Monarch looked on, unmoving.

Using the brass key on his watch fob, Fitzroy unlocked the cabinet door. He reached for Rose's arm.

With a scream, she reared back. She smashed her head forward into his face. The crack resounded across the room. The illusions flickered. They snapped into white light and disappeared.

In the street, the fighting went silent for a long moment. Then the men outside loosed a great roar of triumph.

Fitzroy staggered back against Mr. Monarch, knocking him to the floor. Half off his own feet, he fell against the desk. Blood streamed from the fresh cut between his eyes.

He had dragged Rose with him. She landed against his chest, still screaming but now with tears clogging her voice.

The true soldiers hurled themselves at Will, knocking aside his pistol, grappling him.

Mrs. Fitzroy rounded the front corner of the desk, past Will, to reach for her husband.

Almost as one, Fitzroy and Rose scrambled to right themselves. Jerking Rose away from him, Fitzroy held her by one arm, hoisted onto her toes.

Screaming louder yet, she beat at him with the other arm, scratching and kicking. Her eyes were dazed, her scalp broken where she had struck him.

Tears coursed down her blotched face. "Bloody devil! Bloody bleeding devil!" She sobbed the words, over and over.

Fitzroy came to his feet, unsteadily.

Will bucked the soldiers. "Release her!"

The soldiers swarmed him, three gripping his arm as they struggled to bring his other hand around and cuff it.

"I agree to your terms!"

Fitzroy didn't look at him. He backhanded Rose across the face, hard enough to wrench her from his grip.

She staggered.

"That's enough!" Will shouted.

Fitzroy caught her again and thrust her back at Mr. Monarch, who was regaining his feet. "She was yours to begin with. See to her."

Mr. Monarch encircled her shoulders with both hands, trapping her against him.

A roar began in Will's stomach. Its heat surged up through his chest. It filled his mouth, and it burst free.

He lunged against the soldiers, yanking free. With a proficiency even Fitzroy would admire, he picked his own pocket and came out with Isabella's stiletto.

He didn't reach for Fitzroy or for Mr. Monarch. He couldn't have touched them before the soldiers closed upon him.

Instead, he caught Mrs. Fitzroy's arm and dragged her to him. He clamped his arm about her waist, her back to his chest. He fixed the point of the stiletto beneath her third rib on the left. The tip pierced the plum silk of her gown, pierced her shift and her stays and whatever else she wore beneath. It touched flesh, and she gasped.

Will looked at Fitzroy. "Free her."

Mr. Monarch pulled Rose nearer. She was blinking hard, straining breaths past her teeth as she tried to regain her wits.

Will looked about at the soldiers. "Back away!"

Watchful of the stiletto, they scrambled aside.

He eased backwards, towards the tall French window. "Free Rose, or I will kill your wife."

Silence weighted the room.

Then Mrs. Fitzroy laughed.

"Do it." She tilted her head against Will's jaw, speaking up at him. The position was strangely intimate. "Do it, arrogant, ignorant boy. Pierce my heart and have done!"

Will froze.

Indeed, no one in the room moved.

She laughed again, shorter and deeper this time. "Can you possibly believe my husband would sacrifice his cause?" A fierce pride edged the bitter words. "He would not. He knows what is important in his life. He has known always."

Fitzroy drew his brows over haggard, handsome features.

It was the first time Will had known him to *look* at her.

Fitzroy shook his head slightly. "Esther . . ."

Beneath Will's arm, her ribcage shuddered. Was it hope? That she was wrong? That her husband would topple all his plans for her?

Will drew his own breath of hope. Let it be so. Let Fitzroy choose—just as Will had chosen Rose when first he stepped into this room. Let it be the choice that would save them all.

Fitzroy straightened his waistcoat. He looked away from his wife, to the window—and his face closed up. His eyes lost focus, the cords in his neck tightened.

Outside, the clamor in the street changed its tenor once more—rising shrieks, shouted warnings. The monsters had returned.

Mrs. Fitzroy breathed out, softly.

In this house, there was no hope. She would know that better than any.

Fitzroy looked at them. His eyes were shot through with broken veins. A crust of blood underlined one eye. He reached slowly for the goblet of physic on the desk.

"Stay," Will ordered. But he held no power here, and they all knew it.

Fitzroy drained the physic to its dregs. His gaze never left Will. It was the expression of a victor about to finish his battle.

Will dragged Mrs. Fitzroy back another step, until the window glass—warm from the fire outside—pressed against his shoulders. He had nowhere else to go.

Mr. Monarch grinned openly.

Will's whole body burned. "Why?" The question was for every single one of them, but he tilted it into Mrs. Fitzroy's ear. "Why do you follow him? What has he ever done to earn your faith? He would allow me to kill you even now. Why?"

Her breath came in great gasps, edging into sobs. She had no wish to die. She wanted to live, surely—to live with a husband who loved her and protected her.

Calmly, Fitzroy blotted the blood from his forehead, his

458 – K.M. WEILAND

nose, his eyes. He bent to retrieve his fallen pistol.

"*Why?*" Will shouted.

Mr. Monarch tsked. "Now, my children, now." The pale blue of his eyes was alight. Gently, he slumped a dazed Rose into a pile against the wall. He walked out from behind the desk, approaching the window. He rested his hands one upon the other, the bandaged one on top. "We must have *calme*." His eyes glittered. "We must not let our rampant *émotion* to get the better of us, yes? Perhaps we may yet all *survivre* to have profit from this night."

Mrs. Fitzroy lurched against Will's arm, nearly pulling free. The stiletto sliced a line through her gown.

"You!" She hurled the word at Mr. Monarch as if it were the vilest of curses. "You have no place in this house!"

Mr. Monarch bowed his head. "I am but a most humble servant to your esteemed husband."

"You believe you can have my place beside my husband? You believe I will die here tonight?" She strained forward, towards Fitzroy. "Perhaps I will."

Will strove to prevent her from ramming against the stiletto.

"But I give you my oath." Her words growled up from her throat. "I will do *anything* to keep you from him!"

Mr. Monarch's face hardened. "My lady." He spread his hands. "I am nothing beside your husband. I stand in awe of him, you know this? I would do nothing but to help him."

She scoffed. "*You* would help him. *You.*" She shifted in Will's grasp, to face Fitzroy once again, even as she continued to speak to Mr. Monarch. "What part of my husband's life has not been the product of his attempts to escape you?"

She was trembling so violently Will fought to hold her.

"I see it now," she said. "I understand. Was there not always a ghost between us? Something dark and malevolent? Something he was forever running away from? Something he must prove he could overcome?"

Fitzroy did not open his mouth or raise his hand to halt her words. His face might have been carved from stone.

Realization struck Will. He pressed his jaw against her temple, enough to see down into her face. "You love him. He doesn't deserve it, he does not even return your affection, but . . . you love him."

A great hiccuping sob caught in her chest. She flung her head back against his shoulder, as if she would collapse. "I," she breathed out, "am so lonely."

Fitzroy frowned, confused almost. "I . . . know this."

She nodded. Her jet earring vibrated against Will's chin. "That is well. I wanted you to know. It is enough."

She thrust herself into the blade. The point resisted for not even half a second. It punctured flesh. Hot blood welled against Will's fingers.

She twisted in his grip. The torque upon the blade turned it backwards, towards him. It scraped her rib, but did not penetrate deep enough to find her heart.

She clamped both hands over his upon the hilt. With a great, primal scream, she levered her weight against the blade. It tore free of her side and it smashed back into Will.

Only his reflexes saved him from death. The blade tore through his coat and his shirt. It nicked between ribs, and fire exploded in his side.

He staggered back, gasping. For a precious second, his mind spun useless revolutions, trying to find any sort of purchase.

She slumped against the window, holding the red-slicked silk beneath her arm and panting, wild-eyed, victorious.

Behind the desk, Rose was struggling to regain her feet. She lurched forward. "Will!"

He could turn his head only slowly.

Too slowly.

Mr. Monarch's bulk rammed into him and propelled him forward.

Will collided with Mrs. Fitzroy, and she with the window. Glass exploded around them. Her wail rose in his ears. Together, they toppled over the sill and plummeted into naught.

# CHAPTER 46

WILL FELL. HEATED, smoke-laden wind engulfed his body. Beneath him, Mrs. Fitzroy smashed to a halt, and he smashed into her. Her scream cut short.

The world swirled around him. He choked. No air would enter his throbbing chest. Blackness filled his vision. The moment stretched to infinity. He could find no thoughts within his brain, no memories.

Was this, then, death?

The moment ended. His chest gave one great heave, like a bellows, and pulled in air foul with smoke. He choked, coughed. His sight returned in a blare of colors and lights. Pain hammered him.

Still gasping, he wrenched himself up. His head struck an iron railing. Far below, the ground eddied. He tried to scramble back from the drop, but he tripped upon Mrs. Fitzroy's gown.

Then the world came 'round full circle, and everything jolted back into sense.

They had fallen only a single floor. The narrow balcony on the fourth story had broken their descent.

God save him. He fought to regulate his breathing.

He glanced up. The broken window was above and to the left. His fall hadn't been straight down.

A shriek, more rage than fear, wafted down.

Rose.

He must see to her safety before he did aught else. He turned, gingerly, to Mrs. Fitzroy.

She lay broken like a castoff doll. Blood yet trickled from the wound in her side, but her bird-like eyes were bright no longer.

His hand shaking, he closed them.

The irony was that she had probably saved him in the end.

"Be at peace," he whispered.

An explosion racked the battlefield below. Soldiers were beginning to flee. The men of the street gave chase, shouting.

Smoke gusted everywhere, flickering through what few illusions remained. Fitzroy probably had little idea the illusions were fading out in the haze. The fire was creeping roundabout his house, gaining ground every moment.

But if time were running out for Fitzroy, it was also running out for Will.

Should Fitzroy escape this night, he would marshal his strength and return—more formidable than ever.

Will eased to his feet. His every bone shot pain through him. At least naught seemed broken. He touched the wet heat in his side. The wound stretched in a line of agony, but was not deep.

He leant back against the railing, looking up.

The upper floor had no balconies to which he could leap. There were only shuttered windows. But the lip of a cornice jutted six feet above his head. He could manage that. God willing, he could still manage it.

Mr. Monarch's voice drifted down. "He has taken her ladyship with him. The loss—it is so great, my boy. But you have now *victoire* too. This Wayfarer—this thorn in your paw—he is gone from you. He cannot stay your hand."

Will jumped. He grasped the cornice with both hands. His arms caught his full weight, and immediately, the gash in his side stretched and ripped.

In his throat, a cry gathered, and he clenched his teeth against it. Kicking hard, he hauled himself up. With all his speed, and before he could lose his balance, he clutched the edge of a shutter and got his feet under him upon the cornice.

"You—" Fitzroy rasped. "You killed her."

With his gloved fist, Will smashed the nearest pane and wriggled through the window into the drawing room, only a few rooms from Fitzroy's study. Smoke trickled beneath the doors.

He tried the entry to the corridor, but the latch stuck fast. Without breaking stride, he swiveled, locating the door to the adjoining room.

In a bound, he reached it and opened it.

The darkness and the smell of leather-bound books engulfed him. This would be the library, the room adjacent to the study.

"You have killed my wife."

Fitzroy's voice was muffled. But even Will could hear the rising damnation.

"No, my child. I would not do this thing. She has killed herself—with the help of this boy."

"You think I would bring you here to harm her? To speak such words to me?" Fitzroy's voice rose. "Do you remember? When I was a boy in your filthy rat hole? You told me to be useful. You would see to my safety as long as I was useful."

"As I will be useful to you now." Mr. Monarch seemed to speak confidently even yet, but his voice, too, rose a notch.

Footsteps scrabbled, and then Rose yelped.

"The chit, she will be of annoyance to you no longer. I will see, for you, that she is dealt with appropriately."

Will reached the adjoining door, tried the latch—locked. He whirled to the corridor door. Locked as well.

He turned back to the smutty orange of the window. Crossing the room through the backlit shadows of chairs and tables, he thrust the sash up so hard the topmost panes cracked. He looked outside.

To his right, only four feet away, shards glinted at the edges of the broken window through which he had fallen.

"No," Mr. Monarch spoke again. He was obviously striving to maintain calm. "You do not need to do this. I am your friend. I am useful to you."

Within the room, shadows flickered.

Fitzroy's voice rose, a guttural growl that became a roar.

Illusions. He was summoning his monsters.

"If you please, there is no *nécessité*." Mr. Monarch began to sound unsteady. "There is no need for this *horreur*. They are not real, they are illusions, I know this." But his voice kept rising.

"Arrest him," Fitzroy ground out the words.

His flesh-and-blood soldiers tromped.

Mr. Monarch squealed, footsteps darting away.

"Pursue him!"

Will crouched on the library's sill. Ducking his head clear of the lintel, he swung around the corner. Momentum carried him into the spin. He reached the end of it, released the sill, and kicked off hard.

With thrust to spare, he caught the far windowsill one-handed and slapped his other hand up to join it. Again, his side screamed wrath upon him.

"And you." Fitzroy's shredded voice was hardly recognizable. He sounded wrung out, manic, beaten even.

Had he loved his wife as much as that after all?

More shadows flickered through the window above Will's head—so many, they all but blacked the light.

"You wretched creature," Fitzroy said. "I will save you from your misery, and in the echoes of eternity, you will thank me for it."

"I ain't afraid of what's not real," Rose said.

The hammer of a pistol clicked. "Then I will show you what is real."

Will inhaled the smoky midnight air. For a wonder, the befouled breath brought fortitude. It filled his blood, his muscles, his bones. The pain in his side faded.

All his remaining strength, all his speed—he channeled into his arms and his legs as he hauled himself over the sill.

The room was black with writhing shadows, staring eyes, reaching fingers.

In the midst of it, Rose stood, her back straight, head up.

The world slowed. It submerged him in impossible silence.

He reached for her. Droplets of blood fluttered from his hand and burned through the nearest illusion in a glitter of golden motes.

Fitzroy stood at the desk's end. Pickpocket reflexes twitched his aim from Rose to Will. The pistol's hammer crashed down. The flint sparked in a flash and a trail of smoke.

Will dodged on instinct. And this time, something was different. He could almost see the ball rolling down the pistol barrel, could almost feel the displacement of air as it burst free. He ducked, spinning.

With a great whump at his ear and a blast of heat against his cheek, the ball passed him by. It struck the wall. Splinters scattered against his shoulders.

His speed carried him onward. He caught Rose by the waist and propelled her before him.

They smashed past Fitzroy, past the open door. Will thrust out a hand to the newel post of the stairs and slung them around it. Half-running, half-falling, he carried her down one flight of stairs, then jumped the railing and plunged to the next landing.

At last, he slammed back into his place within the world. His breath roared in his ears, but the beat of his heart was certain, steady. It pumped power throughout his body, vanquishing pain to the rearmost part of his consciousness.

The house below was in an uproar. Soldiers were running, people shouting. Tite the butler bellowed orders to evacuate the servants.

Will unwrapped Rose from his arms. "Are you injured?" His voice cracked around the smoke.

She looked up at him, wide-eyed. In the shadows, her face and hair glowed. For once in her life, she failed to respond.

"Are you well?" he asked again.

She nodded, slowly. "Are you then?"

"You know I have to leave you. I must go after Fitzroy."

"Sure." She pushed back from him. "You think I can't get out of here?"

"Last I knew, Lifty was at the entrance, milling with Bull. If you can find him, tell him to leave too, before the entire house is aflame."

From past the blood and the bruises on her face, she looked at him solemnly. "I knew you'd do it." Then she turned away.

God help him, but he hadn't done it. Not yet.

The most uncertain part lay ahead. He had saved her this time, but he had no assurance he would be here on the morrow to fulfill the rest of his promises.

Before she rounded the corner of the stairs, he caught her arm. "Rose." He fumbled in his coat pockets, wasting precious time until he found what he wanted.

She shook her head, fidgeting, wanting to be gone, as well she should.

He withdrew the lopsided mask she'd loaned him in Blackfriars. "Here." He tied it around her head. "You have always been my partner, you know that?"

She stood motionless, not even smiling. Too little, too late between them perhaps. Or perhaps she was yet too woozy to care about such things.

Below, another explosion shook the street. The smokers going off, no doubt.

He hesitated, not knowing what else to say, and having no time in which to say it. "When this has ended, you're to find Lady Isabella. She'll see you cared for."

He started to rise.

"Will." She flung herself at him. Her skinny arms came around his neck and closed fast. She burrowed her face into the corner of his collar. "You're the only good thing that ever happened in my whole life."

He wrapped his arms about her and held her tight against him, never mind the pain in his side. If God allowed he should live past this, he would take her with him—wherever he went—whatever happened or did not happen with Isabella. He would care for her, as the little sister who had appeared in his life to replace those he'd lost.

"I'm sorry," he said. "I'm sorry I let this happen to you. Sorry for what you heard me tell Tom."

She pressed deeper into his collar. "Please don't die," she whispered. Then she pushed away. In her eyes, unshed tears shimmered.

He had no words. He could give her only a firm nod.

She backed up, licking her lips, refusing to let the tears fall.

Would that he could remain with her. He straightened and took a step back, dragging his feet. He had freed her from Fitzroy and Mr. Monarch, only to leave her in the frenzied hell of this waning battle.

She raised her chin. "Go on then, eh? I'll be the one finding you when 'tis over." Flashing a weak grin, she turned 'round the newel post and clattered downstairs.

She was giving him permission to leave her.

He did not allow himself to think on it. He turned away, and he leapt between flights, back to face what had always been his to face.

# CHAPTER 47

B ACK ON THE fifth floor, Will slowed only for a single glance into the mirror that yet hung across from the open door to Fitzroy's study.

Framed within the cracked glass, Fitzroy stood at the gun cabinet, reloading his pistol. A tall, curtained window backed his shoulders.

Will entered and lunged at him.

Fitzroy had scarcely time to raise his head.

Will closed his arms about him. They crashed through the curtains, through the window, through the unlatched shutters.

Fitzroy House was the tallest on the street, but it was tightly packed against its neighbors. This fifth-floor window opened directly onto the adjacent roof.

They skidded across the flat stretch of lead roofing.

Will rolled into a crouch, balanced on one hand.

Fitzroy smashed to a stop against a great brick chimney. He shook his head, as if trying to clear it, and scrabbled for his pistol—ramrod still in its barrel.

Will rushed him and kicked aside the pistol. Up here, the advantage was all his. Up here, Fitzroy was trapped.

Catching Fitzroy beneath the arms, Will hauled him forward. He hurled him over the gap between this roof and the next, then leapt after him. He couldn't risk Fitzroy climbing back through the smashed window into the study.

Fitzroy rolled to a stop. Blood streaked his chin. He blinked, dizzily. Then his eyes darkened. He looked across at Will, as one slavering dog might watch another in the pit fights.

"Well," he said, "and who might have foreseen you and I should come to this?"

"Don't." Within Will rose a weary rage. "Don't speak. Your words have brought to me naught but destruction."

Wiping blood from his chin, Fitzroy pushed to his knees. "Pray, do not disappoint me with naïveté." He spread his arms to London's glittering skyline. "Who gave you all this, if not I?"

The rage centered, a burning coal, in Will's stomach. He flung himself at Fitzroy. He pounded a fist into the man's jaw. Clenching Fitzroy's hair, he thrust his head back, forcing him to look up at him. "And Tom?" The words burned his throat.

Fitzroy glared at him, passive.

Pain closed in upon Will, heating his blood. He could kill Fitzroy, snap his neck and hurl him to the street far below.

Then it would be over. He would have won.

And Tom would yet be dead.

That would not change tonight, even if Fitzroy died. Will was going to have to carry on, to hold that burden within him and bear it for every day to come.

He didn't want to merely kill Fitzroy. He wanted to tear him apart, to sustain his life for as long as possible, to make him suffer as Will suffered.

But that wasn't what he had asked of his men earlier tonight.

He thrust Fitzroy away. Retreating to where the pistol had landed, he took it up.

"You will kill me now?" Fitzroy asked, still passive.

"Yes." But he would do it with dignity.

For the first time, Fitzroy's eyelid tremored. "Tell me—what of Esther?"

"She's dead." He pulled the ramrod from the pistol barrel and cast it aside. "And for what?"

In Fitzroy's face, the shadows deepened. He closed his eyes. His jaw churned.

"You remember what you told me when first we met?" With his free hand, Will withdrew from his pocket the golden sovereign. He flung it between them.

It clinked, spinning, against the roof.

"You told me *that* was how a man bought respect in this

world. Are you pleased with what you've bought?"

On that sun-streaked day back in the village, he had revered Fitzroy. He had believed him. If he had not, would this all have occurred?

"Look at us," he said. "We've both of us sacrificed all that mattered in pursuit of a lie. Why? *Why?*"

"A lie." Fitzroy opened bloodshot eyes. The broken veins were uncanny in the flickering light. He laughed without humor. "And what did you desire instead? The truth?" He sat back on his heels. "A man can spend all his life in pursuit of the truth, and he will never find it. It is something too great—too pure—for any of us to understand." He clenched his fists upon his knees. "Every *truth* you think you believe? It is a lie in some part, if only because your mind cannot grasp the whole of it."

The time had come. Will had talked too long already. He tightened his finger against the trigger.

But first he asked what honor demanded: "Will you surrender to me? I'll offer but once. Will you do it for the memory of your wife, and for your son? For the only *true* things you ever possessed in your life?"

Fitzroy exhaled hard, furiously—blowing drops of spittle. "My *wife*, my son." In the corners of his eyes, blood began to well.

"No," he said.

The illusions came, as Will knew they would.

He pulled the trigger.

But these were not the shadow monsters from the streets, nor the soldiers, nor the doubles. They did not advance upon him with the steady movements that mimicked reality.

These hurtled at his head. From every direction, they swarmed him. Every hideous thing the world had ever known: snakes, spiders, bats, rats, soaring through the air.

A rat leapt into his face, its eyes coal-red, its bared teeth dripping black blood.

In his hand, the pistol exploded.

Fitzroy cried out and grasped at his shoulder.

Too high. Will's only shot had missed Fitzroy's heart.

Instinctively, he swiped at the rat, even knowing it was naught but air. He lurched into a run, straight at Fitzroy. He was slower than he should have been, his aching joints grating.

In every direction, the world warped. Buildings at either side shot up impossibly. They towered over him. They closed in all around, boxing him in, tighter and tighter. They blacked the fires.

The suffocation of confinement caved in upon him.

He ran on. He would out-pace the illusions—run *through* them.

But the buildings moved with him. Overhead, they crashed together. Their peaked ceiling sank lower and lower, until it almost touched his head.

He could not run forever. Soon he must reach the end of the roof and plunge over the edge. He ground to a halt.

The buildings dropped into a void. Before him, a precipice loomed.

For an instant, he leant into it.

The dizziness. If the height could trigger his dizziness, he might see through all the illusions.

But, no. His gaze held steady. Mr. Losborne's physic burned within his veins. At this moment, he required a mirror or smoke, same as any other man. How long until the smoke from the street rose high enough?

He turned. "Fitzroy!"

Let the man reveal himself. Will required only a sound—Fitzroy's voice or the scrape of his shoe. Then he could pass through the illusions in pursuit of the sound.

"Will."

The voice was not Fitzroy's.

It was Rose's.

The roof became a dark expanse, cut off from houses and streets.

At the far side of that expanse, Rose dragged herself towards him, on her arms alone.

She wept. "Save me. Why didn't you save me?"

He breathed out hard and took one step.

Before him, the precipice opened once more.

He pulled back. "No." He shook his head, hard. It wasn't

Rose. Couldn't be her. But when had Fitzroy learned to cast sound as well as sight?

"Will."

That was Isabella.

He turned again.

She stood in naught but her shift, golden hair shorn ragged. Blood streaked her arms and legs. Outstretched hands trembled.

Others appeared.

Lifty. Pish. Postelwaite. A multitude. All of them bleeding, suffering, dying. All of them screaming his name.

*Will Will Will Will Will Will Will*

Movement flickered at his shoulder, and he flinched.

Out of the darkness, his own figure emerged, dressed in rags, eyes blank. He stumbled towards the others. He looked like his father had on the day he was dispatched to the workhouse. He looked like Will's nightmares.

It was a lie. He *knew* they were all lies.

But there was truth here too: the truth of his own fears.

His heart pounded as if he were running at his top speed. Sweat burned his face. He could not gain a clear breath.

"No." He shook his head again. He forced himself to listen to his words. "'Tisn't true."

"Is it not?"

At last, Fitzroy flickered into view: dozens of him. His multiple selves swarmed Will. His face had blanched to white, and his blue eyes glowed in the darkness.

"*IS IT NOT?!*"

He encircled Will.

"I will tell you what is true, Will Hardy. You are *nothing*." From all directions, he closed in, leering. "You were born nothing, and you will die nothing."

One of the illusions would be Fitzroy, *must* be Fitzroy. Will lunged at the nearest. His fist punched naught but a scorched hole in the darkness.

"You want truth?" Fitzroy said. "You desire respect?"

Will flung himself about, striking wildly, hitting at every one of them.

They bore down upon him, stifling him, laughing at him.

"This is truth," Fitzroy said. "*This* is respect. Respect is fear."

"No." Will might have accepted that once. "I don't believe that anymo—"

A blow caught him behind the ear. He staggered. His vision warped. For but a moment, dizziness overwhelmed the effects of the physic.

In that moment, the illusions all blinked into nothing.

He managed to drag a breath into his lungs. He straightened, and he turned.

But it was not Fitzroy he faced.

From out of the darkness walked Tom. He looked Will up and down, and he clamped his jaw.

"Ah, Will lad, you disappoint me."

# CHAPTER 48

THE ROOF BENEATH Will's feet seemed to tilt. He staggered. The back of his head felt hollow. White sparks danced in his vision, the result of Fitzroy's blow to his head.

Before him, Tom stood straight and whole.

But it wasn't Tom. It couldn't be.

It was an illusion like all the rest.

Tom shook his head. "Did I raise you up to such a night as this, Will?"

"You're dead." The words dropped like hammers to an anvil.

"Yes. I'm dead." Tom drew his brows. "Why am I dead?"

*Because I wasn't fast enough. Because I didn't listen.*

"Because of Fitzroy." He bade himself breathe. He could not afford this argument. "You're not real."

Tom advanced, hands extended. "I'm dead because of you. You made the wrong choices."

Will straightened. "I know I did."

Tom's voice—and angels help him, it *was* Tom's voice— sounded as if it were coming from Tom's own mouth. Did that mean Fitzroy was disguised behind the illusion? Did he hope Tom's face would protect him?

Will stepped forward. "You died because you made a choice to save me. You died because Fitzroy and Mr. Monarch murdered you. And that I cannot let pass."

Tom shook his head. "What would you do? Avenge my death. You think I desire that?"

Will could not seem to make himself move with speed. He

*knew* the illusion was Fitzroy's. Yet he continued on, talking to Tom. "You desired me to protect others from what Fitzroy will do to them—is doing."

Tom dropped his entreating hands. "Will, lad. Don't you understand? 'Tis too late for that." He snorted, softly. "No one will see what happens on this rooftop tonight. No one will honor you, no one will thank you—not even if you die for them."

Will raised his chin and looked Tom in the eye. "I have no care if the people acclaim me."

These were the words Tom had been wanting to hear all this time. Tom—if he were the real Tom—would look Will back in the eye and grin that slow grin.

He *did* look at Will. Slowly, he did smile. The smile lit up his face and crinkled the corners of his eyes.

Within his chest, Will's heart halted.

*Tom . . .*

Out of the darkness, a blow pounded Will's wounded side. The world turned to white fire. He gasped and skidded to his knees, retching.

Then Fitzroy had *not* been inside the illusion of Tom? He had cloaked himself in the darkness.

Will strained to gain his feet. Black spots swarmed his vision, and he blinked, over and over, trying to clear them.

He was too slow.

Another blow clouted him, a fist behind his ear.

Again, he stumbled.

Tom approached. "Ah, Will. Lie down, lad. You've fought longer and harder than you need to."

He didn't lie down. He struggled back upright. Fitzroy's invisible fist cracked into his mouth. He kept his feet this time, but the inside of his lip sliced against his teeth. He tasted a wash of blood and gagged.

Before him, Tom halted. "Don't you see? You can never redeem yourself to me. 'Tis far too late." A black spot bloomed against his homespun shirt. It grew and grew. It turned from black to shattering scarlet.

Tom looked down at his chest. When he looked back up, his eyes were wide, pupils dilated. "You see." He choked and coughed flecks of blood. "You see, Will. It is too late." He rasped. "No one will ever know what you do tonight. You will die or you will run—and 'twill all be for naught."

This time, Will felt, more than heard, the whisper of movement behind. He summoned what speed was left to him, and he dodged.

The spin carried him forward. Only a hand's span separated him from Tom.

"Too late," Tom slurred past the blood in his mouth.

*No.* Will couldn't marshal his thoughts in a straight line any more than he could his body. His head filled with that one word: *No.*

*Don't make me watch him die again. Don't make me hear these words—and the godforsaken truth of them.*

It *was* too late. There was no lie to that. Tom would never witness the choices Will made here tonight, for good or ill. He would not see if Will were to live or to die.

Rose would not see. Isabella would not see. Will could give up everything to do the right thing—and who would know? Was that truly worth anything?

And then, through the fog in his brain, a new word:

*Yes.*

Yes, it was worth it. Yes, it mattered not if Tom did not see, if no one saw. It mattered not if the world were to decide, after the wreckage of this night, that he was indeed an outlaw.

Was he so great he believed himself more than a cog in the clockwork? Was he more than any other man facing down the only choice with which man is ever faced: do right or do not?

It was as if a white light flared all through him. As the final piece fit solidly into place within him, he almost gasped with the correctness of it.

Then Fitzroy hit him again.

He had acquired a weapon—the empty pistol perhaps. He slammed the cold, hard length of it into Will's ribs.

Will heard them crack.

He staggered forward, through the flickering illusion of Tom. He could not protect himself from the second blow, to his back. He toppled and only scarcely got his hands up to keep from smashing his face against the roof.

Unthinkable pain overwhelmed him. The world felt as if it were tipping sideways. Even with his eyes closed, dizziness churned.

From behind, Fitzroy panted. "Did you know, that first day I saw myself in you."

Will spat blood. He eased over onto one elbow.

Even now, Tom was the only one standing over him.

But Tom flickered, blurring to gold at the edges.

Will shook his head, hard. The pain and the giddiness swirled his vision. This time, when he looked at Tom, he saw not one man, but two.

At last, Fitzroy stood within the illusion.

"I desired a legacy," Fitzroy said. "I thought perhaps you might have become it. But, no."

It wasn't the pistol he held after all: it was a lead-lined gutter, jagged at the end.

"I see now what I failed to see then." Fitzroy sounded utterly weary. "You are no better than any of them. No better than Mr. Monarch. No better than that little street urchin you saved to grow up to a life of prostitution and yet another generation of abandoned bastard children." He knelt, still flickering, before Will. "You will never be worthy of respect."

Back in Affery, Will would have dueled Richard Grainger over the bare insinuation he would not be found equal to men of wealth, fame, and breeding.

Now, strangely, he found—*it did not matter.*

The respect of such men was hardly the point. It had never been the point, had it? That's what Tom tried to tell him all along.

What the world knew of his actions could not change the truth of the actions themselves.

Fitzroy crouched beside Will. He believed himself yet invisible. His face was haggard. Blood streamed from his eyes, his nose, his ears. He was about to win, and yet he looked more broken even than Will.

He extended the jagged point of the gutter to Will's throat. "Tell me," he rasped. "When you die here tonight, who will care? Who will even know?"

The energy of purpose filled Will. It pushed aside the pain, pushed aside even the dizziness.

He raised his head, and he looked Fitzroy in the eye. "Only me." Then he surged forward.

Fitzroy had an instant to register shock that Will could see him.

Then Will hurled himself at Fitzroy's chest, heedless of his own broken ribs and the wound in his side. He caught Fitzroy beneath the arms, and in a last burst of energy, all his speed fired within him. He shoved off with his legs, and he ran, bowling Fitzroy along before him.

At every side, the illusions faltered. The orange of the street fires slashed through the false darkness. To the right and ahead, the eaves flashed.

He gathered himself, and Fitzroy with him, and he leapt.

Below, flames devoured the adjacent roof. More illusions swarmed. They surged up towards Will. They bared cavernous black mouths, eyes a glare of blood.

Will opened his arms and thrust Fitzroy away from him.

For a second, their eyes met. Panic flayed Fitzroy's face. He scrabbled for a hold in Will's clothing.

Even still, he fell.

Will's interrupted momentum scarcely carried him far enough. He smashed into the edge of a chimney. It caught him in the stomach and slammed all the air from his body. Pain roared. Blackness closed upon him.

An instinct for survival kept him scrabbling for a hold against the hot brick. Another sort of instinct drew his gaze around, over his shoulder.

Fitzroy landed on his back upon the flaming roof. He stared up at Will, blankly. His illusions converged all about him.

The roof gave way. Fitzroy fell. Still, he stared at Will, his mouth a round hole. The illusions fell with him and exploded in a burst of white light.

Will nearly lost his grip. When he dragged open his eyelids once more, the last of the false darkness had disappeared. The only sound was the roaring fire below.

He craned his head to catch a glimpse of the street.

Past the smoke, men stood frozen and confused—shocked

perhaps. As quickly as that, the illusions had vanished.

Running steps began striking against the stones. The red of soldiers flashed through the smoke.

With a great shout of conquest, Will's men gave pursuit.

Will clamped his eyes against the dizziness and faced forward. It was over then.

Over.

Of a sudden, he was more done up than ever he had been in his life. Too done up to go on breathing.

But he must. He must find Rose, find Isabella.

Groaning with the pain of it, he climbed up and over the wobbling chimney and gained the next roof. He stayed there, doubled over, rasping, for too long. Beneath him, the roof trembled—whether with his own unsteadiness or the compromised integrity of the building.

He moved one foot before the other. He made it back to Fitzroy's study. The broken glass inside the windowsill sliced his coat sleeve. It mattered not. After this night, perhaps he would never again wear it.

He found one of his cutlass-pistols on the floor and took it with him, empty though it was.

Smoke clogged the house. He coughed, and his cracked ribs stabbed into him. The fire here was not over-hot. Someone had worked to put it out, or perhaps the soldiers had protected this house, not realizing their master had departed.

Now it was empty. Every sound echoed back up at him.

He clomped down the stairs instead of leaping down the flights. He held one hand against his bleeding side and leant his shoulder against the wall all the way down.

Had Rose got out in time? Had she found Lifty? Had Lifty even survived?

He swallowed and gathered his voice. "Rose!" The word rasped in the smoke.

Below, something scrabbled.

"Rose?"

He clattered down the stairs.

One flight up from the ground, he turned the corner into a blinding cloud of smoke.

He choked and tripped. Against his foot, something clattered—the tiny barrel of a still-gushing smoker—and he kicked it aside.

It rolled two feet, then bumped against something.

In the corner, a gun barrel glinted near the ground. Slowly, a hammer locked.

His dulled reflexes were still fast enough to whip his empty pistol around to point at the threat. "Stay!"

Rose burst from the smoky corner, pistol in hand. "Will!" She rushed him, arms coming around his waist.

The pain of it nearly wrenched him off his feet.

She jerked back. "Corblimey, Will." She stared up, eyes wide.

She was safe. Somehow that thought overcame even the wash of pain.

Gasping, he gripped her shoulder, as much to keep her near as to prevent her touching him again. "I told you to find Lifty, to leave." The words came out gruff.

She pinched her eyebrows. Her eyes darkened. She eased in nearer and looked over her shoulder.

He saw it then, past the smoke.

A body lay heaped against the wall of the landing. A sheen of green silk glinted.

*Mr. Monarch.*

He had found Rose? He had returned for her? Will tightened his grip on her shoulder. But—she had escaped, she had . . . killed him?

He leant in. She resisted, and he allowed her to remain behind.

Mr. Monarch lay on his side, hands above his head. Long, bloody marks scored his face.

Will glanced back.

Rose raised her chin. "'Twas the illusions. Rats. Hundreds of 'em, coming after him, climbing all over. He clawed up his own face, didn't he? Trying to get 'em off."

"He lit the smoker?"

She nodded. "He dasn't leave the protection of the smoke."

And so he'd suffocated?

Will breathed out—the first true breath since he'd met the man. "He's dead."

Rose worked her hand spastically around the grip of the pistol. "Not dead enough." She raised the pistol, still cocked, and pointed it with both hands at Mr. Monarch's splayed body.

Will caught the barrel. "He's gone, and we're here—and that's what matters. We need to leave this place, else we'll end as he is." He couldn't stifle another cough—or the wince spasming his ribs.

She dragged her focus from Mr. Monarch's body and took in the state of him.

"Fitzroy?" she asked.

He merely nodded.

She took one breath of her own—in, then out. She reached for his hand. "Come on, then." She quirked her mouth sideways. "And shouldn't I have known you'd tear yourself all to pieces afore night's end?"

He let her lead him out. He left Mr. Monarch without a backwards glance, just as he had left Fitzroy.

It was over.

*Over.* Fitzroy's threat was over. The battle was over.

And in so many ways, didn't it feel as if his life were over?

Rose fussed over his wounds and his clothes. "And look at your smart clobber now, will you?"

Bodies littered the stairs, shoved aside by fleeing servants. Blearily, he examined every face. He thought he saw Bull. But no Lifty.

Please, let it be. When he walked away from this night, he didn't want to leave everyone he cared for lying on the cobblestones behind him.

They crossed the foyer.

With both hands, Rose pushed aside the mangled door.

In the doorway, he halted. He blinked against the firelight.

A thunderous sound filled the street. Everywhere, men and women were whirling about, singing, shouting.

He scanned the street.

*Let them be here.*

Across the way, a familiar shovel hat bobbed amongst the exultant shadows beneath a lamppost. Lifty caught sight of Will, and an expression that might almost have been relief crossed his face. Then he grinned, wide enough to show the missing teeth in back. He'd lost another in front from the look of it. Bull's handiwork no doubt.

But he was alive.

Will scanned again. His heart beat harder. This was the last place in the world he should have left Isabella. Anything might have happened to her.

Rose tugged at his hand

Even that hurt. He pulled his head around to follow her nod.

There at the end of the street, amidst the glittering rubble that remained of the mirrors, Pish emerged from a building. He turned to help someone out over the debris.

In the reflected light of the mirrors, her hair glinted gold.

She was safe. They all were safe.

The sudden relaxation of his muscles flooded him with exhaustion. The world tilted.

Isabella saw him. She closed her eyes, then opened them. Her smile shone past her tears. *"You did it."* He couldn't hear her over the clamor, but he could read her lips.

He had done it. They had done it.

"Come on then." Rose clamped a hand over his where it leant upon her shoulder. She supported him into the street. "Time we leave."

He walked after her, one foot before the other. Again, darkness threatened to close down the corners of his vision. He concentrated on the cobblestones directly before him.

He didn't hear it at first, through the rush of his pulse in his ears. And even then, it took a moment to register—for it was no sound a'tall. It was silence.

He looked up.

With every step he took, the celebration fell silent around him. The people watched him. They whispered, one to another, and their whispers became a hum backed only by the whistle of the cold autumn wind and the crackle of the remaining fires.

Halfway down the street, Gamp waited. In his face, something had shifted. He nodded, slowly at first. Then he looked Will in the eye and nodded again.

It seemed a promise. A promise that this wouldn't turn to

the bad? That Gamp would do as Will had asked. No looting, no more violence. Perhaps this night would be one none would remember with shame.

Will managed a nod in return.

Gamp's expression didn't alter, but he pulled off his hat.

Others followed his lead, in silence.

Rose tightened her grip upon Will's hand.

He plodded on. He could do nothing else. But within his chest, his heart overflowed. Fitzroy had been wrong. These people—they *did* know what he had done for them tonight.

And . . . it still didn't matter.

The satisfaction he had thought once to feel did not rise within him. He did not deserve their acclaim—no more than when they had reviled him yesterday, no more than when they would, likely, revile him again tomorrow.

He eased his hand from his wound to wave aside their gesture.

Behind him, a voice—Lifty's?—raised a shout.

The crowd picked it up, eroding the silence.

*Wayfarer Wayfarer Wayfarer*

At street's end, Rose turned him around to look back.

She raised her face to him. "See that. You saved them."

"I almost didn't." His voice cracked.

"But you did. You remember that, eh? For the rest of your life."

If there was going to be one thing he carried away with him for the rest of his life, it wouldn't be saving *them*.

He looked down at her. "Let us go."

"Just you and me?"

"You and me."

# CHAPTER 49

WILL MET PISH in secret.

They found each other in a narrow Southwark alley not too distant from the Marshalsea. Side by side, they stood before a tavern stall that wasn't anything more than a window cut into the wall of a building.

Will leant his elbow upon the window's broad shelf. With the hand that wasn't nursing his ale, he casually shielded his face from passers-by and other customers.

"I'm ashamed of it, I'll admit that," Pish said. "But as a logical man, I can't rightly say I'm surprised."

"Scarcely your fault." Will slanted him a glance. "I was heartily glad to hear you'd been reinstated at Bow Street. And commended by the magistrate, I think?"

Pish's scowl deepened. "Oh, it's rubbish—all of it. Those chaps up top they've no notion how to decide their own minds even. And they're in charge of us all? Makes a man tremble down to the buckles on his shoes." He straightened, and his scowl softened. "What they're trying to do to you—there's not a spot of justice in it. And not even two full fortnights since you were saving the whole worthless city."

Will shrugged. "They presented me a reward."

"Hah. Lucky you used every last crimp, or they'd be wanting that back too."

In all honesty, Will remembered little of the first week. The wound in his side, although not deep, had left him with a roaring fever for a full four days. He'd spent all of it sequestered in Tom's old room at the Marshalsea, with Rose for nurse.

People had come and gone, but no one had been allowed in.

When finally he'd got his head back, he woke to discover he was rich. In a burst of clarity and resultant goodwill, Parliament had awarded him the entirety of Fitzroy's estate.

Lifty had been the one to tell Will, crowing jubilantly.

Rose had shooed him from the room, and Will had promptly fallen back asleep.

That was the first week.

By the end of the second, Parliament was beginning to fully realize the ramifications of this extraordinary battle between two men with unprecedented abilities. Where there were two, might there not be more?

Three days ago, the official proclamation had come down. Any demonstration of unnatural abilities was strictly forbidden, punishable to the full extent of the law, howsoever the judge should see fit.

In short, Will was now officially an outlaw.

"Confidentially," Pish said, "I've been assigned your arrest warrant. They're saying no one will be comfortable sleeping until you're accounted for."

Will took a long swallow of ale. "Think you can catch me?"

Pish smiled. It was a strange, crooked expression. "Not so confidentially: *no.* And quite personally"—he leant in—"I'm to give you the highly unofficial thanks of certain Bow Street officers."

"I'd rather that in the end, I think."

"I had my doubts, you know. Brazen little devil, I says to myself, first I met you. Thinks he's above the law, he does, and we'll just have to see about that." He smiled again, then sobered. "But you proved me wrong, lad, you did that."

Will pushed up from the shelf. "Do you think any man ever really proves himself? I used to believe it was something we worked up to all our lives until finally we accomplished it." He turned up the high collar of his new coat—bought with Fitzroy's money. "But now—" He couldn't quite put it into words. "Now I think perhaps we must go on proving it every day."

Pish held out his angular hand. "Good day to you, Mr. Hardy. I might say I should like to have sight of you again, but that would be the day I'd have to be serving a warrant, wouldn't it?"

"Farewell, Mr. Pish. You have my thanks—for everything."
He flashed a grin. "And I wish you the luck of your chase."

"I'm certain I'm to need it." Pish tilted his tankard in a small toast, then turned his back to drink it off.

Will accepted the hint and disappeared around the corner before Pish could turn and look again.

---

Of late, the Marshalsea was empty to the point of desolation. Those casualties of the battle, like Will, who had been nursed here were largely gone. Even most of the debtors had gone.

Postelwaite roamed the Lodge with a besom, twitching it against the floor at the slightest pebble or fragment of dirt. He saw Will through the grated door and scrabbled for his keyring.

"Mr. Hardy, sir, and I was hoping you would return to us to say a last farewell."

"Of course." Will removed his hat and opened his collar. He was among friends here, little as he might have believed it when first he'd entered this place in search of Tom. "I needed to see Rose."

"You *are* leaving then?"

"It grows too dangerous here for the time."

Postelwaite mashed his cap in his hands along with his keys. "But where will you go?"

"Back to Affery for a stop." There were things he needed to see there, if only once more. And perhaps some*one* as well.

Lady Isabella and her grandfather—who had been wounded in the siege upon his London house—had returned to their Lightwood estate in Surrey.

"After that"—he shrugged—"I'm not certain. See the world, I daresay." He grinned. "The journey roundabout will take me considerably less time than most, I'll warrant."

"Yes, indeed, sir." Postelwaite shifted. "I'm sorry you'll be leaving us, you know. You were the most remarkable thing ever to happen to this poor place. And you were correct—'twill be a story to tell my family until I'm an old, old man."

Will extended his hand. "You played your role valiantly, Mr. Postelwaite."

"Thanky." Postelwaite sighed. "'Twon't be much in the way of excitement here for quite an eon—especially after what you done for all those who had debts." He blinked. "Not that it wasn't grand of you, and with your own reward money too."

Will waved it off. "Parliament would have reclaimed it long ere now, had I kept it."

Postelwaite hastened to unlock the far door to the empty yard.

Will turned to Tom's building.

Near to the door loitered a man in a smart rig—sunshine-yellow waistcoat, shiny brown beaver hat, embroidered pocket-handkerchiefs.

Lifty, of course. He grinned, flashing gold teeth in both front and back now. He twirled a knobbed cane, bobbled it, and settled for tucking it beneath his elbow.

"I say, me jolly mate, and what d'you think of the new clobber? Toppin', ain't it? Wouldn't even recognize ol' Lifty Lefty, would you?"

Will let himself smile. "Then things are going well?"

"Blimey. Ain't they? Could've blowed me down if ever you told me this day was coming. But with Mr. Monarch and"—he cleared his throat—"Bull from the way, that leaves a famous hole to be filled. Who's to fill it better'n me, I'd like to know?"

Will coughed. "And you're certain you wouldn't want to come with me—with Rose and me?"

"You want my advice—mate to mate—I'll tell you a sprightly cove like you's balmy to tie himself down with a chit. Same as you was balmy to be giving up all that reward you could have been sharing with your deputies."

"Seems you're doing well enough without it."

"Yes, well, back to my point. You don't need little Rose to be a burden on your back, now do you? My new enterprise could make use of someone quick as her. She might even be my partner someday, never mind she's a biddy."

Will shook his head.

"I'll tell you something else. My new enterprises? They're going to be legitimate."

"And what are your new enterprises?"

"Still to be worked out. But you've my oath, don't you?" Lifty touched forefinger to temple. "*Legitimate* Lifty Lefty, that's my new name around here."

Will attempted not to laugh. Truly he did. But he couldn't help the twinkle in his eye. "I believe you mean it."

Inside the building, someone clattered down the stairs.

"Well, then?" For an instant, Lifty looked in dead earnest. "I'd care for her, you know. I always have, haven't I?"

Will hadn't the heart to tell him the truth, so he slapped his shoulder. "She can remain if she wishes."

She emerged, laden with a pack almost as large as herself. Her eyes were shining, all the brighter now that her face was scrubbed clean. She had combed her hair and plaited it down the back of the new blue frock Will had sent her out to buy before he'd distributed the rest of the reward.

"Well, then." She beamed up at Will. "Ready, are you?"

Lifty, for once, was wise enough not even to ask. He nudged her with the cane. "Don't forget your old mate Lifty, eh?"

"Ain't likely, is it? Best you find a smart mort what can watch out for you, now I'm gone."

He laughed, louder than necessary. Then he shouldered his stick and tipped his hat. "Well, then, if I don't see your names in the papers first, you see if you can't find mine, what?" With a wink and a cluck, he sauntered off.

Rose looked up at Will. The sparkle in her eyes sobered. "To Affery?"

He took her pack. "To Affery."

———

The strangest part about crossing the village bridge was that Affery looked no different. The stone cottages and shops were still small, still packed one upon another all down the single narrow street.

He had been gone so little time, and yet everything in the world had changed. Some part of him had expected that at long last sleepy Affery should have changed too.

Rose peered about. "This is where you're from then?"

"The forge is yonder." Would *that* have changed? His chest tightened. He couldn't say if he wished it to or not.

She swiveled on her heel, looking in all directions at once, then skipped to catch him up. "Ain't like nothing I ever seen, is it? It's like . . . a little fae town."

The dirt of the road had once again smudged her face, but her eyes were clear and her cheeks, if not exactly peachy, had at least gained a dusty pink.

"You don't miss London?" he asked.

She shrugged. "Not yet."

They passed Pirrup Inn—with its faded portrait of the old King George jutting over the street.

The door opened, and the portrait wobbled in its breeze. Richard Grainger stepped out. He glanced at Will once, then again—perhaps more because of the strange sight Will presented in his necessary eye-shields than because of any recognition.

Grainger curled his lip at Rose. Then he looked again to Will, and *then* he recognized him. "Well."

The tone was impudence itself.

The familiar heat of wounded pride rose within Will. The scar from Grainger's horsewhip across his face burned as of old. He halted.

In days past, he couldn't have touched Grainger—in more senses than one. Even were it not for his standing, Grainger was the taller and the heavier.

Now, Will was the quicker by far. And wasn't he already an outlaw? Today, he had naught to lose by finally teaching Richard Grainger the lesson he so badly needed to learn.

Grainger came forward. "Little Will Hardy. I truly prayed we had seen the last of you when you ran from here like a worthless yellow cur."

"Oh, gawn," Rose said.

"Your master is dead, I hear," Grainger said. "That leaves you no name but that of orphan and pauper." He stepped nearer. "Vagrant, even. Move along, now. There is nothing else for it. Otherwise, I fear it will be the workhouse."

Will's heart beat hard. One blow to Grainger's face. It would be enough. Then he would walk away. Seemed he should be owed that much for all the foul words over the years.

Rose snorted. "And you're a daft puppy, ain't you? Don't know what happened in London, do you? What almost happened to the whole bloody country? And Will's the one what stopped it, ain't he?"

Grainger ignored her. He had no regard for her opinion of him. She was nothing to him.

And, suddenly, Will realized: that was exactly how he felt about Grainger. What did it matter what a cub like this thought of him, one way or t'other? After all that had passed . . . Richard Grainger mattered naught.

Will pushed Rose to start her down the road. He took a last look back and managed a grin. It started out false enough, and then—it wasn't.

He grinned at Richard Grainger and he touched the tip of his hat. He caught one glimpse of Grainger's astonishment before moving on.

At the edge of the village, Rose looked at him. "Who's the cully?"

"No one." 'Twas the truth.

———————

The forge was locked, great padlocks upon both front and back doors.

Will stood before the house door and merely looked. Behind him, the millstream chuckled. Tip the bulldog was nowhere to be found. One of the neighbors must have taken him in.

He had expected the memories to bowl him over—the ghosts of Tom and himself hammering in the forge, fishing in the stream, shoeing horses in the yard.

But there was naught. There was only this place, peaceful and beautiful as ever.

Rose clanked the padlock against its heavy chain. "Want I should pick that for you?"

He shook his head.

Whatever of his belongings remained held no significance. The only thing that had ever mattered here was now gone.

He had thought he needed to return to finally bid Tom good-bye. But now he was here, he found he'd already done so. The separation was long over. All that remained was the ache of loss.

He reached above Rose's head to press his palm against the door. He closed his eyes. He didn't pray anything, didn't think anything. There were no words left, only an understanding.

Still, he spoke: "Goodbye, Tom."

Then he pulled back.

Rose shifted. "Now where?" She bit her lip. "To see her ladyship?"

He looked eastward, to where the Lightwood estate lay several miles distant. Even now, he could hardly walk up to the front door and announce himself to the footman. Lord Carstone would probably be as inclined as ever to throw him out on his ear.

But he couldn't leave without seeing Isabella.

He turned to the stream. "First, we'll visit the old farm."

They crossed the stream, Rose by the footbridge, Will in a single bound.

Few of the golden autumn leaves remained now. Will could see past the naked trees to the field—and farther on, to the charred skeleton of the old Hardy barn.

*That* did raise a skein of anger in his heart.

He would yet have words with Dr. Silas about that.

Halfway across the field, Rose stopped. "What's all this then?"

He squinted past his eye-shields.

Amidst the rubble, half a dozen men labored with shovels and picks.

At the knoll above, a tall man in genteel dress leant heavily against two canes, watching the work. Lord Carstone, come to observe the restoration of his property?

Will's heart missed a beat, half as much with the old instinct of revulsion as with a sudden burst of hope.

A few feet from the stile, Rose halted. Her face was somber, a little fearful even. She pointed into the midst of the rubble.

Even before he turned his head, Will knew it was Isabella.

She was the only woman amongst the workers, dressed in a plain brown frock with a white apron and a wide-brimmed straw bonnet. She stood from examining the ashes and raised her hand to her eyes.

So the moment had come—and much more easily than he had feared. Still, he'd no idea what he would say to her.

He glanced at Rose. "You'll wait for me?"

"Might be a tolerable long wait, seems to me."

"Rose."

She raised both hands in defeat and clomped off to sit at the stile. "'Course, I'll wait."

He set one hand upon the stone fence and leapt over—considerably more gracefully than upon the day when first he'd met Isabella in the road.

He crossed to the opposite fence and hoisted himself over that as well. He looked at Lord Carstone and hesitated. He had naught to say to the man. But neither did he wish to slight him, not anymore.

Lord Carstone watched him. He made no move to approach Will or even to beckon. But he unbent his neck, ever so slightly, and inclined his head.

Will returned the gesture, bowing at the waist.

Isabella met him in the house garden, beyond the hearing of her workers. She reached out and clasped his hand with both of hers. "You look well."

"So do you."

"Yes, well, I was not the one who nearly died, was I?"

Ever since he woke from his fever, he had been practicing words for her. Now, in this place, none of those words would leave his tongue. "I—"

She released his hand, properly, and looked up at him, her eyes soft, serene—expectant even. Never had she looked at him like that, not even that night under the moon. She looked as if she might say *yes*—to whatever he would ask.

He swallowed and then took a chance and removed his eye-shields, so he might look her in the eye. His hat brim blocked the most direct rays, and he ignored the burn seeping around the edges. He was almost growing accustomed to it.

"My lady."

She smiled, genially. It was the smile of knowing comradeship. "Yes?"

Suddenly, he found himself grinning. A measure of discomfort seeped away. They had been through too much together and seen too deeply into each other to hide behind this façade of formality.

"I—" The words he wished to say returned to him. "I wanted to tell you, with your permission, what I think of you."

She raised both eyebrows in that expression of practiced amusement. "I am not certain I am brave enough to hear such."

"Bravery has never been your lack."

The practiced smile didn't falter, but something softened in her eyes. "My grandfather would say—and indeed has, of late—I am quite foolhardy."

"That too." Will tempered his agreement with another grin. Then he sobered. "Pray, listen. At one of the last occasions we were together, we spoke words."

She sobered as well. Perhaps she could hear already the whisper of what he was about to say. "We did."

"I wanted to see you again, here, to tell you I meant them."

She smiled, for real this time.

"But also"—he hastened on—"that I have not, as yet, the right to say them."

She watched him steadily, but she did not look as surprised as she might have.

Now came the most difficult part. "I think—someday—that I might very much appreciate the opportunity and the permission to tell you that . . . I care for you."

She seemed neither shocked at his impudence nor frustrated by his hesitance. "Someday?"

"Yes. When I am worthy."

"And when will that be, Will Hardy? If not today, after what you have done, then when?" She stepped in nearer. "My grandfather understands us better now than I think ever he will. I have put matters to him—more or less. He would not be averse to . . . discussing the situation. And from him, I hope you know, that is a good deal?"

"Indeed."

The news was as heady as a glass of mulled wine. If ever someone had told him Lord Carstone should be open to even a *discussion*, he would have laughed in the teller's face.

It was all here within his grasp: everything he'd wanted. Isabella. A fortune. Stature.

And he was handing it all back. Perhaps he *had* been born a fool to die a fool.

He shook his head. "I can't ask him now. It isn't about the timing, or what I've done—or not done. It's because I have pursued you for all the wrong reasons."

For the first time, she raised her chin, uncertain.

"I sought you first for your position, for your beauty, for your wealth. Because the world would think better of me for having won such a prize." He shrugged. "Because I would think better of myself."

Her eyes flickered, absorbing that. "And now?"

"Now, I believe I need time to seek you for yourself. And to do something to truly earn your respect—and your grandfather's."

Disappointment crossed her face.

He could have kissed her for that alone. "You don't have to wait for me." He nearly choked on the words. "But I wanted you to know I am coming back—once I have worked things out a little better. I will see you again."

He took her hand, and when she did not resist, he kissed it gently.

He looked up from under his hat brim.

The faintest glitter of a tear welled in her eye. With her free hand, she briefly touched his. This was as bold as they dared be. Indeed, it was passing bold enough.

"Bless you, Will Hardy."

They broke contact and stepped apart.

For an awkward moment, there was nowhere to look and naught to say.

Then he cleared his throat and gestured to the barn rubble. "I hope your grandfather is not to take on another tenant here. You've told him of the danger?"

"In not so many words." They started back to the road. "In fact, he has rather given the farm to me, for the time being." She pointed to the workers. "Hence the industry."

"You're not to go to Dr. Silas in Paris?"

"Not yet. As you know, my grandfather is not well after the ball he took to his limb. I must bide with him for the time."

"And while you do, you will continue Dr. Silas's work here?"

"There is much I do not yet understand. Perhaps it is I who will find you a cure."

At the first stile, he halted. "You will have more care than Dr. Silas, I trust?"

"Let us hope so. When you return, perhaps I will have good news." She looked across to the opposite stile.

Rose had walked several paces down the road to poke at a coney with a stick.

"And you?" Isabella asked. "Do you go to Paris now?"

"As soon as ever I'm able. I've yet enough of the reward money saved for passage." He hesitated. "But also, I want to take this thing that's been given me—however much longer I have it—and see if I can do something good with it."

"Even though you have been outlawed?" Her eyes twinkled. "I did not tell my grandfather about that bit, you know."

"Tom would think this the right thing to do. And he was usually correct."

There seemed no more words to be said. "Well." He slipped his eye-shields back on. "Farewell, my lady."

"Fare thee well, Will Hardy."

If he stayed another moment, he would undoubtedly tarnish her reputation forever by leaning down and kissing her.

Instead, he swung over the stile. He managed to hold himself to a single backwards glance on his way down the road to Rose.

She remained squatting with her stick, even though the coney had fled. "Still coming with me then?"

"Never any doubt of that."

She cast aside the stick and rose to rattle the dust from her skirt. "Why come with me when you could stay with the likes of her?" She peered up at him. Above the guarded set of her mouth, her eyes were impossibly vulnerable.

"Because, for the time being, my girl, it's you and me for the road. That suit you?"

She watched him for a second, as if testing whether he truly meant it. Then a grin swept over her face. "Don't it though?"

He swung both her and her pack onto his back. "Then let us go a-wayfaring."

**Note From the Author:** Thanks so much for coming along with me on the journey of the *Wayfarer*! Did you know reviews are what sell books? If you've had fun reading this book, would you consider rating it and reviewing it on Amazon. com? Thank you!

Join the discussion: #Wayfarer

**Don't want the fun to end?**

# CLAIM YOUR FREE E-BOOK!

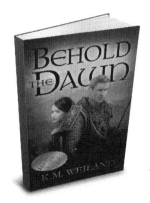

# ACKNOWLEDGMENTS

MANY SMART, SUPPORTIVE, enthusiastic, and generally wonderful people helped me put before you the book you've just read.

One of those people might even have been you. So many of you contact me every day. You encourage me. You remind me to never give up on the things worth doing. You put a face and a voice to the often faceless, voiceless audience that joins me in the shared imaginative spaces of my stories.

I thank you, just as I thank the many stellar individuals who have contributed their time and skills even more directly by reading and commenting on early drafts.

My particular thanks and love to my long-time critique buddy Linda Yezak, who has been walking beside me almost from the beginning of this journey.

Thanks to London Crockett, Braden Russell, Kate Flournoy, Lorna G. Poston, Liberty Speidel, Lynette Ward, M.M. Ballasch, and Daeus Lamb for their insights, humor, and stalwartness.

To my Wordplayer and Super Reader groups on Facebook, who help me through all the toughest decisions, such as choosing book covers and refining advertising blurbs, as well as pumping me up with their daily zeal and positivity.

Sincere thanks to fellow geek Dave Chesson for his kindness, generosity, and good advice.

My gratitude, as always, to my killer cartographer Joanna Marie, who continues to contribute to my growing collection of personalized maps.

Special thanks to my brother Jared, who always sees through all my plot  holes.

To my parents, brother Derek, brother-in-law Timothy, and my adorable niece and nephews for their endless love and support.

And to my sister Amy (because I once promised she would always get a mention as my as my "#1 fan.")

Thank you all for enriching my life, asking me to be a better person, and showing me how to be a better storyteller.

K.M. Weiland

## Also by K.M. Weiland

What if dreams
came true?

Sometimes even pilots
have to wing it.

*www.kmweiland.com*

# ABOUT THE AUTHOR

K.M. WEILAND LIVES in make-believe worlds, talks to imaginary friends, and survives primarily on chocolate truffles and espresso. She is an award-winning and internationally-published author, whose novels include the medieval epic *Behold the Dawn*, the portal fantasy *Dreamlander*, and the dieselpunk adventure *Storming*. She is a native of western Nebraska. Visit her website kmweiland.com for updates about her books.

**Also by K.M. Weiland:**

*A Man Called Outlaw*

*Behold the Dawn*

*Dreamlander*

*Storming*

Printed in Great Britain
by Amazon